NO TIME FOR DOUBLE-TALK

Fritz and Hugo marched the Hardy boys down the corridor.

"I wonder what's waiting for us," Joe said to Frank as they walked along.

"I have a strong hunch that they have a big surprise in store," replied Frank. There was an odd mocking tone in Frank's voice, but Joe didn't have time to wonder about it.

"In there," said Hugo from behind.

As they entered the room, Frank said in the same strange tone, "Hi, Joe."

"Hi, Frank," answered the young man waiting inside.

Joe looked into the face of that young man—and suddenly wondered if he had really come out of his drugged trance, or if maybe he was as crazy as the inmates at the Lazarus Clinic used to be.

The young man he was staring at was himself!

Books in THE HARDY BOYS CASEFILES® Series

Available from ARCHWAY Paperbacks

THE LAZARUS PLOT

FRANKLIN W. DIXON

AN ARCHWAY PAPERBACK
Published by POCKET BOOKS

New York   London   Toronto   Sydney   Tokyo   Singapore

AN ARCHWAY PAPERBACK *Original*

An Archway Paperback published by
POCKET BOOKS, a division of Simon & Schuster Inc.
1230 Avenue of the Americas, New York, NY 10020

ISBN: 0-671-73995-6

First Archway Paperback printing June 1987

14 13 12 11 10 9 8 7 6

THE HARDY BOYS, AN ARCHWAY PAPERBACK and
colophon are registered trademarks of Simon & Schuster Inc.

THE HARDY BOYS CASEFILES is a trademark
of Simon & Schuster Inc.

Printed in the U.S.A.

IL 7+

THE LAZARUS PLOT

Chapter

1

"GOT YOU!" FRANK HARDY smiled grimly. Once again, the older of the two Hardy boys had made a capture. In this case, the capture was a fish.

Rushing water came up to the top of his hip-high boots as he braced himself against the current of the Allagash River. Above the tall pines on both banks of the river, the early fall sky was a dazzling blue. Frank felt a million miles away from the world of crime fighting and danger in which he and his brother, Joe, lived—and had nearly died. The fanatic followers of the Rajah and his *Cult of Crime* had done their best to fit Frank and Joe for matching coffins.

The Hardys had survived, however, and decided that a vacation was definitely in order. They'd packed their fishing and camping gear into

Joe's latest pride and joy, a 1958 station wagon complete with wood paneling, which he'd lovingly reconditioned. Next stop, the Maine north woods, for two weeks of peace, quiet, and fishing.

"Whoa, big fella," Frank muttered as his fishing rod began to bend. He let out some line as the fish fought to escape. From the feel of the line, the fish was a big one. Then he saw it leap into the air—a trout!

Just the right kind of adventure, he thought. Trout give you a challenge, put up a fight, and don't carry guns.

He fought the fish on his hook, letting out the line, then reeling it in, bringing the fish ever closer to his net. Already, he could picture it grilling over the campfire.

This is just what we need, he thought. Two weeks without having to look over our shoulders. Two weeks without racing against time to head off some disaster. Two weeks without mayhem, mystery, or murder. He grinned to himself. But will Joe be able to last two weeks without girls to chase?

His smile faded as he thought about Joe, back in town buying supplies. Frank had always kidded his brother about belonging to the "Girl-of-the-Week Club." But he knew that Joe had really and truly loved only one girl—Iola Morton. Then terrorists had bombed the Hardys' car, and Iola had disappeared in a fireball. It looked as if Joe was never going to get serious about another girl again.

Would he ever get over it, Frank wondered, or would he be haunted by Iola's memory forever? Crashing noises from the nearby forest brought Frank whirling away from the riverbank. He turned just in time to see Joe Hardy tearing through the underbrush.

Frank shook his head. "You made me lose a fish," he complained. Then he saw his brother's face. "What's wrong? You look like you saw a ghost."

"I did," Joe said, still gasping for breath. "*Iola.*"

"That's impossible," Frank said patiently. "Your mind is playing tricks. Iola's *gone*, Joe." Frank began to get worried. Had too much hardball with the bad guys scrambled Joe's brains?

"I know what I saw," Joe said, stubbornly shaking his head. "I left the car and was heading back here through the woods. And suddenly she stepped out from behind a tree less than ten yards from me. I saw her face as clear as day. She was wearing a sweater and jeans, just like the ones she was wearing before . . . before . . ." Joe's voice trailed off.

"You've got to face what happened," Frank said, putting his hand on Joe's shoulder. "Nothing was left of the car but a few hunks of molten metal after that bomb went off. There's no chance that Iola could have survived."

3

"But remember: *They didn't find a trace of Iola's body,*" said Joe.

Frank saw the gleam of hope in Joe's eye. A crazy gleam, Frank thought, for a crazy hope.

"The police said the heat was so intense that it left no traces of her," Frank reminded him gently. "Except in your memory, Joe."

Joe's face tightened. "That wasn't a memory I just saw. It was *her,* as real as you or me."

"But did she say anything or do anything to make contact with you?" Frank asked. "The real Iola would have."

"She was about to say something," Joe said. "She saw me and opened her mouth to speak. Then all of a sudden she looked confused, like she didn't know where she was or what she was doing. Her eyes went blank, and she turned and ran. Before I could move, she'd disappeared in the forest."

"Vanished—just like that," said Frank skeptically.

"I don't care if you believe me or not. That's what happened," said Joe, now openly angry. "When I couldn't find her, I came back here to get you to help track her. She needs help, Frank. And if you won't help her, I'll have to do it alone."

He turned away from his brother and strode back into the forest.

"Joe! Wait!" said Frank, hurrying after him. "Stranger things than this have happened and turned out to be real. I'll come along if you want me to."

Joe flashed a smile at his brother. "I figured you wouldn't be able to resist a mystery. Come on, Sherlock. Together, we'll be able to pick up her trail."

"How will you find the spot where you first saw her?" Frank asked as they made their way through the forest. Sunlight filtering through the branches dappled the ground. The only sounds were the crunching of pine needles under the Hardys' feet, the buzzing of insects, and the occasional call of a bird.

"I dropped my pack with the supplies when I saw her, so it should still be lying there," said Joe. He squinted through the trees. "There it is now."

They stood beside the discarded pack.

"So where did this girl . . . Iola . . . come from?" Frank asked—and then he heard it.

Just a small sound.

A twig snapping, maybe, or pine needles crunching.

But it was a sound that somehow didn't belong, that made him want to dive for cover. Frank got a hold on himself, smiling at how on edge his nerves were. They were safe in the woods.

But Joe didn't think so. He grabbed Frank's arm and dived to the ground, dragging Frank with him.

5

"Joe—" Frank began, but a much louder sound drowned out his words.

Rifle shots exploded.

Bullets whizzed inches over their heads.

"It's a trap," Joe rasped. "And we're sitting ducks!"

Chapter

2

"GOT TO FIND cover," Frank whispered into his brother's ear as they lay side by side, facedown, hugging the ground. There were more rifle shots, more bullets whizzing above them.

"Good thinking," said Joe, already starting to roll himself along the ground toward the nearest large pine.

Frank followed him. They reached the side of the tree away from where the shooting was coming, and cautiously raised themselves to their hands and knees.

More shots. A bullet thumped into the tree, and another ricocheted off it, showering splinters of bark.

The Hardy boys hit the ground again. Wiggling on their stomachs, using their elbows to propel them, they retreated farther away from whoever was using them for target practice.

The rifle shots ended. As Frank strained to cover ground, he kept his ears wide open for sounds of pursuit. But he heard none. Just the sound of Joe and him going over the blanket of pine needles, and the sound of their increasingly heavy breathing as their lungs began to burn.

Finally, it seemed safe to stop.

Concealed behind thick undergrowth, they again raised themselves to their hands and knees.

With the back of his hand Frank wiped away the sweat coating his forehead.

"Whew, close call," he whispered.

"Hey, remember what you told me about this trip?" Joe whispered back.

"No. What?" said Frank.

" 'No bad guys, just good times,' " said Joe.

Frank shrugged. "Okay, so I was wrong." He edged his face toward a gap in the undergrowth to peer into the forest. "Looks like they're not coming after us."

"Then it's time for us to go after them," said Joe. His eyes were flashing like warning lights. People taking potshots at him triggered his temper.

Frank didn't have Joe's hot temper. Instead he had cool-headed logic. But he did share his brother's dislike of running from a fight—and Joe's determination to come out on top no matter what the odds.

"From the number of shots, it's a good bet there's more than one guy," Frank said. "We can't go straight at them, because it won't do any good to go charging into the barrels of their guns."

"We'll make a circle and approach them from behind," said Joe.

"Just what I was thinking," replied Frank. "And it would be even better if we split up. It'll double our chances of spotting them. If one of us does, he can give a signal. How about this?" Frank pursed his lips and whistled a whippoorwill call.

Joe replied with one of his own.

"It'll do," said Frank, nodding. We'll gamble that our pals out there won't know that whip-poorwills do their calling at night."

"We won't even give them the time to think about it," said Joe. "We'll make sure they never know what hit them."

"We'll have surprise on our side," Frank agreed. "They'll never figure that we're coming after them." Frank checked the compass on his watch, and Joe did the same. "Okay. You go five hundred paces to the southwest. I go the same distance southeast. Then we trade directions, so we meet in another five hundred paces—unless one of us makes a sighting first."

"Catch you later," said Joe. He moved off, quiet as a cat, his expression alert and intent, like a tiger on the prowl.

9

Frank was just as alert. As he moved silently through the forest, he did a mental check on himself, as his karate teacher, Kim Sung, had told him to do in the moments before possible combat. He made sure his breathing was smooth and deep, his muscles relaxed and supple, his heartbeat slow and steady. That done, he went into the final stage of readiness, wiping all thoughts from his mind, so that his senses of sight, hearing, and smell would be clear and he could instantly react to danger.

Then he saw it—the glint of sunlight striking metal.

He knew what that metal was. It was the metal of a rifle.

Frank pursed his mouth to whistle, but it was too late.

A man stepped out from behind a tree. He was big, bald, and black bearded, over six feet tall and a good two hundred pounds. He looked like he had been outfitted from head to toe by L. L. Bean, complete with red-and-black-checked flannel shirt and hunting cap. But Frank barely noticed what the man looked like. All he was interested in was the rifle in the man's hands, pointed straight at him.

Frank had only a split second to make his move—and he made it. He stepped toward the man, raising his hands in surrender.

Then, without a break in movement, his leg shot upward, the tip of his boot catching the man

10

square on the chin. The instant Frank felt his boot make solid contact, he twirled to one side, away from the rifle. His flow was perfect. Kim Sung would have been pleased.

The rifle dropped from the bearded man's hands as the man went down as if pole-axed, right into a thick patch of wild blueberries.

Direct hit, thought Frank—and that was his mistake.

Too late he remembered another of Kim Sung's teachings. Never let success distract you. Never congratulate yourself on doing well, because when you do that, you relax your guard.

Too late Frank realized someone had come up behind him. He only had time to half-turn before he saw the face of an angry man, his hands high above his head, and then the blurred shape of something—a rifle barrel, perhaps—coming down.

Then there was a sharp pain, and blackness.

Joe, moving silently through the forest, heard a crashing noise.

It might have been an animal running through the undergrowth.

On the other hand, it might have been a body falling to the ground.

Joe headed in the direction of the sound. He watched every step he took and kept close to every tree he went by.

After a moment, he heard voices and headed

toward them. The voices became more and more distinct, but he couldn't understand a word.

A foreign language, he thought as he pressed against a thick tree, then peered around it.

He saw two men—a big, bald, bearded one, with hands bleeding from some kind of scratches, and a wiry, redheaded one—standing over a body on the ground.

Joe recognized the body at the same time that he recognized the language the men were speaking.

It was Frank who was lying on the ground.

And it was French the men were speaking.

Were the men survivors of the French gang that the Hardy boys had broken up in their case *Evil, Inc.?* Were they out for revenge?

Joe let out his breath in relief when he saw Frank's head make a slight movement, his body give a tiny twitch. At least Frank was still alive.

The bearded man grinned. While the other man kept his rifle trained on Frank, the bearded man unhooked a canteen from his belt and poured water from it onto Frank's face.

Frank shook his head as he opened his eyes. Then the bearded man leaned down, grabbed Frank by the arm, and lifted him to his feet like a limp doll. When he let go, Frank stood there, weaving groggily, like a battered fighter set up for a knock-out punch.

As Joe grimaced in horror, he saw the wiry man get set to deliver it.

The man parted his lips in a snarl, lifted his rifle, and pressed the tip of the barrel against Frank's head, just behind his ear.

Joe could wait no longer. He moved out from behind the tree and charged.

He had never moved faster in his life—not on the football field going for a touchdown, not on the baseball diamond stretching a single into a double, not on a track heading for the tape in his specialty, the hundred-yard dash.

But even as his knees pumped and his feet flew faster and faster, he knew he couldn't reach Frank in time.

At the first crunch of Joe's feet on the pine needles, the wiry man wheeled around and leveled his gun at Joe.

This was one race Joe couldn't win.

He couldn't move faster than a bullet.

All Joe could do was brace himself to die.

Chapter

3

Joe did not hear the rifle shot he was expecting. He did not feel a bullet slam into him.

Instead he heard the wiry man with the rifle gasp, "Aghhh!" as Frank karate-chopped him on one forearm, then the other, in a blur of motion. The rifle dropped from the man's paralyzed hands, and the man dropped on top of it, after Frank chopped at the back of his neck.

The bearded man reached for the hunting knife on his belt, but he never made it. Joe hit him in a flying tackle, smashing him back against a tree, then let him go and backed off a step. When the bearded man reached for his knife again, Joe lashed a right hook to the jaw. The man went down like a sack of flour.

"Good work," said Frank as he removed the

wiry man's belt and set about tying his hands behind his back with it.

"Good work yourself," said Joe, doing the same thing to the bearded man. "I thought I was a goner. I thought you were, too. You woke up in the nick of time."

"Actually, I came to a couple of minutes before, but I didn't see any sense in letting those guys know it," said Frank, squatting as he made sure the wiry man was securely tied. Then he stood up.

"Playing possum, huh?" said Joe, giving his man a final check and standing up, too.

"Right," said Frank. "I figured it might be interesting to hear what they had to say to each other when they thought I was unconscious. And of course, it would be a lot easier to make my move when their guard was down."

"Did they say anything?" asked Joe.

"Yeah, but I didn't understand what," said Frank.

"They were speaking French, I think," said Joe. "You must have understood *something,* unless that A you got in French class last year was a joke."

"I just caught a stray word here and there," said Frank, shaking his head. "They were speaking with some kind of weird accent. Plus they were talking real fast, and my head was still ringing, so it all sounded like Greek to me."

Joe laughed, then became serious. "We'll just have to wait until they come to before we find out what they're up to."

"We can speed up the process," said Frank, unhooking his canteen from his belt. "I'll do to them what they did to me—give them a water cure."

A minute later, the men were standing on their feet, shaking their heads.

"*Sacre bleu, qu'est-ce qui s'est passé?*" mumbled one.

"*Ma pauvre tête,*" groaned the other.

"Either of you speak English?" asked Frank.

"Yes, of course," the bearded man said with a heavy accent.

"Certainly," replied the other one, with a similar accent. "We come from Quebec. We French-Canadians must speak both French and English."

"Then you can start talking," said Joe, in a hard voice.

"Why were you taking target practice on us?" said Frank.

"On *you?*" said the bearded man. "Why should we shoot at you?"

"Think hard," said Joe, raising his fist menacingly. "You should be able to remember. It was just about fifteen minutes ago."

"*Mais non*, that was *you?*" said the wiry man. He turned to his companion. "I told you that you were mistaken when you said you saw deer. You are always so quick on the trigger."

"When you hunt, you must react instantly," said the bearded man defensively. "Otherwise, the deer, they get away. I saw the motion, I was sure it was the deer. Needless to say, I apologize."

"I must apologize, too, for hitting you over the head," the wiry man said to Frank. "But when I saw you attacking my friend Henri here, I had no choice. Who knew what kind of criminal or madman you might have been?"

"Jacques had to do it," Henri agreed. "After all, you attacked me without any reason."

"That gun you pointed at me seemed like reason enough," said Frank.

"I heard you coming through the undergrowth, and naturally I thought you were a—"

"Don't tell me—a deer," said Frank. "Listen, before I untie you, promise you won't make any more little mistakes. The woods aren't safe with trigger-happy hunters like you around—especially before the season officially starts." Smiling grimly, he took the bullets out of the rifle he was holding, picked up the other rifle and emptied it, then frisked the men, removing all the bullets from their pockets. Meanwhile, Joe searched their backpacks, which were lying nearby, and removed the rest of the ammunition from them.

"I suggest the two of you try fishing this time of year. It's safer for everyone concerned," said Frank as he and Joe untied the belts from Henri's and Jacques's wrists.

"You cannot do this," said Henri indignantly as he rubbed circulation back into his hands.

"It is outrageous," agreed Jacques.

But they took a look at Frank's hands spreading flat in readiness for another karate chop, and Joe's hands balling into fists, and limited further protest to Henri's saying, "You have not heard the last of this."

"We will notify the authorities," said Jacques.

"You do that," said Joe.

"Yeah, please," said Frank. "Once they hear our side of the story, you guys can forget about hunting again, unless you want to do it without a license."

"Okay, okay," said Jacques. "Maybe we do lose our tempers a little. And maybe we were a little too quick on the trigger—especially Henri. I have to admit, it is not the first mistake he makes today. Less than an hour ago, he almost shoot at another person."

"I tell you, she look just like a deer," muttered Henri.

"'*She*'?" Joe asked instantly. "You saw a *girl*, near here, a little while ago?"

"She is wandering around like a lost one," said Jacques. "I have no idea what she is doing here in the middle of the woods. Certainly she is not dressed for it. She is wearing new jeans and a pretty sweater, like she is at a school picnic."

"Jeans and a sweater," said Joe, trying to keep his voice calm. "Tell me, what did she look like?"

"A pretty girl, on the petite side, with a face like, how you say, a pixie, and dark hair," said Jacques.

"Yes, dark hair, like an elk," said Henri.

"But you didn't shoot at her?" said Joe.

"No, of course not," said Henri.

"I grab his rifle just in time," said Jacques. "Then I call out to the girl. I think maybe she needs help. But when she hear me, she turn and run."

"Which direction?" asked Joe urgently.

"That way," said Jacques, pointing.

"Come on," Joe said to Frank. Without waiting for a response, Joe jogged off in the direction that Jacques had indicated, toward an opening in the trees and thick foliage.

"So long," Frank said over his shoulder to the two men as he followed his brother.

"Looks like we're on some kind of abandoned trail or road," said Joe as he jogged along at Frank's side.

"A road to nowhere," commented Frank. "It hasn't been used in years."

"Yes, it has—by that girl," said Joe, keeping up a fast pace until he halted abruptly. He picked a scrap of torn blue woolen material from the branch of a sapling where it had snagged. "I'd know this blue anywhere. It's the same color as the sweater Iola was wearing when I saw her before—and the last time I saw her, when . . ." Joe trailed off, wincing at the memory. Then his

19

voice grew urgent. "Let's speed it up! We're on her trail."

"But we're coming to a dead end," said Frank, peering ahead.

A hundred yards down the overgrown road was a tall wire fence topped by barbed wire. On a gate in the fence was a large sign. The Hardy boys were too far away to read the lettering, but they could make out the picture on it. A skull. The universal symbol of death.

When they reached the fence, Frank read: "Warning. Electrified fence. Property patrolled by armed guards and attack dogs. Trespassers will be shot on sight."

Joe refused to let that stop him. "Iola must have gotten through this fence—or been *taken* through it—somehow. The only other place to go is deeper in the woods and I don't see why she'd do that. We've got to get in there." He reached for the gate latch.

Frank grabbed his arm. "Careful. The electric current might be on. And even if it isn't, you can bet it's locked."

"We have to get through it," said Joe, peering through the wire mesh. On the other side was what had once been a handsome lawn and garden, but had become a jungle of high green grass, tall weeds, and a rainbow of flowers gone wild.

"Well," said Frank reluctantly, "I see three options for getting in. We could get a ladder and go over it, but getting past the barbed wire on top would be tricky, and we would be sitting ducks if any guard spotted us. We could cut through the fence, but that would be hard with the current on, and any disturbance in it might set off alarms. That leaves one other way."

"Going *under* it," said Joe. "We could get a couple of shovels and tunnel through and have good cover at the same time."

"Tonight. When we have the cover of darkness," said Frank firmly. "But this is ridiculous, Joe."

"I hate to wait that long. Something might happen to Iola by then," said Joe.

"See any other choice?" asked Frank.

"You and your logic," replied Joe, shaking his head. "Once, just once, I'd like to see you go with gut feeling and not brains."

"I'd rather use my head and save our necks," said Frank. "Anyway, there aren't many other places in this forest to go. If someone went inside, they're still there. Come on." Frank sighed. "Let's get to the general store in the village and buy a couple of shovels. Big ones. We'll have to do some heavy digging tonight. And while we're at the store, we can do some digging there. We can find out if anyone knows anything about this property."

Two hours later, after a jog back to the station wagon and a drive to the village, the Hardy boys had gotten both the shovels and some information.

The storekeeper was a tall, lanky, gray-haired man, who was as close-mouthed as most of the citizens of Maine that the Hardy boys had met. But the sight of the money that Frank and Joe laid out for a pair of high-priced shovels warmed him enough to loosen his tongue when they asked him about the fence in the forest.

"Figure that must be the old Lazarus place," he said, counting the money twice, then ringing it up on his antique cash register.

"The Lazarus place?" Frank repeated.

"Fact is, they called it the Lazarus Clinic," said the storekeeper. "Folks around here, though, got a different name for it. Lazarus Loony Bin. Some fancy New York doctor opened it and had a lot of rich patients for a while—until the folks paying the bills got tired of seeing no results, and the place went out of business."

"What's it being used for now?" asked Frank.

"*Ain't* being used. Hasn't been for two, three years," said the storekeeper disdainfully. "Crazy place for a crazy house, in the middle of nowhere. Lost a bundle, that doctor did."

"Thanks for the information," said Joe. Then he said to Frank, "Time to move."

"Hey, mister, you're forgetting your shovel," said the storekeeper as Joe dashed for the door.

"I don't think I'll need it," said Joe.

"Well, mister, our policy is no refunds," said the storekeeper.

"Don't listen to my brother. We'll take them both," said Frank, picking up the two shovels and following Joe, who was already halfway out the door.

As soon as they were in the station wagon, Joe said, "If that place isn't operating, the electric current won't be turned on in the fence. There won't be armed guards or dogs. We can go right in with a pair of wire cutters, if the gate is even locked. No wonder Iola disappeared so fast. She must have gotten in easily."

"I'm not so sure," said Frank. "That fence seemed to be in awfully good repair, and that warning sign looked freshly painted."

"We'll see when we get there," replied Joe, pressing down on the accelerator.

Night had fallen and the stars were out in a moonless sky when the Hardy boys arrived at the fence again.

"Now we'll check this thing out," said Joe. Before Frank could argue, Joe splashed some water from his canteen onto the fence.

"See? No current," Joe said triumphantly. "We could have been inside hours ago and have caught up with Iola by now, if you weren't so cautious. Frank, you have to learn that sometimes you just have to go for it."

With that, Joe turned the handle on the gate and gave a shove. The gate swung open.

"Easy as pie," he said. "Let's find Iola now."

"Hey, slow down," said Frank. "Joe, if there's anybody inside at all, it *may* be some girl, but don't you know that it can't be Iola? Not after what happened. She's gone. You're just setting yourself up for . . ." Frank trailed off.

Joe wasn't listening to him. He was already moving through the overgrown garden, toward the dark shape of a massive building. Frank, shaking his head, had no choice but to catch up with his brother and try to keep alert to possible danger for both of them.

"She's in there, I *feel* it," said Joe. He shined his flashlight on the massive oak door of what seemed to be a Victorian mansion.

"The storekeeper was right—this is a crazy place," said Frank.

"When we were kids, we would have called an old heap like this a haunted house," said Joe. "Except it's not a ghost we're looking for." He reached for the doorknob. "Now we—" Suddenly Joe gasped. "Wha—?"

He and Frank were caught in blazing light that seemed to come from every direction. It blinded them, but they could hear a voice near them quite well.

"Freeze—or you will be the dead ones!"

Chapter

4

BLINKING, THE HARDY boys turned toward the sound of the voice. But the glare of a spotlight prevented them from seeing whoever was talking.

"You seem to be interested in entering the Lazarus Clinic," the voice said. It was remarkable in just one respect: There was nothing remarkable about it. It was without an accent of any kind. "Allow us to give you a guided tour. But first, raise your hands."

Two men dressed in black slacks, black sweatshirts, and black athletic shoes stepped forward. They carried military assault rifles poised and ready.

Frank and Joe raised their hands.

"I am glad to see you are being cooperative," said the voice. "Hugo and Fritz have nervous trigger fingers. Now we must have a quick examination of your persons. Hugo, frisk them."

While Fritz trained his rifle on the Hardy boys, Hugo took their hunting knives from their sheaths, then gave them a swift but professionally thorough going-over, from their ankles to their shoulders.

"Good, you are clean," said the voice. "Take them inside."

Hugo swung open the door, and prodded by Fritz's assault rifle, the Hardy boys went inside.

From behind them the voice said, "Please do not turn around to look at me, unless you want a rifle barrel smashed into your face. Instead take a look around you. This building is unique. It was originally built ninety years ago by an eccentric millionaire, who later went bankrupt. It was converted into a mental clinic sixty years later by an even more eccentric psychologist, who went bankrupt in turn. It is now perfect for my organization to use. Not only did we buy it dirt cheap, but we are assured of privacy here. Our work demands a great deal of privacy."

"Pretty sloppy of you to leave your front gate unlocked then," said Frank.

He got the answer he half-expected.

"It was no accident that the gate was unlocked—for you," said the voice. "Rest assured, it is locked now."

"So we walked into a trap," said Frank. "And Iola was the bait."

"I was told you were an intelligent young man," the voice said.

"So it *was* Iola!" Joe exclaimed. "She *is* here! Tell me where she—" Forgetting himself, he wheeled around to question his captor.

He didn't get to finish his question—or see who was doing the talking.

All he saw was Fritz's rifle barrel slashing toward his face, while in the background, a figure darted out of sight behind a high-backed chair.

At the same time, the lightning reflexes that made Joe an ace athlete went into action. Before the rifle barrel could touch his face, he grabbed it and pulled it, letting Fritz set himself off balance by his own forward momentum. Then he viciously shoved it away, sending Fritz sprawling backward into Hugo's rifle.

"Run for it!" Joe shouted to Frank while he himself dashed through a nearby doorway and down a corridor. Behind him he heard shouts and running footsteps.

At the end of the corridor was a winding stairway. Joe went up it three steps at a time. On the second floor, he raced down another corridor, rounded a sharp turn, and found himself facing a closed door. The door was metal, in sharp contrast to the old wood of the house and the faded floral carpeting on the floor.

Joe heard the footsteps of his pursuers. He hesitated for just a moment before grabbing the door knob and giving it a turn.

The door opened easily. Joe stepped inside—and felt his knees go weak.

Stunned, he could only gasp, "Iola."

She was sitting in a chair facing him, looking exactly the way she did when Joe had last seen her—her face, her hair, even the clothes she was wearing.

But now there were electrodes fastened to both sides of her head.

Leather straps bound her wrists to the arms of the chair.

And her eyes stared blankly at Joe.

Iola wasn't alone. Four men were in the room. There were a distinguished-looking elderly man with a thick white crew cut and a livid scar across his pale forehead; a short, stout, middle-aged Oriental; a tall, thin youth in his twenties with a freckled face and horn-rimmed glasses; and a massively built man with a shaved skull. All wore white lab coats and the same startled expression as Joe barged in.

Joe, though, had eyes only for Iola.

"What are you doing to her?" he cried. He clenched his hands into fists and moved forward menacingly. "Take those electrodes off her head! Get those straps off her wrists!"

He didn't know what he was going to do if they refused—and he never got to find out.

Too late he heard a sound behind him.

Before he could turn, an arm snaked around his neck.

Then he felt a jabbing pain in his arm.

A needle— was all he managed to think before the room and Iola's face blurred as Joe slid down the chute to oblivion.

Oblivion, Joe decided, was like a sleep without dreams. There was no way of telling how long he was out. It might have been a minute or a day later that he opened his eyes and saw Frank's face looking down at him with concern.

"I was hoping you had gotten away," said Frank. "No luck, huh?"

"I was hoping you'd made it, too," said Joe, putting his hand to his forehead, which was aching from the aftereffect of whatever drug had knocked him out. Then he said, "Ouch!"

It wasn't his forehead that had pained him, though. It was his thumb. Only then did he notice that his thumb was wrapped in a thick bandage.

The next thing he noticed was that Frank's thumb was bandaged in the same way.

"Our thumbs," Joe said. "What happened to them?"

"I've been wondering the same thing ever since I came to after they drugged me," said Frank. "All I know is how much it hurts—too much to risk taking the bandage off."

"Cautious as usual, but I guess you're right," said Joe. "Anyway, we've got more important questions to answer. Like where are we, and how do we get out of here? I can't even tell what time of day it is. They took my watch away, along with

29

my clothes. The sweatshirt and pants they put on me are two sizes too big. You're lucky. At least they left you with your clothes.''

"They left me with my watch, too," said Frank, glancing at it. "It's ten P.M. We were knocked out for a whole day.''

"Unless they fooled around with your watch to confuse us," said Joe. "In this room, there's no telling." His eyes traveled around the blank white walls of the windowless room. The only opening was a viewing window of unbreakable plastic in the metal door.

"Good thinking. We have to watch out for dirty tricks," said Frank, nodding. He looked around the room. "I can't see any way out of here. This must have been a high security cell for disturbed patients when this place was an asylum.''

"We'll have to wait until they take us out of here, and then make a break for it," said Joe. "One of us has to make it. It isn't only for our sakes. Iola is here. I saw her, right before they caught up with me.''

Frank leaned forward, his eyes gleaming with excitement. "That can only mean one thing. The Assassins are involved in this. They're the only ones who could have gotten their hands on Iola right before the car blew up.''

"So you're finally convinced she's alive?" asked Joe.

"I can't deny the evidence," said Frank. "They must have yanked her away from the car door a split second after she opened it and a split second before that device triggered the bomb."

"It's like I told you—I never actually saw Iola get in the car," Joe said eagerly. Then he paused. "But why would the Assassins want to kidnap her?"

"Who knows what plans they have?" asked Frank. "The only thing we can be sure of is that they're still operating all over the world. Exposing one of their plots and nailing a few of their killers was like chopping one tentacle off an octopus." He set his face in determination. "We have to get out of here. We have to alert the Network."

"But first we have to rescue Iola," said Joe, a touch of anger in his voice. It was just like Frank to think of the Network first and Iola second. Frank had his dogged sense of duty to the Network—even though that top secret government agency and its contact agent, the Gray Man, had made it clear that they'd rather do without the Hardys, if only the Hardys hadn't proved so valuable.

Joe was slightly mollified when Frank said reassuringly, "Of course we'll get Iola out of here. I'm not some kind of monster. But we have to make contact with the Network fast. We have to warn them about what's going on out here in the middle of nowhere."

"I guess you're right," said Joe reluctantly. "As long as Iola gets number-one priority."

"Of course I'm right," replied Frank, and

31

when he saw Joe's reaction to his smug tone, he again added, "And of course Iola comes first. But we can't just go with our emotions. We have to make plans to cover all possibilities. Like what if just one of us makes it out of here? What does he do then?"

"He has to waste a lot of time getting back to Bayport," said Joe. "That's the only place we can contact the Network from."

"We may not have that much time, if we don't want the Assassins to skip out of this crazy house," said Frank. "We have to figure out a way to contact the Network from here."

"Look, you were the one who insisted we take a total break from crime fighting," said Joe. *You* decided to leave our connection with the Network at home. Without that modem the Network gave us, we're totally cut off from them."

"It was dumb of me, I admit," said Frank. "But look, give me a rundown of how you'll make contact with them. Not that I don't trust you. But I want to make sure you'll do it exactly right if I'm not around. The Network won't tolerate the smallest error. They're really strict about total security."

Joe nodded. That made sense. Frank was the one who handled the computer hook-up that connected them to the Network's central Washington office. But Frank had taught him how it worked—

in case of emergencies like this one. Joe went over the procedure in his mind, opened his mouth, and then closed it.

"What's the matter? Your mind go blank?" Frank said. "Take a couple of minutes. See if you can remember it without my helping you."

"It's not that. I can remember it perfectly," said Joe. "But there's a good chance this place is bugged. That drug must have messed up your head. You're usually the one who thinks of things like that."

"Of course I did. I checked the place out," said Frank impatiently. "What do you think I am? An idiot? Let's not waste any more time. They might be coming for us at any minute. Just tell me the procedure so I can feel secure."

Joe looked at his brother more closely. Frank actually looked angry. The drug must still have been affecting him, or else his nerves were shot. Joe felt funny, being the cool, levelheaded one, instead of Frank. But if Frank wouldn't admit that there was no way to detect really sophisticated eavesdropping equipment, then Joe would have to be the one on guard.

"No dice," he said. "The Gray Man told us never to risk revealing the contact code. You know that as well as I do."

To Joe's amazement, Frank's eyes glowed with fury. Then he relaxed, and shrugged. "Okay, if that's the way you want it. Conversation over."

"Glad you've come to your—" Joe began.

Suddenly the door swung open. Fritz and Hugo were there, with their guns.

"Let's go," said Fritz.

Joe kept a sharp eye out for any chance to jump them, but they were too alert and professional. As they marched the Hardys down the corridor, they kept a perfect distance from Joe and Frank—too far away to be attacked, but not far enough away for the boys to escape.

"I wonder what's waiting for us," Joe said to Frank as they walked along.

"I have a strong hunch that they have a big surprise in store," replied Frank.

There was an odd mocking tone in Frank's voice, but Joe didn't have time to wonder about it.

"In there," said Hugo from behind them as they came to an empty door.

As they entered, Frank said in the same strange tone, "Hi, Joe."

"Hi, Frank," answered the young man waiting inside.

Joe looked into the face of that young man—and suddenly wondered if he had really come out of his drugged trance.

Or if maybe he was as crazy as the inmates at the Lazarus Clinic used to be.

The young man he was staring at was himself!

Chapter

5

FOR A SECOND, all Joe could see was his own face staring into his, as if he were looking into some kind of crazy mirror.

Then he saw more.

He saw that the double facing him was wearing Joe's own clothes—which must have been why Joe was wearing the gray sweatshirt and pants.

He saw that his brother Frank, the *real* Frank, was not standing beside him, but was strapped in a chair in the center of the room. Frank was wearing gray sweat clothes, too, while his own clothes were on whoever it was who was posing as Frank.

Joe didn't try to figure out what it all meant.

Instead he shot out a right cross aimed at the chin of the double facing him.

But the double reacted just as fast, blocking the

punch with his left arm and lashing out with a right hook.

Joe knew it was coming. He slipped it by pulling his head back sharply and dived at his opponent.

He missed and hit the floor with a jarring crash.

His double leapt on him but did not make contact. Joe rolled out of the way in the nick of time.

The two of them lay sprawled side by side on the floor. Then, at the same time, they jumped to their feet and stood facing off, panting and looking futilely for an opening in each other's defenses.

"That's enough," said a voice over a hidden speaker system. It was the voice of the unseen man who had directed the Hardy boys' capture. A voice without accent or inflection. A voice that could have been produced by a computer—or by somebody who wanted to give no clue to his identity.

"The experiment is over," the voice continued. "You two could keep fighting for an hour without either of you gaining an advantage. Joe Hardy number two is a success, a perfect replica of Joe Hardy number one, right down to the last reflex. Okay, men, take care of Joe One, before he exhausts himself trying to knock himself out."

Fritz and Hugo, who had been watching the fight with big grins, stepped forward and grabbed Joe by both arms. They shoved him into a chair next to Frank I. Frank II, grinning as well, used the straps on the chair arms and legs to tie Joe in.

Careful not to let his movements show, Joe flexed his muscles to test the straps. They held tight—no chance of a breakout. At the same time, he glanced around the room, and caught sight of the lenses of TV cameras in openings in all four walls, near the ceiling. Doubtless the cameras showed everything that was happening in the room to whoever was in command.

The voice came over the speaker again. Frank and Joe, listening closely, could detect a note of very human triumph in the mechanical tone. "Now that you are both comfortably settled in, allow me to introduce the team responsible for our successful effort. I'm sure that if your hands were free, you would want to applaud them. Gentlemen, you may come in."

The men who entered were the four Joe had seen in the room with Iola.

The voice first introduced the distinguished-looking elderly man with the crew cut.

"Meet Dr. Helmut von Heissen, one of the most brilliant plastic surgeons in the world. Unfortunately, the world does not know of the remarkable advances he has made in skin grafting techniques, since he was unable to publish the results of the splendid scientific experiments he performed while a young doctor at a Nazi camp.

"Our organization, however, fully appreciates his genius. We have given him a free hand and unlimited resources to pursue his efforts ever since we discovered him living in forced obscurity. The results you see before you—Frank Hardy Two and Joe Hardy Two—are your perfect doubles, all the way down to your thumbprints.''

Involuntarily, Joe and Frank looked at their bandaged thumbs.

Seeing this, Dr. von Heissen smiled. ''Do not worry, young men,'' he said, in English that was blurred only slightly by a German accent. ''Your skin will grow back to normal in a couple of weeks, providing, of course, you live that long. On the other hand, if I may use that phrase, your prints will be fully operational on Joe Two and Frank Two in a day.''

''You've got to be kidding,'' said Joe. ''I've heard of mad scientists, but . . . '' Joe shook his head.

The doctor's face hardened for a moment into a chillingly ruthless mask of hate. Then it relaxed into a superior smile again. ''I assure you, my methods have been perfected. I only wish I could publish the results of my years of trial and error. But the world is not yet ready to accept the necessity of using human beings as guinea pigs to speed the pace of progress.''

''You must be patient, Doctor,'' the voice on the speaker said soothingly. ''The time will come when the Lazarus Clinic will be revered around the world as a shrine to your magnificent achievements.''

Then the voice went on with its introductions.

"Of course, molding the body means nothing unless the mind is molded—and we have experts on that, as well," it said. "Meet our colleague, Colonel Chin Huan, formerly chief of the indoctrination section of the Red Army. It was he who engineered the remarkably successful brainwashing program used on American prisoners in the Korean War.

"If he had not chosen to side with the wrong political faction in the power struggle after the death of the Chinese leader Mao Zedong, he would doubtless still occupy a high position in his native land. But as it is, we have been able to let him utilize and further expand his expertise in controlling and programming the human mind. By this time, it may be safely said that a person's mind is putty in his skilled hands."

Chin bowed in the direction of the speaker. "Thank you for your praise, but it was impossible to achieve without the technical help of my comrade Peter Clark." He bowed again, in the direction of the tall, thin, freckle-faced young man with horn-rimmed glasses who stood behind him.

Peter Clark stepped forward to join Chin, and the speaker introduced him. "Mr. Clark was formerly employed by a pioneering electronics firm on the West Coast, until it was bought by a larger corporation and its pure research budget was slashed."

"They took away my laboratory, just when I

39

was getting into some really interesting stuff," Peter Clark complained in a high-pitched whining voice. He sounded very much like a five-year-old tattling on somebody who had stolen his toys.

"Fortunately, we are able to supply Peter with all the equipment he wants. In return he has supplied us with the most advanced techniques for computerizing and electronically implanting information into the human brain," the voice said.

"Really neat stuff," added Peter, with a pleased expression.

"Now you see what the staff of the Lazarus Clinic can do," said the voice.

"You mean you created two guys who look like us, and then programmed them to think like us?" asked Frank.

"Not created—recruited," replied the voice. "We found two young men with the right body types. Then, using our excellent file on your personal lives, we programmed that information into your doubles. We've also recorded your voices and videotaped your activities, and then programmed your speech patterns and motor abilities into Frank Two and Joe Two. But there is a difference between them and you. A big difference. They think what we want them to think. And do what we want them to do."

"You jokers have gone to a lot of trouble—but why?" asked Joe.

"That is for us to know and for you not to live

long enough to find out," answered the voice.

"But you must want us for something. Otherwise you wouldn't have bothered to let us live this long," said Frank.

"You're right. But since you obliged us by walking right into our hands, we have decided to use your presence as an opportunity to pump every bit of information out of what is left of your lives."

"Pump away—you're not getting a thing. Let Chin try his brainwashing stuff and see how far he gets," said Joe defiantly.

"Joe's right," Frank said, and added with calm logic, "You blew whatever chance you had of making use of us when you told us you're going to kill us anyway. Bad move."

The voice, however, did not sound disturbed by the Hardy boys' resistance.

In fact, it seemed to be enjoying its cat-and-mouse game.

"Let me assure you, Frank, there are far more painful things than death—things that can make death seem sweet. And let me inform you, Joe, that there are far swifter and more effective means than brainwashing to get what we want out of you."

The voice paused a moment to let its words sink in. Then it continued, "But I still haven't introduced the fourth member of our team. How rude of me. Let me do it now. Gentlemen, meet Ivan Boshevsky."

With that, the big bearlike man who had been standing behind the others stepped forward. His shaved skull gleamed in the light. His smile gleamed even brighter. His grinning lips parted to display a set of bizarre false teeth, a mingling of gold, silver, and stainless steel.

"Comrade Boshevsky was employed by the Soviet KGB during the regime of Joseph Stalin," the voice went on. "Unfortunately, after Stalin's death, certain of his methods of interrogating prisoners were called into question, and he was not only discharged, but forced to spend several years in the same labor camps where he used to send others.

"Needless to say, as soon as he was released, he sought other employment for his extraordinary skills, and we were only too happy to hire him. His work for us has more than justified our confidence. He has been invaluable in extracting the most jealously guarded bits of personal information from the most reluctant subjects. As I have indicated, he is a true master of making any human being in his hands beg for death."

Boshevsky stood in front of the Hardy boys. He gave them another hideous smile. Then he extended his hands in front of him. They were huge. He put them together and flexed them to limber them up. The sound of his knuckles cracking was like pistol shots.

In a voice eager with anticipation, he said, "I am ready to begin."

Chapter

6

FRANK LOOKED AT the torturer standing in front of him and steeled himself. He remembered what his karate master told him about handling pain. Concentrate on the pain when it comes, rather than try to ignore it. By focusing on the pain and judging exactly how intense it really is, your mind becomes occupied so that fear cannot enter it. It's fear that makes pain truly unbearable, and by eliminating fear, you can stand far more pain than is ordinarily believed possible. Frank hoped his karate master was right. He would soon find out.

Joe braced himself, too. He thought of the times that linesmen had piled up on him on the football field, or baseballs had bounced off his ribs when he was batting. Each time something like that had happened, he hadn't quit or even backed off. He'd just seen red and gone after the opposition even harder.

"Do your worst—and see how far you get," Joe said to Boshevsky and to the unseen person who was directing the horror show.

"If you think we'll cave in, you're crazy," Frank added.

The speaker sounded amused. "I wouldn't dream of hurting two fine young men like you. I realize how courageous and dedicated you are. Breaking you down would be a waste of Boshevsky's energy, not to mention a loss of valuable time. Especially when there is a much easier way to get the information we want." Then the voice barked a command. "Bring her in."

Joe looked toward the door, and his breath caught in his throat. He wanted to believe what he was seeing, yet didn't want to believe it. He felt joy—and pain.

"Iola," he whispered.

A guard had led her into the room, his hand gripping her upper arm as he half dragged her to stand beside Boshevsky. When the guard let her go, she made no move to escape. Instead she stood there with a dazed look on her face.

"Say hello to your boyfriend, Iola," said the speaker.

"Joe, what are you doing here?" Iola said. "What are they going to do to you?"

"Forget about me," said Joe. "What have they

44

done to you? Are you okay? I can't believe you're actually alive!"

But before Iola could answer, the speaker cut in. "Don't worry about what we've done to Iola, Joe. Worry about what we *will* do to her if you don't tell us what we want to know."

"You wouldn't—" Joe began.

"You don't think so?" the speaker said. "Men, convince Joe that we are serious."

Smiling, the Hardy doubles unstrapped Joe from his chair, grabbing his arms firmly when he tried to lash out in a desperate bid for freedom. He felt their grip and realized that they were as strong as he. That made sense, he thought. Doubles were doubles. Joe II had to be Joe's match, and Frank II had to be at least as well conditioned as Frank, who was in top shape.

Meanwhile, the guard shoved Iola into the chair in which Joe had been sitting. He strapped her in, and Boshevsky stepped forward. Once again he flexed his huge hands and cracked his knuckles. Then with the serious look of a craftsman at work, he reached out with one hand and grasped one of Iola's earlobes, giving it a sharp twist.

Iola screamed.

Joe felt his knees turn to water and his blood turn to ice.

Boshevsky was reaching for Iola's other earlobe when the speaker said, "That's enough for the moment. Joe has had a hint of what will

45

happen to Iola if he does not cooperate. Believe me, Joe, what you have just seen cannot compare with Boshevsky's ingenuity and enthusiasm in inflicting pain when he *really* goes to work. But perhaps you don't believe me. Perhaps you want to see more."

"No, no more," said Joe. He kept his eyes on Iola and avoided looking at Frank. He didn't want to see how Frank would react to surrender. Because Joe was about to give in. He would do anything rather than hear Iola scream like that again. "You win. I'll tell you what you—"

"Not so fast, Joe. Think for a second," said Frank, before Joe could continue. "How do you know this is the real Iola? Remember, these guys specialize in creating doubles."

"But her clothes, her voice," said Joe.

"The clothes would be easy," said Frank. "And clearly they can program voices. That would be no trick with a computer to analyze and reproduce voice prints. They could have tapped our phone to get our voices, and as for Iola, remember how she liked to send tapes instead of letters to her friends? They simply got their hands on one of those tapes."

Joe wavered. He looked first at Iola, then at Frank. Whom should he believe? His brother—or his own eyes and ears?

"Very good thinking, Frank," said the speaker. "We were told you had a fine deductive mind, and indeed you have. Unfortunately, even the

46

best of minds can be wrong. And fortunately, it will be easy to prove it in this case. Joe, ask Iola anything you want, no matter how personal it is. If she is not able to tell you things that only you and she could know, you are free to believe that this lovely girl is not the girl you love. Do you have any objection to that, Frank?"

Frank was silent a moment. He bit his lip, thinking hard. Finally he reluctantly admitted, "I guess not."

"But I do," said Joe. "The stuff I ask Iola isn't anything I want anybody else to hear—especially your goon squad here. I'm not going to have Iola perform in this human zoo."

"You want to spare your true love from embarrassment as well as pain. How very touching," said the speaker mockingly. "But I will agree to your request. You may speak with Iola alone in a room. But I warn you against trying to escape. It would be quick death for both of you."

The speaker needn't have issued his warning. The room into which Joe and Iola were led made thoughts of escape impossible. Like the cell Joe had been in before, it was without windows, and the locked door was made of steel.

As soon as the door slammed shut, Joe and Iola turned to face each other. They would have liked to touch each other, too, but their hands were cuffed behind them.

"A man yanked me away from the car just before it exploded," Iola said desperately. "Then

47

I was blindfolded, and I wound up here. I've been kept prisoner ever since. It seems like forever."

"It wasn't so long ago," said Joe, looking into Iola's eyes. "It seems like just yesterday we were together. Maybe that's why, deep down, I wasn't surprised you're alive. I mean, in my heart, I never *really* believed you were gone. It's so great to find out I was right. It's so great to find you. One thing's for sure. I'm never going to lose you again, not if I can help it."

He could see no answering spark of joy in Iola's eyes, though. It was clear why. Iola was still reliving her ordeal.

"I didn't know what they wanted to do with me," she said, her voice filled with remembered hurt. "Then, a couple of days ago, they told me you and Frank were camping nearby. They ordered me to lure you two into a trap. They threatened to let Boshevsky loose on me if I refused. But when I saw you in the woods, I couldn't do it. I turned and ran."

Iola shook her head at the memory. "I was praying you wouldn't be able to follow me here. But you did. I guess I knew you would. You and Frank make quite a team. But this time you were too good for your own good."

Iola was obviously in agony over their plight. Joe ached to take her into his arms to comfort her. It hurt him that he couldn't. And what he had to do next hurt him even more.

"Look, I don't want to ask you a bunch of

48

questions to prove who you are—but I have to," he said. "I mean, *I* know you're *you*. No other girl has ever made me feel the way I feel now. That kind of thing can't be faked. But I owe it to Frank to do what I said I would. You know Frank. He doesn't go by gut feelings. He needs facts, and he won't go along with me to save you from Boshevsky unless he has some."

"I understand," said Iola. "I wish now that I *weren't* me. Or that I had the nerve to say I wasn't or to tell you not to tell them anything even if they torture me. But I can't. I'm just too scared. You see, they made me watch Boshevsky work on somebody once. I know what he can do—and I can't face that happening to me."

She paused, then went on. "But I don't even know what they want to get out of you. Maybe if it's important enough, I'd be able to stand up to them."

"There's only one thing they could want to get out of Frank and me," said Joe, "and that's how to contact the Network."

"The Network?" repeated Iola, puzzled.

"It's a government agency that fights criminals like these," said Joe. "Frank and I hooked up with them after a group that calls themselves the Assassins blew up the car and kidnapped you. We helped the Network stop the Assassins before they pulled off a political murder—Senator Walker's, as a matter of fact. The man you were campaigning for when the car exploded.

"Anyway, the Network sort of let us halfway into their confidence. They gave us a way to contact one of their agents, a guy called the Gray Man, in emergencies. Frank's double tried to fool me into telling *how* we contact the Network, and I bet that *my* double tried to fool Frank the same way. They failed, so now they're trying this."

"But why would they want to contact the Network?" wondered Iola, her brows furrowing.

"Beats me, except that it has something to do with our doubles," said Joe. "They could do a lot of damage."

"So your secret is important," said Iola.

"It's important—but it isn't as important as you," said Joe, looking hard at the only girl he had ever truly, deeply loved. Then his mouth tightened. "If you *are* you."

"How can I prove it?" asked Iola with a helpless look in her eyes, as if she could see Boshevsky coming closer.

"Remember our first date?" said Joe suddenly.

"Of course," replied Iola. "I remember how I told you I thought you were rude for showing up late, and stuck-up for thinking I'd still go out with you."

"And remember how I apologized right then and there and won you over?" said Joe.

"You did not!" said Iola indignantly. "I *didn't* go out with you, and it wasn't until the next day when you said how dumb you had been and how sorry you were that we started getting to be

50

friends. But I don't see what—" Then she paused, and her puzzled face brightened. "I see now."

"That's right," said Joe, and went on with his questions. He asked about the first time they had kissed, about their first quarrel, of dream dates they had had and ones that had been absolute disasters. He asked about movies they had seen together, their favorite snacks, plans they had made. He ransacked his memory, and Iola remembered everything as well as he did.

After half an hour he said, "I'm convinced, you *are* you. The trouble is—" He paused, unable to finish his thought.

Iola did it for him. "I know. The trouble is, you don't know whether to be happy or sad about it. Because now you have to choose between me and this Network of yours."

Joe's jaw tightened. "There's no choice. You're the one I have to think about. The Network can take care of itself."

He went to the door and gave it a kick to signal the guards who were waiting outside. They opened the door and led Joe and Iola back to join the others.

"What did you decide?" the speaker asked.

"You win," Joe said, keeping his eyes fixed straight ahead. He didn't want to have to see the pained look on Frank's face. "What do you want me to tell you—as if I didn't know."

"Not very much. Merely your procedure for

contacting the Gray Man at the Network," the speaker said.

"Don't—" Frank started to say, only to receive a jarring slap of Boshevsky's hamlike hand across his mouth.

Instinctively Joe started to move to his brother's aid. The guards at his side grabbed his arms instantly.

"Don't lose your head, Joe," the speaker cautioned. "Remember what will happen to Iola if you do anything foolish."

"Right, right," said Joe, and forced himself to relax his tensed muscles.

"And now, the information," said the voice.

Joe spoke quickly, as if he wanted to get it all out before he had second thoughts. "We contact the Network through a special modem, which at the moment is hooked up to Frank's computer in his bedroom back home. The access code is Z-slash-two-three-four-one-one-slash-M-O-slash-six-six-three. The response identification code is T-I-slash-four-three-three-slash-seven-seven. Our identification code is H-A-slash-two-two-two-slash-eight-six."

"I am happy you have been so sensible," the voice said. "Since you are so sensible, I need hardly inform you that if you prove to be lying, Iola will pay the consequences."

"I know," said Joe, gritting his teeth.

"Good," said the speaker. "And now that you have kept your part of the bargain, I will keep mine. I promised you that you would feel no pain after you told us what we want to know, and you won't."

Joe felt the guards' hands tighten on his arms as Dr. von Heissen opened a black medical bag. He removed a hypodermic needle and a vial filled with amber liquid. Then he filled the needle and turned to Frank, who looked defiantly at him, determined not to show any fear.

Swiftly, expertly, the doctor gave Frank an injection. Frank's eyes widened for an instant, then closed as his head dropped and his body slumped.

"Frank," said Joe, barely able to choke out his brother's name.

So this is how we meet our end, Joe thought as the doctor reloaded the hypodermic and moved toward him.

"Gute Nacht," said the doctor as he stuck the needle in Joe's arm and pressed down the plunger.

That means "Good night" was Joe's last thought before he plunged into blackness darker than any night.

Chapter
7

THIS HAS TO be a dream, Joe thought.

It was like a dream—a dream that kept repeating itself.

Once again he was being shaken awake. Once again he was in the windowless cell. Once again he saw Frank's face above him.

But this time Frank was dressed as Joe was, in gray sweatpants and shirt.

And Frank's face wore the same slightly dazed expression that Joe's did.

"It is you, isn't it?" Joe asked.

"Sure is," replied Frank.

"And we're not dead?" said Joe.

"If we are, this isn't my idea of heaven, and I hope we didn't foul up enough to go the other way."

By now Joe was fully awake, his mind functioning.

"I wonder why they didn't kill us on the spot," he said. "I can't think of any more use they might have for us."

"They must have wanted to keep us alive but safely under control long enough to make sure that what you told them was true," said Frank.

He looked hard at Joe, and Joe had to avert his eyes as the awful events flooded back to him.

"Look, I'm sorry, but I had to do it," said Joe.

Frank tried to keep his expression rigid with disapproval, but he couldn't. His face softened. "I know you had to," he said. "I know how much Iola meant to you."

"You don't have to use the past tense," said Joe. "She's alive, remember."

"I'm still not totally convinced of—" said Frank, but when he saw Joe getting ready to argue, he dropped the subject. There were too many much more pressing matters to iron out. "I wonder how long we've been knocked out. I wonder if it's been long enough for our doubles to start doing their dirty work, whatever it is."

"I think we're about to find out," said Joe as he heard a clicking noise. "Somebody's unlocking the door."

The door opened slightly and the barrels of two hunting rifles poked inside.

"Hello again, my little deers," said a voice with a strong French-Canadian accent.

"You two back up against the far wall," said another French-Canadian voice.

The Hardy boys obeyed, and the two hunters who had nearly bagged them in the forest stepped into the cell—Henri, the bald and bearded one, and Jacques, the wiry one. Both still wore their hunting clothes.

"I guess I should be surprised to see you, but I'm not," said Frank. "Your story sounded a little fishy."

"It was a cover story that we didn't think we'd have to use," said Jacques, shrugging. "We thought we'd knock you off right then and there, and that would be that. But we had strict instructions to be sure to eliminate both of you at the same time, or it was no go. It was vital that no one find out that you had been wiped out."

"That makes sense," said Joe. "Otherwise those doubles of ours would be worthless. Nobody would believe they were us."

"And when you failed, you fell back on your second plan," added Frank. "You put us on Iola's trail."

"Which led us into this trap." Joe finished his brother's train of thought.

"They told us you two were smart," said Jacques, nodding.

"But not smart enough," said Henri. "Come on, let's get this over with."

"What are you going to do with us?" asked Joe.

"First, we are going to take a little walk in the garden," replied Jacques. "And after that—but we'll let you find out."

"Yes, we will make it a surprise," said Henri with a nasty smile.

Frank and Joe exchanged quick glances. They didn't need words to tell each other what they both clearly saw. Henri and Jacques were still angry at having been beaten in the forest. They were aching for revenge. Frank and Joe would have to be careful not to rub their itchy trigger fingers the wrong way.

The Hardys meekly followed orders as they were marched at gunpoint out of the cell, through the empty corridors of the clinic, and out a door into the abandoned garden. It was night, and the garden looked like a ghostly jungle under the full moon.

"You don't mind if we ask you some questions," said Frank as they walked. "I don't figure you intend to let us live long enough to tell anyone the answers."

"You figure right," replied Jacques with satisfaction. "This time you will not escape our bullets. Just do not try to make any false moves—or you will die even sooner than planned."

"Before that, I'd like to know who it is that's outsmarted us," said Frank in a resigned tone. "I bet it's the Assassins. They're your bosses, and they set this whole operation up to get revenge on us for fouling up one of their plots."

"You're right about us being members of the Assassins," said Jacques.

"But you're wrong about everything else," said Henri.

"I don't get it," said Joe. "How can you be working for the Assassins, yet *not* working for them?"

"The Lazarus Clinic borrowed us from the Assassins to do this job," said Jacques.

Joe still looked puzzled. "Borrowed you? You mean, like somebody borrows a lawnmower from a neighbor?"

"Exactly right," said Jacques. "The Lazarus Clinic wanted to cut you down, and the Assassins had the tools to do it. Us."

"Like you said, the Lazarus Clinic and the Assassins are neighbors, good neighbors," added Henri. "The clinic has helped us many times in the past—for large amounts of money, of course—and we were happy to return the favor, naturally, also for a fee. The clinic had no trouble paying it. They run a very profitable business.

"You would be amazed at how many people want to change their faces and their identities. You would be even more amazed to know who some of them are. And the size of the bonus we are getting for this job would absolutely astonish you.

"The clinic couldn't afford to haggle with us. This was too much of a rush job," said Henri.

"The Lazarus people had been shadowing you two for a long time, developing a foolproof plan to snatch you and rub you out in your hometown, with nobody being the wiser. But when they discovered you were coming so close to them, in the Maine woods, it was an opportunity to eliminate you that they could not pass up, even if it meant pushing their plans ahead of schedule and laying out big bucks for us."

"This was a golden chance to get rid of you without a trace," Jacques elaborated. "They could take care of you in the forest, and if that failed, they could lure you here. They are very careful people. They always have a back-up plan."

By then the hunters and the Hardys had reached a small clearing in the garden. The hunters told the boys to stop, raise their hands above their heads, and turn and face the hunters. In the moonlight the Hardy boys could see the rifles aimed straight at their hearts.

"So they needed two killers in a hurry, and they got you two from the Assassins," said Frank. He kept his voice calm as he repeated what the hunters had said. He didn't want it to sound as if he was desperately playing for time as he tried to figure a way out of this jam.

"That must be why Iola looked so confused when she saw me—they hadn't had time to complete her brainwashing," said Joe.

"What a smart young man you are," said

Jacques with thick sarcasm. "Yes, you are right. The girl was merely supposed to pretend to run away, so that you would go get your brother and come looking for her. Then when you both came back together, she was supposed to reappear and distract you enough to make sure you were sitting ducks for us."

"Instead, she really did run away, and you were alert enough to save yourselves," said Henri. "I tell you, that failure will not look good on our records when promotion time comes around."

"Still, it did not end badly," said Jacques. "I heard the Lazarus people saying that though your coming here to the clinic presented a slight element of added risk, it also had its good side. They were able to get a very useful piece of extra information from you by capturing you alive."

"I just hope they tell that to the Assassins—so our performance rating is not hurt," said Henri.

"I'm sure they will, after we make sure these two are never a danger again," said Jacques.

"But there's something I still don't understand. What interest does the Lazarus Clinic have in the Network?" said Joe. "Why should they be so eager to have our doubles make contact with them?"

"They did not tell us, and we did not ask," said Henri. "Our job isn't to ask questions, but to follow orders."

"Already we have wasted too much time talking," said Henri. He gave the Hardy boys a nasty smile. "Don't think we don't know that you two have been stalling for time. We have merely been playing a little game of cat and mouse with you. But now your time has run out."

"That's right," said Henri. "We were called off an important job in Quebec to come down here, and we must get back there quickly. We are scheduled to plant a bomb tomorrow."

"So we get this over with right now," said Jacques.

"Yes," said Henri. "I suggest you stop staring down the barrels of our guns and look down at the ground."

"We're not scared of facing you," said Joe. He was getting ready to make a leap at them. He might not stand a chance, but it beat just standing there and taking it.

"Don't get any smart ideas, Mr. Tough Guy," said Henri contemptuously. "I said look at the ground, and I meant it. To your right, next to that rose bush."

Lying there in the moonlight were two shovels.

"You brought those shovels here—and now you will get to use them," said Henri.

"That's right," said Jacques. "To dig your own graves."

"Pick up those shovels and start digging," ordered Henri, motioning with his rifle.

"We'll tell you when to stop," said Jacques.

"And when to die," added Henri.

61

Chapter

8

SWEAT SOAKED FRANK'S clothes as he dug. He and Joe had been deep in trouble before, but never three feet into their graves and getting deeper every minute.

Digging in the hole next to Frank, Joe was thinking the same thing. There had to be a way out. But all he could see was the dirt on his shovel. The dirt that soon would be shoveled back over him.

Then both Hardy boys heard the words they were dreading.

"Okay, boys, you've dug enough," said Jacques, motioning with his rifle for them to stop.

"I thought graves were supposed to be at least six feet deep," said Frank. "This one is barely up to my waist."

"Still stalling for time, I see," said Henri. "Well, we don't have any more time to waste. We have to cut out of here for Quebec quickly, the minute we're finished with you. And these holes are plenty deep enough."

Jacques nodded in agreement. "They will not have to hold you standing up. You most certainly will be lying down," he said.

"And nobody is going to come digging for you here," said Henri.

"So goodbye, Hardy boys," said Jacques, taking aim with his rifle.

"Let me dig just one more shovelful—to even out the bottom. I always like to do a job right, even if it's the last job I ever do," said Frank.

He didn't dare look at Joe. He could only hope that his brother picked up on his words.

Joe didn't dare look at Frank. He could only hope that he was hearing his brother right.

The Hardys looked at the two Assassins and felt a surge of relief when Jacques shrugged and nodded, and then Henri shrugged in accord.

Instantly the Hardys turned to the work at hand. They took firm holds on their shovels, turned, bent down, and dug deep into the black earth. Then they straightened up, with their shovels carrying full loads.

"Maybe you will be rewarded for your labors. Maybe they will plant roses over you so that your blood will nourish beautiful blossoms. You will become what in the sixties they used to call

63

flower children," said Henri, chuckling at his own grisly joke.

"It's a pity this has to end so fast—playing cat and mouse with you has been fun," added Jacques, smiling, too.

"Yeah, a pity," said Frank. "I'd much rather be the one who has the last *laugh*."

Praying that Joe interpreted his raised voice as a cue, Frank flung his shovelful of dirt at Jacques, who was nearest to him.

His prayer was answered.

Joe's shovelful of dirt smacked Henri in the face at the same moment that Frank's hit Jacques.

Both Hardy boys followed up instantly, coming out of their holes with raised shovels. They smashed the shovels down on the Assassins' skulls with equal force—and with equal results.

Frank and Joe stood side by side, catching their breath and looking down at the two knocked-out killers at their feet.

"Good thinking," Joe said.

"Good thinking yourself," replied Frank.

"Now what?" asked Joe.

"Now we have to move fast," said Frank. "We have to catch up with our doubles, and that'll be hard. We can be sure that they've already checked out the information about the Network connection; otherwise the clinic wouldn't have decided that they were finished with us. I wonder how long we were knocked out."

Joe bent down and took a watch off Henri's limp wrist. As he had hoped, it was a calendar watch. "We've been out for a whole day," he said. "No wonder I'm starved." Then he grinned and added, "Of course, action like this always gives me an appetite. What I'd do for a burger and some fries right now. Or maybe a double-thick shake."

"You'll have to forget about food," said Frank. "We have to figure out what to do with these two bozos. Then we have to figure out how to escape."

Joe looked down at the two Assassins. "I've got an idea. They were talking about planting bombs. Instead, *we'll* plant them."

Frank nodded, "Right. But before we do, let's change clothes with Jacques and Henri. That way we might be able to get past any guards at the gate, which will save us the time of trying to tunnel under the fence. And we need to save all the time we can."

"Let's get to work on these holes," said Joe, grabbing his shovel again.

Twenty minutes later, Joe and Frank were in the Assassins' hunting clothes, and the Assassins were in the Hardy boys' sweatsuits. The two killers, bound and gagged, were also in dirt up to their necks. All they could do to express their feelings was make faint noises while their eyes bulged with fury.

" 'Bye now," said Joe, picking up one of their

rifles. "I hope this doesn't get you in trouble with your bosses. I'd hate to think of you spending the next few years cleaning dirty weapons and stuff like that."

"I hope the guards at the gate don't check us too closely," said Frank, picking up the other rifle. "I don't want to have to shoot my way out of any tight spots."

"Risk is the name of the game," said Joe cheerfully as he headed toward the gate.

For what seemed like the millionth time in their adventures, Frank had to shake his head at his brother's enthusiasm for taking on danger.

On the other hand, Frank had to admit to himself, life would be pretty dull without the kick of overcoming odds.

For instance, when they reached the gate and gave the guard stationed there a casual wave, and in turn were waved through by him, the surge of triumph and relief made the jittery sensation beforehand worthwhile.

Unfortunately, the feeling of triumph lasted only as long as it took them to reach their camping site.

By the time they arrived, after a half-hour of jogging along the overgrown forest trail in their heavy hunters' boots, they were breathing hard. By now the eastern sky was brightening with the first hint of dawn. Joe looked at where their tent and equipment had been, shook his head, and said, "They've cleaned out everything. They didn't leave a trace that we had ever been here."

"I guess we should have expected this," said Frank. "Let's check out the station wagon, though I've got a strong hunch what we'll find."

He was right. The spot where they had parked the station wagon was empty.

"What now?" asked Joe, still looking regretfully at where the station wagon had been. "Two months of hard work on the engine and a new paint job down the drain."

"We need wheels. We have to get back to Bayport fast," said Frank. "That's where our doubles must have gone—to access the Network on our computer. We have to try to catch up with them before they use it. And if we can't do that, we have to alert the Network before our doubles pull off whatever dirty trick they're planning."

Joe wiped his dripping forehead. Already the chill of the Maine night was wearing off as the sun cleared the horizon. It was shaping up to be a scorcher. "It feels like we're chasing our own shadows," he said, looking down the deserted blacktop road.

"Let's make it to town and see if we can rent a car there," said Frank. "Good thing Henri and Jacques had wallets stuffed with cash. I guess the Assassins don't believe in credit cards." Frank started jogging down the road. "Come on. It can't be more than a six-mile run."

Joe jogged beside him, matching him step for step, even though Frank kept pushing up the pace.

"Aren't you glad now I made you go on all those training runs with me last winter?" Frank asked his brother.

"Give me sprinting any time," panted Joe. "Or at least give me a pair of running shoes. I think somebody slipped lead into the soles of these boots."

Thirty-five minutes later, Joe spotted the general store where they had bought their shovels.

"There should be a crowd cheering us on—like at the end of the Boston Marathon," Joe said, gasping for air. "I could use some encouragement about now."

"Come on, slowpoke," said Frank, pushing up the pace still more. "Let's just hope that we find someone up this early."

Fortunately, the storekeeper kept country hours. He was sitting in a rocking chair inside his store, sipping coffee.

"Morning, young fellows," he said. "Back so soon?"

"Seems so," said Frank carefully. He gave his brother a warning glance not to say anything more, just in case the storekeeper wasn't talking about them, but about their doubles.

Joe nodded almost imperceptibly. He got the message.

"What happened, your car break down?" said

the storekeeper. "I told you that old heap couldn't be trusted when I filled it up with gas yesterday. You should have listened to me and taken my price for it and that car rental deal I offered you."

"Yeah, I have to admit, you were right," said Frank, thinking fast. "It gave up the ghost just ten miles from here. Some local farmer bought it for junk and put us up in his barn for the night. As soon as it got light, we hiked back here to take you up on that car rental."

The storekeeper looked the Hardy boys over and said, "A little ten-mile stroll, and you boys are sweating like that? Why, when I was your age, I could do that without breathing hard. Trouble with young folks today, you don't take care of yourselves."

"Right," said Joe, grinning. "I plan to turn over a new leaf. But at the moment, I'm not in shape to make it home by foot. About that car rental you mentioned . . .?"

"Come with me," said the storekeeper, getting out of his rocking chair.

He led them out of the general store and down the single main street of the tiny town. They reached a car rental agency, and the storekeeper unlocked its front door and ushered them inside. Then he put on a cap with lettering that read We Aim to Serve You Better for Less, and said, "Now, what model do you want?"

"The fastest you have," said Frank.

" 'Fraid that's going to cost you quite a bit," said the storekeeper. "Now, for a lot less, I can give you our special wreck-of-the-week bargain, guaranteed to get you there or your money back."

"We'll still take the fastest," said Frank.

The storekeeper's face was torn between the pleasure of making a nice profit and the pain of seeing money squandered. "Well, I reckon it's your money," he said with a shrug. "What'll it be, American Express, Visa, or MasterCard?"

"We're paying in cash," Frank said, pulling out a wallet bulging with hundred-dollar and fifty-dollar bills.

"Sorry about that," said the storekeeper. " 'Fraid I can't take cash. Against the franchise company's rules."

"Look, we'll pay extra," said Joe, pulling out a stuffed wallet from his pocket.

"Rules are rules," said the storekeeper, shaking his head. Then he looked at the bulging wallets in the Hardy boys' hands while his tongue worked itself thoughtfully around in his mouth. " 'Course, I happen to have a car I just might be willing to *sell* you . . ."

A half an hour later, the Hardy boys were rolling down the highway in a 1955 Buick Roadmaster, with tail fins that seemed to reach halfway to the sky.

"I hope this whale makes it to Bayport," said

Joe, at the wheel, pressing down as hard as he dared on the accelerator.

"Good thing we still have some cash left," Frank pointed out. "We're going to have to stop at every gas station on the way. This car must get about a hundred yards to the gallon."

It was early afternoon and ten refueling stops later, when the car engine wheezed to a stop. But by that time it had done its job. The Hardy boys were just four blocks from home.

They climbed out and pushed the car to the curb. Joe gave it a quick final look. "This baby is going to keep me busy for at least five months."

Just then a voice behind them said, "Man, Joe, don't you ever get enough?"

Frank and Joe turned and saw their pal Chet Morton. He was grinning at them, his mouth stained brown from the chocolate triple-dip ice cream cone in his hand.

"Just this morning you drove by in that ancient station wagon of yours," said Chet. "Now you've got another antique. What you plan to do, open up a museum?"

Frank and Joe exchanged quick glances.

"It was a bargain, I couldn't resist it," said Joe.

"Hey, you guys want to go to the pizza parlor with me?" asked Chet.

"Some other time," said Joe. "We've got a couple of things to do right now. Anyway, what about that diet you were going on?"

"Like you said, some other time," replied Chet. "I've got things to do, too, like try the new peppers-and-pepperoni special." Chet patted his ample stomach with anticipation, gave a goodbye wave of his hand, and headed for lunch.

"So our doubles arrived here this morning," said Frank. "Let's make it home fast."

But they had covered only a block when they were stopped again.

It was Frank's girlfriend, Callie Shaw.

"You're still in town?" Callie said. "When I saw you a couple of hours ago, you said you had to make some kind of trip, so we couldn't see each other tonight. And why on earth have you and Joe put on those hunting outfits?" There was a hurt look in her eyes. "I know you're involved in a lot of mysterious activities, but you've let me in on them before. What's the matter, don't you trust me anymore?"

"Look, Callie, I promise I'll explain everything as soon as I can," said Frank. "But not now, okay?"

"If that's the way you want it," Callie said, and turned on her heel and strode away.

"Sometimes I wonder what you see in her," said Joe. "Every time we get a case, she wants to horn in."

"You've got to be kidding," said Frank. "I wouldn't mind Callie's help right now, except I can't see how anybody but ourselves can help us out of this mess. I'm getting more and more jittery thinking about what we're going to find out at home."

"Too bad Dad's not around," said Joe. "*He* could help us."

But Fenton Hardy, the great detective who was the boys' father, was away with their mother, Laura Hardy, on a well-deserved Hawaiian vacation.

The only one at home was the Hardy boys' aunt Gertrude.

When she saw the boys come in, a worried look appeared on her face—a not uncommon occurrence. The smallest thing could set off alarm bells inside Aunt Gertrude—and her nephews provided unending sources of concern.

"What happened?" she asked. "Some kind of trouble? You raced out of here just a few hours ago without a word of explanation. And now you're back, wearing different clothes."

"No trouble," Frank assured her as he headed for the stairs to his room.

"Just a little change of plans," Joe added, and followed Frank up the stairs, three steps at a time.

Frank and Joe went straight to Frank's room.

"We've got to warn the Network," said Joe as Frank warmed up his computer. "It's a shame we had to ditch that scrambler radio they gave us." The Hardys had had to leave the radio behind while being pursued through the Adirondack Mountains by followers of the *Cult of Crime*.

"There's still the computer modem," Frank said, tapping the code numbers on his keyboard. But the screen went blank.

"What the—?" he burst out, opening up the computer's case. Then his face got bleak. "The modem is gone. Our twins must have used it and taken it with them."

"Then we have no way to get in touch with the Network," said Joe.

Frank nodded. "Not by electronic connection—and certainly not in person. If only they trusted us enough to let us know where their headquarters are . . ."

His voice trailed off as the computer's disk drives began whirring. "Hey, I didn't start any programs."

"Get back!" yelled Joe as the computer went up in a blinding flash.

Chapter

9

FRANK'S CHAIR TOPPLED as he threw himself backward. He hit the floor hard, then rolled to his feet.

Joe charged the rogue computer with Frank's bedspread in his hands, ready to smother any fire.

But Frank had already reached the wall and pulled the plug.

With a sizzle of electricity, the computer died down.

The Hardys stared at the smoldering wreck. "Looks like our twins didn't just steal the modem. They set up a nasty surprise if anybody tried to use it." He waved away a thin wisp of smoke. "Even if they didn't nail me, they certainly nailed my computer."

"Maybe the Network will give you a new one," suggested Joe.

Frank's face was grim. "Yeah. If we could get in touch with them." He slammed his fist against his palm in frustration. "If we just had a clue to where they are."

"It's the Gray Man's fault," said Joe angrily. "He should have told us where to find him, instead of keeping us at arm's length, like we were a couple of kids who'd spill the beans at the drop of a hat."

"The trouble is, he wasn't so wrong," said Frank. "After all, we did give the Lazarus goons the information they wanted."

"You mean *I* did," said Joe. "Okay, I admit it, so don't rub it in. But I'm not apologizing. I'd do it again, if it meant saving Iola. If that makes me a wimp, then I'm a wimp."

"Nobody's blaming anybody, and nobody's calling anybody a wimp," said Frank, putting his hand on his brother's shoulder. Frank sometimes got mad at Joe, but when it came to a pinch like this, he wasn't going to see Joe hurt. "Let's not worry about water under the bridge. We have to worry about what happens now."

"What happens now is we stare at your computer and it stares back at us and—" Joe shrugged and said, "We're beat."

But Frank wasn't about to throw in the towel. "When you're stumped by a problem, it means you have to look at it from another angle," he said. "We have to stop looking at this useless computer and look in other directions, starting with going through this room."

Joe shook his head. "What do you figure we'll find? Think our doubles left us a note telling us where they were going?"

Suddenly Frank said in an excited voice, "They just might have. Take a look at this."

He was examining a notepad on his desk.

Joe hurried over, took a look, and then said with disgust, "Come on, Frank, this is no time for kidding. That's nothing but blank paper."

"You know how I like to keep my desk neat— as opposed to yours," said Frank.

"That's putting it mildly," said Joe. Frank's desk was always a model of efficient organization, while Joe's looked like the aftermath of a tornado.

"This notepad is out of place, sitting here in the middle of the desk," said Frank. "One of our doubles must have used it."

"So what?" said Joe. "He took whatever he wrote with him."

"Let's see if he did," said Frank. Without explaining further, Frank emptied his pencil sharpener onto his desktop.

Joe leaned forward to watch. This had to be important, if Frank was soiling his precious work space.

Ignoring the shavings of wood, Frank took a pinch of graphite powder between his thumb and

77

forefinger and sprinkled it on the notepad. Then he shook the notepad very gently, the way gold prospectors used to shake their pans when hunting for gold in streams, to separate grains of precious metal from the silt.

"Pay dirt!" Frank exclaimed, peering down at the paper.

The paper was no longer blank. The graphite dust had settled in indentations in the paper made when something had been written on the paper above it.

"Now if we can just read it," Frank said, squinting hard. What he saw was: 7864 9 St. "And then there's a couple of letters," he added.

Joe peered at the paper, his eyes straining to make out the faint black markings. "There's an *S* and an *E*."

"That's it. Seventy-eight sixty-four Ninth Street, Southeast. We've got it!" said Frank triumphantly.

"One little problem," said Joe. "We know the number, we know the street, but we don't know the city."

"But we can make a good guess," said Frank. "Washington, D.C., is the only city I know that has addresses like that. Its streets are designed to form concentric circles, and they're divided into different compass points."

"Anyway, it makes sense that the Network is located there," said Joe eagerly. "What are we waiting for? Let's go!"

"Let's do one thing first," said Frank, grabbing Joe's arm before he could dash out the door.

"What?" said Joe. "We're wasting time."

"Let's change clothes," said Frank. "We want to keep a low profile, and I kind of think that two guys in hunting clothes, carrying Remington hunting rifles, might attract a tiny bit of attention boarding the New York-Washington shuttle."

"Okay, but make it quick," said Joe, already on his way to his room to change.

Five minutes later he was back, wearing a pair of clean but very worn jeans and a white shirt with the sleeves rolled up.

"My good pair of spare jeans is missing," he said. "Guess who must have taken them."

"I found the same thing," said Frank, who had been forced to put on an old pair of corduroys rather than the pressed Levi's he saved for special occasions.

When they got downstairs, their aunt Gertrude confirmed their suspicions.

"I don't know what's come over you boys," she said. "Used to be that you wore the same clothes for months, until they had to be peeled off you. Today you come back in fishing clothes, go out in your best jeans, come back in hunting clothes, and now you've made another change."

"It must be a stage we're going through," said Joe.

"You could look it up in a psychology book,"

said Frank, and paused. "Look, Aunt Gertrude, could we ask a little favor?"

"What is it?" she said.

"Could we borrow your car for the day?" asked Frank. "We have to take a little trip, and ours broke down."

"I don't wonder," said Gertrude with a small sniff of triumph. "I always said you boys were foolish, spending all that time with those ancient cars that Joe digs up. No surprise that they keep breaking down. That's why I keep trading mine in every two years for a new model. I never have the least trouble."

Joe didn't mention that the main reason his aunt never had car trouble was that she never drove over thirty miles an hour and seldom drove more than ten miles at a stretch. He just said, "Well, maybe this has taught us a lesson."

"I certainly hope so," replied Gertrude.

"But, anyway, can we borrow your car?" asked Frank.

"Well . . ." Gertrude pretended to be thinking it over. But as the Hardys well knew, she had never denied her favorite nephews anything they asked. "If you promise to be careful, and to drive very, very slowly," she said.

"Definitely," said Joe as Gertrude opened up her handbag.

"Of course," said Frank as she handed him the car keys.

It was true what used-car salesmen claimed about cars that were owned by timid, elderly ladies. Aunt Gertrude's car was in great shape, at least at the start of the drive to New York. By the time Joe drove it into the parking lot at La Guardia Airport in New York, several years had been taken off its operating life.

But it had done its job. The Hardys were able to catch a shuttle flight to Washington just before the boarding ramp was wheeled away. And less than an hour later, they were hailing a cab at Washington National Airport.

As the cab drove up, Frank said, "Seventy-eight sixty-four Ninth Street, Southeast, please—and fast. It's an emergency."

The driver turned around to look at them. "You *sure* you want that address?"

Frank double-checked the address he had written down on a piece of paper. "That's it. Seventy-eight sixty-four Ninth Street, Southeast."

The driver shrugged. "Okay. It's your money," he said in a tone that clearly meant, "It's your funeral."

When they arrived at their destination, the Hardy boys saw why the cabbie had sounded so skeptical.

Seventy-eight sixty-four Ninth Street, Southeast, was in the heart of the Washington, D.C., slums, the part of the city that visitors to the capital seldom saw or wanted to see. The street was lined with decayed or abandoned buildings, and idle men lounged on street corners or in front of bars, looking as if they were aching to rip off any stranger. The air reeked with poverty and the violence that poverty bred.

"Want me to wait?" the cabbie asked. "You won't be able to hail a cab in this neighborhood. And you might not get one even if you phone."

"We'll take our chances," said Frank as he paid the man. "We might be awhile."

He waited until the cab drove off before he turned to Joe. "I wonder what our chances are. I've got a strong hunch we've fouled up. This doesn't exactly look like official Washington."

"Sure doesn't," said Joe, glancing at 7864 Ninth Street, Southeast. It was a five-story brick building that looked as if it had been built around the turn of the century and not been repaired since. Graffiti was scrawled on its walls, missing panes of glass had been replaced with dirty cardboard in many of its windows, and paint was peeling from its door. "Know what I'm thinking?"

"I'm afraid so," said Frank.

"We've got the wrong address," said Joe. "Which leaves us—"

"Nowhere." Frank finished his thought glumly. "But we might as well make sure."

He pressed the buzzer.

The front door was opened by a white-haired

man who was clearly the building super. He was wearing paint-splattered, grime-covered, tattered denim work clothes. But what was most noticeable was his size. He was at least six-feet-eight and close to three hundred pounds.

"What do you want?" he said in a hostile voice, looking meaningfully at the baseball bat he held in one hand.

"Uh, guess we have the wrong address," said Joe, stepping back.

"Yeah, sorry to have disturbed you," added Frank.

"Ain't got no use for strangers 'round here," the man muttered, and slammed the door.

"Well, that's that," said Joe. "We're back to square zero."

"Not quite," replied Frank.

"What do you mean?" asked Joe, with sudden hope. He knew the look in Frank's eyes. He could practically hear wheels spinning in Frank's brain. Frank had seen something.

"You notice that guy's work boots?" said Frank.

"No. I was too busy looking at his baseball bat," answered Joe. "Why? Something funny about a super wearing work boots?"

"Nothing funny about *ordinary* work boots," said Frank. "But those work boots had a high polish. The kind of polish the army likes its men to have. Or the secret service or the CIA or the

FBI or any other kind of organization. Some habits are hard to break, and shined shoes is one of them."

"So this guy could work for the Network, and this place could be a front," said Joe, nodding.

"It would be a perfect cover."

"It's easy enough to find out," added Joe. "We just have to buzz him again and tell who we are and ask to see the Gray Man."

"Think a second," said Frank. "How can we prove who we are? Our doubles have our IDs." He looked down at his bandaged thumb. "They even have the thumbprints that are on our IDs. That guy would never let us in."

"We could try to overpower him," said Joe. But he didn't sound enthusiastic about their chances of overcoming that man-mountain.

"There are some things even karate can't do," agreed Frank. He thought a moment. "But we could fake him out."

"What do you mean?" asked Joe.

"I'll show you." Frank picked up an empty bottle that was lying in the litter-filled gutter. Then he walked over to a boy who was standing nearby, looking at the Hardy boys curiously. The boy was about ten years old, wearing worn-out-at-the-knees jeans and a ripped T-shirt. His eyes lit up when Frank waved a ten-dollar bill in front of his face.

"Like to earn some easy money?" Frank asked him.

84

The boy looked hard at the money, then shook his head. "I ain't getting into anything illegal, mister. No way."

"Nothing illegal," said Frank. "And no danger—not if you can run fast."

"Fastest kid in my class," said the boy with pride. "What do you want to do? Put me in some kind of race?"

"That's right," said Frank. "A kind of race. See, the super in that building has been boasting to me how quick he is for his size, and how he doesn't have to lose weight. I want to show him he's wrong. So I'm setting up a test for him. You stand right here, and when he opens the door, make sure he sees you, and then you start running."

"He won't catch me, not in a million years," said the boy, pocketing the bill.

By now Joe had gotten the idea. "Let me have that bottle," he said to Frank. "I've got a stronger pitching arm than you."

"Just remember to duck out of sight fast," Frank said as Joe started his wind-up.

Joe's throw was perfect. The bottle smashed through a front window, and the Hardy boys were crouched behind a next-door stoop by the time the super appeared.

The boy was honest—he earned his pay. He waited for the super to spot him, then tore down the street.

The super went after him.

"That white hair has got to be fake," said Joe, watching him. "That guy moves like a pro half-back."

"We'd better move fast, too," said Frank, leading the way through the front door that the enraged guard had neglected to close.

"Wow," said Joe as he looked around him. "Who would have thought it?"

They weren't in a decaying tenement. They were in a modern office complex, with brightly lit corridors leading past rows of gleaming doors. In front of them on the wall was an office directory.

"Could this be it?" said Frank, his eyes scanning the list of names. " 'Edward Gray. Operations chief. Four twenty-two.' "

"Sounds worth checking out," Joe replied.

"Let's get in that elevator before somebody comes along and spots us," said Frank.

They entered the small elevator near them and rode to the fourth floor. There they followed the numbers on the doors until they reached 422.

"We won't bother to knock," said Frank. "It's a little late in the day to worry about being polite."

He swung open the door and entered, with Joe right behind him.

Joe breathed a sigh of relief. Their gamble had paid off.

The Gray Man was sitting there, behind the desk.

Even better, the Gray Man's eyes lit up when he saw them.

"Frank and Joe Hardy," he said. "What a surprise. Good to see you. What can I do for you?"

Joe grinned. Their troubles were over.

Except that Frank didn't seem to see it that way.

Joe's mouth dropped open as he saw Frank dash toward the Gray Man. Frank hurtled himself over the desk. He smashed into the Gray Man, toppling him out of his swivel chair. Then he sat on the Gray Man's chest and raised his fist menacingly over his deathly gray face.

Frank had gone crazy—or had he?

Suddenly Joe had a horrifying thought, and his blood turned to ice.

Was this really Frank, or was this—?

He didn't bother finishing his thought.

Instead he moved forward, his fists clenched, as he asked harshly, "Who are you anyway?"

Chapter

10

FRANK, STILL SITTING on the Gray Man's chest, looked up at Joe and grinned.

"Relax. I'm still me," he said. "And I haven't gone nuts."

"But—" Joe looked quizzically at the Gray Man, who was unsuccessfully struggling to get out from under Frank.

"I saw him reaching for his desk buzzer," said Frank. "He was going to sound the alarm and bring in guards to haul us away." He looked at the Gray Man, who had given up struggling. "Am I right?"

"You'll never get away with this," the Gray Man said, glaring defiantly at Frank.

"What's gotten into him?" Joe asked his brother.

"It's not what's gotten into him. It's *who's*

gotten *to* him," said Frank. "Our doubles must have arrived here already and convinced him they were us. So when we arrived, he thought we were imposters. Right, Mr. Gray?"

"Very clever," said the Gray Man. "But not clever enough to fool me."

"See what I mean, Joe?" said Frank. "That's why I didn't want him to call the guards. It would have taken too long to convince everybody that we're really us, especially if they tossed us in jail instead of hearing us out. I couldn't risk that. We have to stop our doubles before they do whatever they're out to do. What *are* they out to do, Mr. Gray? You must know. What did they come to see you for? We have to know their next move so we can stop it."

"I'm not talking," the Gray Man said, his jaw clenched with determination.

"Look, we're *us*," said Joe. "Can't you *tell?*"

"I can tell that those are convenient bandages—now we can't check the thumbprints in your files," said the Gray Man. "And I can tell that you're trying to bluff your way through this masquerade even though you've found out I'm on to your game."

Joe looked helplessly at Frank. "What can we do? The guy won't listen."

Frank's brows furrowed. Then they relaxed as he made his decision. But the grim look on his face made it clear that he wasn't happy with what he had decided to do.

"We can't waste time talking, Mr. Gray," he said. "We have to take more direct action."

Joe stared with shock as Frank stood up and hauled the Gray Man to his feet. In the same motion, he grabbed the Gray Man's arm and bent it behind him.

The Gray Man couldn't hide a grimace of pain as Frank gave his arm a slight twist.

"Frank!" Joe protested. He didn't mind doing what he had to do in a fight, but this was different. Torture wasn't his thing. He could take it and he had. Handing it out, though, was something else.

Frank ignored him. "Make up your mind—fast," Frank said to the Gray Man. His voice was rock hard.

"Look, Frank, we can't—" Joe began.

Frank cut him off sharply. "We do it this way. We don't have a choice."

"I don't see why," said Joe, giving his brother a searching look. Maybe he had been right the first time. This couldn't be Frank, who hated to see anyone or anything suffer.

"I've got a hunch that what our doubles are planning has to be stopped fast," Frank said impatiently. "If it means playing as rough as they do, that's the price we have to pay. We can't afford to lose time. It's a rotten trade-off, but it's the only option we have."

Frank's words didn't make Joe feel any less queasy, but they did tell Joe that this was his brother. He recognized their logic, the kind of logic that made Frank so different from him. Joe went by his feelings, and they told him that torturing a man for any reason was dead wrong. But Frank believed in using his head, and arguing with the way Frank summed up a situation was as hard as arguing that two plus two made five.

All Joe could say was, "Maybe you're right, but I can't watch this." And he turned his face away.

"Okay, Mr. Gray," Joe heard Frank say. "Tell us what those guys wanted, and spare yourself a lot of pain."

"Not on your life," the Gray Man shot back.

"Then don't say I didn't warn you," replied Frank.

His eyes still averted, Joe winced in anticipation of what he would hear next.

But what he heard was his brother's defeated voice, "Okay, Mr. Gray, you win. I can't do it. I thought I was tough enough, but I guess I'm not tough that way."

Letting out a deep breath of relief, Joe turned to see that Frank had let the Gray Man go and was standing with his shoulders slumped and a defeated look on his face.

Then Frank's face brightened as the Gray Man put his hand on Frank's shoulder and said, "You win, too, Frank. You've convinced me."

"We have?" said Frank, totally puzzled.

For once Joe could see something that his brother couldn't. "I get it, Mr. Gray. You figured that *real* imposters wouldn't mind torturing you to get the information they wanted. But *we* wouldn't. And you were right."

"I know I'm right," said the Gray Man, his usual decisive authority returning to his voice. "You boys have a lot of courage, but there are some things you can't bring yourselves to do—which is one of the reasons the Network can never completely rely on you. We, like our enemies, sometimes have to play dirty to win."

"And that's one of the reasons we'd just as soon not get hooked up too tightly with you," said Joe. "We'd rather fight crime our own way, with our own rules."

"But right now we're in this fight together," said Frank. "And we have to stop our doubles."

"First of all, tell me about those doubles," said Mr. Gray.

"It's a long story," replied Frank. "But to make it short, there's an organization that makes doubles for clients who need them for crime. They made doubles of us, even down to our fingertips, and they forced us to tell them how to contact you."

"But I made you swear never to—" the Gray Man began, then paused. "I suppose they used torture."

Frank shot Joe a quick glance, then said,

"Right. Torture. I'd rather not go into the details."

"Don't feel bad," said the Gray Man. "Everybody has his breaking point. But tell me more about this organization. What's it called? Where's it located?"

Frank was about to answer when Joe cut in quickly, "There's time for that later. Right now, we have to stop our doubles."

Frank nodded. "Joe's right. What are they up to? Why did they contact you?"

The Gray Man nodded, too. "We *do* have to stop them fast, and that'll be hard. They're clever, I have to hand it to them. They contacted me through the computer hook-up and told me they had to see me personally with information they couldn't risk anybody finding out about through electronic eavesdropping.

"After they got here and after they passed through all the security checks to be able to see me alone, they told me they'd gotten wind of a plot that concerned the life of the President himself. But when I asked them what it was, they said they couldn't tell me. And can you guess why?"

"I'll take a wild guess," replied Frank.

"Go ahead, Sherlock," said the Gray Man, with a smile. "That's what your brother calls you, if I remember correctly."

"Our doubles told you that they couldn't trust

you because there was an organization that made doubles of key figures and you might be one of them."

The Gray Man tried not to look surprised. "And how did you figure that out?"

"You didn't seem as surprised as you should have when we told you about the Lazarus group—like you'd heard it all before," answered Frank.

"So they're called Lazarus," said the Gray Man, thoughtfully.

"But what did they want with you?" Joe interrupted impatiently.

"Oh, right. Back to the subject at hand," said the Gray Man. "They said they could only speak to the head of the Network because they could be sure that this was one person whose identity this Lazarus group could not know. You see, I am the only one in the Network—and one of only a very few people in the highest level of government—who knows who the head is."

"And you revealed it to them?" said Frank.

For a second the Gray Man's air of assurance faded. He looked ashamed, apologetic. Then he pulled himself together. "I did. It was a snap decision and I made it. They claimed the President's life hung by a thread, and only the Network head could stop that thread from being snapped very, very soon. So I told them. Or rather, I told *you*. You see, though I have a lot of doubts about your maturity and efficiency, I have no doubts at all about your honesty."

"Thanks," said Joe.

"Anyway, there's a good chance we can stop them before they do any damage," said Frank. "You can contact your boss immediately."

"If only it were that simple," said the Gray Man. "But you see, one of the methods we've employed to keep our head's identity a total secret is not to have any mechanical lines of communication with the boss.

"I think, especially after seeing how hostile forces succeeded in finding out the link between you and me, that you can see our wisdom in doing that. Only I have contact with our head, in ways that no one shadowing me can suspect. That's just part of the security system that our head has personally devised, and it's proved to be the most effective cover a secret official has ever had—until now, anyway."

"Then you'll have to rush some of your men to cut off the doubles," said Frank.

"Letting our own agents in on the secret would break the system wide open," said the Gray Man. He went to his desk and pulled out a Browning automatic pistol and put it in a shoulder holster that he also took from the desk. He removed his jacket, fastened the holster, and put his jacket on again. "There's only one way to do it. We have to go ourselves."

"What a good idea. Let's all go together."

It was Frank's voice—but it came from the doorway.

Silently the door had been swung open, and Frank II stood there, with a Beretta pistol leveled. As he stepped into the room, Joe II followed, an identical pistol in his hand.

"Brother Frank is right," said Joe II. "I'm sure our twins here are simply dying to meet the Network head."

"Well, maybe we can arrange that," said Frank II, with the kind of sharklike grin that had never appeared on Frank Hardy's face. "First, they'll see the head. And then they'll die."

Chapter

11

"GOOD THING WE checked with home base before we proceeded with the plan," said Frank II as Joe II relieved the Gray Man of his pistol and pocketed it, then frisked the Hardys for weapons.

"Yeah," replied Joe II. "They told us that you two bright boys had escaped and might be coming after us. We were ordered to double back, wait outside this place in case you arrived, and then put you and Mr. Gray out of action."

"Contingency Plan A," added Frank II. "The boss covers all bases when he sets up a job."

"Thanks to you boys, we had to junk our original mission," said Joe II.

"A real shame." Frank II shook his head. "It was a doozy of a scheme. The boss's best ever."

"But at least we'll accomplish something,"

said Joe II. "We'll get rid of the head of the Network, Mr. Gray, and of course you two."

"You'll never get away with this," said the Gray Man. "You'll never even get out of this building."

Frank II smiled. "I don't think we'll have any trouble."

"The boss told us what to do," said Joe II. "We just walk out."

"With you and the Hardy boys," added Frank II. He was wearing Frank's favorite seersucker jacket. He put his pistol hand in the pocket but kept the gun pointed at the Gray Man.

Joe II put his pistol hand in the pocket of the windbreaker he had taken from Joe's closet. He, too, kept his weapon on the Hardy boys.

"Now let's walk out of here together, nice and slow," said Frank II.

"And what will the guard think when he sees two pairs of Hardy boys?" asked the Gray Man.

"The boss thought of that—like he thinks of everything," replied Joe II. "He said this was one place where nobody would even blink."

"Yeah, he said Network people would be used to seeing weird stuff," said Frank II. "They'd figure using doubles was just a new trick of the trade."

Their boss was right. The guard didn't blink an eye when he saw them. In fact, he opened the door for them to go out.

The doubles shepherded Mr. Gray and the

Hardy boys down the street and around a corner. There a large black Mercedes waited for them.

"You guys do things in style," remarked Joe.

"Money is something we don't have to worry about," Joe II replied.

"Yeah. Whoever said that crime doesn't pay never heard about us," said Frank II. He pulled his gun out of his pocket and motioned for the Hardys to sit in the backseat. Then the doubles got in front, with Mr. Gray squeezed between them.

"Don't you two get any funny ideas back there," said Joe II. "My gun is going to be pressed against Mr. Gray here the whole ride. One false move from either of you, and he gets it."

"Just sit back and enjoy the scenery." Frank II pressed the starter and the engine purred to life. "It's your last trip, so you might as well make the most of it."

Frank and Joe exchanged looks, each hoping to see in the other's eyes a gleam of inspiration, a bright idea for getting out of the jam. But there was nothing.

They turned away from each other and looked out the car window as they drove out of the city slum and over a bridge spanning the Potomac River. Soon they were traveling through a countryside that seemed a world away from the mixture of grandeur and grime that was the nation's capital. They saw green fields divided by low stone walls, untouched stands of forest, rippling brooks, and large mansions set far off the highway.

"Pretty cool, huh?" remarked Joe II. "Fairfax County, Virginia. This is where the rich folk live. You know, the fox-hunting set."

"Except we're doing a different kind of hunting," said Frank II. "Head hunting."

"You guys are real jokers," Joe replied sarcastically.

"Yeah, a riot," added Frank.

"Glad you think so," said Joe II. " 'Cause then you can die laughing."

"And you won't have long to wait for the punchline," said Frank II as he turned the Mercedes off the main highway, passing a sign that read Allingham Manor, and onto a narrow blacktop road that cut through a stand of forest.

"Wow!" exclaimed Joe as the road emerged from the forest and he saw an immense, beautifully tended lawn gleaming emerald in the late afternoon sunlight. In the distance was a large, white mansion with Grecian columns.

Joe peered at the house as they approached it. "It looks like something George Washington could have lived in at Mount Vernon."

"Or Jefferson, at Monticello," added Frank.

"But definitely not the kind of place that the Network head would live in," said Joe II. "Pretty shrewd."

"But not shrewd enough." Frank II stopped the car on the white-pebbled circular driveway in front of the mansion.

"This is where we get out," said Joe II. With his gun pressed against the Gray Man, he eased out of the car and his "brother" did the same. They motioned for the Hardys to follow. When they did, the doubles put their pistols back in their jacket pockets, but kept them at the ready.

"And how do you figure on getting past the guards here?" asked Frank. "What kind of brilliant plan did your leader come up with?"

"That's the beautiful part," replied Joe II, smiling at a private joke.

"No plan needed," said Frank II with the same kind of grin. "You tell them, Mr. Gray. If I did, it would crack me up."

The Gray Man, a pained expression on his face, cleared his throat uncomfortably and said, "Unfortunately, there are no guards here."

"No guards?" repeated Joe, baffled.

"But you must have some kind of security," said Frank, and then paused, not wanting to say more. He didn't want to tip the Gray Man's hand. Maybe the Gray Man had been on to their doubles from the very first and was laying a trap for them.

"No, he's not fooling you—or us," said Frank II, as if he had been reading Frank's mind.

"Come on, Mr. Gray, explain the setup here to

these two bright boys, just like you explained it to us when you thought we were them," said Joe II, enjoying the Gray Man's discomfort.

"It's the chief's idea," said the Gray Man defensively. "Actually, it's quite brilliant. The idea is that the best security system is no security system at all. Even the most cleverly disguised guards can be spotted through their own lapses or through leaks in the organization that hires and trains them. So the chief does without all the usual protection and lives completely in the open, which is the most ingenious cover ever devised."

"Talk about being too smart for your own good," said Frank II. "Your boss takes the cake."

"Our boss told us this job would be no sweat," added Joe II, "but even he didn't suspect how easy it would be."

Frank II rang the front doorbell, and a formally dressed butler answered. When he saw the Gray Man, he bowed his head slightly in recognition.

"Come for a visit, sir?" the butler asked.

The Gray Man glanced at the pistol bulging in Joe II's jacket, then said, "That's right, Harvey."

The butler ushered them inside and said, "Please wait in the drawing room while I announce your arrival."

The butler left them and started up a winding stairway while the Gray Man led the others into a large, elegant drawing room. It was painted a delicate robin's-egg blue and was furnished in the style of the eighteenth century, complete with a gleaming harpsichord.

"Your boss has refined taste for somebody in such a tough racket," Frank II commented, looking at the paintings on the wall.

"A lot of things about the chief would surprise you," said the Gray Man.

The Gray Man was putting it mildly.

At that moment, the Network head entered the room, after dismissing the butler at the doorway.

The doubles' jaws dropped open. The Hardy boys were just as startled.

"What brings you here, Gray? Our next meet isn't scheduled until the fox hunt on Saturday," she said.

There was a sharp glint of suspicion in the eyes of the slender, white-haired woman as she looked at the Gray Man and then at the Hardy boys and their doubles.

"What is this? Some kind of masquerade?" she asked. Her hand moved toward the expensive purse she was carrying. It was slung from the shoulder of an exquisitely tailored summer tweed jacket that made her look as if she had stepped out of a fashion ad for gracious country living.

"Freeze, baby," said Frank II as he whipped his gun out of his pocket before she could open her bag.

"Toss that bag here—closed," ordered Joe II, pulling out his gun, too.

The woman's face did not change expression,

as if facing a pair of guns was the most natural thing in the world. With a slight shrug, she tossed the bag to Frank II.

He opened it immediately. "A Browning automatic," he said. "That's a pretty big piece for a nice little old lady to be carrying."

"Cut the jokes," she said. "What's going on here, Gray? Did you foul up?"

"Let me explain how it—" the Gray Man began.

"Yeah, he fouled up," Frank II interrupted.

"Don't worry, though," said Joe II. "He's going to pay for it."

"Unfortunately, lady, so are you," said Frank.

"This must be some kind of mistake," the woman replied. "My name is Laura Van Appels and I have no idea what you want with me. If it's loot you're after, please just take what you want and go. I'm sure Mr. Gray has somehow divulged that you can ransack this place without fear—I detest guards and burglar alarms. They're so vulgar. That's why I carry that dreadful gun in my purse, though I hardly know how to use it."

"Nice try, Laura baby, but no cigar," said Frank II.

"But don't feel bad, you had a great cover," added Joe II.

"No way would we have cracked it without help from your friends here," said Frank II.

"But all good things have to end." Then, in a curt voice, Joe II commanded, "All of you sit down against the wall, cross-legged, three feet from one another, with your hands tucked under you."

Laura Van Appels and the Gray Man obeyed immediately, but Frank and Joe hung back. Each was desperately looking for a way to get the guns out of their doubles' hands.

But the guns stayed in those hands, pointed dead at the Hardy boys.

"Come on, you two, move it," Joe II ordered, and Frank and Joe joined the others sitting cross-legged against the wall.

They watched helplessly as Frank II removed a roll of thin wire from his pocket, along with a wire cutter, while Joe II kept the captives covered.

Swiftly and expertly Frank II bound the hands and feet of the Gray Man and his boss.

"Don't move, and the wire won't cut into your skin," he advised them as he stood up and inspected his handiwork with satisfaction.

Then he turned to the Hardy boys. "Now for you two," he said.

Frank and Joe had the same thought. Maybe when Frank II tried to bind them up, they'd have a chance to—

But their plan died before it could be born.

"Get to your feet and stand in the middle of the room," Frank II ordered.

After the Hardys had reluctantly obeyed, Frank II said, "Now to finish setting the scene." He pulled the bell cord to summon the butler.

The butler was right on the job. Two minutes later he came through the door, and Frank II, pressed against the wall next to the door, brought his pistol butt down on the butler's head.

The butler dropped in a heap on the carpet.

"I bet you wonder what we're doing," Joe II said, grinning at the Hardy boys.

"I can guess," replied Frank, who had been following the sequence of events keenly, putting it together like a jigsaw puzzle in his mind.

"Okay, tell us, if you're so smart," said Frank II.

"You shoot the butler and the two tied up over there with your Berettas. Then you shoot us with the Browning. Next you put the Berettas in our hands, and the Browning in the butler's hand so when the police arrive, it looks as if we killed the Gray Man and Laura, then were surprised by the butler, whom we had knocked out, but who came to before we thought he would. He shot us, but not before we shot him. I bet you even have an extra gun in your pocket to plant on the butler, since you couldn't have counted on Laura packing one."

"*Very* good. It's like you can read my mind," said Frank II, pulling out the spare gun from his pocket. "But I guess I shouldn't be surprised. After all, your mind *is* my mind—of course, they left out your goody-goody conscience." He smiled. "Let me tell you, it's a real pleasure being programmed to be as smart as you. The boss told me that I would have the brains to come up with something good on the spot, and now I know where those brains come from."

"Yeah," Joe II said to Frank. "It's a real pity you aren't a little smarter."

Frank II agreed. "It's a crying shame. But I've thought and thought, and even with all your brains, I can't figure out how you can get out of this alive."

Chapter

12

SOMETIMES BRAINS AREN'T enough to save you.

Sometimes you need luck. Pure, dumb luck.

That fact was brought home to Frank Hardy at the very moment when he had given up trying to use his brains.

He heard a groan from the butler, who was lying on the carpet, and saw the man start to sit up.

Joe heard and saw the same thing.

So did Frank II and **Joe** II.

None of them had time to think about what they were doing.

Both Frank II and Joe II instinctively turned to handle the butler.

And in that split second, Frank and Joe made their move.

Frank karate-chopped Frank II's gun hand, sending the Beretta flying.

Joe slammed into Joe II, knocking him off balance. Before Joe II could recover, Joe had twisted his arm behind him and forced him to drop his gun.

So far, so good.

But then the Hardy boys ran into trouble.

Double trouble.

Frank's double easily parried what should have been a knock-out chop and stood facing Frank, looking for an opening to deliver a blow of his own.

Joe's double freed himself from Joe's hold by suddenly relaxing his muscles, then yanking his arm loose in the split second when Joe was readjusting his grip, a ploy that Joe himself had often used in the past.

Facing Joe II, Joe remembered the slugfest he had had with his double back at the clinic. Neither of them had been able to come out on top before the fight had been broken up.

Joe looked Joe II in the eyes and saw the reflection of his own face in those eyes that could have been his own. It was crazy, he thought, like looking down some kind of fun house hall of mirrors, seeing endless reflections of himself, until he hardly knew who he was and where he was. He felt dizzy.

Joe had to get a hold of himself. He clenched

his fists, cocked his right hand, and threw it. But Joe II easily blocked the punch, and then followed with a lightning right cross of his own.

Joe jerked back his head just in time and felt the fist whiz by an inch from his chin. Instantly he countered with a vicious left hook. It hit empty air as Joe II jerked his head back.

Again they faced each other, and Joe II grinned. "Just like before. You can't lay a hand on me," he said. "I've got all your moves and all your speed. But maybe they've programmed a few tricks into me that you don't have. This is going to be a real interesting fight."

Meanwhile, Frank and Frank II were circling each other, feinting, trying to find or force a chink in the other's defenses. Finally Frank lashed out with his foot in a kick that his teacher would have applauded, only to be caught easily by Frank II and thrown to the ground.

But when Frank II tried to follow up his advantage by jumping on top of Frank, Frank rolled out of the way and leapt to his feet. Frank II instantly followed, and once again they were circling each other warily, both breathing hard.

"Logically, neither of us can win," said Frank II. "Unless, of course, the clinic gave us a winning edge over you."

"We'll have to find that out," said Frank, refusing to stop hunting for some way to get at his double, while carefully keeping up his guard.

But it was Frank II who made the next move—a dirty move.

He leapt back, grabbing a sherry decanter from one of the elegant tables. With one motion, he whipped out the stopper and threw the wine into Frank's and Joe's eyes, blinding them.

But even through the pain, Frank's first thought was for his brother. He turned his head to see Joe II cocking his right hand for a savage punch.

At the same moment and in the same pain, Joe instinctively checked out his brother's safety. He saw Frank II readying a killer chop that could snap Frank's neck like a brittle twig.

Frank forgot his pain as he leapt to his brother's defense, catching Joe II's right arm with a chop that paralyzed it, then following it with a chop that sent Joe II to the floor. Joe II twitched once, then lay there unconscious.

Meanwhile Joe had jumped Frank II, who saw his fist coming a fraction too late. A moment later, Frank II was out on the floor, with Joe standing over him, blowing on his bruised knuckles.

"They forgot to program one thing into my double," Frank said. "They didn't know how often I have to get you out of trouble."

"*You?* Get *me* out of trouble?" cried Joe indignantly. "If I hadn't come to your rescue all those times with my right hand, you'd be a long-gone karate kid by now."

"Anyway," said Frank, "the clinic apparently doesn't know what it means to be brothers. Our doubles had a blind side."

"And we blind-sided them. No sweat," replied Joe, sounding a lot more cocky than he felt. He had been as close as he ever wanted to come to feeling he couldn't win a one-on-one fight.

Laura Van Appel's voice cut into their conversation. "Save the self-congratulations for later, boys. Get us out of these wires. We have work to do. We have to clean out the rats' nest that spawned those two." The authority in her tone told the Hardys why she was head of the Network. She was definitely a person who expected her commands to be obeyed instantly.

"Right," said Frank, moving toward her and the Gray Man.

"Hold it, Frank," said Joe sharply. "I have to talk to you about something."

"Talk to me? About what?" replied Frank, puzzled.

"And in private," Joe added.

"Hey, what are you waiting for?" said Laura Van Appels, with a touch of annoyance.

"Come on, kids, let's not fool around." The Gray Man suddenly looked uneasy.

"Let's talk in the next room," said Joe. "But first, let's tie up our doubles and the butler, too. We don't want them coming to before we get back in here."

"I can see tying up the bad guys, but why the butler?" asked Frank.

"I'll explain—in private," was all Joe would say. The serious look in his eyes made it clear that he didn't want to explain further.

"I hope you have a good reason for this," said Frank, as he and Joe set about tying up the butler, who was half-conscious now, and the doubles, who were still out like lights.

"Trust me," said Joe.

"Do I have a choice?" asked Frank.

By then both the Gray Man and his chief were fuming.

"Free us this minute!" Laura Van Appels commanded in a voice that was close to a bellow of rage.

"Wait until I get my hands on you crazy kids!" exclaimed the Gray Man.

Joe cut their voices off as he led Frank into the hallway and shut the door.

"What's with you?" asked Frank. "This better be important."

"It *is* important," Joe said fervently. "Nothing could be more important. Don't you see, we can't let them know all about the Lazarus Clinic—not when Iola is still prisoner there. I don't want to think what could happen to her if the Network launched an attack on the clinic."

"But I'm sure the Network would take all possible precautions," said Frank.

"Are you kidding?" Joe cut him off. "The Network's not going to do anything that would hurt their chances of wiping out Lazarus. You know as well as I do how the Network looks at things. If Iola got hurt during their attack, they'd just call it an unavoidable trade-off."

Frank wanted to disagree—but he couldn't. That *was* the way the Network operated. It might be good for national security, but it left a bad taste in his mouth just as it did in Joe's. There were some things the Hardy boys couldn't swallow, and sacrificing individual human beings in the name of the greater good was one of them.

Still, he couldn't help protesting, "We could get in a lot of trouble if we didn't tell the Network everything they want to know."

"And since when has trouble started scaring you?" asked Joe. He grinned at his brother. "Besides, I would have thought figuring out a plan to get Iola out of the clinic before the Network went in after Lazarus would appeal to you. I mean, you're always saying how dull life is without challenge and adventure."

Frank grinned back. His brother knew him too well. Iola might be Joe's weakness. Figuring out how to beat dangerous odds was his. Already his mind was racing, like a computer whirring into operation.

"I might just be able to come up with a scheme . . ." he said thoughtfully, and slapped the palm of Joe's hand.

"Ouch," said Frank, playfully flexing his hand to make sure it was still intact.

"That's nothing compared to what your jaw would have felt like if you hadn't agreed," said Joe. "Nobody, including you, is going to stop me from saving Iola."

"No way could you get past my guard," said Frank. "It's lucky you didn't have to try. And even luckier that you have me to figure out how we pull this off. On your own, you'd probably have broken into the clinic like you hit a football line—and gotten thrown for a dead loss."

"I won't argue, Coach," said Joe, "just so long as you get busy at the blackboard and draw up a touchdown play."

Frank had formed his plan by the time he and Joe returned to the drawing room ten minutes later.

Laura Van Appels and the Gray Man were seething.

"Cool it," said Joe, ignoring their demands to be freed. "I'm sure somebody will come along to untie you in a couple of hours or so. You must have a flock of servants in a monster mansion like this."

"We were thinking of calling the cops after we left here and having them come," said Frank. "But we figured you wouldn't want your cover blown. This way, you'll only have to explain things to the servants, and I'm sure you can come up with a good story."

"At least you're sane enough to have thought of that," said Laura Van Appels, her voice dripping with sarcasm.

"You'd better believe we know what we're doing," replied Frank. "And you'd better listen hard to what we want you to do. As soon as you're able, assemble a mobile strike force that can move fast by helicopter. Then have someone in this house ready to answer the phone and relay our message to the strike force when we contact you, since Network headquarters can't be reached by phone. We'll get the number on the phone in this room. Understood?"

"You'll never get away with this!" the Gray Man roared after them as they headed out the door.

Joe paused in the doorway and said over his shoulder, "You'd better pray that we do."

Chapter

13

THE HARDYS HAD recovered their credit cards and wallets from their doubles, which made travel much easier. They took a plane from Washington to Boston. There they rented a car for an after-midnight drive to Maine. The sun was just clearing the horizon when they pulled up in front of the general store where they had bought their shovels, and then the Buick Roadmaster.

As before, the proprietor was up early, sitting in his rocking chair, sipping coffee.

As soon as he saw them, he said, "Now, if it's about that Buick, I didn't make any guarantees. You bought it fair and square, and the store policy is clearly posted." He pointed to a tiny sign half-hidden behind a stack of bags of fertilizer. It read No Refunds.

"No problem about the car. It's a beauty," Joe reassured him.

"We're here to buy something else," Frank said.

"Well, what can I do for you boys?" the store-keeper asked, instantly getting to his feet. "I can offer you a great buy on a Pontiac convertible in the garage. Nineteen forty-nine model. Let me tell you, they don't make cars like that anymore. Needs a tiny little bit of work, of course. That's why I'll give you a real good price on it."

"Maybe another time," said Joe.

"Right now what we need is two shovels," added Frank.

The storekeeper gave them a look usually re-served for small children.

"Two *more* shovels?" he asked.

"Right," replied Frank. "We liked the first ones so much we want to give some to our friends as gifts."

"Good idea," said the storekeeper warily, keeping an uneasy distance from them. "I'm afraid, though, the price has gone up a little bit."

"But we just bought those shovels a few days ago," protested Frank.

"Got the manufacturer's notice in the mail yesterday," said the storekeeper.

"Okay, no argument," said Joe, pulling out his wallet. "And give us some rope, too. Real strong rope. I hope inflation hasn't hit that, too."

"Matter of fact, I just got the word about that, too, in the same mail delivery," said the store-keeper.

Carrying their purchases, Frank and Joe headed back to the car.

"It's not only open season on deer around here, it's open season on tourists," said Frank.

"Forget about those few bucks, tightwad," replied Joe, "because it's open season on the Lazarus Clinic for us."

Frank saw the eager, reckless look in Joe's eyes and cautioned, "Remember, don't go off half-cocked when we get there. Stick to the plan. Both plans, if necessary."

"You and your plans," said Joe. "One plan isn't enough. You have to come up with two. Myself, I'd rather play it by ear."

"We'll play it to win," Frank answered. "Developing plans and back-up plans is a good idea. So we go with plan A, and if we get into trouble, we switch to plan B. That gives us two chances instead of one to get Iola out of there."

Joe shrugged. "If that's what it takes, then that's what we'll do."

After parking their car and following the over-grown forest trail to within a few hundred yards of the fence gate, Frank and Joe put plan A into operation.

They left the trail before they came in sight of any guard who might be posted at the gate, worked their way through the forest until they reached a remote section of the high wire fence, and then started digging.

"I wish we could have waited until night," Frank said as he and Joe fell into the rhythm of their work. First Joe would dig a shovelful of dirt. Then, while he was tossing it over his shoulder, Frank would take one. The dirt flew, the hole under the fence grew, and the sweat poured from both boys.

"We can't stop," said Joe, grunting with effort as he drove the blade of his shovel into the earth with all his strength. "Every minute counts. We have to take our chances and trust to luck."

"And if we run out of that, we have to trust to plan B," said Frank. "Let's hope we don't have to. We'd really need luck to get away with that one."

It took two hours of backbreaking work before the boys managed to dig under the fence. Then, leaving their shovels behind, they wiggled through on their stomachs. They were careful not to let their bodies touch the bottom of the fence. They didn't know what kind of alarm system might be in place.

"So far, so good," said Joe, brushing himself off.

"That was the easy part," said Frank. "Remember, keep down. Somebody might be on lookout."

They kept low to the ground as they made their

way toward the mansion, moving from bush to bush in the overgrown garden. They passed the spot where they had left Jacques and Henri. All that remained were two empty holes.

"I wonder how long they had to wait until somebody found them," whispered Frank.

"No matter how long, it couldn't have happened to two nicer guys," Joe whispered back.

By then the boys had reached the side of the clinic. They began to check the windows.

"Just as I figured, they're all locked," said Frank after they had worked their way around the mansion.

"The back door, too," said Joe. "Maybe we could break open one of the windows. We could throw in a rock wrapped with cloth to muffle the sound."

"Too risky," replied Frank. "This place is bound to be wired with alarms. We'll stick with the original plan. We'll go in through the front door."

Still hugging the side of the mansion, they moved to the large front door.

"Okay, you stand on one side, I'll stand on the other," said Frank. "We'll wait for somebody to come out, then jump him before he can close the door behind him. We'll tie him up and gag him, leave him in the bushes, and go in. After that, we'll do it your way. We'll play it by ear."

"All right. I'll try the door." Joe gave the big brass knob a turn, and the door swung open.

"Nothing beats helping yourself," he said, turning toward Frank to give him a triumphant grin.

But the look on Frank's face wiped his grin away.

He turned to find himself staring at Fritz and Hugo.

And at the assault rifles in their hands.

He didn't have to look at Frank again to know that plan A had just come to an abrupt end. It was time for plan B—fast.

"Hi, guys," he said to the Lazarus gunmen. "It's great to be back."

"Yeah, the job wasn't the snap it was supposed to be, not after those kids busted out of here and complicated things," Frank chimed in. Behind his back he dropped the coil of rope he was carrying. With an almost imperceptible motion of his foot, he shoved it under some shrubbery.

"Good thing we had a back-up plan," Joe added.

"Yeah, and it worked fine," said Frank. "We cooled the whole bunch of them."

Fritz and Hugo lowered their rifles.

"The boss will be glad to hear that," said Fritz. "He was getting a little worried—not hearing from you."

"There were some complications," Frank explained. "You know how it is. Even with the best-laid plans, little things can go wrong. Nothing important, though. We'll explain it all to the boss when we see him."

"See the boss, that's a laugh," said Fritz.

Frank remembered the voice of the Lazarus leader over the intercom—and his absence from view. "I mean, *talk* to him, of course."

"Yeah, like they say, take us to your leader," said Joe with what he hoped was a winning grin.

As Hugo and Fritz turned to lead them into the mansion, Frank and Joe exchanged quick nods. Then they moved.

Frank attacked Hugo from behind, and Joe attacked Fritz. Both Hardy boys used the same efficient punch on the back of the neck to knock the men out. Swiftly Frank retrieved the rope, and within minutes Fritz and Hugo were bound, gagged with their own shirts, and placed out of sight in a front hall closet.

"So far, so good," Joe remarked.

"Good?" exclaimed Frank. "We got through by the skin of our teeth."

"We've still got a crack at rescuing Iola," said Joe. "That's good enough for me."

"Now all we have to do is find her," Frank pointed out. Then his look of concern changed to a broad smile, and he said, "Hi, Ivan, how's it going? Broken any arms or legs lately?"

Ivan had emerged from a room off the hallway and stood staring at them. His mountainous body seemed to fill the doorway.

The Hardy boys didn't even have to look at each other to know what to do. Joe hit him low, with a tackle around the knees, and as Ivan bent

123

over to grab Joe, Frank hit him high, with a chop that sent Boshevsky toppling over like a huge tree.

Then, muscles straining, the Hardy boys dragged his body back into the room from where he had come. They closed the door behind them.

"Looks like this is Ivan's workshop," said Frank, taking in the operating table complete with straps to hold down a victim.

"I think we can give big boy here a taste of his own medicine," said Joe.

With a mighty heave, Frank and Joe swung Ivan on the table and strapped him down.

"Time to wake up," said Joe, gently slapping the giant's cheeks until his eyelids flickered open.

"Talk and talk fast," said Frank. "Where is Iola?"

"You cannot get away with this," Ivan snarled, immediately realizing that his captors were the real Frank and Joe, and not Frank II and Joe II. "I will not say a word."

"I think you will," said Joe, and he let his gaze rest on a row of sharp metal instruments neatly laid out on a stand beside the operating table.

"She is in a room upstairs, on the second floor, the third door to your right," Ivan Boshevsky said quickly. "I am telling the truth, believe me. You don't have to—"

Frank cut off his speech with surgical tape he found next to the instruments.

"Never fails," he said to Joe. "The biggest bullies are always the biggest cowards."

Joe wasn't interested in philosophy. "Come on, let's move."

"Not so fast," said Frank. He opened the door to the room cautiously, and eased his head out. "Okay. The coast is clear. All systems go."

He and Joe ran up the stairway three steps at a time. Joe was the first to reach the door to which Ivan had directed them. Saying a silent prayer, he tried the knob. The door swung open.

Joe felt dizzy with joy when the girl sitting at a desk with her back to him turned around, and he saw that she was Iola.

"Joe, Frank, it is you, isn't it?" she cried, and the same joy lit her face. "This isn't another one of their tricks?"

"It's us all right," Joe said. "And we're getting you out of here."

"Oh, it's too good to be true," she said in a dazed voice. "How—?"

"We don't have time to explain it now," said Frank. "Let's hurry."

"Of course," Iola agreed, nodding. She stood up. "But before we go, let me just go get one thing."

"Iola, you haven't changed a bit," said Joe. "Every single time we were going to go out, you remembered something at the last minute and had to go back for it."

125

"That's right, I haven't changed at all," Iola replied, and opened a drawer in a table by her bed. "Well, maybe I've changed just a *little* bit. I didn't use to know how to use *this*."

Iola turned, a Luger pistol in her hand.

It was pointed straight at Joe's heart.

Chapter

14

JOE GRINNED. "HEY, Iola, watch where you're pointing that thing. It could go off. Remind me to teach you how to handle weapons sometime."

Iola didn't return his grin. And her weapon didn't waver. "You two do what I say. I don't want to have to use this. But one false move from either of you, and I will."

The voice was Iola's—yet it wasn't. Joe began to detect a mechanical sound to her words, as if they were being played on a tape.

"What's wrong with you, Iola?" asked Joe.

But Frank had already seen what Joe was unwilling to see. "We'd better do what she says, Joe. She means business with that gun."

"But—" Joe said.

"You have to face it," said Frank. "They've

succeeded in brainwashing her. They've made a puppet of her. She's in their hands.''

"And right now you're in mine, and don't forget it," said Iola. Still covering them with her gun, she pressed a button on an intercom machine on her bedside table.

"What is it?" a voice answered.

At the sound of the voice, Frank and Joe exchanged glances. The voice seemed strangely familiar. It belonged to someone they knew, but who? The answer stayed maddeningly out of reach, even though both Hardy boys strained to come up with it as the conversation over the intercom continued.

"The Hardys busted in here, but I got the drop on them," said Iola. "What do you want me to do with them?"

"You're sure they're *the* Hardy boys and not *our* Hardy boys?" the voice replied, its tone charged with sudden alertness.

"I'm sure," Iola said. "Unless you were giving me some kind of test."

"Of course not. We have absolute confidence in you," said the voice. Then it paused, before going on, "That means something went wrong, very wrong, with plan B, after their escape fouled up plan A. We'll have to switch to plan C—the doomsday scenario."

"What's that?" asked Iola.

"You'll find out soon," the voice answered.

"Bring the boys to the conference room. I'll gather the others. It's time to wind things up here."

There was the click of the intercom being turned off, and Iola turned to the Hardy boys. "You heard the boss. Let's go."

"Is that your boss?" asked Frank. "You've had a change of leadership since we were here last. He sounds different."

"You'll see," was all Iola would say, and an impatient gesture with her gun stopped any more questions.

The conference room turned out to be the room where Frank and Joe had been questioned during their first visit to the clinic. Familiar faces greeted them when they entered.

There was the arrogant face of Dr. Helmut von Heissen, the impassive face of Colonel Chin Huan, and the pouting face of Peter Clark.

One more person was in the room. He was a man of average size and weight, wearing the same white lab coat as the others. But he was far different from them in one respect.

He had no face.

Or rather, his face was covered by bandages wrapped mummylike around his head, with gaps at the eyes, nose, and mouth.

But his voice identified him instantly. It was the voice that had spoken to Iola over the intercom. The Lazarus leader.

"I couldn't locate Fritz, Hugo, and Ivan," he said. "But I'm sure the Hardy boys here can tell us where they are."

"Talk," Iola ordered them.

Frank and Joe looked at the gun in her hand and then at the look in her eyes. Her pitiless gaze told them that her finger was tight on the trigger.

"Fritz and Hugo are tied up in the front hall closet," said Joe.

"And Ivan is strapped down in his torture chamber," added Frank.

"Get them," the Lazarus leader ordered his men. Von Heissen, Chin, and Peter Clark hurried off.

"We'll wait until everyone is assembled here," the leader said.

They didn't have long to wait. In less than ten minutes, the entire team was in the room.

"I wanted all of us to witness our latest triumph," the leader began proudly. "It will be good for our morale to see what achievements we are capable of—especially now, when we have suffered a slight setback. It will help inspire us in the period ahead, when we will have to suspend our operations until we find a secure new base."

He nodded to Dr. von Heissen. "My good Doctor, I will let you do the unveiling, since it is your superb skill we will be admiring."

"You do me a great honor," Dr. von Heissen said crisply. He removed a pair of surgical scissors from his worn black leather medical bag and, with practiced expertise, snipped the bandages around the leader's head and carefully unwrapped them.

"It can't be!" exclaimed Joe, his jaw dropping.

"I knew that voice sounded familiar," said Frank, trying to remain cool and ignore the feeling that his brain was being scrambled.

Standing in front of them was the Gray Man.

"You see what a good job you did," the leader said to Dr. von Heissen.

"I must admit, I was a little worried," the doctor said. "Those snapshots I had to work from were not of the best quality, even though the Assassins claimed they were the best available."

"And your voice passed the test as well, Peter," the leader continued.

"It would have been even better if they'd given me better tapes," replied Peter Clark, his pale face flushed with pleasure.

"It is a shame that we could not get the information about this Mr. Gray that we needed from the Network head so that you could have programmed it into me, Colonel Chin," the leader told his chief brainwasher.

Chin shrugged. "Life is a balance of victory and defeat. One must accept both."

"I'm afraid we'll have need of your philosophy in the dark days ahead," said the leader.

By now Frank had stopped listening to the conversation. He was too busy trying to figure things out.

"So you planned on kidnapping the Network head and getting information from her about the Gray Man," he said to the Lazarus leader. "Then, after you were programmed well enough, you—" Frank paused, not wanting to say more. He suddenly felt a little sick.

"Very good," the leader said with a smile. "Please continue. I want to see how smart you really are."

"Yeah, go on," said Joe. "I'd like to make some sense out of all this, too."

"All right," replied Frank. "After you got the information you needed from the Network head, you planned to rub her out. Then you'd get your hands on the Gray Man, who was her natural successor. You'd rub him out, too, and take his place. And you'd be head of the most powerful undercover security force in America."

"Beautiful, isn't it?" said the leader. Then he shrugged. "Such a pity it didn't work out—this time. Dr. von Heissen will have to go to the trouble of giving me yet another face, for a while. I must decide if I want my old one, or a nice new one. I always did want to look like Robert Redford."

"Why not Count Dracula?" asked Joe. "It would be perfect for somebody who likes to suck the life out of the living." Angrily Joe looked at the Lazarus leader. Then he looked at Iola. She was still covering him with her pistol and looking at him with dead eyes. Joe could not believe what Lazarus had done to her.

The Lazarus leader smiled and turned to his team.

"I think we should let Joe in on the truth, don't you?" he said. "It is only fitting that he and his brother should appreciate how magnificent your work is, even though they might not applaud."

"What do you mean?" asked Joe, but Frank suspected what was coming.

"You tell them, Dr. von Heissen," ordered the leader.

"Iola here is one of my greatest successes," said Dr. von Heissen. "Of course, I had a great number of excellent photographs to work from. Iola's parents had a superb photo album of their late daughter."

"Their *late* daughter. But—" began Joe.

"See how astonished Joe is? How he still cannot believe this girl is not really his beloved Iola?" the Lazarus leader exclaimed. "And he knew her so well. Doctor, Colonel, Peter, your work has passed the ultimate test with flying colors."

"You can't kid me," said Joe. "Nobody but Iola could have known that stuff about all the times we were together by ourselves."

"There is one thing you did not know about Iola," said the Lazarus leader. "Your girlfriend kept a diary. An extremely detailed diary. It lay untouched in her room, along with her photo albums. All we had to do was get into her room while her parents were away, make copies, and use them to create the Iola you see before you, her looks, her voice, her memories absolutely true to life."

"But who are you?" Joe asked the girl in a stunned voice.

"I am . . . I am . . ." the girl paused and looked to her leader for help.

"Unfortunately, it was necessary to wipe out the memory of her previous identity to ensure total success in the transformation," said the leader. "Iola Two here only knows the part she is supposed to play, like an actress who has memorized her lines, and that she is to follow my orders without question. Am I right, my dear?"

"But you can't just make puppets out of people," Joe protested. "Human beings aren't made out of some kind of putty."

At that everyone except Iola II smiled—the leader, the team of scientists, and the two guards, all enjoying Joe's refusal to admit the truth of what he was seeing and hearing.

Iola II remained expressionless, her eyes blank, as she awaited orders.

Still smiling, the Lazarus leader said, "I see you are still not convinced, Joe. But maybe I can offer you final proof. I and the others are about to leave you alone with Iola, so that you will not be able to imagine she is acting out of fear of me. It would rob us of the full pleasure of our triumph if you were not totally convinced. Besides, I'm sure my scientific team here would welcome this excellent test of their work. It will prove valuable in future assignments."

The leader turned to Iola. "We are leaving now. I want you to wait fifteen minutes, then leave, too, and join us at the clearing in the forest. A helicopter will be waiting there to take us across the Canadian border to the hunting lodge."

Frank glanced at his watch to see what time the countdown was beginning.

The Lazarus leader caught the gesture.

"Are you in a hurry to go somewhere?" he asked Frank sarcastically.

"I'm just seeing how much time you have left," lied Frank, thinking fast. "The Network has this place surrounded. You might as well give up."

"You really expect me to believe that the Network would jeopardize an attack on the clinic by letting you try to rescue Iola?" The Lazarus leader laughed cruelly. "How amusing. The Network may be many things, but they are not fools. Nor am I. Your coming here could have only been inspired by something as idiotic as Joe's love for his girlfriend. I'm sure our young Romeo did not tell the Network our location. He wouldn't do anything to endanger his dear Iola."

"I wouldn't, but my double might have," said Joe. "I'm sure the Network has already made our doubles spill the beans about your location. You're not the only ones who play rough to make people talk."

"The Network can play as rough as they like with the doubles, but it will do them no good," said the leader. "Colonel Chin will tell you that."

"They are programmed not to reveal anything under any circumstances," Chin agreed.

"So you see, there is really nothing more to talk about—or to hope for," said the leader. He turned to his men. "Okay, let's get out of here."

But Iola stopped him. "Sir, you haven't told me what to do with the Hardy boys."

The Lazarus leader pretended to sound surprised. "Oh, didn't I? What an oversight. But I forgot, I can't leave it to your imagination, because you don't have one."

Then his voice hardened. "I'll tell you very simply what you are to do. After we leave, kill them, Iola. Kill them."

Chapter

15

THIS IS NOT *Iola. This is not Iola.*

Joe kept telling himself that as he looked at the girl who held him and Frank at gunpoint.

He saw her look at her watch. She must have been trying to decide exactly when she should squeeze the trigger. She would have to squeeze it just two times. No chance of her missing. The range was too close. Her gaze was too unwavering. Her gun hand was too steady. She was a machine perfectly programmed to kill.

And yet—

This is not Iola, Joe said to himself again.

The others must have left the house now. In a few minutes, it would be all over for the Hardy boys. In a few minutes, Iola—no, Iola II—would be running to join her leader and the others.

This is not Iola. But why then was the feeling

that surged through him the same as when he and Iola had been together? When Iola had been alive? When they had loved each other?

Joe remembered it all so clearly. He felt like a man seeing his life pass in front of him in his final seconds. He was seeing all the times he and Iola had shared. All the memories they had shared.

All the memories.

Suddenly Joe said, "Remember the time we went on that picnic and made plans to go to college together? Remember the way we kissed? Remember how we said we would never break up?"

Almost despite herself, Iola II replied, "Of course I remember."

"And remember the time we had that fight and we broke up? Remember how lousy we both felt? Remember how finally we both called each other at the same time and got busy signals and thought the other one was talking to somebody else? Remember how we laughed about it when we were back together again? Remember how wonderful it felt to be going steady again, after we thought we had lost each other forever?"

"And I gave you that ring and you gave me those earrings and we—" Iola II began. Then she paused, blinking her eyes, as if unsure where she was, in the present or the past.

By now Frank had realized what Joe was doing.

"I remember how great you two looked at the prom," he said. "In fact, I remember how great you looked all the time, whatever you were doing, whether you were walking or talking or sharing a pizza. It was like you weren't just going together, you *went* together. There was a kind of harmony between you. Everybody who knew you felt that. And you two felt it most of all. It was the kind of thing that happens between people just once in a lifetime maybe, if they're lucky. You have to remember that."

"Being together *was* special," Iola II agreed dreamily, looking into Joe's eyes. "I did love you so . . ."

"Why don't you give me that gun, Iola, before it goes off by accident," Joe said, extending his hand.

Iola II drew back. The gun, which had been drooping in her hand, steadied. "No, I can't. I'm supposed to—"

"Forget about that," Joe said. "I know you've got a conscience. Remember who you are, Iola. Remember who I am. Remember what we mean to each other."

"But I'm not—" Iola II began.

"How can you say that when you remember so clearly who you are, and how in love you and Joe were?" asked Frank.

"Right. Remember. All those times. All that love." Joe extended his hand again.

"But . . . I . . ." Iola II's voice, which had sounded confused, grew strong again. "But I do remember. How can I forget?"

She held the gun out to Joe, and as Joe closed his hand around the cold steel of the barrel and drew the weapon out of Iola II's unresisting hand, he felt a chill run through him.

It was as if Iola's love had come back from the grave to save him.

It was as if he stood in the presence of Iola's ghost.

Except that the girl in front of him was no ghost. She was very real and once again was very confused, not knowing who she was or what she was supposed to do. All she knew for sure was that the memories inside of her would not let her kill the boy she loved so much.

Joe and Frank exchanged glances.

"Those Lazarus people did quite a job," said Frank.

"Lucky thing they did," agreed Joe.

"I'd love to see the expressions on their faces when they find out how successful they were in planting all those memories," Frank went on.

"Maybe we'll get that chance," said Joe. "Maybe the Network will let us be in on the operation when they close in on the Lazarus group in Canada. Believe me, I'm going to ask for that favor."

"But first we have to get out of here fast,

before anyone gets suspicious about Iola not showing up," said Frank.

"You mean, Iola *Two* not showing up," Joe corrected him. He took the girl's arm and said, "Come on, Iola, we have to make a run for it."

"Whatever you say, Joe," she replied. "I know I can trust you."

"More than you can trust Lazarus," said Frank, who was already at the door. "This door is locked."

"But why—?" Iola II asked, more confused than ever.

"A better question is, how do we get out?" said Frank.

"Yeah," said Joe. "I've got a hunch it'd better be fast."

Frank examined the lock. "This is an old-fashioned model, probably put in by the original owner. There was no reason for Lazarus or the shrink who took over this place to change it, since the room wasn't meant to house patients or prisoners."

"We don't have much time," said Joe. "Stand aside, everybody."

Frank turned to see the Luger in Joe's hand. He followed orders.

"This might be crude, but it'll do the job," Joe said grimly, and blasted away the lock. He gave the door a shove. It swung open. Then he tossed the gun aside and led the others out of the room and into the deserted corridor.

"They've all gone, everyone but us," said Iola II. "This is so creepy, like a grave."

"Like a grave," agreed Frank, and then repeated in a sharper voice, *"Like a grave."* His tone became one of command. "Come on, let's run for it."

"What's the hurry? There's nobody to—" Iola II started to ask. But Joe had already grabbed her arm and was pulling her along as he broke into a run, following in his brother's flying footsteps.

They reached the front door.

Frank tried it.

"Good, they didn't bother to lock it," he said, and dashed out.

"They probably figured Iola wouldn't make it that far," said Joe as he and Iola followed.

They didn't stop running even when they were outside. They were thirty feet down the front path before they were stopped by a gigantic roar—and by a shock wave that sent them sprawling face forward onto the pebbles.

They felt a blast of heat on their backs, as, lying on their stomachs, they turned to see that the clinic had erupted in a mass of flames.

"The place exploded like a bomb," said Frank, after checking to see that Joe and Iola II had suffered no injuries other than the minor cuts and bruises that he had. He looked at his watch. Ten minutes had passed since the Lazarus group had left Iola II in the room to dispose of him and Joe. "Iola wasn't supposed to leave for five minutes yet."

"But they still locked the door in case she tried to leave early," said Joe. "Just like them."

"Typical," agreed Frank. "They always have a back-up plan."

"They wanted to kill me?" Iola II asked dazedly.

"They didn't need you anymore," replied Joe.

Iola II looked with horror at the sea of raging flames. Then her face hardened. "Those rats."

"Let's not get mad," said Joe. "Let's get even."

"Right," said Frank. "We'll find a telephone and try to contact the Network. We've blown the cover off the Lazarus criminals, and now, no matter how far they go, there'll be no place for them to hide."

"Are you in good enough shape to run a couple of miles?" Joe asked Iola II.

"I always could keep up with you," she answered, "or don't you remember?"

Joe looked at her, a lump forming in his throat. "I remember," he managed to say.

"Then let's do it," said Frank, and the three of them started running in easy strides. They ran through the front gate that had been left open by the fleeing Lazarus group and down the overgrown forest trail, dappled with sunlight filtering through the trees.

Suddenly Frank, Joe, and Iola II came to stumbling halts.

Frank had time for only one thought.

I should have figured it. They had one more back-up plan.

Stepping out of the trees to block their path was the Lazarus leader.

There was a big smile on his face.

And a big gun in his hand.

Chapter

16

INSTANTLY JOE KNEW what he had to do.

He charged straight into the barrel of the Lazarus leader's Smith and Wesson .38—a pistol that looked as big and as deadly as a cannon.

Joe didn't kid himself, though. He knew he didn't have a chance.

But he also didn't have a choice.

Maybe, just maybe, Frank could seize the advantage while Joe was being blown away.

It was worth trying, better than nothing. And their chances would be nothing if they surrendered.

Joe charged, waiting for the bullet to rip through him, wondering how bad the pain would be and how long it would last before it all ended.

But it didn't happen. Joe heard no pistol blast, felt no agonizing impact, as he covered the space between them, reached the Lazarus leader, slammed into him, and connected with a right cross that sent the leader staggering backward even as his mouth flopped open in an unsuccessful attempt to say something.

Suddenly men poured out of the forest, assault rifles in their hands. They surrounded Joe, Frank, and Iola.

"Sorry, I did my best," Joe said to the others. "But they've got a small army here."

Then, to his amazement, he saw Frank's face break into a giant grin.

"What's the joke?" Joe asked.

"Don't you see?" Frank answered maddeningly.

"See what? That we've had it? That Lazarus has won? I see all that okay," said Joe.

"Lazarus? You think these guys are from Lazarus?"

Joe took another look at the men surrounding them. This time he saw more than the rifles in their hands. He realized that none of them had been at the clinic. He saw that though they wore the outfits of deer hunters, their boots were highly polished. Two of them were helping up the man he had knocked to his feet, and the man was shaking his head groggily, then advancing on Joe with his hand out rather than his gun.

Joe's eyes widened. "Look, I'm sorry, I didn't know it was you," he said to the Gray Man.

"That's okay, Joe, it was an honest mistake. I

was thrown for a loss myself when we captured the Lazarus leader. He could have fooled me, if he hadn't been pretending to *be* me. In this game, there's no way you can tell the players without a scorecard."

"So you caught him and all the others?" asked Frank.

"Including the two who were piloting the helicopter," said the Gray Man. "A couple of French-Canadians."

"They wouldn't be called Jacques and Henri, by any chance?" said Joe.

The Gray Man nodded. "You know them?"

"We ran into each other," Joe replied.

"You'll be able to pump them for information about both Lazarus and the Assassins," said Frank.

"I assure you, we'll get everything they know out of them," said the Gray Man. "We have our methods."

"I guess you do," said Joe. "I've got to admit, I don't like some of them, but this time they sure came in handy." He laughed. "Lazarus was so confident there was no way you could get our doubles to talk."

"Actually, Lazarus was right," said the Gray Man. "We must find out their programming techniques. We could use them to make sure our own agents never break down. Those doubles wouldn't crack."

"Then how did you find us?" asked Frank.

"Child's play," replied the Gray Man, smiling. "All I needed to do was remember that the word *Lazarus* came up a couple of times during our little adventure in Washington. I fed that into our computer, along with the fact that you two had been on a fishing trip to Maine. The printout about the Lazarus Clinic appeared one minute later. Never underestimate the Network data bank. We've had this place totally surrounded for hours. In fact, we were just readying a full-scale assault when the Lazarus crew came running out, right into our arms."

"Glad they came out in time," said Joe. "Your attack might have been a little messy—for us."

The Gray Man cleared his throat. "Well, sometimes in our business, there are what we call unavoidable trade-offs. But of course, since you boys aren't professionals, you wouldn't understand."

Joe shot Frank a quick, triumphant glance. Then he said, "Oh, we understand, all right. Maybe that's why we're *not* professionals."

The Gray Man shrugged, the superior look on his face undisturbed. "I'm afraid you're not cut out for this kind of work. Still, I must admit that you've proved quite valuable."

"Can I ask a favor in return?" said Joe, a thought suddenly striking him. "Can I see the Lazarus leader one last time before you cart him away?"

"Sounds fair to me," the Gray Man answered.

"You come with me, Iola. This concerns you," Joe said to the girl, who stood beside him looking totally lost. Apparently, she had at last fully realized that she did not have a clue who she was or what she should do.

"What about me?" asked Frank. "Am I allowed to come, too?"

"As if I could keep you away from a mystery," said Joe.

The Lazarus leader, stripped down to his underclothes to avoid confusion with the Gray Man, was being held with his team under armed guard in a clearing. In the clearing, too, was the large helicopter that was supposed to fly them to safety.

"Tell me," Joe said to the leader. "Who is this girl? We have to give her back her real identity."

"And why should I tell you?" There was a look of pure hate in the eyes of the Lazarus leader. "You Hardy boys have ruined everything—my perfect plans, my great organization. All those years of work are down the drain."

"I'll give you one good reason to tell me," said Joe, and bunched his fist in front of the man's face.

"You can't stand by and let him threaten me like this," the Lazarus leader protested to the Gray Man, who was watching the exchange with a smile on his face.

"It would not upset me in the least to see your features rearranged," the Gray Man said.

149

"Talk fast," Joe ordered, cocking his fist.

"She was a high school student by the name of Sally Collins," said the Lazarus leader. "We needed a girl of Iola's size, and we found and kidnapped her. There was a newspaper story about her disappearance. Then there was a search, and then—nothing."

"At least we know who you are, Sally," Joe said to her.

"But what good will that do me now?" the girl cried. "I've got someone else's face and mind. I'm not Sally Collins; I'm not anybody."

"But *they* can do something about it," said Joe, indicating the Lazarus team. "If they destroyed Sally Collins, they can bring her back again." He turned to the Gray Man. "What do you think? Will you do that? Will you make *them* do that?"

"It's a brilliant idea, Joe," Frank said to his brother. He turned to the Gray Man. "You have to see how good it is. Not only can you use the Lazarus team to restore Sally's looks and memory, but you can make them change your double back to his original identity—unless of course you enjoy having two of you around, one good and the other evil."

"You kids come up with the craziest ideas," said the Gray Man, shaking his head in wonderment. "But I have to admit, this notion isn't bad. Especially since the Network might have a few other uses for these people as well. Yes, I can think of a number of situations in which they could be handy, under the proper supervision, of course."

"I hope I haven't created some kind of monster," Joe said.

"All's fair in the war against our enemies," the Gray Man said, his eyes gleaming at the thought of the new weapon in the Network arsenal.

"That's what I was afraid you'd say," replied Joe, and shrugged. He turned to the girl. "Anyway, Sally, you'll soon know who you are again."

She smiled gratefully at him. "Thank you, Joe." Then her smile faded. "But does that mean I won't remember anything that happened to me since I was changed?"

"I don't see how you could, or why you'd want to," Joe answered, wondering why she looked so concerned. "They'll probably arrange to have you found wandering around dazed, as if you had suffered some kind of blackout. Partial amnesia, I think they call it."

"Then I won't remember anything," she said, regret coloring her words. "I won't remember all that's happened between us."

"That's right," agreed Joe thickly. "It'll be all over. You won't be Iola anymore. Iola will be gone forever."

He looked at the girl and the girl looked at him. He felt as if a distance were already opening up between them.

The girl broke the silence. "Goodbye, Joe. And thanks for everything. I wish I could say I'll never forget you."

"Right." Joe was unable to continue speaking. He was losing Iola for the second time.

His fist clenched, he turned abruptly to the Lazarus leader. "Iola *is* gone, isn't she? Just as you said she was."

The Lazarus leader glared at him. "You'd like to know for sure, wouldn't you? You'd like to put your mind to rest, one way or the other. Well, I don't care if you beat me to a pulp, I'm not giving you your precious answer. Any pain you cause me will be only temporary—while I can leave you to agonize over your missing girlfriend forever."

Motionless, they faced each other. Then Joe unclenched his fist. "One-way fights aren't my thing," he said, and turned away. "But I'm not giving up," he told his brother. "Iola *is* alive, I can feel it. I couldn't feel this strongly about someone who was dead."

"Then I won't tell you to give up hope," Frank said softly. He put his hand on Joe's shoulder. "Anyway, solving mysteries is what we do best—and Iola is at the top of the list."

"You bet she is," said Joe, and he and Frank shook hands on that.

Frank and Joe's next case:

The Hardys are proud of Fenton Hardy's past as a New York City cop. But when an enemy from the old days turns up, Frank and Joe face a danger that could kill millions—starting with their kidnapped father!

Hidden bombs in the air conditioning systems of Manhattan skyscrapers are set to go off. The explosions will spread a deadly virus to everyone in the buildings. It's a monstrous revenge and a deadly challenge. Can Frank and Joe stop this plot and save their father? Find out in *Edge of Destruction,* Case #5 in The Hardy Boys Casefiles.

P9-DHK-251

VELVET PASSION

Michael found herself staring at Ethan's naked back, at the angle of his shoulder blades, at the tautness of his skin. She wanted to run a finger down the length of his spine. She wanted to trace it with her lips.

Ethan turned around. Michael was just pulling the nightshirt modestly over her knees. She almost looked prim. Almost. But there was her hair which had been loosed from every confining pin and lay across her shoulders and back in all its magnificent splendor. There was the delicate hollow of her throat which was laid bare by the open collar of his nightshirt. Then there was the way her lips came together as she swallowed her smile. His blue-gray eyes slid over her hair, her throat, and came to rest on her mouth.

"I'm about tired of sleeping on the floor," he said in a low voice. Then he came toward her.

Michael raised her face. Her eyes held his.

"This is when you should tell me to stop," Ethan said.

Michael blinked once. Her mouth parted slightly. No sound came.

"Can you?" he asked, his voice just above a whisper.

"No."

HEART STOPPING ROMANCE BY ZEBRA BOOKS

MIDNIGHT BRIDE   (3265, $4.50)
by Kathleen Drymon

With her youth, beauty, and sizable dowry, Kellie McBride had her share of ardent suitors, but the headstrong miss was bewitched by the mysterious man called The Falcon, a dashing highwayman who risked life and limb for the American Colonies. Twice the Falcon had saved her from the hands of the British, then set her blood afire with a moonlit kiss.

No one knew the dangerous life The Falcon led—or of his secret identity as a British lord with a vengeful score to settle with the Crown. There was no way Kellie would discover his deception, so he would woo her by day as the foppish Lord Blakely Savage . . . and ravish her by night as The Falcon! But each kiss made him want more, until he vowed to make her his *Midnight Bride*.

SOUTHERN SEDUCTION   (3266, $4.50)
by Thea Devine

Cassandra knew her husband's will required her to hire a man to run her Georgia plantation, but the beautiful redhead was determined to handle her own affairs. To satisfy her lawyers, she invented Trane Taggart, her imaginary step-son. But her plans go awry when a handsome adventurer shows up and claims to *be* Trane Taggart!

After twenty years of roaming free, Trane was ready to come home and face the father who always treated him with such contempt. Instead he found a black wreath and a bewitching, sharp-tongued temptress trying to cheat him out of his inheritance. But he had no qualms about kissing that silken body into languid submission to get what he wanted. But he never dreamed that *he* would be the one to succumb to *her* charms.

SWEET OBSESSION   (3233, $4.50)
by Kathy Jones

From the moment rancher Jack Corbett kept her from capturing the wild white stallion, Kayley Ryan detested the man. That animal had almost killed her father, and since the accident Kayley had been in charge of the ranch. But with the tall, lean Corbett, it seemed she was *never* the boss. He made her blood run cold with rage one minute, and hot with desire the next.

Jack Corbett had only one thing on his mind: revenge against the man who had stolen his freedom, his ranch, and almost his very life. And what better way to get revenge than to ruin his mortal enemy's fiery red-haired daughter. He never expected to be captured by her charms, to long for her silken caresses and to thirst for her never-ending kisses.

Available wherever paperbacks are sold, or order direct from the Publisher. Send cover price plus 50¢ per copy for mailing and handling to Zebra Books, Dept. 3743, 475 Park Avenue South, New York, N.Y. 10016. Residents of New York and Tennessee must include sales tax. DO NOT SEND CASH. For a free Zebra/ Pinnacle catalog please write to the above address.

WILD SWEET ECSTASY

JO GOODMAN

ZEBRA BOOKS
KENSINGTON PUBLISHING CORP.

For BHGH, Inc.

ZEBRA BOOKS

are published by

Kensington Publishing Corp.
475 Park Avenue South
New York, NY 10016

First printing: May, 1992

Printed in the United States of America

Prologue

She was not the sort of woman he usually noticed.
Ethan Stone's shaded glance was more likely to alight
on a woman with a quick and easy smile and a bit of invitation in her eyes. There was nothing the least invit-
ing about this woman. For one thing, she was serious.
Her mouth was flattened by the weight of her thoughts
and there was a small vertical crease between her eyebrows. He could not make out the color of her narrowed
eyes but the expression was grave and focused somewhere on the wall behind him. If he moved a little to the
left her eyes would bore directly through his shoulder.
He shifted his weight on the desktop where he was
lounging, hitching one leg higher and stretching out the
other. The slight movement did not attract her attention
and Ethan continued his leisurely assessment, fascinated in a way that was not particularly flattering to his
subject.

She wore a pair of gold-rimmed spectacles that sat
low on her nose. He didn't see many women wearing
glasses, so that she had them at all made her something
of an oddity. The manner in which they perched on the
end of her nose suggested she didn't need them for any-

5

thing but reading and writing. Certainly, by the way she stared out over the top of the thin wire frames, she didn't require them for deep thinking.

Her skin was pale, her complexion smooth, and it was possibly her best feature. Her hair *could* have been her best feature but it was a nest for pencils. Ethan counted three of them buried there. Pencils aside, her hair was quite magnificent. She had done what she could, he thought, to make it seem less so. That she was not entirely successful led Ethan to believe it was her one true vanity. An effort had been made to scrape it back tightly, to make it ruthlessly conform to the shape of her head, but pride or sanity had caused her to stop short of that cruelty to herself and to those who looked at her. Rather than being molded to her head, her hair was a soft coppery penumbra of light, a frame of deep red and chestnut for her face. By accident or by design, slender, curling threads of hair had escaped the loose chignon and gently brushed her forehead, her cheeks, and shimmered in the gaslighted room.

The thick, lustrous quality of her hair was at odds with the severe, starched white blouse she wore, the equally stiff black skirt, and the tight, forbidding set of her serious mouth. As much as that mouth of hers put him off, that hair drew his interest.

Amused, one corner of Ethan's mouth lifted as he watched the woman's hands absently search the surface of her desk, sliding over a stack of papers, several books, a leather notepad, and patting down a half dozen loose sheets of paper scattered across the top. Unable to find what she wanted, the flattened line of her mouth shifted to one side in an expression of disgust, and her shoulders heaved once with an impatient, silent sigh. Tearing her gaze away from the point beyond Ethan's shoulder, she began searching in earnest, lifting books, the notepad, and sifting through the stack of papers. She pushed her spectacles up the bridge of her slender nose and repeated the search, but more methodically this

6

time. She appeared about to give up, slumping back in her chair, the starched white blouse not looking quite so stiff now, when she cupped the side of her face in her palm and her fingers touched one of the pencils in her hair.

The shape of Ethan's mouth was only fractionally altered but it was enough to replace amusement with derision. The woman plucked the pencil from her hair, but instead of applying it to paper, she held it in the manner of a cigarette, stuck the tip between her lips and inhaled as if she were smoking. Ethan shook his head, not quite certain he believed what he saw. He didn't know any women who smoked. Well, there was Caroline Henry, but she worked in a saloon. After regular hours she might smoke in the privacy of her bedroom, usually after she had been energetically engaged, but she always asked permission.

Ethan's thoughts came back to the woman across the newsroom. She didn't look as if she asked anyone for anything. He tried to imagine her in bed. He couldn't get past the cameo brooch closing the collar of her starched white blouse. The thought of throwing up that stiff black skirt was unappealing, and probably impossible.

She took the pencil out of her mouth, exhaled softly, and leaned forward over her desk. The pencil was rapped lightly against one of the books, a steady tattoo that kept the beat of her tapping left foot. The spectacles slid slowly down the length of her pared nose as she bent her head over her work. Except for a rabbit-like wrinkle to keep them in place, she didn't seem to be bothered by their position. She began writing in earnest, her hand fairly flying across the paper in an effort to keep pace with her thoughts.

Ethan's blue-gray eyes settled again on the crown of her beautiful mahogany hair. The two remaining pencils were a nuisance, but he refused to let them spoil his pleasure. It was her hair, after all, that had first cap-

7

tured his attention. That, and the fact she was the only woman in a room of two dozen men.

It made sense, he supposed, that in a city the size of New York there would be women working outside their homes. He was used to seeing women in saloons, dance halls, on the stage, perhaps even managing a hotel. Occasionally a woman might help her husband run his store or teach at the local school house. Since coming East, though, Ethan had seen young women working as clerks in large department stores, employed as professors at one of the private universities, and even as doctors in some of the hospitals. It shouldn't have been so surprising then that the *Chronicle* counted one lone female among its secretarial staff—even if she probably did use her luncheon time to sneak a cigarette. Ethan considered it was a good thing to be confronted with this vision of a modern city woman. It was the final confirmation that he didn't belong in New York. He was thirty years old, born in Nevada, raised all over, and except for some time in Pennsylvania for schooling, and a few years in the south during the war, he'd rarely been east of the Mississippi. He was ready to go home.

"You can go in now, Mr. Stone."

Ethan heard the voice but the words didn't register immediately. Her hair really *was* magnificent. He wondered how old she was. Twenty-three, twenty-four? In spite of her serious air she did not look old beyond her years. "Hmmm?" he murmured idly.

The secretary cleared his throat as he stood behind his desk. "This way, Mr. Stone. Mr. Franklin and Mr. Rivington have already stepped inside. Mr. Marshall's a busy man and I'm afraid he's behind schedule as it is."

There was very little that Ethan did in a hurry. Drawing a gun and sizing up a person's character were possibly the only two exceptions. It was his general opinion that everything else could wait. That included the publisher of the *New York Chronicle* and the men who had insisted he accompany them to this meeting. He came to

8.

his feet slowly, offering the lazy, derisive smile that was never meant as an apology to the efficient, no-nonsense secretary, and turned his lithe frame in the direction of the publisher's office. "By all means," he said, faintly drawling over the words, "schedules must be kept." Ethan couldn't wait to board a train west.

Mary Michael Dennehy came out of her work-induced trance just as Ethan was turning away. She cocked her head to one side, glimpsing the strong three-quarter profile before she was left to stare at his back. Her gaze skimmed over him then dropped back to her work. She heard the door to Logan Marshall's office close and she dropped her pencil, stretched her arms above her head, and sighed.

She called above the general din of the newsroom, making herself heard to Logan Marshall's secretary. "I suppose I was just squeezed out of my 1:30 appointment by that man."

Samuel Carson held up three fingers. "Men," he said, shaking his hand to indicate the number of them. "That particular man was a marshal."

A Marshall? wondered Mary Michael. The publisher had an older brother who didn't do much with the paper any longer, but she wasn't aware of any other relatives. What chance did she have in the face of nepotism?

"And," Samuel Carson continued, "you never had an appointment, Miss Dennehy."

Mary Michael smiled. A dimple appeared on either side of her wide, generous mouth. It would have riveted Ethan Stone's attention. It made color rise in Samuel Carson's neck, starting just below the stiff cardboard and fabric collar of his shirt, until his entire face was flushed. He felt the heat, reminded himself that he was married with four small children, and abruptly went back to his work.

Oblivious to her smile's effect on Samuel Carson, Mary Michael finished stretching and returned to her hunched position over the desk. A pencil loosed itself

9

from her thick hair and dropped on the paper in front of her. The wondrous smile became a quick, self-depreciating grin as she rummaged through her hair and found the last pencil tucked in the coil at the back of her head. She stared at it a moment, shrugged, then slipped it behind her ear in case she needed it later. It was inevitable that she would.

Brushing aside the pencil lying on top of her work, Mary Michael continued writing. The small crease appeared between her brows again and her mouth flattened in concentration. She wrote furiously, as if there had been no interruption. Indeed, her conversation with Samuel was forgotten now and her attention to the task in front of her total.

It was a full thirty minutes before she finished. Her neck was stiff and her hand was cramped. She raised her head, tilted it to the right, then the left, forward, then backward. Prying her fingers from around the pencil, she shook out her hand. The circulating blood actually tingled. Mary Michael took off her spectacles, folded the earpieces carefully, and laid them on top of her finished work. She absently rubbed the bridge of her nose with her thumb and forefinger, closing her eyes. Finally she slid fully back into her chair and stretched her legs under her desk.

"No rest, Miss Dennehy," Fred Vollrath said, dropping a stack of letters on her desk. The pile leaned precariously for a moment, then collapsed in a neat and silent avalanche. "These just came for you."

One eye opened. It glanced at the aftermath of the avalanche of letters then rose to meet the city editor's frank gaze. "You're not serious, Mr. Vollrath." But she saw that he was. Her other eye opened and she abandoned her relaxed posture. "I can't possibly answer —"

"Can't? I'm certain I misunderstood. You didn't say 'can't,' did you?"

She had known it would be like this when she came to the *Chronicle*. Known it and accepted it. But she had

10

been an employee for nearly fifteen months and there was hardly any lessening of pressure or trials. It had been expected that she would quit at one week, a month, then two months, later six. When she was still working after a year many of her fellow employees believed she had done it to spite them. Mary Michael knew there was an ongoing wager in the press building as to how long she would stay. She had been there so long one naive copy boy actually forgot what he was collecting for and asked her to place a bet and name a date. She did. To the astonishment of everyone in the office she gave him two bits and said, "When hell freezes over." The next day someone left a small block of ice on her desk with the word hell carved on its surface. She let it melt.

Had she but known it, she won some grudging respect that day. Her guard up, she could not feel the lessening of tension around her. "No, sir," she said quietly. "I'll do them before I leave tonight."

Fred's thick brows lifted. "Not the whole pile, Dennehy. I never said do it all. That was *your* assumption."

She grimaced as he walked away. He was right, she realized. She always thought she had to do more, be better, prove something. "I *was* working on something else," she said under her breath. She saw the city editor stop as if he had heard her muttering, hesitate while she held her breath, then keep on going. Mary Michael released a heavy, discouraged sigh and sliced open an envelope at random with her letter opener. She began to read. Minutes later, her own project pushed aside, she began to write.

It was four-thirty when she looked up at the clock. She had made a little headway into the pile of correspondence, answering a dozen letters. It wasn't particularly satisfying, especially when she glanced around the newsroom and saw how others were engaged in important, significant assignments. What was satisfying, however, was seeing that Samuel Carson was absent from his desk and the pathway to Logan Marshall's office was now open.

Mary Michael managed a calming breath. It was as good a time as any to corner the publisher. Although she saw him nearly every day, there weren't all that many chances to talk to him. What she wanted to discuss couldn't be done in the cavernous newsroom where voices carried to all corners. It often appeared everyone was engaged in his own activity, but let some juicy bit of gossip get out and it spread with the capricious energy of a wildfire.

Sticking the stems of her glasses in her hair, Mary Michael let the frames rest against the crown of her head. She picked up her leatherbound notepad, added the papers she had been working on earlier, and stood up. The decision made, she didn't hesitate until her hand rested on the doorknob to Marshall's office.

"You can't go in there," Samuel yelled from the entrance of the newsroom. "He's still —"

Mary Michael took a deep breath in the same moment she twisted the knob and stepped inside the *Chronicle's* inner sanctum. Closing the door behind her quickly, she marched directly to the front of the publisher's desk.

To the casual observer Logan Marshall's office was a tribute to chaos. Floor to ceiling shelves on opposite sides of the room sagged beneath the weight of files, correspondence, newspapers, and books. Photography equipment, unused in several years and mostly outdated, was propped in one corner collecting the occasional cobweb. The publisher's desk was littered with the most recent financial dealings, notes from the accountants, and memorandums from the lawyers. A stack of wooden boxes on the edge of the desk were marked for incoming and outgoing business. They were jammed to overflowing with things that begged Marshall's attention.

Logan Marshall himself was supremely comfortable

12

amidst the confusion. Indeed, there was no confusion as far as he and every other staffer on the *Chronicle* were concerned. Mary Michael had seen him lay his hands on a particular piece of information in a matter of seconds, to the utter astonishment of visitors and neophyte reporters. Samuel Carson's position as secretary to the publisher was secure by virtue of the fact he *never* touched anything inside the office.

Marshall's chair was swiveled toward the windows behind his desk when Mary Michael entered. His chin rested on the points of his fingers, his hands pressed together in an attitude of deep thoughtfulness or prayer. Mary Michael hoped it was the former. She needed all the prayers on her side.

Swiveling around at the interruption, Logan's dark brows lifted in question. He was a handsome man in his thirties, with a hard cast to his features and cool pewter eyes that were constantly assessing. Mary Michael took it as a good sign that he didn't seem angry, merely amused. "There's something you want, Miss Dennehy?"

So he *did* know her name. Sometimes she wondered. After he had hired her she thought he had forgotten her existence. Except for the usual greeting he gave anyone he passed on his way to his office, he never seemed to notice her. She swallowed, her tongue cleaving to the roof of her mouth. Any moment, she thought, Samuel Carson would interrupt, apologizing for her entrance in the first place. "It's about the Harrison court case coming up this week," she said. "That's the one where Sarah Harrison shot her —"

Marshall lifted his head and indicated with a short wave of his hand that she should jump ahead to her request. "I'm familiar with it. William Pearson's been assigned since the beginning."

"Yes, sir, but Mr. Pearson's been out these past four days with some illness and it doesn't appear he'll be recovered in time to —" She was interrupted again, this

13

time by Marshall waving his secretary back out of the office as soon as the door opened. For the first time since marching into Marshall's office, Mary Michael believed she had a chance of getting what she wanted. She opened her mouth to state her case when Logan leaned back in his chair and announced the story she wanted to cover had been given to Adam Cushing during the morning assignments.

Disappointed, but trying not to let it show, Mary Michael pressed her case. "I've already been working on some background, sir. An angle that Mr. Pearson didn't have and I'm certain Mr. Cushing doesn't know about."

"On whose authority?" Logan demanded bluntly.

That gave Mary Michael pause. When she hesitated a beat too long the question was rapped out again. "My own authority," she answered stiffly, heat rising in her cheeks as she tried to hold her ground.

Logan pointed at the notepad she held in front of her like a shield. "Are those your notes?"

She nodded, passing them across the desk when he held out his hand. She stood rooted to the floor as he skimmed them, watching for every nuance of expression on Marshall's impassive face. There was only the merest flicker of interest, but it gave Mary Michael reason to hope again.

"They're good," he said finally, handing them back to her. He saw the brief light in her eyes, the beginning of a smile that could have knocked him over even though he was married to one of the most beautiful women in New York. He deliberately crushed it. "Give them to Vollrath. If he likes what he reads, he'll give them to Cushing to use in his coverage of the trial."

"But I —"

"Give them to Fred," Logan repeated softly, brooking no argument. "If you want an assignment you go to the city editor like everyone else, Miss Dennehy. Not over his head to me. If you develop a piece without authority then expect to give it up to someone with more experience working the court beat. Those are the rules. I enforce them."

Mary Michael's fingers pressed whitely into her notepad. She took his reprimand on the chin, knowing it was well-founded. She had taken a chance and she had lost. She may have even set herself back months. The city editor was going to be livid when he discovered she had gone straight to Marshall for an assignment. She took a step backward from the desk, waiting to flee the room at his dismissal.

"Another thing you may want to observe," he went on casually, "is the civilized ritual of knocking before entering or clearing your way with my secretary. That way, Miss Dennehy, you wouldn't enter my office while I'm in the midst of another meeting and make yourself a target for public criticism."

Until that moment Mary Michael had no idea she and Logan Marshall weren't alone in his office. Blinded by humiliation, she glanced over her shoulder and saw the three leather chairs clustered in the corner behind the door were all occupied. She had a vague impression of tall, dark, and handsome—an adjective for each man—and then her mind went blank from mortification at her error.

"Pardon me," she murmured to the room at large, then without waiting for direction from her employer, she turned on her heel and quit the office.

Ethan Stone found it in himself to feel a little sorry for her. Marshall had been hard but fair. He respected her for handling the thinly veiled criticism so well. Still, a woman with hair like that, using it as a nest for pencils and pair of spectacles . . . it was sign of changing times for which he had no liking.

Throughout the mostly one-sided exchange he had observed her slender back, narrow waist, and boyish hips and found nothing to suit his taste. Standing, he could see that she was taller than he had expected, but still average for a woman. She held herself as stiffly as

15

she sat, her spine rigid, her frame unyielding. It was only when she turned to leave and he saw the full curve of her breasts, tautly defined above the notebook she held pressed to her midriff, that he thought she might be worth the time it would take to get past the brooch on her starched white shirt. As soon as the thought crossed his mind, he dismissed the idea as ludicrous.

Carl Franklin was the first to breach the silence following Mary Michael's exit. He was a gruff man, a score of years older than any man in the room, and angular in the extreme. He represented the majority stockholder in Northeast Rail Lines who was looking toward western expansion. His client was easily one of the richest, most influential men in the city, and Franklin spoke bluntly of what was on his mind. "I didn't know she was working here. What were you thinking when you hired her?"

Still thinking of the notes he'd read, Logan didn't respond immediately. "Actually," he said at last, "it was my wife's idea."

John Rivington was a government man, looking for a way to promote the western territories by getting eastern money to put down rails. Fresh out of college with a law degree, he was still wet behind the ears, anxious and eager to serve the newly appointed Secretary of the Interior. His sandy brown hair fell over his forehead, his smile was full and gleaming white, and he charmed women with his unaffected good looks. "I suppose it might be all right for a woman to be a secretary."

Logan's smile was faint. "It might be," he allowed thoughtfully. "If that's what she wanted to be. But you see, gentlemen, Miss Dennehy is going to be one of this paper's very best reporters. She just doesn't realize I know it yet."

Ethan Stone set down his coffee cup. He was the man who could make the dreams of Franklin's client and Rivington a reality, who, if he agreed to risk his life in their mad scheme, could probably get Logan Marshall to invest some capital as well. Leaning forward, resting his forearms on his knees, his blue-gray eyes hinting at dry amusement, Ethan said, "Shall we attend to the business at hand?"

Chapter One

Engine No. 349 strained to pull its load up the curving path carved through the Rocky Mountains. The engineer called for more steam and the fireman obliged by shoveling furiously, feeding No. 349's seemingly insatiable appetite for coal. Clouds of black smoke poured from the main stack, drifted and dispersed in the air, and finally settled as a fine gray powder on the snowbanks, on the tops of the cars and, filtering through the windows, on the clothes of the Union Pacific passengers.

No. 349 carried 158 passengers, most of them day travelers who would ride only short distances in their second class cars. The discomforts of second class were relatively minor when compared to the difficulties of traversing the Rockies on pack mules and horseback, especially when snow came early to the mountains or never left at all. There were a few cowboys, farmers, and whole families among the way travelers, but the bulk of them were miners looking for some excitement in the next town or the one after that.

Two third class cars on No. 349 carried through travelers, emigrants who had started their journey on the far side of the Atlantic. Taking the eastern rails west, they slowly made their way from New York or Philadelphia to Pittsburgh, Cincinnati, and St. Louis. The Union Pacific Railway would take over at Omaha, but instead of the four-day trip that a first class passenger could enjoy to Sacramento, the emigrants often found themselves sidetracked with the freight while the express trains and their rich human cargo rolled on by.

To the emigrants it often seemed more whim than design when they were finally moved from the sidetrack to become part of a larger passenger train. They could hope then that it would be the last time they would be pushed aside. It rarely was.

Three plush Pullman cars carried the first class passengers. While the second and third class travelers were not allowed beyond the confines of their crowded cars, the men and women in first class had the freedom of the entire train. The dining car offered them better fare than any of the depot restaurants and the Pullman sleeping berths were infinitely more comfortable than the benches and boards other passengers were forced to use.

No. 349 had the requisite mail car, carrying letters and packages from the East. It also carried silver bullion and the payroll for the entire contingent of miners at St. Albans camp in Colorado. Two guards, hired to protect the shipment, lounged in the mail car and polished weapons they hoped they never had cause to use.

As important as the mail car was, the real pride of No. 349 was in the four private cars preceding the caboose. Commissioned by the *New York Chronicle,* the cars were designed by George Pullman with every amenity for the comfort of the *Chronicle* staffers in mind. The least decorative of the four cars was the one which held the photography equipment and the darkroom. It also carried supplies for the reporters and illustrators, reference books, surveying tools, extra baggage, rifles, and maps.

Furnished with inlaid walnut paneling, damask curtains, and stained glass skylights, the staffers enjoyed better accommodations than in their New York hotel apartments. The sleeping berths were wide and firm, the seats were thickly cushioned and covered in soft attractive fabrics, and the dining area in the hindmost car was as cozy as a favorite aunt's parlor. Each car had a cast iron stove to provide warmth, hurricane oil lamps for light, and a toilet for life's necessary inconveniences.

By agreement of the six staffers, the photography car was the site for working, the two sleepers the site for quiet contemplation, and the dining car the site for the best traveling poker game anywhere in the world.

Drew Beaumont tapped his cards against the table top, thought a moment longer, and finally folded. His high, broad forehead was ridged with the bent of unhappy thoughts. "Where the hell is Mike? I need a loan."

Bill and Dave Crookshank, brothers who often were mistaken for twins, shook their heads simultaneously, cinnamon-colored hair falling forward across their brows.

"Not likely," Bill said. "Maybe take you for thirty dollars, but not make a loan of it."

"Mike's wandering anyway," Dave added, tossing his money in the pot. "Said something about getting some personal stories from those emigrants we took on yesterday." He turned to the *Chronicle's* illustrator on his left and motioned toward the pot. "In or out, Jim?"

Jim Peters flicked his cards with his thumbnail. His lower lip was thrust out as he sighed and placed his hand face down on the table. "Out. I suppose Mike will have half a dozen pathetic faces for me to sketch to go with each story."

The *Chronicle's* other illustrator and part-time photographer, Paul Dodd, threw his money in the pot and disagreed with his colleague only on the numbers. "A full dozen faces. Half of them probably related to one another. Mike's a sucker for a family story."

The conversation had come full circle back to Drew

21

Beaumont. "And our esteemed publisher is a sucker for Mike's stories," he groused as the play passed him by. When he didn't get any sympathy from the others he knew he had overstepped himself. He shifted uncomfortably in his chair and finally pushed away from the table altogether. After a few minutes he left the dining car.

Dave and Bill Crookshank exchanged knowing looks with the remaining staffers. "Drew still can't accept Mike's a better reporter," Bill said.

Jim laughed. "Drew still can't accept *Mike*."

"Except when he needs a loan." Paul poured himself a drink, watching Bill draw the pot toward him. "You could have lent him the money, Bill. You're the big winner tonight."

"That's because Mike's not here."

"Game's not quite the same, is it?" Dave noted, shuffling the deck.

Everyone agreed. The cards were dealt, the wagers made, but it wasn't quite the poker game it could have been with Mike Dennehy.

No one had ever called her Mike before. Up until the time she had boarded the *Chronicle's* private touring cars for the trip West, she had been addressed as Miss Dennehy by all her fellow employees. It was probably her fault, she reflected later, that things changed on the train. She had indiscreetly confided that in her own family she was never called Mary or even Mary Michael. She was simply Michael. With four sisters all having the same first name, it was only the eldest, in this case Mary Francis, who answered to Mary. Mary Margaret, Mary Renee, Mary Schyler, and Mary Michael were simply Maggie, Rennie, Skye, and Michael.

Michael accepted the informal moniker from her colleagues as the first sign that she belonged. She knew it started in an attempt to needle her, to point out that she would never be part of the reporting staff no matter what Logan Marshall thought she could accomplish on

22

the Western Tour. Calling her Mike was meant to ironically emphasize her femininity and keep her separate — in what the men perceived to be her place. At some point, however, the tone became affectionate, accepting, and eventually a little awed. Michael felt she had earned the right to the name and the byline which headed all the dispatches she sent back to New York. She had lived up to Logan Marshall's expectations and laid to rest the concerns of most of her male colleagues.

It had only taken three months, 14,000 miles, and 200 hours at the poker table.

Michael's mind wasn't on the poker game as she listened to Hannah Gruber tell her story. Marveling that the woman had strength to talk, troubled as she was by shortness of breath and a cold in her chest, Michael made notes in her pad about the Atlantic Crossing, the impersonal, even degrading inspection upon entering the United States, and the slow and hazardous journey the Gruber family was now making across the country. Hannah cradled a baby in her arms while one of her toddlers slumped against her shoulder. Sitting stoic and silent beside his wife, Joseph Gruber held the other toddler in his lap and watched his wife carefully.

Michael was touched by the concern she saw in Gruber's face, the way his eyes wandered to his wife's careworn features and the tired slope of her shoulders. She felt his disapproval when Hannah agreed to speak to her, but he did not forbid his wife the opportunity to spend time with another woman. He might have spoken in place of Hannah but his knowledge of English was too poor. Michael also suspected he wanted to give his wife this one small pleasure. Since leaving Germany there had been far too few of them.

The stench in the emigrant car was a force to be reckoned with. Even after nearly an hour Michael wasn't accustomed to the smell of unwashed and ailing humanity. It was too cold to open the windows and the air was further befouled by the uncovered oil lamps and the stove which burned the dirtiest and cheapest of coals. The car was so crowded that it was impossible for Michael to sit without someone giving up their seat. The uncovered benches were too narrow to comfortably accommodate anyone but the young children. The aisle was cluttered with belongings that could not be contained overhead or under the seats, and the toilet was a curtained-off affair that did little to secure one's privacy or dignity.

It was not the first emigrant car Michael had visited and though she found the conditions deplorable, she also found them to be fairly typical. Forty dollars did not buy much in the way of comfort. It bought hope.

Journey of hope, she thought. It had possibilities. She scrawled the title across the top of her notes on Hannah. Listening for a few more minutes, Michael closed her interview when she saw Hannah was tiring to the point of complete exhaustion. Perhaps California's warmer climes would bring Hannah relief for her lung congestion, but Michael wasn't convinced Hannah would make it that far. It was rare for an immigrant *not* to experience some infection, by virus or vermin, during the cross country trek, but dying from it was not the norm. Michael remembered a doctor she had spoken to briefly in one of the first class cars. Perhaps he could be persuaded to examine Hannah and recommend something for her cough.

Michael shut her notepad, slipped a pencil behind her ear where it joined another, and pushed her spectacles up the bridge of her nose. Slipping a gold piece — part of her poker winnings — in the small dimpled hands of the Gruber toddlers, she thanked Hannah and her husband for their time and threaded her way down the aisle to exit the car.

Outside, the relief was both blessed and brief. No. 349 was moving slowly through the mountain passes, but at their present altitude the air was bitterly cold even without the wind whipping around her. Michael

24

slipped the notepad into the pocket of her duster and went forward to the next car. After just a few moments in the fresh air, the odor in the second immigrant car was nearly intolerable. It took an incredible act of will not to screw up her features in distaste as she wended her way through the car. She was largely ignored by the passengers, used as they were to curious first class passengers coming through to discover the plight of the poor. Most of the comment she caused was simply due to the fact that her face didn't register contempt or derision or sympathy. She merely appeared accepting. A change of clothes and she could have been one of them.

It was more difficult to move among the second class passengers. She was propositioned three times by two miners and a cowboy, all of them declaring eternal fidelity until they reached the brothel in Barnesville. Michael merely gave them a hard look over the top of her spectacles. That look did not invite additional comment.

My God, Ethan Stone thought, she still wore pencils in her hair. He lifted his hand to shade his mouth and control the urge to speak to her as she passed. At least her spectacles were on her nose where they belonged. Counting backward on mental fingers, Ethan realized it was a little more than six months since the one and only time he had seen her. He wondered at himself for remembering her so quickly. He was good with faces. In his line of work it could make a life and death difference, and often did. But this was something different. Seeing her again, he recalled more than her face. He remembered the solemn and sober set of her mouth, the shape of her shoulders as she sat hunched over her desk, and the stiff way she held herself as she accepted Logan Marshall's reprimand.

As she walked past him on her way to the first class cars, Ethan felt himself struck once again by her determination, her hard sense of purpose. He was also struck by the slender line of her body, a waist he thought his hands could span, and breasts that made him reconsider that he had once thought her figure rather boyish. It wasn't completely surprising that she was propositioned three times as she wended her way through the car. She was the first decent, unattached woman most of the men in the car had seen in a month. There was a lot they were willing to overlook. Like the pencils. But then, when it was too late to discover the answer, he found himself wondering about the color of her eyes. It was not a comfortable thought.

Ethan pushed his long legs into the narrow aisle and stretched as soon as she was gone. Until he felt the tension uncoil from his neck, shoulders, and back, Ethan hadn't fully appreciated how nervous Miss Dennehy's presence had made him. Recognition on her part could ruin everything. It made him wonder how good *she* was with faces.

Ben Simpson nudged Ethan with his elbow. Ben was a gaunt, bony man and the poke caught Ethan in the ribs. Ben flinched when Ethan turned and gave him a sour look.

Clearing his throat, Ben said quietly, "Check the time, will ya?"

"It's two minutes later than the last time you asked me. Relax, Ben. Everything's planned right down to the kerchief you're wearing around your neck. Houston saw to it himself."

Ben's thin body was filled with restless, nervous energy. He tapped his fingers on the bench in the space between Ethan and him. He wanted to check the inside of his coat once again, just to feel the reassuring shape of his Peacemaker. He didn't do it because Ethan would have given him that belittling look again. Ben wasn't certain he liked Ethan, or trusted him completely, but he did respect the way the man had with a shooter. Considering what they were going up against, that counted for a great deal in Ben Simpson's book.

"Seems like we've been climbing the side of this

26

mountain forever," Ben said, staring moodily out the window. Darkness made it impossible for him to the see the sheer drop on his left but he knew it was there. Long before the railroad had come to the Colorado Rockies, Ben Simpson had explored the length and breadth of them on horseback. "I once had a mule that could do it faster."

Ethan closed his eyes, ignoring Ben's complaining, and reviewed in his mind the steps necessary to make Nate Houston's plan successful. His own success depended on making things work.

Ben poked him again. "You ain't asleep, are you?" Then, without waiting for an answer, "Check your damn watch."

Ethan took his time about sitting up and made a small production of patting down his vest pockets to find the one with the watch. "9:30," he said slowly, not showing his surprise. Perhaps he actually had fallen asleep. "It's time."

Ben was already on his feet, stepping over his partner and heading toward the car door. He didn't have to look back to know Ethan was following him. It was part of the plan.

Once they were outside and standing on the small balcony of the car, they didn't waste anytime getting to the ladder of the car in front of them. Ben went first, making the climb to the passenger car's roof quickly and with a lightness that mocked his fifty years. Ethan waited until Ben cleared the ladder, then followed. Although No. 349 was in a steep climb and moving slowly, the cars bucked and wind swirled icily around him. The clear night sky was brilliant with starshine but only a sliver of new moonlight. Eventually the night would afford them the protection they needed as fugitives. Now it posed a danger. Ben and Ethan braced themselves, feet apart like sailors on a rolling ship, and waited until their eyes had adjusted to the darkness before they began moving toward the express mail car.

27

Hannibal Cage had been an engineer with the Union Pacific for three years. He had worked his way through the ranks, starting as a switchman, then a brakeman for four months, and finally as a fireman. He was a bull of a man, broad-shouldered and thickly muscled, and fully aware his strength was nothing compared to the power he wielded in the cab of Engine No. 349. He was completely in control of 35 tons of steel and steam, the final authority over his brakemen, fireman, and porters, and the guardian of the passengers' safety. He survived by taking his job seriously. He respected No. 349, treating her delicately in regard to the amount of coal and water his fireman gave her. He worked her slowly up a grade, never pounding her, and knew how to keep her to the curves on the sharp, treacherous descent down a mountain.

It was a matter of some debate whether Hannibal Cage loved his locomotive more than his own life. On the night of October 22 it was a moot point. When Hannibal saw the bonfire laid across the tracks as No. 349 cleared the grade, he threw the Johnson bar into reverse, signaled his brakemen with three short blasts of his whistle, and commented calmly to his fireman that he figured somebody was up to no kinda good.

The two guards in the express mail car were on their feet as soon as the train shuddered to a halt. Underneath them, along the entire length of the train, the wheels shot off sparks and screechingly protested the abrupt application of the engine's reverse lever. In anticipation of being boarded from the front, the guards raised their shotguns toward the car's large sliding door. It was an unfortunate assumption. Ben Simpson and Ethan Stone used the regular doors at either end of the car to enter simultaneously and surprise their victims.

Ethan's Colt .45 was leveled directly at the back of the stockiest of the two guards. His voice was low and even, rough in a whiskey-whispered sort of way. "You'll want

28

to put those shotguns down, gentlemen, and you'll want to do it carefully. I'm not anxious to kill you, but I can't speak for my partner here."

Behind the kerchief that hid half his face, Ben Simpson bared yellowed teeth in a happy grin. "Can't say that I'm anxious, boys, but I ain't reluctant, if you take my meanin'."

The guards took his meaning quite well, placing their shotguns on the floor of the mail car and pushing them toward the robbers without ever turning around to face them.

Kicking the weapons out of the guards' reach, Ethan approached them cautiously. Fairly certain they had relied on their shotguns for protection and carried no pocket revolvers, he motioned Ben to close in. "You wouldn't want anyone to think you made it easy for us, would you?" he asked. He saw both of his victims wince as they anticipated what would come next. Ethan made the blow as sharp and clean as possible, bringing the butt of his Colt down hard on the back of one guard's skull. Ben's man flinched at the last second and had to be clubbed twice before he dropped unconscious to the floor.

"They're not going anywhere," Ethan said as Ben poked both men with the pointed toe of his boot. From the deep pockets of his coat he pulled out a stick of dynamite. "C'mon. We have work to do."

In the engineer's cab Hannibal Cage did not go down as easily as the express car guards. He had no intention of resisting the robbers until he was asked for the one thing he couldn't give: No. 349 herself. He fought like the man he was, hard and fair, and he gave as good as he got until Jake Harrity managed to get his gun between their twisting bodies and fire off one shot. When Hannibal slumped to the floor the fireman surrendered his shovel and complied with Jake's order to remove the engineer from the train.

"You'll never make it down the mountain on your

own," the fireman warned Jake as he tended to his friend's grave chest wound. "No. 349 will take you right over the side."

Above his kerchief Jake's brown eyes raked the blackened and greasy face of the fireman. He shrugged, unconcerned by the railroader's warning. "We got us a man, tallow pot."

In the caboose the conductor and two brakemen were easily overpowered by another team of robbers before they could respond to the engineer's whistles. After tying up the brakemen, Happy McCallister and Obie Long began moving forward with the intention of relieving passengers of whatever struck their fancy.

The *Chronicle's* poker game proved to be a bonanza. Dave Crookshank thought he was going to be the big winner of the night. He and his fellow staffers took little notice of the train's halting. After three months riding the rails, they considered themselves rather jaded travelers. On the prairies they had witnessed a swarm of locusts that brought the illusion of night to the afternoon sky and stopped their train cold. In the Sierras an avalanche blanketed their cars and kept them stationary for two days. Bridge washouts, Indian tampering, and the occasional herd of buffalo had meant abrupt halts and unplanned delays.

When Paul Dodd suggested off-handedly that one of them investigate the current reason for stopping he was largely ignored. Bill Crookshank reminded him that Drew had gone in search of Mike and between the two of them they would come back with the story. "If it's worth anything," Bill added, watching his brother rake in another pot. "Damn, Dave, but you need your nose tweaked tonight. Too proud of yourself by half, taking our money the way you have."

At that moment the door at the rear of the car opened and Happy McCallister announced he'd be pleased as a preacher to pass his hat and collect their offerings. The fact that he was cradling a shotgun in his arms encour-

30

aged the stunned newspaper men to follow instructions.

"Reckon you fellows will have quite a story to tell your paper," Happy said, watching from the doorway as his partner gathered the winnings. " 'Course that wouldn't be wise. Me and my friends ain't in this fer the glory like them James boys. None of us would want this in that big city paper of yours."

Dave Crookshank, irritated at being cheated of his hard won money, laughed a little bitterly. "And how do you propose to keep us silent?" Although his brother kicked him under the table, Dave continued to stare defiantly at Happy.

"Well," Happy drawled, his eyes thoughtful below the brim of his weathered hat and above the line of his kerchief, "it seems to me I could kill you now."

"We're not going to write anything," Bill said.

"Or I could kill you later," Happy went on, ignoring the hastily given promise. "Generally, though, that involves trackin' you down, and I don't cotton much to trackin'. Some boys is good at it, but I've never been one of 'em." Happy's sharp eyes scanned the circle of men at the table. He waved the barrel of his shotgun in the general direction of the empty chair. "Where's the other one of you?"

No one answered.

"Doesn't really matter if you tell me or not," said Happy. "My partner here can spot a newspaperman like a vulture spots carrion. Not much difference in his mind. Nor my mind, come to think on it. Neither one of us needed your paper's name painted on the side of the car to realize what you are. Unfortunate all the way around." Happy motioned to Obie to finish quickly and head for the forward door. "See ya, fellas. 'Course it'd be better for everyone if I didn't."

For a full ten seconds after the robbers moved out of the car and disappeared into the next one, none of the *Chronicle* staffers said a word. Jim Peters pulled a handkerchief out of his pocket and wiped his wide brow.

"God, for a moment there I thought they meant to kill us."

Dave pushed away from the table, his chair scraping the floor. He did not look particularly relieved by Jim's words. "I think I better go have a look in the caboose. There's no telling what they did before they got here."

His brother waved him off. "What about Drew and Mike?" Bill asked the others. "Do you think they'll be safe?"

Jim finished mopping his brow. "They were bluffing about being able to spot a reporter." He looked around the table for reassurance. "They had to be. Anyway, Drew can take care of himself, and who in their right mind would suspect Mike?"

"Who in their right mind holds up a train?" Bill asked dryly.

Paul Dodd reached for his sketchbook lying on the table behind him. Taking out a pencil, he began to draw. "Would you say the one with the shotgun was taller than the other or just about the same height?"

Bill grabbed Paul's pad. "What the hell do you think you're doing?"

"Illustrating the story you're going to write."

"Not me," Bill said. "And not anyone else at this table, including you. You heard what he said. He'll track us down."

Paul laughed a little uneasily under his breath. "Yeah, but he said he wasn't very good at it."

Happy and Obie didn't stop moving forward until they had gone through the last private *Chronicle* car and assured themselves there were no reporters in hiding. "Nice accommodations they got for themselves," Happy observed as he and Obie stepped onto the small balcony outside the equipment and printing car. "Seems almost a shame to wreck it all."

"Sure we should?" Obie asked, pushing back the brim of his hat. "Houston might not like it. It was never part of the plan."

32

"That's because Houston didn't know about the *Chronicle*. These cars must have joined the train back in Cheyenne. If he had known . . ." Happy let his voice trail off and allowed Obie to draw his own conclusions. When he was certain they were of the same mind he pointed to the link-and-pin coupling and said, "Let's take care of this, shall we?"

Obie jumped off the balcony and onto the roadbed, moving between the cars carefully. The link-and-pin coupling which held the cars together proved to be a stubborn affair and Happy leaped down to assist. Working together they managed to pull the pin free.

"Nothing's happening," Obie observed.

"The grade's not real steep here," Happy said. "Give it a few minutes. These cars'll start rollin' back. You'll see. Right down the mountainside. First curve comes and—" He didn't have to finish. He made a diving motion with his hand to indicate what would happen to the accelerating cars when they reached the curve.

"Maybe gravity needs a boost," Obie said, grinning. He pulled himself back up on the balcony of the car and made certain the handbrake wheel was fully loosened. "Let's give it a push. C'mon. Throw your back into it."

In the dining car Bill Crookshank's legs shifted under him momentarily. He looked at the others. "Did you feel that?"

"What?" Jim asked.

There was another lurch and this time Bill stumbled a little. "That. What the hell's going on?"

"Seems like we're on the move again," Paul said. "Robbers must have left and they're firing up ol' No. 349."

Jim Peters turned his attention from his sketchbook to the windows. It was too dark to see clearly outside but it only took him a few moments to get the sense of car's movement. "We're rolling again all right," he said without emotion. "It's a hell of a thing though, we're rolling the wrong way."

33

After Happy and Obie watched the cars drift away, gathering momentum with each passing second, they hopped back on board the stationary train and entered the emigrant car. The stunned foreigners stared silently at the men as they moved quickly through the car.

"Smells worse'n cattle," Happy said when they left the second car. "Can't taken nothin' from 'em cause they ain't got nothin'. And if they did have something worth takin', the smell of it would bring a posse down on us faster than you can say 'Miss Hearts eats tarts.' "

"Pay attention," Obie warned his partner as they opened the door to the second class car. "These fellows won't be so obligin'."

Obie's assumption was not entirely on the money. The cowboys, farmers, and miners were a subdued lot thanks to the sawed off shotgun Nathaniel Houston was holding on them. A single blast of buckshot from his weapon could cut a man in half. The passengers knew it and the pile of weapons at Houston's feet bore testimony to that fact.

Houston had his lean frame propped negligently in the forward doorway of the car, as if he were bored with the proceedings rather than impatient. Only his darting black eyes indicated his watchfulness. He pinned Happy and Obie with his hard glance when they entered the car. It was enough to let them know they had taken too long.

"Complications," Happy said, gathering up the collected weapons. He threw them out an open window on the cliffside of the car. When he was done he tipped his hat in a mocking salute to the passengers and bid them good evening.

Covering Happy and Obie's back, Houston didn't lower his weapon until they were out of the car. "What complications?" he asked in a low, sibilant voice. He handed Obie the shotgun and took up the younger man's carbine.

34

"Reporters. The *Chronicle's* had four cars attached to this train."

"Had?"

Happy nodded. "Obie and me took care of 'em."

Houston didn't say anything for a moment. He pulled his hat lower on his forehead, hiding the shock of blond hair that had fallen across his brow. "All right."

"All but one," Obie amended. "There's still one of 'em somewhere on the train. There was an empty chair at the poker table."

Just like every member of his gang, the lower half of Houston's face was covered with a kerchief. Still, the movement of his chin was evident as he jerked his head in the direction of the second-class car. "One of them?" he asked.

"Not likely," Obie said.

"First class, then," Houston said. "Let's go."

Drew Beaumont was amused. He hadn't meant to be. He thought that what he really wanted was to be back at the poker table with his fellow staffers. As things turned out, first class was proving to be vastly entertaining. Michael Dennehy was making a spectacle of herself and Drew always found that good for a laugh. In this case he thought he may be able to get thirty dollars out of it as well.

The fact that the train had stopped was a minor annoyance. Drew didn't give it another thought after he realized it meant a longer card game and therefore a better chance of recouping his losses. He had finally met up with Michael as she was leaving the emigrant car on her way to find the doctor in first class. When she mentioned her mission to Drew he saw his chance and bet her thirty dollars she couldn't get the good doctor to move from first class comfort to the malodorous emigrant car. It was not the sort of challenge Michael was likely to refuse.

Drew covered his mouth with his hand to hide his self-satisfied grin. Michael was finding the doctor to be unsympathetic. She had already plucked both pencils from her hair and had broken the tip of one while twisting it in her hand. Embarrassed by her badly concealed impatience, Michael had thrust the other pencil in the pocket of her duster. Drew could see her hand working spasmodically around it while she tried to reason with the doctor.

"It won't take more than a few minutes of your time," Michael said, trying a different approach. "I can't think that I've made myself clear as to how much Hannah Gruber needs your attention."

Thomas Gaines avoided looking Michael in the eye. He remained sitting with his newspaper opened in front of him. He shook the pages again, hoping to remind her that she was interrupting.

Michael was unfazed by the paper rattling. "Would a little Western hospitality go so against your grain?"

"I'm from Boston, young lady, and I won't be lectured by some snippety do-gooder half my age."

"One-third your age," Michael retorted. You old billy goat, she thought. Indeed, with his white Vandyke beard, shaggy haircut, and long, thin face, he looked like a billy goat. "I wouldn't presume to lecture you, Dr. Gaines, but does the name Hippocrates mean anything to you?" Out of the corner of her eye Michael saw Drew Beaumont nearly convulse with laughter at her sheer effrontery. She shot him a quelling glance.

"You are an impertinent young woman, quite rude actually, and I imagine a constant thorn in your husband's side."

Michael was about to reply sharply to the doctor's observation when the door at the rear of the car opened. Momentarily distracted by the interruption, all the passengers turned.

Houston's carbine preceded him into the car. He was followed by Happy and Obie carrying drawn weapons.

36

Behind his kerchief Houston smiled at the play of emotion on Michael's face. "Ma'am," he said softly, nodding in her direction. He touched his Stetson with his forefinger as a greeting to all the passengers. Before he could say anything though, Michael found her voice.

"This is perfectly outrageous," she said, squaring off in the aisle. She stared hard at the intruder over the rims of her spectacles.

"How's that, Ma'am?" Houston asked. For the first time since stopping the train he allowed himself to enjoy the moment. There was always the unexpected to contend with when taking on a job like this. First it had been the *Chronicle* cars, now it was an outraged, priggish schoolmarm who didn't have the good sense to be quiet. He had been watching her through the rear door's window almost a full minute before he entered the car. She was obviously distressed by her conversation with the seated gentleman and it amused Houston to think that he had it in his power to put things right for her. "You were saying, Ma'am," he prompted.

Michael found herself held still by a pair of dark eyes shaded by thick lashes and the brim of a black Stetson. Lines radiated from the corner of each eye and grew slightly deeper as Michael returned the stare. She suspected the robber was laughing at her. Visibly straightening, pulling herself away from the black eyes locked on her, Michael found her voice. "I said this is perfectly outrageous. You *are* intending to rob us, aren't you?"

"That's why we stopped the train," Houston said easily. He gestured to Happy and Obie to begin collecting valuables from the passengers. "Do you have a problem with that?"

Michael blinked once, betraying her astonishment at the cool inquiry. "Now I know you're laughing at me, though I hope you'll understand that I fail to see the humor. Of course I have a problem with what you're doing. Every decent person on this train thinks the same way."

Beneath his kerchief Houston's smile flickered once. "But you seem to be the only decent person with enough gumption to say so."

"My mother says I'm horribly forthright."

"Your mother would know."

Michael snorted, her lip curling derisively. "I see I'm amusing you again, when it's not my wish at all. I don't suppose you'll cease your unlawful operation here?"

"No," Houston said. "I don't suppose I will."

"Well, then . . . you may as well use your gun for some good purpose. I've been trying to convince this doctor that he should attend a young, sick mother in the emigrant car. Apparently none of my arguments have been persuasive enough."

Behind Houston Happy McAllister paused in taking up his collection. "Can hardly believe that," he said under his breath. "Bet she can talk butter off bread."

Obie Long sniggered, nodding his head in agreement. He relieved an unprotesting male passenger of a gold and diamond stickpin.

Looking beyond Houston's shoulder, Michael watched the robbers gather valuables. Drew Beaumont had just lost his stickpin. He glared at Michael, gesturing to her with his eyes that she should sit down and shut up. She was not in the habit of taking Drew's advice on any matter. She pushed her spectacles up her nose. "Well, Mister . . ." She hesitated, hoping the leader would supply his name. When he offered none, she pretended it didn't matter. "Are you going to help me or not?"

Before Houston could respond, the doctor stood, drawing himself up with a stiff and rather pompous posture. His newspaper slipped to the floor. "There is no need to point that weapon in my face, sir," he told Houston. "I shall see to the young woman in question immediately." He took a step into the aisle as Michael happily moved out of his way. His second step was cut off abruptly. The doctor found himself staring down the long twenty inch barrel of Houston's Winchester .44 carbine.

"Not so fast," Houston said with pleasant menace. He kept the calibrated site leveled at the doctor's chest. The carbine was accurate to about 200 yards. At his present distance, Houston could have fired all thirteen rounds into the doctor blindfolded and he was satisfied his target knew it. The doctor's brow beaded with sweat and his complexion was mottled by equal parts anger and fear. He nervously shifted his medical bag from his right to left hand.

"Your eagerness speaks well of dedication to your profession," said Houston. "Yet I wonder if your change of heart is quite what it appears to be." His glance shifted to Michael for a moment, his black eyes held hers briefly, a question in them. "Ma'am? I wonder if you'd be so kind as to hold the good doctor's valuables while he makes his mission of mercy?"

His request brought predictable results. The doctor's shoulders sagged as he realized he could not escape to another car with his possessions intact and Michael was clearly appalled that she was expected to hold the booty.

"I will not be so kind," she said firmly. She felt the compelling black eyes on her again. "You can't ask that of me. It's not . . . it's not . . ." — she struggled, searching for the right word — "it's not gentlemanly."

Obie and Happy hooted and exchanged disbelieving glances above their kerchiefs. "It's not gentlemanly," Happy mocked in a credible falsetto as he examined a platinum watch fob. He dropped it in his pocket then moved carefully around Houston in the aisle and began collecting possessions from the forward passengers. He moved past the doctor and Michael as if they weren't there.

Houston raised one brow at Michael. "Well?" he asked. "How much do you want to see the woman in the emigrant car receive help?"

Frustrated, Michael stamped her foot. "Of course I

39

want her to have help . . . but to be made part of your robbery . . ."

"I'm sorry if I gave you the impression I was a gentleman," Houston said. "I thought the Winchester would dispel those assumptions. Apparently I'll have to carry the shotgun next time. As a weapon, it's a trifle less civilized." He indicated Obie. "Show the lady."

Michael refused to look in Obie's direction. "Laugh all you want."

I will. I have the gun."

Michael realized that somehow she had become the entertainment. The passengers were watching her with various degrees of astonishment and amusement. More to the point, there was none among them who was inclined to rescue her. Even Drew Beaumont had stopped rolling his eyes at her. Her colleague sat slouched in his seat, arms folded on his chest, and practically *dared* her to say another idiotic thing to the robber leader. There was a deep vertical line between Drew's brows, a sure sign he was thinking hard, committing every exchange to memory, and all of it would find its way in the next edition of the *Chronicle*. Michael had a sudden vision of herself as the object of unrestrained laughter in the New York newsroom. It moved her to action.

She held out her hands, palms up, to the doctor. "You'll have to give me your valuables," she said calmly. Her head tilted once in Houston's direction. "He has the gun."

Doctor Gaines took out his pocket watch and slapped it in Michael's hands. "I wouldn't be at all surprised to learn you were part of this," he muttered, reaching for his billfold. "You've distracted anyone from making a move against these fellows and you're much too familiar with them. Too calm by half, I say."

"Calm?" Her eyes dropped to her shaking hands. A gold wedding band was dropped into the heart of her palm. "Are you quite mad?"

"The doctor has a point," Houston said reasonably.

40

"You do appear to be taking events in stride, ma'am. Aren't you scared at all?"

"That, without a doubt, is the most incredibly inane thing that's ever been said to me." She walked directly up to Houston and thrust the doctor's valuables at him. He was so surprised by her action that he almost lost his grip on the carbine. As it was, he teetered a little on his feet. As he recovered his balance the Winchester's site bobbled from the doctor's chest to a female passenger's feathered hat, and finally to the floor. For one incredible second he thought Michael was going to try to wrest the weapon away from him. She didn't. After pushing the billfold, ring, and watch at him, she simply turned around and marched back to the doctor's side.

"Of course I'm frightened," she said angrily. "In fact, if I had the least idea of how one could properly faint in this crowded car, I'd have done so by now. I just don't know how it can be managed without injury."

"Ma'am," Happy said as he took up his post at the forward door of the car, "if it'll loosen the grip on that voice throttle of your'n, me and my friends'd be right tickled to make a space for you. Never thought I'd hear a woman what could talk more than my Em, but you've edged her out. And so much sass, too."

"That's enough," Houston cut in. "Finish with these passengers while I escort the lady and the doctor to the emigrant car." He gestured with the barrel of the carbine toward the forward door and Michael and the doctor obliged him by moving in that direction. As they stepped outside the car Houston paused behind them and spoke softly to Happy. "Find that damn *Chronicle* reporter by the time I get back. Ten minutes." He slipped quickly through the door.

Ethan Stone leaned out of the mail car's sliding side door and looked up and down the track. He squinted, straining to see something in the blue-black night air. Oil lamps from the passenger cars gave off an eerie

41

yellow glow but did little to illuminate the track.

"I can't see anything," Ethan told Ben. "Maybe you should finish loading the bullion and I'll go back and see what's keeping them. Will you be all right?"

"Sure." He pointed to the two unconscious guards and the remaining payload. "No problems here. I'll have this stuff on the mules before you get back. Fire off a round if there's trouble. Can't say that I like it that Houston's not here yet."

"Can't say that I like it either." Ethan jumped out of the car. Gravel shot out from beneath his feet as he landed. A stone ricocheted off one of the car's steel wheels and Ethan found himself instinctively ducking for cover at the sound. "Good reflexes," he whispered to himself. It made him feel a little less foolish.

He didn't encounter anyone on his walk to the rear of the train. He supposed it was a good sign. Houston, Happy, and Obie must have things under control. There was no screaming or shouting that he could hear which suggested the passengers were, if not entirely accepting of their fate, then at least resigned to it. It wasn't until he reached the last car and stepped aboard that he realized something totally outside the plans they made had taken place. The caboose was gone.

Ethan checked the coupling and found the pin lying between the railroad ties. Happy or Obie? he wondered. Had Houston ordered it or had they acted on their own? "Goddamn," he swore softly. There wasn't supposed to be any killing. He'd done everything in his power to see that there wouldn't be and in the end it wasn't enough. He swore again, more loudly this time and watched the single epithet take on substance as his breath misted in front of him. He watched it disappear before he pulled up the scarf to cover his mouth again. Colt raised, angered and frustrated by his own helplessness, Ethan walked the length of the train again and entered the foremost first class car.

Even though it was rendered at gun point, Hannah Gruber was grateful for the doctor's care. The emigrant passengers sat stone still while Thomas Gaines examined his patient.

"They're all very quiet," Houston said to Michael. "Do they know what's going on? Don't they speak English?"

"You could have saved your breath when we came in here," she said, looking pointedly at Houston's gun. "They're familiar with the universal language of thuggery."

"You *are* more sassy than Em." He paused, smiling genially. "That's a mule by the way. No one's sweetheart."

Michael pretended to ignore the comment, but she could feel the tips of her ears growing red. She spoke to the doctor instead. "Have you determined what's wrong with her?"

"Pneumonia." He straightened and opened the black leather case one of the Gruber children held up to him. "I'll give her what medicine I have. If these cars don't get side-tracked too many more times, it should last until she reaches California." He took out several brown bottles, brusquely explained how much of each she was supposed to take, and closed his case. "There's really nothing more I can do for her. She needs rest that she'll never find in this car."

Houston's head tilted to one side and he pushed back the brim of his hat a notch. "Perhaps you'd consider giving the lady and her family your space in the first class car?"

The doctor's eyes narrowed angrily. "Are you going to insist?"

Houston appeared thoughtful for a moment. "No, I don't think I am." He indicated that the doctor should move out of the way. When that was done he reached over the seat to Hannah and dropped the doctor's valuables in her lap. "A gift, Mrs. Gruber. Welcome to America."

Hannah looked at Michael, uncertain what to do.

Michael, in turn, rounded on Houston. "Now why have you done that? Those things weren't yours to give away."

"Pardon me," Houston said, "but I recall having them given to me only a short time ago."

"You know very well—"

Houston made a slashing motion with his free hand. "Enough. Tell her to keep them else I'll be insulted. Our doctor here doesn't need them. Unless I miss my guess, he's still got pockets worth emptying."

The doctor's reddening face betrayed him.

"See what I mean, ma'am? There's honest and then there's honest." His black eyes were smiling at her again. He stepped to one side and motioned to the doctor and Michael to precede him. The doctor moved quickly and went first, leaving Michael to contend with the Winchester pointed at her back. Behind her she heard Houston's low chuckle at the doctor's cowardice. When she stiffened her spine in response, she heard the laughter again.

At the door to the first class car Houston told the doctor to go back inside. He stopped Michael when she made to follow.

"Let go of my arm," she said with credible calm.

Houston's fingers dropped away. "Your valuables, ma'am. Everyone else gave to the cause."

Michael thought of several names she wanted to call him and by the look that passed over the visible part of his face, he apparently was reading her mind. "Oh, very well," she said, rooting the deep pockets of her duster for her poker winnings. Her fingers touched on three pencils and a note pad before coming up with the money. "I wish you'd give this to Hannah Gruber and her family."

Houston took the money. His eyes dropped to the cameo pin at Michael's throat. "The brooch, too," he

44

said.

Michael's hand flew to her collar of her white blouse and there was real pain in her eyes. "It's not valuable."

"It is to me." A memento, he was thinking, of a very interesting encounter.

"Bastard," she said softly.

"So I've heard."

Michael frowned, uncertain what he meant by his last comment. Her fingers trembled slightly as she unhooked the brooch and she closed her eyes briefly, turning away in the same moment she placed it in Houston's gloved hand. She didn't see him give it a long, almost regretful look, before he dropped it in his pocket.

"I thought you might stab me with the pin."

"It occurred to me." Without waiting for Houston's order, Michael opened the door to the first class car and stepped inside.

Ethan Stone wondered if his shock was visible. He felt as if he'd been kicked by a mule when he saw the woman who preceded Houston into the car. He thought he had successfully avoided her altogether. Now, here she was, staring at him straight on, her surprise a palpable thing.

He watched as her brows drew together and her mouth became flat and serious. Her frown of concentration touched every one of her features. Her spectacles had slipped to the tip of her pared nose. Her eyes — dark green, he noted now — were clouded as she tried to place his face. Her teeth caught her lower lip and worried it gently, causing her chin to wobble slightly. Ethan saw her struggle to grasp the elusive memory that would allow her recognition of another place, another time, and he didn't release his breath until he saw annoyance cross her face as she couldn't do it. The moment had stretched as an eternity in Ethan's mind. In reality it had taken mere seconds.

Michael shook her head as if to clear it. Something

niggled at the back of her mind but she couldn't bring it to consciousness. In the next moment her attention was brought to focus on another matter entirely and the thread of memory was broken.

Happy McAllister was holding Drew Beaumont at gun point.

Michael began to march forward, only to be brought abruptly back by Houston's hand on the collar of her duster. "What's he doing? What's this all about?"

Houston ignored her. "That the one?" he asked Happy.

Happy nodded. "Sure is. Hell of a time findin' it out. Didn't say a word until he saw you coming back. Figure that shook him up a little."

Ethan knew now what had shaken Drew and it wasn't Nathaniel Houston. Until *she* had stepped into the car the other *Chronicle* reporter had maintained a stoic silence. Apparently Drew didn't trust his colleague to maintain the same discretion. Wise man, thought Ethan. She looked about ready to say something incriminating any moment.

"What's going on?" Michael demanded again. This time she wrested herself away from Houston's grip and got several steps closer to Drew. Happy's gun held her off. "Drew? What's this about?"

"You know him?" Houston asked.

"Of course I know him. He's—"

Ethan felt his breath catch again.

Drew interrupted. "We met on the train. As you're probably aware, her company's quite entertaining."

"Drew?" Michael's brows knit. "Why are you—"

"Don't worry about me," Drew cut in again. "These men don't seem to like reporters and they've found me out. They were sure they could find a newspaperman right off, but I must look more like a parson than I knew. Took them a while to get to me." His smile was self-depreciating. "Hell of it is, my mother wanted me to be a preacher."

"Drew, I still don't —"

"Seems this fellow here and his friend uncoupled the *Chronicle* cars and the caboose."

"Uncoupled the cars?" Michael couldn't take it in immediately. What Drew was telling her was too horrifying.

"They're dead," Drew said quietly, holding her eyes, willing her to be cautious. "All dead."

There wasn't any more space in the first class car than there had been earlier. Injury was still a possibility but it no longer mattered. Michael dropped in the aisle like a stone.

Chapter Two

In a way it was a relief, Ethan thought. She was out cold, curled and crumpled in the aisle like a dry leaf. For the moment at least she couldn't say anything stupid. Now he could concentrate on the matter of Drew Beaumont. With a little luck he could make it work.

Houston hunkered down at Michael's head. "Get that damn reporter out of here," he barked at Happy, "and take care of him."

Happy hauled Drew out of his seat and pushed him into the aisle. Drew tripped on Michael's outstretched leg and nearly went sprawling himself. Ethan caught him and pulled him upright. "I'll take him out. You help with the lady." He felt the restlessness of the other passengers. A stony stare and a single wave of his gun put all of them back in their seats. "Obie, you watch them carefully. We don't want any heroes. One damned complicating female is enough for any robbery."

"I second that," Happy said feelingly.

Ethan let Drew step in front of him and leveled the barrel of his Colt at the reporter's back. "Let's go." Once they were outside the car Ethan directed Drew to jump down on the mountain side of the track. "Keep going. Walk to the end of the train."

Drew glanced back over his shoulder and sneered.

48

"Thanks to your friends, a shorter walk than it used to be."

"Are you foolish or brave?"

"Neither. Just realistic. You're going to kill me. I've a mind to say whatever occurs to me."

Ethan nudged him when his steps slowed as they reached the rear car. "Keep going. About another hundred feet or so. Stop before the curve. If someone wants to watch I want it said I did my job." He looked around him, feeling the inky night closing in. Could anyone from the train see him at this distance? A witness would be helpful. It could seal his reputation with the others. There were those who still did not entirely trust him.

"That's far enough," he said. "Don't even think of making a break for it or I'll have to shoot you down."

It was an odd thing for him to say, Drew thought, when it was clear the fellow intended to kill him anyway. Drew turned. He could see the last car of the train, the emigrant car, beyond the robber's shoulder. There were faces pressed to the glass in the door, peering out into the night to get a glimpse of the execution.

"What is it you fellows have against some newspaper coverage?" Drew asked. "Some gangs would be grateful for it."

"The James boys perhaps. Not us." Ethan cocked his Colt. The clicking of the hammer sounded unnaturally loud in the still night air. "No one here tonight has any desire to become a folk hero."

"That's too bad. If you'd tell me something about your gang I could write a sympathetic piece."

"Either you're a liar or a man without a single principle. Have you already forgotten your colleagues? How many were in the cars when the coupling was released?"

Drew was shaking with equal parts cold and fear.

49

He thrust his hands into his pockets. "Four from the *Chronicle*. I don't know how many were in the caboose. Their deaths were senseless." Drew's eyes darted nervously. He wondered if he could make a break for it afterall. There was sparse covering on the mountainside to his right and a steep, rocky descent on his left. "My friends weren't armed, for God's sake. They were no threat to any of you."

"Not everyone sees it that way," Ethan said. "How many cars did the *Chronicle* have?"

"Four."

Ethan swore softly. "Did you come on at Cheyenne?"

"Yes."

It did little to ease Ethan's conscience that he couldn't have known about the presence of the reporters. It was a variable that couldn't have been predicted with years of preparation. They had had no such luxury of time in their planning. Ethan shifted his weight from one foot to the other, lowering his Colt slightly. He pulled at his kerchief, letting it fall around his neck and reveal his face.

Drew Beaumont braced himself for the gunshot. When it didn't come immediately, fear made him angry. "Get it the hell over with, you son of a bitch."

"Listen to me carefully," Ethan said calmly. "When I fire I want you to clutch your chest, fall, and roll toward the drop. I'll kick you over the side. You're on your own from there."

"The fall will kill me."

"Perhaps. There's lots of rocky outcroppings where you can gain purchase. I'm not going to push you hard. You probably won't roll more than twenty, thirty feet." Ethan sensed another complaint coming from his hostage. "Look, when you consider the alternative is a bullet through your heart, I think I'm offering you a good deal."

Drew swallowed hard. "Why are you doing this?"

"I have my reasons," he said quietly. "Before you write one word of this for your paper, contact your publisher." Ethan's eyes narrowed. "Are you getting this, mister? Not one word before you contact Marshall. Tell him what happened and let him make the decision of what's to be printed. Don't take it upon yourself."

Drew was about to ask why it was so important when he saw the rear door of the emigrant car open and Michael Dennehy step out. His eyes widened. "Oh God, it's her."

Ethan glanced over his shoulder quickly. She wasn't alone. That he could have dealt with. Obie was following her with his shotgun, chasing after her in his loping stride while she charged ahead like No. 349 herself. "Damn. This changes things."

Drew's eyes widened in alarm. "You don't mean—"

Ethan nodded. "More kick than a mule." He raised his gun again and fired. He watched Drew waver on his feet for a few seconds. Behind him Obie and the woman were approaching fast. "Fall, you stupid bastard! Now!"

Drew's knees buckled under him. It wasn't until he hit the gravel roadbed that he realized he hadn't been shot at all. He rolled closer to the drop and sprawled. He heard Michael scream but he didn't have time to think about it. Ethan's booted foot was shoved in his ribs and the force of it drove him over the side. He slid on his belly, rolled, scrambled for purchase, then slid and rolled some more. Bits of gravel, rock, and snow, clumps of wiry bushes, and a discarded railroad tie, made the journey with him. Something hit him on the head and his vision was suddenly blacker than the night. His last thought before losing consciousness was that being shot probably wouldn't have hurt as much.

Before Ethan could swing around from the drop he

was attacked from behind. Michael managed to get her entire forearm under his chin and press it against his throat. For a moment it seemed the impetus of her charge would send them both over the drop. Instead they fell backward onto the tracks with Michael under Ethan. He turned quickly and pinned her down, straddling her waist with his thighs and holding her wrists on either side of her head.

Air had been driven completely from Michael's lungs. It was the only reason she wasn't swearing like the man above her. She stared into a face that was so hard with rage a muscle worked spasmodically in each lean cheek. Now that the cursing had subsided the mouth was drawn flat, the teeth clenched. The chin was strong, the jaw square-cut and rigidly set. It occurred to her suddenly that she was seeing the lower part of his face for the first time.

But not for the first time. She struggled again to hold onto the memory that would put that face in the proper place. She had seen him before. She was certain of it. But where?

"You killed Drew," she said accusingly. "I saw you."

"I killed him."

Obie stood over both of them with his shotgun. "Lady, you're lucky he didn't kill you, too."

"Perhaps he will when I tell you who I am."

Ethan sighed. "Aww, hell. You just can't keep your mouth shut, can you?"

Michael ignored him. "Drew wasn't just a friend, he was my—"

Ethan clipped her on the jaw.

"Whaddya do that fer?" Obie asked. Michael's head lolled to the side, her eyes closed. Her spectacles rested askew on her face. "Who the hell is she?"

Ethan stood, gave Obie his gun, then pulled Michael to a half sitting position before he bent and lifted her in his arms. "My wife," he said and started walking toward the train.

Michael woke in pain. The entire left side of her face throbbed. Initially she was disoriented, unable to place her surroundings, the steady movement under her, or the object that was holding her so securely she couldn't move. Several minutes passed before she understood she was traveling on horseback at night and the man who nearly broke her jaw was the same one holding her.

"You're awake," he said.

His tone gave nothing away, she noted. He seemed neither pleased nor upset by the fact that she was conscious again. She turned her head slightly, leaning away from her captor to see the terrain and count her companions. There were three other men on horseback, two of whom she remembered from the train. The robber who had forced the doctor to help her, the one she assumed to be the leader, was nowhere in sight.

The ground they were covering was treacherous, steep and rocky. Patches of ice and crusty snow made the climbing slow and the sudden, sharp descents frightening. The man she rode with had positioned her securely in front of him, her hip wedged intimately between his thighs. The saddle horn bore uncomfortably into Michael's flesh as they rode but beside the pain in her jaw it didn't deserve, and didn't get, a second thought.

In addition to the horses and men there were pack mules. Their braying echoed in the narrow passes when they stubbornly refused to follow the lead. The sound of the flicking whips was chilling.

Michael worked her jaw slowly from side to side, realizing for the first time that it wasn't broken. "Where are we?" she asked.

Ethan didn't answer right away. He wanted to enjoy the silence a little longer. It was his opinion that the mules were more sweetly tempered than the woman in his arms. "Rockies," he said.

She sighed. "I *know* that. I want to know where."

"Colorado."

She knew that, too. "Is that the best answer I can expect from you?"

"From me or any of the others."

"We're going to your hideout then?"

"Something like that."

His terse, evasive answers were annoying. Michael's hold on the threads of her patience was tenuous at best. "Why am I with you?" she demanded. The effect of her snapping tone was lost as she winced with pain. She tried to raise her hand to nurse her aching jaw and found it trapped by her captor's arm. "May I?" she asked, gritting her teeth as tears gathered in her eyes.

Ethan loosened his grip and allowed her the use of one hand. It was easier to ride when she was unconscious, or at least unmoving. He needed all his concentration to negotiate the narrow passes and ledges and keep himself, his hostage, and his horse upright.

Michael cupped the side of her swollen face. She imagined she would be black and blue for days. "Why am I with you?" she asked again.

"Because I told Obie you were my wife."

"Your wife!" She had meant to scream the words but Ethan was too fast for her. His hand clamped over her mouth and nose and the words were caught in the heart of his palm. The pressure of his hand nearly caused her to faint from pain and lack of air.

"Shut up and listen for a change!" he said with low, rough menace. "You don't need to comment on everything I say. I'm trying to save your miserable life.

Don't make me regret it." He felt her resignation in the relaxing of her posture. She shuddered once as she slumped against him. Ethan moved his hand away cautiously and heard her sip the air gratefully for breath.

When the trail widened, Ethan hung back and let the others go forward. There was some good-natured ribbing when the men became aware of what he was doing. It was the most anyone had talked since leaving No. 349.

Ethan didn't say a word until he was certain they could not be overheard. Even then he kept his voice low. "I told Obie you were my wife because it was safer than what you were going to say."

Michael tried to remember her last words before she was cold-cocked. Frowning, she asked, "How do you know what I was going to say?"

"Because, lady, you're about as easy to read sometimes as a headline. You were about to blurt out that that reporter was your colleague." His tone dared her to say otherwise. "Isn't that right?"

She offered a reluctant yes. "How did you know?"

"He told me," Ethan lied. "When you came running out of the train, hell bent on martyrdom, he told me. Begged me to save your life."

"And you couldn't refuse a dying man's last wish."

"Something like that."

His cold, neutral tone grated on Michael's nerves. "You're really an amoral bastard, aren't you?"

Ethan refused to be riled. "If you say so."

They rode in silence a little while. Ethan knew she was crying, but whether it was for herself or for Drew, he didn't know, and didn't care to know. Eventually he gave her the kerchief from around his neck. "Here. Blow."

Michael accepted it, wiped her eyes, and blew her nose. When she tried to return it her gesture was acknowledged with a terse, "Keep it." She stuffed it in the pocket of her duster.

"Couldn't you have left me behind?"

"I don't see how. Telling Obie that you're my wife seems to guarantee that you know who I am. I couldn't leave you once he thought you recognized me. It would put all of us in danger."

Michael levered her head back a little and stared at the hard cast lines of her captor's profile. "It's odd," she said slowly, softly, "but it's as if . . . I'm not sure . . . as if I do know you."

Trust her to worry an idea to death, Ethan thought, disgusted. He could see now that she was not going to rest until she placed him. "I don't see how that's possible."

"Neither do I," she admitted. She rested her head against his shoulder again, too tired to think clearly or plot her escape. "What do I call you?"

"Ethan Stone." For the first time in hours he smiled. "It lays better on the tongue than Amoral Bastard."

"So you say."

"I think I better have a name for you," Ethan said when she didn't offer hers.

"Mary Michael Dennehy."

"Dennehy," he repeated softly. God, he had wracked his brain trying to remember her last name. "Irish?"

"On my mother's side. County Clare.

"Catholic?"

"Could Mary Michael be anything else?"

"Well, Mary Michael, I think we'd—"

"It's just Michael. No one calls me Mary."

Ethan's lip curled to one side. "It figures."

"What's that supposed to mean?"

He didn't answer her. "I think we'd better put our story together before we get questioned separately and come up with sixes and sevens."

"You make it up. I haven't decided if I'm going

along with anything you're doing."

Ethan reined in his mount sharply, nearly dislodging Michael from the saddle. One gloved hand slipped around her throat and drew her back where he could look at her face clearly. His lightly colored blue-gray eyes reflected the cool wash of starshine. "You can't possibly be more stupid than I already think, can you? There isn't any choice of going along or not, not if you want to see the sun rise. Tell me now that you're going to fight me every step of the way and I'll break your neck right here and leave you for carrion."

Michael shivered as much from the whiskey-whispered promise of his tone as the flinty hardness of his eyes.

"Is there anything you don't understand?" he demanded, searching her face.

She replied with a small negative shake of her head.

"Good." He released her throat. "You'd do well to keep in mind that your life doesn't mean half as much to me as my own."

"I'll remember," she said, her voice so small he had to strain to hear it.

"Then you just may come out of this alive." Ethan nudged his horse forward. He opened a few buttons on his leather and sheep's wool coat. "Slip your arms inside. Your hands must be like ice by now."

They were numb with cold but Michael wasn't certain she wanted to be that close to Ethan. Her hesitation was a clear signal.

Ethan shrugged and began to button up again. "Suit yourself."

"No . . . wait. I am cold. Nearly stiff with it actually."

She didn't feel stiff, Ethan thought as she slid her arms under his coat and around his back. Her movement wedged Michael tighter against him and he was miserably aware of the curve and pliancy of her flesh.

He comforted himself that any female this close to him, practically molded to him, would elicit the same response. It wasn't possible that his body was stirring in reaction to *her*. He needed to think about something else. Quickly.

"Any loose teeth?" he asked.

Michael had already run her tongue across her teeth several times to assure herself they were intact. She did so again. "Nothing loose."

He tried not to sound relieved. "I clipped you pretty hard."

"Hmm-mm."

"I'll have Detra tend to your face once we get where we're going."

"Detra?"

"She looks after us."

Michael wondered if she might find a sympathetic ally in the other woman. "Who are 'us'?" she asked.

"Try to keep your reporter's curiosity in check," he cautioned. "Everything in good time." Ahead of him he saw Happy McAllister approaching. He gave Michael a warning squeeze. "Happy's coming this way. What ever comes up, follow my lead." He felt her cheek brush his chest as she nodded her agreement.

"Something wrong, Happy?" he asked.

"Can't think of a thing," the older man said. He leaned his wiry body forward in the saddle. " 'Cept for that bit of sass you got in your arms, I'd say we done ourselves as planned. Trust a female to muck up the works."

Ethan's sentiments exactly. "Michael has that way about her." He felt her stiffen in his arms. Did she think he was going to defend her?

"Michael," Happy said, scratching his stubbly cheek thoughtfully. "Odd moniker for a woman. Can't recollect you ever mentioning her or the fact that you was married."

58

"That's because I haven't mentioned her. Truth is, Happy, tonight's the first time I've seen my wife in four years."

That made an impression on Happy. He shook his head from side to side. "Well, of all the dag-burned luck. No wonder she didn't recognize you when she clamped eyes on you in first class. Four years. That's a damn long time."

Ethan nodded. "I offered to take the reporter out just to get out of her way. I thought I was safe when she fainted. When she saw me outside without the kerchief I knew I couldn't take any chances. Not after killing the reporter."

"Who was he to her?" Happy asked. "Obie said she tried to tell you both something about him before you punched her."

Ethan searched for something to say.

"Drew Beaumont was my fiancé," Michael interjected. In her ear she felt rather than heard Ethan's low hum of disapproval. "When one hasn't heard from one's husband in four years it's not unnatural to suppose he's dead."

"Or hope that he is," Ethan said, cutting her off before she created a story at odds with what he had already told the others. "I walked out on her, Happy. There's no love lost on her side."

"Hard to believe," Happy said. "You two cuddled there like nip and tuck."

"I haven't been given any choice," Michael said coldly.

"That so?" Happy grinned, showing a line of straight but tobacco-stained teeth. "You could ride with me for a while, Miz Stone."

Before Michael could form a proper protest or retract her statement, Ethan agreed to the plan. "She'll be more comfortable with you anyway, Happy. More room on the saddle."

The two men drew their horses close and Michael was summarily transferred from Ethan's mount to Happy's.

"Mind your manners," Ethan said. The words were not as significant as the look he shot her. Michael felt the blue-gray eyes bore right through her. Without another glance in her direction he urged his horse ahead and was out of earshot in a matter of seconds.

"Well," Happy drawled. "This is cozy."

Michael bit her lower lip. "Mmm, yes. Cozy is the word." Ethan had done it to punish her. She felt certain he had known she didn't want to go with Happy. He had to have felt her reluctance to be passed around like so much baggage. "How long have you known my husband, Happy? I heard Ethan correctly, didn't I? Your name's Happy."

"It's not my disposition," he said. "Picked up the name when I was greenhorn cowhand. Cut myself in the face with a bullwhip. Can't see the scar much now, what with the stubble and all, so there's no point in lookin'. Doc said I severed a nerve. Cut it clean in two, he said. Folks were like to point out then that I always looked like I was smilin'. Called me Happy. Just seemed to stick. But like I said, Miz Stone, it's not my disposition."

"I'll try to remember that."

"See that you do." Happy took a pouch of tobacco out of his coat pocket, pinched some off with his thumb and forefinger and packed it between his lower lip and gum. "Known your husband nigh on five months now. That's how long he's been ridin' with us. Newest man. You'll understand if that makes me a tad skeptical of what he says or does."

Michael could only summon a murmur. She wondered how long she could stay in the saddle. Even propped against Happy she was finding it difficult to stay upright. Her fingers ached with cold again and

60

Happy hadn't made the same offer to warm them that Ethan had.

"Now Ben up ahead," Happy went on. "Him and me go way back. He's my half-brother. Same mother, different gamblers. He's a Simpson. I'm a McAllister. Obie Long's been with the gang 'bout two years now. Good kid. Not much fer talkin', especially 'round the ladies, but it don't seem to bother them none. Still waters and all that."

Looking ahead on the trail, Michael was able to determine which of the men was Happy's brother. Obie, she knew, was the one who had followed her when she ran out of the train to find Drew. He was riding beside Ethan now. Her eyes scanned the darkness for one more man. "Where's the other?" she asked. "The man who was giving the orders."

"You must mean Houston. He and Jake took the engine down the tracks a piece. That'll keep the passengers from followin'. The Union Pacific won't know about the holdup until the train's late comin' to Barnesville. Even then they're like to think it's snowbound."

"There won't be anyone following us, will there?" Though Michael tried to keep her voice neutral, a note of despair touched her question.

"Not tonight," Happy said frankly. "Probably not tomorrow either. By the time the locals mount a posse, snow will have covered our tracks."

"What about the railroad? Won't the Union Pacific send men out after you?"

Happy leaned back in his saddle so that he could get a better view of Michael's face. "It don't seem to me, Miz Stone, that you're real pleased about this reunion with Ethan. That pretty much the way of it?"

Michael felt Happy's eyes on her and she avoided looking at him. "That's pretty much the way of it," she

61

repeated softly. "You must know I don't want to be here."

"Can't say that I favor it either, ma'am."

For a moment Michael was hopeful. "You don't? Then you would help me get—"

Happy cut her off. "Don't ask it, Miz Stone. You mistook my meanin'. I sure enough don't want you here, but 'cept fer bein' dead and buried, there really ain't no other place for you."

Michael felt cold in her soul. The shiver that swept through her had little to do with the bitter icy wind swirling around her. "Please," she said lowly, teeth chattering violently, "I want to go back to Ethan."

"Just a bit longer," Happy said. "If you're cold you can put your arms around me the way you did Ethan."

"I'll manage," she said tightly, repulsed by the offer. She crossed her arms in front of her, slipped her hands under her armpits, and tucked her head deeper into the raised collar of her coat and away from the stinging wind. "You're the one who uncoupled the *Chronicle*'s cars, aren't you?" She fully expected him not to answer or deny the charge. "You killed them."

Happy shrugged off the accusation. "Obie helped, but it was my idea."

Michael was stunned that he would admit it to her so easily. "Why would you tell me that? Or anything else you've said? You must know that—"

Again he interrupted her, this time placing a hand inside her coat and laying it on her thigh. "I figure it this way, Miz Stone: the more you know, the more you know you ain't goin' nowhere. Ethan, bein' your husband and all, probably has it in his mind to protect you. I don't feel honor bound to do the same. You're either with us or agin us. There's no fence-ridin'. With us, you live. Agin us, you die. That plain speakin' enough for you?"

She nodded.

"Good. Now, seein's how you're not exactly warmin' up to me, I'll set you back with Ethan. I can't think there's much point tellin' him about our conversation, can you?"

"No."

Happy smiled. Flakes of tobacco clung to his front teeth. He spit. "Good for you, ma'am. Mebbe you'll stay with us after all."

In a few minutes they caught up with the others. Ethan was deep in a conversation with Obie and Ben until Michael and Happy came within earshot. Michael's transfer to Ethan's mount was done in a brisk, impersonal fashion.

"Think I'll ride on ahead," Happy said. "Kinda look out fer Jake and Houston. Shouldn't be too much longer afore they meet up with us." He kicked his horse and called back over his shoulder. "She's a good handful, Ethan. She fits real nice agin me. Don't know what you were thinkin', leavin' her alone all those years."

Michael felt Ethan stiffen slightly at Happy's words but he made no reply.

"Don't mind Happy," Ben said. "He don't mean nothin' by it. Cold's most likely addled his senses a little. I'll just go on up yonder and have a talk with him. Obie, why don't you take up the rear for a while?"

Obie reined in almost immediately and let the others get in front of him. The staggered line of sure-footed pack mules followed.

"What did you and Happy find to talk about?" Ethan asked when he and Michael were alone.

Michael had no intention of answering Ethan's questions or even talking to him more than she absolutely had to. She realized that before today she had never experienced fear or fatigue. Now she felt the mind and body numbing effects of each like a paraly-

63

sis of spine and spirit and when she slumped against Ethan it was because she couldn't help herself.

"Michael?" Ethan asked. He gave her a little shake but there was no response. He thought at first she was faking. Slipping a gloved hand beneath her coat, Ethan cupped her breast. She didn't stir. He grinned and dropped his hand. His captive had nerves of steel and starch, but she wouldn't have let him touch her if she could have prevented it. Mary Michael Dennehy had fallen deeply asleep.

Two more hours passed before the party halted for the night. It was the sudden cessation of movement that woke Michael. Groggy and disoriented, she was still aware of the new voices that had joined their group. She had almost immediate recognition of Houston. There was amusement, even civility, in his tone as he spoke, and danger and menace in the slight rasp that edged his words. The other voice drawled deeply and she was able to put a name to it: Jake.

"Your lady's plumb tuckered," Jake Harrity said as Ethan eased Michael down from the saddle. He grinned as Michael slid heavily down the length of Ethan's long frame. She was limp with exhaustion and unsteady on her feet. Ethan had to hold her upright. "Here, I'll see to your horse." He unfastened the bedroll and tossed it on the ground beside Ethan. "You'll need this."

"Thanks, Jake." Ethan slipped one arm beneath Michael's crumbling knees and lifted her high against his chest. He carried her to an outcropping of rocks that gave shelter from the wind on three sides, set her down, and went back for his bedroll and horse blankets. "We've got some tinder for a small fire but it won't provide much warmth. You'll have to share the blankets with me if you expect to get through the night." When she didn't reply, not even whimper in protest, Ethan poked her with his foot. "You're awake, aren't you?"

Michael jerked her leg away. "I'm awake."

"Good." He dropped the bedroll and blankets beside her. "Lay these things out as best you can. I'll see to the fire."

Michael's fingers were stiff and clumsy with cold. Tears stung her eyes and lay icy and wet on her cheeks as she forced herself to work against the ache in her hands. Out of the corner of her eye she watched Ethan build the small fire at the head of their shelter. When tiny flames began licking at the wood, Michael's last vestige of reason vanished. She scrambled toward the fire on her hands and knees and thrust her hands into the flames.

"What the hell!" Ethan dropped to his knees and pushed Michael away. "Of all the stupid . . ." His voice trailed away as he stared at her. She was huddled against the cold inner face of their rocky shelter, her head bent low, her shoulders hunched, and her fingers jammed awkwardly in her mouth. He had difficulty remembering the stiff and starchy woman he had first seen in the offices of the *Chronicle.* "Here," he said roughly, moving toward her, "let me see what fool thing you've done to yourself. You can't put your hands in the fire and not expect to get burned." He pulled her fingers away from her mouth and examined them in the dim light. They weren't burned but Ethan began to suspect the onset of frostbite. "Why the hell didn't you say anything? I would have given you my gloves." She started to pull away at the taut impatience of his tone. "For God's sake, come here! I'm not going to hurt you."

Ben Simpson came upon them. "There some problem here?" he asked, throwing another blanket at their bed. "Thought you might want that.

Anything I can do to help?"

"Thanks, Ben. I'll take care of it myself. My wife's gone stupid with cold."

Ben chuckled at that description. "Ain't you the lucky one, gettin' to warm her up and all. Well, I'll be just yonder if you need anything." He disappeared beyond the rocks.

"Would you rather Ben warm you up?" Ethan asked. "No? Then come here so I can do something about it."

Michael didn't move but she was unresisting as Ethan pulled her toward him. He took off his own gloves and placed his hands between hers and blew on her fingers. After a few minutes he carefully levered her hands near the fire. "Not too close," he cautioned. Taking the extra blanket Ben had given them, he pulled it around Michael's shoulders and raised it along the edge to protect her ears. "You should have told me how cold you were. I could have done something about it."

Through chattering teeth Michael said, "I don't want anything from you."

Ethan found the kerchief he had given her earlier and wiped at the tears that lay frozen on her cheeks. "Of course you don't."

Michael briefly closed her eyes, exhaustion taking its toll again. "Don't patronize me," she said quietly. "You killed Drew. Happy admitted he killed the others. Paul, Jim, Bill, and Dave. All of them gone now . . . because of you and your friends. I don't want anything from you." Her voice dropped to a whisper and then she only seemed to mouth the words. "I want to sleep. I want to die."

Ethan stuffed his kerchief back in his own pocket. "You're a piece of work, Miss Dennehy," he said softly, shaking his head from side to side. "Quite a piece of work."

66

It took him several minutes to get them bedded down for the night. He sheltered Michael with his own body and the blankets, drawing her close inside his open coat and against his chest. Even in her drowsy, semi-conscious state, she was stiff and unyielding, her every muscle tense with cold and fear of his intentions. She shivered into his shoulder and tremors ran the length of her spine.

Michael heard his voice coming to her as if from a great distance. It was quietly encouraging, gentle, and best of all, warm on her face. "Sleep," it said. "Just sleep."

She dreamed she was back in the dining car, playing poker with her friends. She had a mountain of chips in front of her and she had drawn three cards to a full house. Drew was there, disgusted with his turn of luck and asking for an advance of thirty dollars. Michael found herself refusing him again and again in spite of her desire to do otherwise. She wanted to take charge of the dream, refashion it in a way that satisfied her, but she couldn't make it happen. The others started asking her for money as well. Paul and Jim drew caricatures of her smoking a cigar and playing tight-fisted with her winnings. Bill and Dave threatened to report her to Logan Marshall. Happy interrupted the game and drew his gun, promising to kill each reporter in turn, and Michael last. Helpless to stop the grisly chain of events, Michael watched each friend face Happy's gun in turn. When the Colt was leveled at her head she closed her eyes . . . and woke up screaming.

Or thought she did. At first she wasn't certain if she was awake or still trapped in her nightmare. Ethan Stone was beside her, one of his legs lying heavily across both of hers. The blankets cocooned them and beyond the darkness of her immediate shelter she could hear the crackle and spit of the fire. Except for that sound, nothing moved or rustled. There was no echo of her scream, no stirring in the night from any of the others. She had dreamed the scream just as she had dreamed every improbable exchange during the course of her nightmare.

She was left with one lasting impression as the details of her nightmare began to fade. There had been no one to save her, no one to stop Happy's relentless pursuit of the reporters. It seemed more than the vagaries of a dream. It seemed an omen.

Michael lay very still and pondered escape. Was it possible? Ethan appeared to be deeply asleep, breathing quietly and evenly. She took no comfort in it or in the warmth he offered. She had spoken the truth when she said she wanted nothing from him. It had occurred to her there was some price for his protection and though Michael had no clear idea what he might demand, she had no wish to pay.

She raised one corner of the blanket slightly to let in the firelight. The play of shadow across the hard cast of Ethan's features lent him an edge of dangerous mystery. Against her will, Michael felt herself drawn to him as she struggled to bring forward the memory that would set his face in place and time. As had happened previously, it was a fruitless struggle. There was no clear recollection of lightly colored, blue-gray eyes, of a hooded, direct gaze, of thick lashes or sunlines fanning the corners. She could not understand why the dark ebony hair, overlong at the nape with threads of gray at the temple, should be vaguely familiar when it was relatively unremarkable. Frustrated that she could not grasp the tantalizing bit of memory, Michael dropped the blanket back into place around Ethan and cautiously eased herself away from him.

She missed his warmth immediately. In spite of the rocky shelter cold air swirled around her as she sat up. She knew then that while escape from the men was a possibility, her chances of escaping the elements were almost nil. She *was* stupid with cold, she thought, because knowing that she might freeze to death in the wild mountains of Colorado didn't change her mind about leaving.

Michael carefully searched beneath the blankets for Ethan's discarded gloves. Finding them, she put them on, then removed the uppermost blanket and wrapped it around her head and shoulders. Michael rose slowly, making certain her stiff and unsteady legs would support her before stepping over Ethan and out of the stone shelter.

The fire the others had built and surrounded with their bedrolls and saddle pillows was a mere pile of embers. Michael stood very still, listening to the shuffle of the horses and the restless movements of the pack mules. She knew her capabilities and admitted that she could never ride one of the animals back to the train, even if she could have mounted. She was likely to be thrown from one of the horses and the mules had been uncooperative even for the men who knew how to handle them. Michael saw no alternative save to set out on foot.

Snow cushioned her footfalls but made walking difficult. She tried not to think of how far she had to go to reach the abandoned train but only of pressing on. After she had been walking awhile she turned around once, just to gauge her distance from the camp, and was discouraged to still be able to see the red-orange glow from the fire. The hundred yards she thought she had walked couldn't have been more than a hundred feet. Michael had considered the possibility of a search party finding her frozen body on the trail. She hadn't considered that she might fall so close to the robbers' camp that they would be witness to her death. It made her angry enough that she was able to increase her pace for the next few minutes.

"Where the hell do you think you're going?"

The voice, seemingly coming from nowhere, but surrounding her on all sides, brought Michael up short. It was Ethan's voice. There was no mistaking the deep, smooth, whiskey tones and the faint drawl. There was also no mistaking the impatience, incredulity, and anger. She clutched the blanket more tightly closed at her throat and squinted in the darkness to find him. She finally located Ethan standing above her on a rocky ledge. For some reason she thought of a mountain goat and giggled. In seconds, for no apparent reason other than she couldn't help herself, she was laughing uncontrollably.

Recognizing that Michael had reached the end of her mental tether, Ethan climbed down from his perch. His large hands clamped her shoulders and his long fingers pressed deeply against the blanket and into her flesh. His shake was forceful and Michael's head lolled weakly on the slender stem of her neck. Her laughter died away. The prelude to silence was a hiccup.

Michael stared wide-eyed and solemnly at her captor, rather surprised at the sound and the fact that it had come from her. She tried to recall if she had had something to drink.

"I should kill you," Ethan said emotionlessly. He could see her well enough to know that she didn't blink. She was either the bravest woman he had ever met or the most hopelessly naive. Ethan voted for the latter. She didn't think he meant it. "As sure as I know anything, I know you're going to bring me grief. I knew it the minute I saw you on that train. I think I knew it the moment I first laid eyes on you." One hand dropped to his gun and his fingers curled around the handle.

"What are you two doin' out here?"

Ethan spun around, gun drawn. Happy McAllister

stood some fifteen feet down the trail. "Jesus, Happy, are you trying to get yourself killed? Don't sneak up on me that way."

"I already got the drop on you, Ethan." Happy slipped his gun back in his holster. "You would have noticed 'cept for your woman there. I'm of a mind to kill her myself for tryin' to hightail it outta here."

Ethan put his Colt away. Behind him he felt Michael begin to sag. Before she could fall he grabbed her by the waist and pulled her around in front of him to face Happy. "You thought she was leaving?" Ethan asked. He managed to sound surprised that Happy would reach that conclusion.

"I saw her sneakin' out with my own eyes."

"Do you hear that, Michael?" Ethan asked, keeping her propped up and steady on her frozen feet. "Happy thought you were leaving and he was going to kill you for it." Perhaps that would shake her out of her stupor. If he hadn't found her before Happy, she would be dead now. "Michael?"

"I was going to . . ." she said quietly, ". . . going to relieve myself."

There was a bit of her brain that wasn't frozen, Ethan thought, and she had managed to put it to credible use. "You have a problem with my wife tending to a call of nature, Happy?"

"No problem," Happy said after a moment's thoughtful pause. "But ain't she a tad fer from the camp?"

"You're welcome to check her trail," Ethan told him. "You'll see for yourself that she was circling back."

With a distressed sigh, Michael realized Ethan's words were true. She had become disoriented in the dark and, at the time Ethan had called to her, she had actually been making her way back to the camp.

"Go on back to camp, Happy. Let me take care of my wife myself."

"Guess that's why you followed her in the first place, is it?"

"Guess so."

Happy shrugged, one wiry brow raised skeptically. "If you say so, Stone. Only I don't recollect ever hearin' a man sayin' he'll take care of his missus by killin' her. Or did I mistake your intention when I came walkin' down here?"

"If you'd ever been married to more than that mule of yours, you'd know that wanting to shake the devil out of your wife is all part and parcel of the arrangement."

"Shakin' ain't killin'," Happy said, turning on his heel. Still mumbling under his breath and scratching the uneven growth of beard on his chin, he walked away.

"He's right," Michael whispered. "You were going to kill me."

Ethan didn't deny it. "I still might."

Michael tore away from the embrace that was holding her upright and began to retrace her steps back to the camp. Her progress was clumsy, almost drunken, and when she veered off the path considerably, Ethan snapped at her.

"Where the hell do you think you're going now?"

"I have to relieve myself."

"Oh, for God's sake," Ethan muttered. He waited with ill-disguised impatience on the trail as Michael disappeared behind a boulder and beneath the sheltering boughs of some spruce trees. When she didn't return quickly enough to suit him he started after her.

Upon hearing his approach Michael quickly righted her undergarments and stood. "I'm coming," she called. She noticed her announcement did not deter him. "I said, 'I'm coming,'" she repeated with as much dignity as she could muster.

72

Ethan didn't hear dignity. "God, but you're pathetic," he said, quickly assessing her appearance. She was huddled beneath the blanket. She had pulled it over her head and she was still shaking so badly she could barely stand. He hunkered down at her feet and touched the hem of her skirt and felt her leather shoes. Both were wet and crusted with ice from her ill-advised trek in the snow. Without telling her his intention, Ethan picked her up and slung Michael over his shoulder. "You need a keeper," he grumbled.

"I had five," she said as blood rushed to her head. "Thanks to you and the others they're all dead."

"Repeat that to anyone else," he told her, "and you'll join them."

She was silent as he carried her back to the site of their blankets. When she started to get under the blankets, he stopped her.

"Take off your skirt and shoes."

Michael couldn't believe she had heard him correctly so she made no move to obey.

Ethan knelt beside her, brusquely grabbed her by the ankles, and began unlacing her shoes. She fought him, kicking him in the chest with her feet. He slapped her lightly in the face with the back of his hand. It had the desired effect of stunning her into compliance. "That's better," he said.

"You hit me," she said accusingly.

There was no apology in his voice. "And I'll do it again if you don't start doing what I say." He pulled off one shoe. "Get the other one off while I get an extra pair of socks from my saddle bag. No arguments. Just do it. The skirt too."

She wondered if he had an extra skirt in his saddle bag, but some fuzzy sense of self-preservation helped her keep silent. By the time he returned she had complied. A pair of thick woolen socks were dropped in her lap with a growled order to put them on.

73

"What did you do with the gloves you were wearing?"

She had had to take them off to work her shoestrings. She found them near the burned out fire.

Ethan took them from her. "Don't take anything of mine unless you ask or unless I give it to you. Understood?"

Michael nodded.

He tossed a pair of jeans at her. "Put these on. They're Obie's extras. Best fit I could manage on short notice. I'll lay your skirt out on a rock. It'll be stiff as a day old corpse by morning but you might be able to wear it again. I'm not so sure about the shoes." Ethan threw some more tinder on the cold fire and lighted it. "Pull the blankets closer to the fire then lie down." He was patient with her while she followed his instructions. When she was situated under the blankets he slipped in beside her. "Don't think about moving 'til morning."

She couldn't think about anything else. Trapped as she was by his arm and his leg, freedom burned in her mind. "I don't need you to hold me," she whispered. "I'm not going anywhere."

Ethan's sigh was weary. "You can understand if I don't believe you."

"I swear it."

"Go to sleep."

Somehow she did. And later, when Ethan turned away from her, it was Michael who groggily pursued the warmth he provided, fitting her body to the planes and angles of his. It was her leg that insinuated itself between his and her arm which curved around his waist. It was her breath which warmed the nape of his neck and the even cadence of her breathing which lulled him to sleep.

It was something nudging steadily at his foot that woke Ethan. He tried to bat it away as he would a

74

pesky fly, but the rhythmic tattoo was intrusive. Opening his eyes he looked down the length of his body to find the source of the disturbance, then up to see Houston standing over him.

There was a wicked smile on Houston's lean face and his black eyes were knowing. "Looks like you had a better night than the rest of us. Quite a tangle here."

Ethan realized it was true. Michael was curved so tightly against him she was like an extension of his own skin. He couldn't remember the last time he had slept so soundly.

"Usually don't have to rouse you," Houston said, stating what Ethan was thinking at that precise moment. "Of course you don't usually have a lady wrapped around you."

Ethan eased himself away from Michael and sat up. Reaching for his gunbelt, he put it on, then stood. "You waiting on us to leave?"

Houston handed Ethan a tin mug of hot, black coffee. "Happy's chomping at the bit to move on, but there's no hurry. Posse's days away from being organized and there's a storm coming. In twenty-four hours there'll be no trail to follow. We're safe."

Ethan warmed his hands around the coffee mug and raised it to his lips slowly, breathing the aroma as if the fragrance alone could warm him on the inside. "I didn't get to hear much last night about what happened with the engine. Did you and Jake have any trouble?"

"You were fairly well occupied with your own problems," Houston said, looking significantly at Michael's sleeping form. "But, no, Jake and I didn't have any trouble. After the track was cleared we uncoupled her from the rest of the cars and took 349 about four miles down the line. She built up some good speed on the downgrade but nothing we couldn't handle. We jumped at Hunter's Point and let the engine go on.

She didn't make the curve." He made a diving motion with his hand to show what had happened. "In the canyon. It was too dark to see clearly, but the sound echoed for minutes."

Ethan sipped his coffee and noted that Houston sounded pleased with the night's work. "It's too bad we didn't anticipate the *Chronicle*'s cars."

"It couldn't be helped."

Although Houston appeared to shrug off the comment, Ethan knew he was angry about the unpredictable events that had made his plans go slightly less than smooth. "No, it couldn't be helped. The murders are going to cause us some problems."

"You worried?"

"No. You?"

"No." Houston pointed to Michael. "What about her? Happy says she was the fiancée of that reporter you killed."

Ethan nodded. "That's right."

"But you say she's your wife."

"She thought I was dead. I suspect she thought it was time to remarry."

"You never once mentioned a wife."

"I understand you had an encounter with Michael on the train."

"That's right," Houston said.

"Well, if you were married to the shrew, would you admit it?"

Houston turned away, but not before letting Ethan see his slow, thoughtful smile. "I might," he said softly to himself. "I just might."

Chapter Three

They talked casually about the robbery as if she weren't there, or worse, as if her presence were of no account. It was an insult to her and an insult to the men who had died because of their profession. Michael made herself remember that—five colleagues had died simply because they were newspapermen. She owed them something. Her story, her account of the robbery, would be the best revenge. She didn't have to live to tell it in the *Chronicle*, she had to live to tell it in the court.

Knowing that kept her quiet and alert. If Ethan or any of the others wondered at her uncharacteristic silence, they never commented on it.

Michael shared Ethan's mount and the fit was uncomfortably tight. Every time she moved she was aware of him, aware of the hard wall of his chest, aware of the supporting cradle of his thighs. She tried not to move. She tried not to think of the way she had clung to him during the night.

The morning grew warmer, making the impending storm more threatening. Michael still wore the jeans Ethan had given her. Her skirt had been as stiff as Ethan warned. Her shoes wouldn't fit over the heavy socks so she carried them in her lap and clutched them because she was sometimes afraid she would clutch Ethan. He wasn't her ally, she reminded herself, no matter that he had made it his business to save her life.

The sky seemed to press against the mountain peaks. The clouds were heavy and thick and gray. The flakes that fell were a complete contrast, light, airy, and white. They drifted steadily to the ground, spaced widely apart, so that it seemed they fell around her but not on her. Yet when she looked at the blanket covering her shoulders there was a fine dusting of snow in the creases.

A bald eagle, disturbed by the passage of the men, horses, and mules, dove from its nest of sticks in a timber pine and made a threatening, elegant pass over their heads then dropped lower and skimmed the surface of a briskly moving stream for fish.

"How much you figure's in those bags agin, Ben?" Happy asked his brother.

"Sixty thousand if there's a penny."

"Damn," Happy said, grinning. "I like hearin' that."

"You must," Jake said, rolling his eyes. "That's at least the fourth time you've made Ben repeat it. There's none of it that's going to get up and walk away."

Happy's lower lip was distended from a wad of tobacco. He spit in the snow. "Hope not," he said. "Hate to think Obie and me stopped a perfectly good poker game for nothin'."

In his arms Ethan felt Michael stiffen. The bruise on her jaw seemed to darken as the rest of her pale face went ashen. "What are you talking about, Happy? What poker game?"

"When me and Obie interrupted the reporters, they were in the middle of a game. Looked like they was enjoyin' themselves, too. 'Course we took the pot and that kinda made 'em mad. Threatened to do a story about the robbery. You know Houston ain't in it for the glory."

As if there was any glory associated with what they had wrought. Michael wanted to scream. Instead she bit her lip until she tasted blood and tears came to her eyes.

"So you took it on yourself to get rid of them," Ethan said, not bothering to hide his disgust.

"You have a problem with that?" Happy asked, spitting to punctuate his question. "Seems I recall you offering to take that other fellow out yourself. Obie says you dispatched him without much fanfare."

Michael waited to see how Ethan would defend himself.

"I acted on Houston's orders," he said. "You acted on your own. Anyway, you know I was anxious to get away from first class because of Michael."

"So you shot her fiancé." He chuckled. "That's a good one."

Houston pulled up his mount sharply and called over his shoulder. "Enough! I don't need to hear a rehash of last night. What's done's done. It's not the first time any of us has killed."

But this time was supposed to be different, Ethan thought. Or what was he here for? He said nothing.

"Please," Michael said softly, her voice expressing urgency as she reached for Ethan's wrist and held on tightly. "I think I'm going to be sick." She started to wriggle out of the saddle even before Ethan had stopped. Her hand came up in a reflex action to cover her mouth. The small choking sound she made was muffled. "Let me down."

Ethan steadied her as she slid from the saddle. Although he dismounted quickly, Michael was already running for the privacy of some pines. He gave her a moment, waiting for the painful, wretching sounds to end before approaching. "Better?"

His question incensed her. As he reached out to touch her Michael slapped his arm away. "Don't put your hands on me. I can't bear the thought of you touching me. What do you think made me sick? You and the others talk about killing as if those lives were of no account." She barely got the words out before she was sick again. "Get out of here," she moaned softly, turning her back on Ethan.

He didn't move. When he was certain she had emptied her stomach he offered her a handful of snow. "Take some of this," he said, unconcerned by her rebuff. "Rinse your mouth out."

Michael ignored him. A small tremor shook her body as she bent and scooped some clean snow herself.

"Jesus, lady," Ethan sighed. "Do you think I really care whether you take the damn snow from me or not? I'm surprised you saw the merit of my suggestion." He turned his palm over and let the snow fall back to the ground. "I never met a woman so purely stubborn as you." That said, Ethan turned on his heel and went back to his horse. He waved the others on when they looked at him questioningly. "We'll catch up in a few minutes," he told them, mounting. "Michael needs a little more time."

Happy rolled his eyes and shook his head slowly from side to side. He spit. "You ask her if she's pregnant?"

"She not pregnant," Ethan snapped.

"Didn't know it would make you so touchy," Happy said, grinning and shying away from Ethan with exaggerated movements. "Guess I'll take myself off." Under his breath he added, "But she *was* goin' to marry that reporter fellow."

Houston interjected, "That's enough, Happy. Move on. Obie. Ben. Jake. You all do the same." When he and Ethan were alone he glanced in Michael's direction with his cold black eyes. "I suppose the talk upset her."

Ethan shrugged as if it were unimportant. "Lots of things upset her."

"Why did you leave?"

It took Ethan a moment to realize Houston was asking about his fictional marriage. "I wasn't as ready as I thought I was to be settled," he said.

Houston looked at Ethan thoughtfully, measuring his response, then he nodded. His eyes strayed to Michael again. She was leaning against the trunk of a pine, her back turned to them. Occasionally she would raise one hand and brush at her cheek. He knew she was crying. "I wish you hadn't had to bring her along," he said.

"Hell, Houston, do you think it's what I wanted? Once I realized she was on the train I did everything I could to avoid her."

"She's trouble."

"I'm not denying it."

"We can't let her go."

"I know that."

Houston nodded again. "Good," he said finally. "Try to keep her in line, Stone." He kicked his horse and rode off to catch up with the others.

Ethan glanced over his shoulder. Michael was approaching. "He says I'm supposed to keep you in line."

Michael raised her arms for Ethan's assistance to mount.

He helped her up and when she was settled he repeated Houston's statement. She made no reply and

81

her silence annoyed him. "He won't ask me to kill you," Ethan told her. "He'll ask one of the others or do it himself. Keep that in mind."

Michael's response was quiet and firm. "I don't know that I'll enjoy your hanging, but I *will* be there."

Snow fell steadily as they rode on. At noon they stopped for hot coffee and cold jerky. Michael chose to eat outside the circle gathered around the small fire. No one asked her to join them or inquired if she was cold. The only time she elicited a response from them was when she needed privacy to relieve herself and began to walk out of their sight. The hot blush covering her face was all the answer they needed when Ben asked her where she was going.

Houston took advantage of her disappearance to discuss how they would handle her presence as they rode into town. "Any of you given it any thought?"

"I'm keeping her with me at Dee's," Ethan said. "I can't let her out of my sight much. If I absolutely have to, I can lock her in."

"You gonna tell folks she's your wife?" Ben asked.

Ethan shook his head. "I don't want a lot of questions. Too hard to explain how I met up with a wife no one knew I had. Detra can know. That's all."

Obie lifted his hat, smoothed back the crown of his thick hair, then lowered his hat again. "I don't know, Ethan. Who you gonna say she is? And how did we come across her?"

"Look," Ethan said lowly. "No one's going to associate her with the train robbery. Obie and I made it look like we killed her. The emigrants in the rear car witnessed it. There'll be a search for the body, but when nothing turns up they're going to think animals got it, not that we have her. If we return to town with a woman, don't you think most folks are going to assume we brought her in for Dee?" His blue-gray eyes focused on each member of the circle in turn. "That's what we tell them then. Michael's one of Dee's girls."

Everyone except Houston chuckled. He was thoughtful. "And what are you going to do when someone wants their turn with her?" he asked.

Ethan didn't hesitate. "She's mine," he said.

"That's not how Dee usually likes to do things," Obie said. "Folks might begin to wonder."

"Dee's customers will just have to get used to it. Michael's not available to anyone until I'm tired of her."

Happy poked his half-brother in ribs. "Whaddya think, Ben? About another twenty-four hours and he'll be passin' her around?"

Except for blinking Ethan didn't move. It was his very stillness that brought Happy McAllister up short.

"Didn't mean nothin' by it," Happy said, glancing at Ethan's gun. He went on defensively. "You're the one what can't seem to figure whether to kiss or kill her. When you make up your mind let the rest of us know." He stood and tossed the dregs of his coffee on the fire. It sputtered and snapped. He stomped off to take care of his horse.

"Happy's got a point," Houston said, breaking the uneasy silence. "It's probably in everyone's best interest for you to decide what you're doing with Michael."

The men moved off one by one, leaving Ethan alone by the fire. "She's mine," he whispered, when no one could hear. He put out the flames with a handful of snow. "Mine."

Michael said nothing as they started their journey but Ethan had his suspicions. "How much did you hear?" he asked.

She didn't pretend not to understand. "Enough."

"Somehow I doubt that. Don't you have any questions?"

One of his hands held the reins, the other rested lightly against her waist, tightening only when the terrain demanded they shift their weight. Michael thought that one of things she hated most was the fact that she was becoming accustomed to the feel and closeness of him. He turned her away from the wind, adjusted the blanket around her shoulders and ears, and without seeming to think about it at all, would occasionally brush snowflakes from her cheeks and forehead. "I didn't think you'd answer my questions," she said.

"Depends on what they are."

"Is Detra a madam?"

"Saloon keeper."

"Then if I'm going to be one of her . . . her girls . . ." Michael folded her arms across her stomach, suppressing the uneasy churning. "That means that I won't be expected to . . . to—"

"I'm not letting you loose with the customers, no. Not the way you mean. I don't trust you that much."

It was about trust, Michael thought, not about protection or what was decent. "I see," she said slowly.

"Somehow I doubt that, too."

Michael didn't ask any more questions. Instead she closed her eyes and pretended to sleep. Gradually it became a fact.

The posted sign at the edge of Madison listed the

population as "700 give or take a few." Except when it came to mining, preciseness did not much concern the town. Fifteen years earlier the population had swelled to 2500 with the discovery of silver. Many of the mines had tapped out quickly, others held their treasure too deeply to be excavated without special equipment which simply didn't exist at the time. Although men by the dozens drifted away from Madison to seek their fortunes elsewhere, their desertion had little effect on the heart of the town. Far from ever being a boomtown, Madison's central growth had been slow and cautious. When miners left they carried their canvas homes on the backs of their mules. People who built homes stayed.

Madison's main street was a wide muddy track in the spring, a frozen, rutted thoroughfare in the fall and winter. The stores were embellished with impressive false fronts and porches that stretched the width of the buildings. There was a feed store and mercantile, a barber shop, boarding house and eatery, a jail, three saloons, a dressmaker's, a livery, and a bank. The lone church was situated at the far end of town, isolated from the stores and gambling halls. During the week it was used as a school house, the minister's wife was also the teacher. Children from the two streets on either side of the town center often met at the penny candy counter in Tweedy's Mercantile and Hardware before setting off together.

The Madison Mining Cooperative met the needs of most of its citizens. Nearly every individual owned shares in the silver mine and had a personal interest in its success. From the surveys that were done on the mines and the equipment that had recently become available, the town believed the mines would continue producing to the turn of the century.

It didn't seem necessary to look beyond that. There was a sense of satisfaction and optimism that pervaded the spirit of the town, a feeling of comfort that one could put down roots and enjoy a modicum of prosperity.

Madison was moving toward respectability. Not respectable enough to run the gambling halls out of town, but respectable enough to want a little order in them. To that end Madison, Colorado had recently elected its first sheriff.

At the edge of town Houston held up his hand and stopped his group. He reached inside his coat, into the breast pocket of his shirt, and pulled out a tin, five-pointed star. He grinned sideways at Jake who was doing the same. "Well, deputy?" he asked. "Ready?"

"Ready, Sheriff."

Ethan was watching Michael carefully, waiting for her reaction. She would have been offended to know she was so completely predictable.

"What the hell is going—"

Ethan's hand clamped over her mouth.

"Shut her up," Houston said at the same time. "If you can't keep her quiet, knock her out."

Ethan nodded, turning Michael's face roughly toward him. "Hear that?" he asked softly. "Your jaw probably can't take another good clip. You speak up now and you may never speak again." He felt her acquiescence in the slow release of tension in her body. Not completely trusting her, he withdrew his hand in small increments. "I thought that might quiet you."

It was the smugness in his voice that infuriated her. "Bastard," she hissed softly.

"You really shouldn't swear. It's unbecoming."

If he hadn't removed his hand Michael would have bit him.

As if he could read her mind, Ethan chuckled. "She'll be fine, Houston."

Houston nodded. "All right, let's go."

They rode into town slowly, Houston and Jake in the lead, Ethan and Michael behind them flanked by Happy and Obie. The pack mules came next with Ben Simpson bringing up the rear.

"Hey, Sheriff!" A voice called to Houston from the entry to the mercantile. A man stepped out of the shadows of the store front. "You found him! Hell, Happy, where'd ya disappear?"

"Storm caught me unawares up Stillwater way. Had to dig in." He grinned sheepishly, as if he couldn't believe it could have happened to him, and spit once in the street.

"Glad they found you." The man gave the passing party a jaunty salute and turned back to the store to spread the news.

As they traveled the length of Madison's unnamed main street, and more people welcomed their sheriff home, Michael began to understand the story that had been fabricated to cover the disappearance of five of Madison's citizens.

Two weeks before the planned robbery of No. 349, Happy McAllister left Madison on the pretext of prospecting. When he didn't return Ben made a point of reporting the disappearance of his brother to the sheriff. Houston organized a search party among the dozens of volunteers and set off with food, water, and medical supplies.

Michael realized there would be no hiding out in the sense that she had imagined it. Houston's men weren't going to spend months in a cave in the side of a mountain or live in an isolated canyon. During the robbery they had worn their hats low and their kerchiefs high. They'd never called one another by name or given a hint about their origins. For all intents and purposes they were unidentifiable. As for the people of Madison, they had every reason to believe their sheriff was coming to the aid of one of their own. The absence of days was explained. There was no need for inquiry because questions simply didn't arise.

The awareness of the planning and preparation that had gone into the robbery created an uncomfortable sense of hopelessness within Michael. Nothing Ethan had said to her, nothing Happy had threatened or Houston had warned, had the same impact as knowing first-hand how carefully they had created their scheme, how cautious they had been in covering their activities. She understood clearly the threat she was to their accomplishment. She. Alone. There was no one else.

They meant it when they said they would kill her.

"It won't be long now," Ethan said, his breath warm against her ear. "We'll fix you up with blankets and a half dozen hot bricks at Detra's."

He must have felt her shiver, she realized. He thought she was cold. He almost sounded concerned. Michael wondered why the hysterical laughter she felt inside never surfaced.

They stopped in front of Kelly's Saloon. Above the porch roof bright green block letters, edged in yellow, proclaimed the name of the business. Managed by Detra Kelly, the sign informed. Owned by Nathaniel Houston.

Michael pointed to the sign. "How convenient," she said as Ethan helped her down. Cold seeped through her thick socks.

"It has its advantages." He tethered his horse then removed his saddle bag. "Let's get you settled first, then I'll help the others."

Her arms had been crossed protectively in front of her, a shoe in each hand. Now she held them up in a gesture of innocence and pretended indifference. "I'm in no hurry. I don't mind waiting to see sixty thousand dollars unloaded."

Ethan didn't hesitate. It didn't matter that her voice didn't carry beyond him, he refused to take the chance that her next comment might. He slung her over his shoulder, carried her into the saloon, and up the stairs to his room at the rear of the building.

"Explanations later, Dee," he called as he mounted the stairs. He almost couldn't be heard above the laughter and ribald observations of the saloon's patrons. As he turned the corner to his room he saw Houston motion to Dee to follow him to the office. Ethan was surprised by his relief. Dee's reaction to Michael's presence worried him. It was better that Houston explained. Detra was, after all, *his* mistress.

Ethan thought Michael was unusually quiet as he paraded her in front of the patrons. She didn't fight him or even voice a protest. Inside his room he sat her down then quickly locked the door. "I'm sorry if I offended your sense of dignity," he said before she could say anything. He dropped the key in his pocket. "Get out of those damp clothes and into that bed. I'll have Dee send someone up with hot bricks and extra blankets. My nightshirts are in the bureau over there. You can wear one." He saw the immediate look of protest in her eyes, the fear and uncertainty. "Or not," he said. "Naked suits me fine."

He half expected she would fly at him. There was no attack of feet or fists, no barrage of words meant to cut him low. His dark brows drew together and his expression narrowed questioningly. She merely continued to stare at him, her blanket drawn protectively around her. Ethan shrugged, unable to make

89

sense of her. "I'll turn down the bed and leave you alone. The window over there's been painted shut. Even so, don't think about prying it open to yell for help. I'm locking you in. Bang on the door or give the girl Dee sends up any trouble, and you'll wish you hadn't." He considered the threat was sufficiently vague to keep Michael compliant.

Ethan stood outside the door for almost a minute listening for some sound that would mean Michael was doing as he told her. The sound never came. He moved away because he heard Happy calling him.

Fifteen minutes later, when the key scraped in the lock, Michael was sitting on the edge of the bed still wrapped in her blanket. A puddle of water from her thawing socks and ice encrusted trousers was forming on the floor, staining the maroon and cream colored carpet.

Seeing the condition of the new girl, Kitty Long sighed as she entered the room. "Ethan warned me you might be a little hard to reason with," she said briskly. Kitty's arms were filled with blankets and a warming pan. She set things down on a cherrywood table just inside the door. "I can't say I hold with locking you in, but Ethan thinks you're not quite right from the cold." She tapped the side of her head with her finger. "Looking at you, I can understand his concern. I'm Kitty Long. Ethan said I should mention that Obie's my brother. Can't imagine why that's important right now."

But Michael knew why. Even if Kitty knew nothing about the robbery, which seemed unlikely to Michael, she was still not apt to turn her brother in. It was Ethan's warning.

Michael's eyes grazed her uninvited guest. Kitty's coloring was similar to her brother, flaxen and pale, and they shared a certain likeness in the fullness of

90

their mouths. While Obie was tall and rather loose-limbed and lanky, his sister was fully rounded, not thick or heavy, but generously curved. She was also not nearly so reticent as her brother.

"Let me have that blanket," she said. As she was already pulling it off Michael in a no-nonsense fashion, it was less a suggestion than a command. "My, your hair's pretty. Bit of a rat's nest now though, isn't it? Here let me dry it for you then we'll get you out of these wet clothes. I'll be careful not to touch your face. That's quite a bruise you got there. Don't worry thought. I got somethin' to cover it right up. Those are Obie's jeans, aren't they? I recognize the patch I sewed for him on the knee. My, oh my, I could never get into them. But look at you. Just a skinny bit of a thing, aren't you?"

On and on it went. Kitty fussed and fretted and never gave an inch. She asked a barrage of questions and never yielded time for an answer. It was comforting in an odd sort of way, and Michael, numb of thought and feeling, discovered that her eyes were damp with tears.

Kitty warmed the bed with a long-handled pan filled with hot coals while Michael slipped Ethan's nightshirt over her head. "Put yourself right in bed," Kitty said. "That's a girl. Careful not to burn yourself. What a few days it's been for you, hasn't it? I'll wager you thought it was a lark comin' west. Lucky they found you at the Stillwater depot when they did. You could have ended up workin' in Angel Madden's establishment." Her rounded features screwed up comically in a look of utter distaste. "That's no kind of place for anyone."

Michael allowed Kitty to pull the thick goose-down comforter up to her shoulders and tuck her in.

"I could brush out your hair," Kitty offered.

Michael shook her head.

"All right. Tomorrow. When you're feeling a little better." Kitty started a fire in the iron stove in the far corner of the room. She gathered Michael's wet clothes, mopped up the floor with her brother's trousers, then let herself quietly out of the room.

It was several hours later, after bounty from the robbery had been divided and deposited in a safe place, that Ethan was able to return to his room. He was bone weary. He wanted dinner, a bath, and bed, and he wasn't even particular about the order.

The tray he carried with the evening meal was laden with large helpings of beef stew, thick chunks of buttered bread, generous wedges of cherry pie, and a pot of tea and two mugs. He juggled the tray carefully while he opened the door to his room with the key. It wasn't until he actually saw Michael in his bed that he realized how much he had wanted to be alone. A powerful surge of irritation swept through him as he set the tray down and locked himself in.

"Wake up," he said roughly. "Your dinner's here." When Michael didn't respond with so much as a twitch, Ethan went to the bed and touched her forehead with the back of his hand. She wasn't hot or flushed. There was some relief in knowing that. He was of no mind to take on the role of nursemaid to anyone, let alone this stubborn, willful, and ultimately ungrateful patient.

His hand slid lower, lightly cupping her jaw and turning her face so he could see the extent of the bruise he had given her. Some faint swelling still remained but the bruise itself was fading nicely. Tomorrow it would be invisible except to those who

92

knew to look for it. Kitty would. It was the first thing she had asked him about when she came downstairs. She made it sound as if half of Michael's face was discolored. Ethan made up a credible story on the spur of the moment that satisfied Kitty. It further annoyed him now that he had to share it with Michael so their telling of events would have some consistency. Resentment made him impatient. His hand went to her shoulder and he gave her a hard shake.

"Wake up. Your dinner's getting cold."

Michael blinked widely as she was roused from a deep sleep. Instinctively she jerked away from the pressure on her shoulder.

Ethan removed his hand. "I wasn't trying to hurt you," he snapped. "Your dinner's on the tray over there. Half of it's mine so don't eat it all. Go on. I'm not serving it to you in bed. You're going to have to learn to fend for yourself."

"I'm used to fending for myself," she said coolly. Michael sat up and pushed the covers down. The borrowed nightshirt was an adequate and modest cover—the hem fell to the middle of her calves—but Michael had her own thoughts about what was proper and asked for a robe.

"Oh, for God's sake." He turned away from the bed in disgust. He wasn't going to let his own meal grow cold. Sitting down in the large wing chair beside the table, he lifted one of the plates of stew from the tray and set it on his lap. "No, I don't have a robe."

"I merely asked."

Ethan's response was a derisive snort. He applied his attention to his plate and began eating. Only a few moments passed before he caught a flash of bare feet and trim ankles as Michael hastily approached

93

the table, took her food, and scurried back to the bed. Once he heard her settle in he looked up. "Were you expecting me to attack you?" he asked.

"Why, no. Of course not."

He thought she seemed genuinely surprised by his question. "Then why was the robe so important?"

"Mr. Stone, —"

"Ethan," he interrupted. "Don't call me anything but Ethan. We're supposed to be married, remember?"

She hadn't forgotten, but she saw no purpose in doing things his way when they were alone. On the other hand, he didn't look as if he were willing to give her any slack on the tether. The deep whiskey roughness of his voice was strained, the faint drawl more noticeable. The creases at the corners of his eyes were more pronounced, the line of his jaw was defined by the growth of dark beard.

The vague sense of familiarity returned. Michael stared hard at Ethan's face and tried to imagine him with a beard. Was that the key, she wondered. Had he altered his appearance in some fashion?

"What are you staring at?" he demanded, knowing the answer all too well.

"What?" Michael came out of her reverie. "Oh. Nothing. I was just thinking."

"Well, before your thoughts put you in a trance, you were explaining to me about the robe." He bent his head, avoiding her steady gaze, and speared a potato and a carrot.

"Yes," she said slowly. "The robe." Shaking her head to clear it, Michael continued, "It's just that I'm not used to parading around in my nightshirt."

"*My* nightshirt." He watched, fascinated by the light flush that pinkened her features. He recalled thinking when he first saw her that she wasn't the sort of woman who would blush easily, yet he had witnessed the reaction several times.

"My point exactly," she said, struggling for composure. "I grew up with four sisters and my mother. I hope you can appreciate that I'm not entirely comfortable."

Ethan nearly choked on the bread he was swallowing. "You've mastered understatement," he said, pouring himself some tea. He washed down the bread. "When I brought you here this afternoon you were nearly frozen with fear."

"With cold," she corrected.

Ethan's hooded gaze rested on her intently. "With fear."

Michael rearranged the food on her plate. "All right," she said finally. "With fear. But I have reason to be afraid, don't I?"

He would have liked to reassure her but even if she knew the truth, the answer to her question was still the same. "Yes. You have reason to be afraid."

She nodded, expecting as much, resigned to it for the moment. In spite of her hunger she had no appetite. She slid her plate onto the table at her bedside then drew the comforter close about her and leaned against the headboard.

"How are your fingers and toes?" he asked. "No frostbite?"

"No frostbite."

"Your jaw?"

"Tender."

"Kitty asked me about it. I told her you got a little hysterical during the trek and I shut you up."

"Close enough to the truth."

He nodded. "There are some other things we have to talk about if there's to be any chance of protecting you."

95

"I don't know why you want to."

Ethan needed to keep Michael off balance and fearful. "I'm not certain I do," he told her. "But there's my promise to your friend to consider. It's not a good reason, but it's kept you alive so far. I wouldn't examine it too closely if I were you." He watched her mouth flatten, a gesture of self-defense to keep him from hearing her gasp or see her lips tremble. He poured a mug of tea for her and took it to the bed. "You look as if you could use some warming from the inside out."

He didn't know why he did it. Perhaps because she looked so pathetic huddled under the comforter and pressed against the headboard. Her widely spaced, dark green eyes were grave, the set of her mouth, solemn. The light, feathery brows that arched delicately above her eyes were drawn closely together the more deeply she thought. It was her hair, however, that drew Ethan's eyes again and again. The shadings of auburn and copper were no longer confined to a neat crown near the back of her head. The bright highlights did not have to compete with pencils. Her magnificent hair was not merely thick and silky, but liberated from its confining pins, it was fairly wild with curls. Her features seemed more fragile somehow, her complexion a shade more translucent when framed by the wonderfully burnished colors of her hair.

He watched Michael warm her hands with the mug, then sip gingerly of its contents. Ethan returned to his chair and exchanged what was left of his stew for the thick wedge of cherry pie. "We've told everyone that I ran out on you four years ago."

"Why did you leave?"

"Because you're a shrew and I didn't like being corralled."

A tiny smile flickered across her lips. "I see we're keeping very close to the truth as you see it."

He felt a certain tightening in his chest as he glimpsed the dimples on either side of her mouth. No wonder she set her mouth so seriously while she thought. She could make men stupid with that smile. "You told Happy you were engaged to Drew. It makes sense that you would have been acquainted with his colleagues, if not a close friend." The brief reminder of her dead friends was enough to make the smile vanish. "I think we should say that we were together only a few months, from March to July, let's say, in '71."

"Where did we meet?"

"In New York. I was there during that time. Were you?"

She nodded. "I've always lived there."

They traded more information. Michael considered lying because she didn't like the idea of Ethan knowing things about her, even insignificant things. She decided against it because safety lay in the truth. She could not be caught out easily later if she kept her information factual. They exchanged birthdays. She was twenty-three. He was thirty-one. He had no family. She had a large one. She had a university education. He told her what he had told Houston and others: he had completed the eighth grade and was self-taught beyond that. Ethan didn't have the luxury of sharing only the truth. He had to keep his story consistent with every one that had come before. For the most part it wasn't a difficult task. Sharing with Michael was a good mental exercise.

"How long was our courtship?" she asked.

"One week. You would have been taking university classes then. It was impulsive on both our parts."

97

"I don't act on impulse."

Ethan looked at her steadily, his eyes shaded by thick lashes. "Neither do I."

"Then why did we —" Michael stopped, hardly aware she was holding her breath as Ethan set his empty plate aside and came to his feet. He crossed the room with the lithe, rolling stride that announced confidence and purpose. His approach was unhesitating, his determination clear. When he reached the bed he braced one knee on the mattress near Michael's hip and leaned toward her, supporting himself by placing a hand on the headboard on either side of her shoulders. He bent his head. His mouth slanted across her. The pressure was immediately hard; the search was hungry.

His mouth was sweet. There was the faint taste of cherries, the warmth of tea. Her lips parted with very little urging on his part. His tongue teased the soft underside of her upper lip and ran across the even ridge of her teeth. He pressed harder and her mouth opened under his. She was responsive, matching his touch, meeting his demands. Her mouth was sweetly ripe. She pushed against him with her tongue, joining the heady battle. Her low hum of pleasure vibrated between them.

Ethan pushed himself away, breaking the kiss. He straightened and took a step back from the bed. The centers of his eyes were dark as he locked his gaze on Michael. "That's why," he said soberly. "We couldn't help ourselves."

Color drained from Michael's face. "Oh."

"Since we're sticking closely to the truth . . ." His voice trailed off as he watched the evidence of her warring thoughts on her face. She was staring at her hands folded tightly around the mug. Her brow was furrowed, her mouth severe. Would she deny her own response to his kiss? Would she deny that against all reason there was some attraction between them?

"I don't think you should touch me any more," she said finally. "I don't like you. You can't expect that I should. I don't like myself much right now. I feel as if I've betrayed everyone important to me, including myself."

"Those sentiments are mutual." He returned to his chair but didn't sit down. He finished off his tea, grimacing at the cool bitterness of it after drinking from the honeyed warmth of Michael's mouth. "I'll be back in a few minutes. Dee's got a tub around here some place."

"A tub," Michael said a shade wistfully. "I'd love a bath."

"I was thinking of me," he said. "But you can use the water after I'm done."

Michael stared blankly at the door long after Ethan had vacated the room. It seemed prudent to remember that her protector was no white knight. She touched her lips with the tip of her finger, tracing the line that Ethan had provoked to swollen, sensitive tenderness. Her mouth still tingled. She could still feel the pressure of his lips on hers.

No, she thought, Ethan Stone was neither gallant nor chivalrous. He was a predator, possessed of a predator's keen hunting senses and motivated by self-interest. Michael wondered how long she could survive once she was targeted as prey.

Ethan was as good as his word, returning in a few minutes with large copper tub. He placed it near the stove on the part of the hardwood floor not covered by the carpet. Kitty fluttered in and out, talking all the while she helped him fill it with steaming water from the kitchen.

"Here," he said, starting to unbutton his shirt. "How about taking these clothes and getting Lottie to wash them? She knows I'll pay her."

Kitty winked at Michael. "Lottie thinks it's a prime pleasure to do his laundry."

"How nice for her," Michael said weakly. She was fighting the urge to dive under the covers as Ethan began to take off his clothes. With a naturalness that did not take her feelings into account, he stripped down to a gray flannel union suit, a one piece undergarment with woolen knitted cuffs. When he started to unbutton the upper shirt Michael pretended great interest in her tea. She was forced to maintain the pretense only a few moments. Whether by luck or design, Kitty, who was standing with her back to Ethan while he disrobed, saw something on the floor which captured her attention. She bent to investigate, saw it was merely a water stain, and when she rose again her body provided an effective shield for Ethan's activities.

Ethan didn't miss the look of relief in Michael's eyes. Over Kitty's head he grinned wickedly as he stepped out of his flannels and tossed them. He was under the water by the time Kitty made a grab for them and stepped away from the tub.

"You're lookin' more the thing," she said to Michael. "No sense lockin' this door, is there?"

"I'll take care of it," Ethan said. "Thanks, Kitty."

"Anytime." On her way out the door she caught Michael's attention and smiled, gesturing quickly to Ethan. "He's beautiful," she mouthed.

Michael smiled wanly.

"You don't think I'm beautiful?" Ethan asked when they were alone.

"You saw her."

"Kitty's sweet," he said. "She's also rather obvious.

Look, I've got to lock the door. Why don't you dive under those covers now while I do it?"

Both of Michael's feathered brows rose in question. "Not so eager to show yourself without Kitty here, are you?"

He shrugged. "Suit yourself. I was thinking of you."

Michael squeezed her eyes shut as he braced his arms on either side of the tub and began to rise. "No, wait! The key was in the pocket of your trousers and your pockets left with Kitty!" Her rapid fire speech was met with silence. A few seconds passed then there was the sound of water lapping against the sides of the tub as Ethan lowered himself again. Michael opened her eyes cautiously. She was struck by the fact that his face had taken on the ruddy hue of embarrassment. "I'm sorry," she said, raising her cup to her mouth to hide her unrepentant smile. "I thought I should save you the trouble of interrupting your bath. You would have realized it after a moment but by then you would have dripped water everywhere."

He gave her a sour look. "You could have said something about the key before Kitty left."

"I could have," she said. "The truth is, I have no intention of running from here wearing your nightshirt. If I wasn't eager to walk across the room in it, you can be certain I'm not stepping foot in the hallway."

Ethan wasn't entirely sure he believed her but it appeared that for the time being she was staying put. He searched the water for the soap and upon finding it, lathered up. "You need to know that only a few people think we're married. Houston, Jake, Obie, Ben, and Happy all believe our story. Your safety depends on them continuing to believe it. Dee

101

knows as well. She's been Houston's mistress going on three years now and she's part of everything that happens. Keep that in mind."

"What about Kitty?"

"I don't know what Obie tells her. I know what we told her. She, like every other person who works for Dee and every other person you'll come in contact with, thinks Dee hired you for entertaining in her saloon. You play the piano, don't you?"

"My father insisted."

"You sing?"

"My mother insisted."

There was something she wasn't telling him. "But . . ."

"All the lessons were wasted. I'm tone deaf."

"Wonderful. Don't you do any normal female things?"

"You can't possibly know how offensive your question is. I take it to mean that you think only men can or should be reporters."

Ethan wanted to avoid an argument. "Forget I said anything. It doesn't really matter if you can't play, sing, or dance—"

"I didn't say I couldn't dance," she said quietly.

Ethan shot her a quelling glance. "Can you?"

"You said it doesn't really matter."

"Can you dance?" he asked again, grinding out the question between clenched teeth.

"Yes. Very well in fact."

"All right then. That's why Dee hired you. I hope to God you're good."

"You'll never know. I'm not dancing in this saloon."

Ethan ignored her objection. He wasn't all that sure he wanted her dancing for the others, but she would if she had to. It was as simple as that. "You

102

were hired by Kitty to entertain her patrons. You answered an advertisement in the *Chronicle*."

"The *Chronicle*. How clever you must think you are. The irony's not lost on me."

He cut her off with an impatient slash of his hand. The soap slipped out of his palm and he had to search under water for it again. "Dee paid your fare from New York. The snow storm stranded you at the depot in Stillwater. We came across you during our search for Happy."

"If I'm the entertainment, then what am I doing with you?"

He was tempted to say, "because you're the entertainment," but good sense prevailed. "Do I need to kiss you again?"

"Oh," she said, the memory making her flush. "That reason."

"As long as everyone believes you're well and truly mine, you won't be bothered much."

"Much."

"This isn't New York," he reminded her. "First and foremost it's a mining camp. There are only about seventy women in Madison and the unmarried ones are younger than sixteen or work in one of the saloons. The men will respect that you're my mistress but that won't stop them from hoping they can change it. You'll have to put up with a little teasing and pinching. An occasional pat on the bottom."

Michael grimaced. "I'd be safer married to you."

Ethan had thought of it. He would have never asked her if she hadn't broached the subject. "Is that what you want?"

"No!" She set down her mug and hugged her knees close to her chest. "Absolutely not. As long as Houston and the others think I'm married to you they'll leave me alone. I know they're the ones I have

103

to fear. I'll try to tolerate the pinching."

"You'll have to tolerate it. I'm not going to draw my gun on someone for nuzzlin' you." Before she could reply to that, he held up the soap. "Do my back, will you?"

"Go to hell."

He shrugged and turned his head away so she couldn't see his smile. Whistling tunelessly under his breath, Ethan finished his bath. He grabbed the towel Kitty had left for him and wrapped it around his waist as he rose from the water. Michael turned her head away. "You can look now. I'm decent."

They had different definitions of that word, she thought, facing him again. He had used the towel to cover, not to dry. As a result, fat droplets of water fell from the curling ends of his dark hair to his shoulders. Water glistened on his arms and chest and the towel clung wetly to his narrow hips. He turned, going toward the bureau and Michael traced the length of his spine with her eyes. The towel contoured the shape of his buttocks and the hardness of his upper thighs. She thought of Kitty's parting words. Ethan Stone *was* a beautiful man.

In the mirror above the bureau Ethan watched Michael watching him. Seeing the brilliance of her dark green eyes, fascination warring with a reluctance to look, Ethan had difficulty bringing to mind the woman in the *Chronicle* newsroom, the woman who looked as starched as the blouse she wore, as severe as the lines of her skirt, and as forbidding as the set of her mouth. In fact, watching Michael now brought a response to Ethan's flesh that the towel couldn't hide.

He opened the top drawer of the bureau roughly, intent on taking his mind from a condition he could not relieve with Mary Michael Dennehy. "You can take your bath now. I'm getting dressed and going downstairs for a drink." Several of them, he thought. He found a pair of cotton drawers and stepped into them, pulling them up hastily under the towel. He tossed the towel at Michael on the bed. "If you lay it by the stove while you're in the tub it should be dry enough to use." Still keeping his back to Michael he rifled the rest of the bureau and came up with a clean pair of jeans, a navy blue flannel shirt, and some thick woolen socks. He didn't sit down until he needed to pull on his boots and even then it was quickly accomplished. He ran a comb through his hair twice, did the rest with his fingers, and left the room as if the entire Sioux nation were on his tail.

Michael wasted little time taking advantage of his absence. Locking the door with the flimsy hook and latch, she eagerly shed Ethan's nightshirt and sank into the water. It was merely lukewarm but Michael had no complaint. It felt entirely refreshing.

She washed her hair, using the half-filled bucket that Kitty left behind to rinse. When the water became too cold to soak she stepped out and wrapped herself in the warm towel. The comb Ethan had used was lying on top of his bureau. She sat on the edge of the bed, her heels hooked on the frame, and worked out the tangles in her hair an inch at a time. When she was satisfied with the result she knelt on the carpet near the stove and began drying her hair as best she could. She was still kneeling, wrapped in the towel and running the comb through her hair in an absent motion as she thought of other things, when the door to her room flew open, smashed by Ethan's booted foot.

"Don't you ever lock me out again!"

Chapter Four

Michael almost burned herself on the hot door of the stove as she moved back and out of the way of Ethan's fury. "You could have knocked. I would have opened it." Ethan spared a glance at the window. His cold eyes wandered so briefly that Michael could have believed it was imagined on her part. She understood the nature of the glance, the thought that guided it toward the window. "I didn't lock the door to mislead you and escape by the window," she told him. She tightened her clasp on the knot in the towel above her breast. "I told you I wouldn't leave in your nightshirt. I surely wouldn't leave dressed like this."

She was immediately sorry for drawing attention to her covering, or lack of it. Ethan's coldly furious eyes grazed over her. She felt them on her wildly curling damp hair, her naked shoulders, the curve of her hip that was turned toward him. His glance did not rest on any particular feature longer than any other; equal attention was given to the length of her legs, the water droplet in the hollow of her throat, the outline of her breasts.

"Don't lock me out." His voice was sharp and cold and clear.

Michael felt gooseflesh rise on her arms and legs. He commanded her complete attention. In spite of her wish to do otherwise, she couldn't look away.

"Ever," he said lowly. He waited for some reply and when he saw her brief, reluctant nod, he freed her from the force of his gaze. "You may want to get dressed. We have company."

Houston chose that moment to step into the room from the hallway. "From where I was looking," he said, "Michael seems most suitably clothed." His black eyes traced the curve of her body from head to toe and he was more than a little intrigued by the soft flush that followed in the wake of his gaze. His small polite smile did not quite match the interest in his eyes.

"Give her a minute," Ethan said, stepping to one side to block Houston's view.

From the hallway a feminine voice drawled sweetly. "Oh, Ethan, you act as if she's modest beyond words." Detra Kelly took one look at Michael huddled near the stove, protectively guarding herself with arms folded across her chest, and revised her opinion. "Well, perhaps she is."

Michael wondered if she looked even a tenth as mortified as she felt. Gathering the shreds of her composure, she said quietly, "I have all my teeth."

Ethan and Houston grinned simultaneously. Detra was unamused. "You're going to have to get used to men looking at you a lot more closely than these two."

Michael thought it best to remain silent. She merely stared at Detra, knowing now there would never be any help from that quarter.

Dee Kelly was a bit more than two inches shorter than Michael, coming just below Ethan's shoulder. Both her slenderness and her bearing gave the impression of height. She carried herself with confidence, her small chin raised just the slightest degree necessary to keep others at a comfortable distance. Her hair, smoothly knotted in a chignon, seemed darker and more lustrous than ebony in comparison to the pale alabaster quality of her skin. Her eyes were deep blue, remarkable in their ability to rivet attention to her features. The mouth was generous, pouting in a sly way even when she was smiling. Her jaw gently rounded out the classic oval of her face. Gold and ebony earrings dangled from her lobes and brushed the slender line of her neck.

Houston put one arm around Dee's shoulders. His hand curved around her upper arm and gave her a gentle squeeze. "I don't think it's possible for any men to look more closely then we are, Dee."

Dee's smile did not reach her eyes; she was plainly unamused. She felt Houston's squeeze become a warning. Reining in temper and jealousy she said, "Perhaps you're right. But it's still no reason for her to act the simpering virgin. She's Ethan's wife, for God's sake." *There,* she thought, that's *my* warning. "You did tell me she's supposed to work for me, didn't you? Ethan says she can dance."

"I haven't decided if I'm going to allow her," Ethan said. He remembered Michael's earlier refusal to dance in the saloon, but he insisted on her realizing it was his decision.

For once Michael didn't mind people talking about her as if she weren't in the same room. As Ethan, Houston, and Dee engaged in conversation their attention wandered away. Michael reached for the nightshirt she had placed over the back of a ladder-back chair, pulled it down, and slipped it on over her head and over the towel. When she poked her head through the open collar she was unhappily aware of recapturing their notice. "Please, don't stop on my account," she said briskly, holding up her hands innocently. "You just go on deciding my fate. Since I met Ethan on the train I haven't had a say in—"

"You say too damn much," Ethan said.

"You haven't changed in four years," she said sweetly, offering him a quick, insincere smile. "I could have managed the rest of my life quite nicely believing you were dead." Michael got to her feet and padded softly over to the bed. She sat on the edge, pulling the comforter over her lap to hide her bare ankles and feet. With a little maneuvering she was able to rid herself of the damp towel. "In fact, I'd rather come to enjoy the thought of you being dead."

Dee's soft drawl filled the room after the long tense silence. "My God," she said. "What were you thinking of when you married her, Ethan?"

It was Houston who replied. "I should have thought that'd be obvious to even you, Dee."

Ethan grinned. His mouth curved in a intimate insult guaranteed to set Michael on edge with the memory of his earlier kiss. "Exactly."

Michael's chin came up, and her eyes narrowed briefly with the depth of her hatred. With effort, she bit back her anger.

Detra slipped out from under Houston's arm. "I don't know if I have anything in my wardrobe that will fit her," she said slyly. "Kitty might have a few things we can alter."

"She's more your size, than Kitty's," Houston said. "You might have to let out a hem."

"*I* won't have to let out anything," Dee said, barely holding onto her temper. "If *she* wants something more to wear, then *she* can alter it."

"Sheath those claws, Dee," Houston ordered. "I don't know exactly what's got your back up, but you'll just have to work it out. Ethan didn't want his wife here. His wife doesn't want to be here. No one's happy about it, but it's the way things are."

Dee's sharp murmur protested the way she was being talked to in front of others. With a last icy glance at Michael, she turned on her heel and left the room. Her skirts swayed, taffeta and silk rustled, and then, except for the faint pinging of the piano below stairs, everything was quiet.

Houston shook his head, considering Dee's behavior. "I guess I've been away too long," he said finally. "She needs a little attention. So does your woman."

Michael bristled. Her head snapped up. "I am not his woman any more."

Ethan smiled grimly. "Looks like I've been away too long, too," he said.

"Appears so." Houston gave Michael a jaunty two fingered salute as if he was tipping his hat to her and tapped Ethan lightly on the back. On his way out the door he examined the lock. "I'll see about getting this fixed tomorrow. Don't worry about interruptions tonight. Even Happy's found himself a woman till morning." He closed the door softly behind him.

Michael waited until the sound of Houston's footfalls faded. "I don't know which I despise more," she said. "You or that smug smile of yours." She mimicked Houston's tone. " 'Your woman could use some attention.' " She shot Ethan a disgusted glance. "And you reply in the same patronizing vein. Do all men think the way you do or is it only my bad luck to keep meeting them? Honestly, for a moment there you both sounded like my—" She stopped abruptly, the drift of her thoughts pulling her up short.

"Like your . . ." Ethan prompted.

"Never mind." Michael scooted back on the bed to

110

get away from Ethan's towering presence. "It's enough you know that I don't appreciate comments like that."

Ethan unhooked his gunbelt and hung it up on a nail just inside the door. He fiddled with the latch just to see if he could secure it again and gave up when he saw the cause as hopeless. He sat down in the maroon and gold wing chair and stretched out his long legs, hooking his feet at the ankles. "Since we're speaking of appreciation," he said with credible calm, "I'm going to tell you what I not only don't appreciate, but won't put up with. I think we've already established that you're not to lock me out of this or any other room again. If the room's secured, it's because I've decided I wanted it that way. I don't want to hear your sass in front of other people. It looks like I can't control you, and if the others think I can't, you're as good as dead. You're alive because I've managed to convince them I can hold onto you.

"As far as Houston goes, stop trying to throw yourself at him. Dee will scratch out your eyes. She may do it anyway, so watch yourself around her."

"I don't know what you're talking about."

Ethan's expression was skeptical. His dark lashes lowered a fraction as he studied Michael to gauge her sincerity. "Didn't you hear the things Dee was saying to you?"

"I heard her. Of course I heard her. I also felt her animosity the moment she came in here. What I don't understand is why."

His voice was harsh, impatient whisper. "How can you be a reporter and be so naive? I thought that was beat out of you right away."

"I'm not naive."

"I see it a little differently. Dee was angry because she recognized your interest in Houston."

111

"There," she said rather triumphantly. *"That's* what I don't understand. What do you mean I was throwing myself at him? I find him as repulsive as I do you."

Ethan's eyes dropped to her mouth, stayed there long enough to remind her of the kiss they shared, then rose to meet her guilty gaze. "I assume I've made my point. Stay away from him."

It was more than a warning. It was a command. Michael gave no indication one way or the other if she intended to follow it. "I was the one at a disadvantage," she reminded him. "If you had knocked I would have had time to dress."

"I did knock. Several times."

Michael frowned, trying to remember back to what she had been doing just before the door was kicked open. She had been brushing her hair, deep in thought. "I didn't hear you." She bit her lower lip. "And I wasn't throwing myself at Houston."

Ethan knew Michael was telling the truth. He had seen as clearly as Detra that the interest was primarily, perhaps completely, on Houston's side. There was likely to be trouble. If Michael encouraged him, there was *sure* to be trouble.

"May I have that comb, please?" Michael asked, pointing to the floor near Ethan's feet. He scooped it up and tossed it across the room. Michael caught it deftly and began running it through her hair. "How long are you going to keep me with you?"

"As long as I have to," he said. Watching her fingers sift through the damp strands of her hair, Ethan was tempted to reply with the truth: "As long as I want to."

"How long is that?"

"I don't know."

"Days? Weeks?"

He shook his head and said carelessly, "Months . . . years . . . forever. It depends."

"Depends? On what?"

"On whether you live that long." He leaned forward in his chair and rested his forearms on knees. "On whether you convince us that you don't mean to turn us in."

There was a pause in the steady motion of Michael's hand through her dark chestnut hair. How would she ever convince any of them of that, she wondered. No one was that good an actress. Her thoughts took a tangential leap suddenly. The only actress she knew was Katy Dakota, Logan Marshall's wife. That in turn reminded Michael of the publisher himself and then of the *Chronicle*. For a reason she could not immediately fathom she found herself staring hard at Ethan Stone again, trying to place his face.

Although Ethan was unaware of the route her thoughts had taken to lead to this direct and steady stare, he knew what she was trying to do. He found himself absently rubbing his upper lip with his forefinger in a way he had done when he had a mustache. As soon as he was aware of the gesture he stopped, afraid it would give her a clue.

He shifted in the chair, throwing one leg over the arm.

"I suppose Detra will have some clothes for you in the morning," he said. "You'll have to alter them. You heard her. She won't do it."

"Then I'll have to wear them as they are. I don't sew."

"Now there's a surprise," Ethan said sarcastically. "Didn't your mother teach you anything?"

"Lots of things. I chose not to learn needlework."

"Were you born ornery?"

113

The realization that she was biting back a smile distressed her. She did not want him to make her laugh. "It's a family characteristic," she said coolly.

"Along with sass and brass."

She avoided his eyes, turned away from the frank assessment that seemed to know what she was thinking and was gently mocking her for it. "The sass and brass may be my own." She caught the glimmer of a smile on his face, a smile that was as a lazy as his walk, as faint as his drawl. Careful to keep her attention elsewhere, Michael pretended great interest in her surroundings.

She had not appreciated earlier what a comfortable room it was. The furnishings were all dark wood, walnut or cherry, rather plain and solid, lacking the intricate finishing detail of a master carpenter, but warm and serviceable just the same. Besides the bed, bureau, and side table, there was the wide-armed wing chair in which Ethan was sitting, the table beside him, an upholstered footstool, two straw seat ladderback chairs near the stove, a wardrobe, and washstand. A large spongeware basin and pitcher sat on the stand's marble top. The room's single window was framed with blue and white checked curtains. The walls were papered: deep violet flowers curving gracefully on a cream background. Except for the mirror above the bureau and Ethan's gunbelt near the door, nothing hung on them. The parts of the floor that weren't covered by the carpet had been swept clean and mopped recently. The entire room, in fact, was neatly kept. Recalling that someone did laundry for him, she wondered if Ethan was responsible for the room or paid one of Dee's girls to provide the service.

Ethan watched Michael's eyes wander about the room and tried to fathom the nature of her

114

thoughts. "Not quite what you're used to, I expect."

Michael didn't answer immediately. "Not what I grew up with," she said softly. "But what I'm used to." She turned to him again, waiting to see if he would pry. He didn't. Perhaps he didn't want to know what she meant. Certainly he had no reason to care. "There's bound to be a search for me," she told him. "The paper. My family. Have you thought of that?"

"I've thought of it. I thought of it when I realized I was going to have to bring you with me."

"What do you mean? What have you done?"

"I made sure the people who saw you run out of the train think I killed you. I don't know what they could see from that distance but they heard the extra shots."

"But they'll never find a body . . . they'll know—"

"They'll know I dropped it over the cliff along with your friend's. They're only going to think they can't find it. After what Happy and Obie did to the *Chronicle*'s cars and the caboose, do you really believe anyone will think I was capable of showing mercy?"

"No."

Ethan hardly knew whether to be relieved or insulted by the quickness of her response. "Exactly." As far as he was concerned the subject was closed.

"I wonder if Hannah's family witnessed it," she said, more to herself than to Ethan. "I wouldn't like to think they had." She thought about the family's journey of hope, about the story she might never write. She didn't need to think about it any longer. She needed to act. "Where's my coat? I had pencils in there and a notepad with the beginnings of a story. And where are my glasses? I can't write without my glasses."

"You're not doing any writing tonight." Ethan

reached in his pocket and pulled out a gold watch. He flipped open the cover, glanced at the time, and closed it again. "It's after eight."

"That's early."

"On some other night it might be, but not to-night. You slept a lot more in the saddle than I did. I plan to pack it in soon."

"I still want my pencils and notepad." Without conscious thought her hands strayed to her hair.

"No pencils there," Ethan said. Thank God, he thought.

She realized what she had been doing. Her expression was sheepish. "Oh. Sometimes I put them there so I can find them later."

Ethan remembered the first time he had seen her. She had searched all over her desk before she chanced upon one of them in her hair. "Well, they're not there now. Your things are safe, I'm sure."

"My glasses?"

"They were in the pocket of the shirt I gave Kitty. They were already a little bent."

"Bent! But—"

"When I knocked you out," he said shortly. "It's a small price to pay in exchange for your life."

It *was* a petty concern, she thought. It *was* the least of her problems. Bent spectacles were merely an inconvenience. Yet somehow the loss of her glasses crystallized the loss of everything and everyone else. Tears welled in her eyes and her chin quivered.

"You're crying about your glasses?" Ethan demanded, disbelief and scorn rife in his tone. "Lady, I don't pretend to understand what goes on in that mind of yours. Your friends have been killed, you've been . . . oh, hell, I don't need to recite the litany of crimes against you . . . and you're crying now be-

116

cause of your spectacles."

She swiped at her eyes and sucked in her breath to steady her nerves and her chin. "It's not the glasses," she said in a small voice. Michael turned on her side away from him so he couldn't see the steadily dripping tears.

Ethan made no reply. He sat very still in his corner of the room, waiting for the soft even cadence of her breathing that would signal sleep. It was more than twenty minutes in coming, but eventually she gave in to the weariness that had made her as fragile as crystal.

Taking his time, Ethan tended to the fire in the stove, adding coals so it would burn reasonably well into the night. He checked his gunbelt, removing the extra ammunition and the bullets from his Colt. Opening the third drawer of his bureau, he dropped the bullets in and hid them under a few shirts. The bottom of the wardrobe had several blankets stored away. Ethan took them out and laid them on the floor beside the bed. After nearly a week of sleeping on the ground he had been looking forward to his bed. He had thought about sharing it with Kitty or Josie or Carmen, but not with Mary Michael Dennehy. Certainly not Michael.

She had both pillows. One she was hugging to her breast, the other was under her head. Ethan gently lifted her hair and her head and pulled. Michael didn't stir. His hand was slow to release her hair. The ball of his thumb passed back and forth across the silky texture. In his mind's eye he saw her sitting at the head of the bed, running the comb through her hair, pulling it straight, only to have it spring into curls the moment she released it. He gave up his hold on her hair reluctantly and only when he realized how she would react if she woke and saw what he was doing.

There was no sense in frightening her anymore than she'd already been frightened.

Stripping down to his drawers, Ethan blew out the lamps and got into his makeshift bed. It was warmer than the ground he had slept on the night before but not any softer. Turning onto his back, his head cradled in the palm of his hands, Ethan stared at the ceiling and considered what he was going to do about Michael Dennehy.

Ethan thought back to the afternoon five months earlier in the *Chronicle's* offices. He was not nearly done with the work he had set out to do for Carl Franklin, John Rivington, and Logan Marshall. The things they had discussed that day, even the things they had suspected, had not prepared Ethan for the depth of the problem he was facing. He owed none of the men anything, not the railroad man, not the government man, and certainly not the *Chronicle's* publisher. Yet it didn't seem that he could quit at this juncture. In light of everything that had gone wrong during the robbery he owed something to the brakemen, conductors, and reporters who had occupied the last five cars of No. 349.

He finally fell asleep thinking about Drew Beaumont and the kick that had sent the reporter over the side of the mountain. Had he survived? And if he did, did he have enough sense to take Ethan's warnings seriously? A story about Michael Dennehy and her real connection to Drew and the *Chronicle* would surely be a death sentence. This time for him as well as her.

It was the weight on her chest that woke her, the suffocating weight that seemed to compress her lungs and wouldn't let her draw a breath. Michael clawed at the weight. She twisted and struggled, pushing upward with her arms and outward with her legs.

"Stop it, Michael!" The husky whisper was also urgent. "Damn you, woman, stop struggling and I'll let you up! I'm not going to hurt you." Ethan was sitting on the edge of the bed, half turned toward Michael but leaning over her. One forearm rested heavily on her breastbone while his hand clamped her mouth closed. The other arm batted her flailing hands away, protecting himself. "Would you please wake up?" he demanded impatiently.

She *was* awake. Not that she could tell him. She was desperate to suck in air, faint with the lack of it now that he had pinched off her nose. Her teeth managed to grasp the fleshy part of his palm. She bit down hard.

Ethan swore. He stopped pinching her nose, jammed the side of his forefinger under the soft part of it and pushed. Michael's mouth opened almost instantly and Ethan freed his hand. He raised his hand to his mouth, sucking on the wound, tasting to see if she had drawn blood, while Michael gulped for air.

"I said I wasn't going to hurt you!" he told her.

"You were doing a credible job of it."

His voice lowered and became even more severe as he explained. "You were screaming at the top of your lungs! Another few seconds and you would have had every boarder in here."

He had barely completed his sentence when there was a knock at the door. Ethan was without patience. "What the hell is it?"

Happy pushed open the door far enough to stick in his head. The meager light from the stove gave an orange cast to his scruffy features. He grinned

119

widely. "You mind pleasurin' your woman a little less loudly, Ethan? Some of us folks done already called it a night."

Michael pushed herself away from Ethan and sat up. "He was *not* pleasuring me," she said between clenched teeth.

Happy's eyes wandered from Ethan to Michael and back to Ethan again. "Well, then, if'n you're gonna beat her, gag her first. No sense keepin' the rest of us up." He nodded once as if to emphasize the point and ducked back into the hallway.

Working herself up to a scream that would shatter Happy's eardrums, Michael threw her pillow at the door. "Why that son of a—"

Ethan's hand found its mark. "You cuss like a man, too. Now, shut up." He waited. "Done?"

She nodded, staring at him wide-eyed above the hand that covered her mouth.

"Good, 'cause I've had about as much as I'm taking from you tonight. There's a few hours left till morning." He lifted his hand cautiously. "Go back to sleep now." Yawning, Ethan slid off the bed and onto the floor. His brief taste of the bed made the floor seem harder than before. He punched his pillow and gave it a sour look when it didn't conform to the shape he wanted. He turned from side to side several times before he found a position that was vaguely comfortable. His satisfaction was punctuated with a sound that was somewhere between a groan and a sigh.

The silence was blessed . . . for as long as it lasted.

Michael scooted to the edge of the bed and looked over. She could make out Ethan's lumpy form beneath his blankets. It was more difficult to tell whether she was talking to his face or his feet. "Was

120

I really screaming?" she asked.

Every part of the sound he made now was a groan. "Ever heard a rebel yell?"

She hadn't, but she got the point. She was relieved to find out she was speaking to the talking end of him. "I'm sorry about waking you. I must have been dreaming."

"Hell of a dream."

She nodded. "It was hell. I mean, that was the dream. At least I think it was. It's difficult to remember now." Shutting her eyes, she could recall a black slippery void that surrounded her, pulsing as if it were a living thing. At times it was as insubstantial as midnight, as smooth as polished onyx, as cold as well water. Then it would become oppressive, thick and heavy, bearing down on her and squeezing her from all sides. There was no escape and the only direction she felt herself go was not up or down, but deeper. Remembering forced a shiver to the surface of her skin. She burrowed under the covers. "It was emptiness," she told him. "I think that's what I was dreaming about."

Maybe, he thought, if he didn't say anything she might go back to sleep now.

"And I couldn't get away from it."

Ethan turned away from her.

"I wonder what it—"

He sat up abruptly. Now his head was almost level with her face. "Lady, listen to me. I don't know about your dream. I don't *want* to know about your dream. Find a fortune teller if you have to know what it means. All I know is you were screaming like it was the end of the world. Now, go back to sleep or, so help me God, you'll wish it *were* the apocalypse." He lay down again, this time on his stomach with one arm propped under the pillow and his head.

Michael bit her lower lip to squelch her giddy laughter.

She would have liked to have fallen back to sleep but the room was cold. Lying there, she could hear the bitterly icy wind whistling past the window. She glanced at the stove and saw by the dying glow of coals that there was little warmth coming from that quarter.

Waiting until she thought Ethan's steady breathing indicated sleep, Michael pushed back the covers and slipped quietly out of bed. She stepped over Ethan, careful not to touch him. The towel that had been lying at the base of her bed was still damp. She draped it over the back of a ladderback chair then knelt in front of the stove to lay a new fire.

She was shivering rather violently when she felt the press of hands on her shoulder.

"Go back to bed," Ethan said. His voice was husky with weariness. "I'll do that."

"Are you sure? I didn't mean—"

"To wake me," he said, finishing her sentence. "I know. Go on."

Michael came to her feet slowly, aware of Ethan's hands still on her shoulders. When she turned toward him he lifted them only fractionally, then rested them again, this time so that his thumbs lay along the line of her collarbone. A different kind of shiver caused her body to tremble. She looked up at him and felt the hot impact of his eyes on her mouth.

He raised his hand. She thought he was going to touch her mouth with the pad of his thumb. She almost closed her eyes in anticipation of the contact. Instead of tracing the line of her lips, Ethan turned her and gave her a gentle push toward the bed.

"Go," he said. "While you still can."

Ethan took care of the stove quickly and returned to his place on the floor. The ache in his groin was a poor sleeping companion. It was small comfort to listen to Michael toss and turn and know she was wrestling with the same demons.

Kitty was a dervish of activity as she entered the room. "Time to rise, Michael. Ethan said I was not to let you sleep past nine. And Dee, well, I can tell you Dee thought you should have been up long before that." Kitty laid a plain hunter green gown, similar in cut and style to the sky blue one she was wearing, over the back of the armchair. "That's for day wear. Dee found it at the back of her wardrobe and I let out the hem. It should be a fine fit." She held up another gown in front of her, sashaying around the room to show it off, clearly oblivious to Michael's sleepy inattention. The gown was pink taffeta, trimmed in white at the bodice and along the hem. It was inches shorter than any decent street dress, coming to the middle of Kitty's calves as she pretended to model it. The bodice was low, off the shoulder, and the short sleeves were rather dramatically puffed. The waist was so tiny the wearer would have no choice but to be tightly cinched in a stiff corset.

"This was Dee's too," she said, putting it with the other one. "A little too small for her now, which is why I think she's letting you have it. You'll have to try it on so I can fit it proper. Ethan says you don't sew. I don't mind helpin' out until you learn. It's a shame about your trunks and such. They're probably on their way to San Francisco by now. I bet you had some pretty things. It always seems to me that

123

Eastern ladies have the prettiest things." Her voice was a shade wistful, her light blue eyes dreamy. The far away look only lasted seconds then she was all brisk business again, clapping her hands once to slough off the fantasy.

Rooting through the pile of clothing items she had placed on the table, she held up a pair of white tights and white kid boots. "These go with the pink gown. We do a very nice number with parasols that I'll teach you after breakfast. I'll have to find you a parasol, to be sure. I think Carmen might have one you can use. Ethan says he intends to get you to the dressmaker some time today. You'll need day dresses and gowns for evening work." She sighed. "You were lucky to find Ethan. He sure seems to have taken a shine to you. I can't recollect him ever takin' so much interest in a single woman before. He put me in mind of a hummin'bird, goin' from flower to flower."

A hummingbird was the last thing that came to Michael's mind when she thought of Ethan Stone. Yawning and stretching and keeping her thoughts to herself, Michael sat up. Kitty was still sifting through the pile of clothing she brought in, holding things up for Michael's inspection. There were more stockings and tights, two pairs of serviceable shoes, cotton and silk drawers, lacy petticoats, corsets, hair ribbons, hair pins, and hair feathers. It was an impressive array of items that Detra had donated. Michael imagined that Houston had had to use some persuasion. She preferred not to dwell on the form that persuasion may have taken.

The bilious and bawdy pink gown had been Detra's way of exacting revenge. Michael was fairly sure of that. If the dress didn't fit Dee any longer, Michael had little hope it would fit her. Detra had offered it as nothing less than an insult.

"Ethan said he wasn't sure he was going to let me dance," she told Kitty. "You may not need to find that parasol at all."

"Oh, pish," Kitty said, waving her hand dismissingly. "Dee hired you, didn't she?"

"Yes." She offered the answer reluctantly, wondering if Kitty were laying a trap. Had Obie told her the truth as he knew it, or did she still believe the story that Ethan wanted almost everyone to believe? Michael saw the ease with which she could be caught in a lie. "Yes," she repeated. "Dee hired me."

"Well, then. There's nothing more to be said. Ethan might keep you here all night but before then you're one of Detra's girls. That's what she told me to tell you. She says she hired you to work and you'd better do it." One pale eyebrow was raised consideringly. "Unless you decide to quit, that is. Can't think it's a good idea though. Ethan may lose interest in you and then where will you be? Sure, you may be able to save a little money after giving Dee her forty percent, but it will be a while before you can get train fare out of these parts again, and you might as well know that if you quit now Dee would as soon see you in the streets as hire you back."

Only one thing made an impact on Michael. "What forty percent?"

Kitty tossed a blood red robe at the bed. "Dee's cut," she said with untroubled frankness.

"I'm not sure I understand," Michael said. "You mean she pays me a wage for dancing and I give her back forty percent?"

That interpretation brought a frown to Kitty's full mouth. Her rounded features screwed up comically as she looked at Michael as though she suddenly saw a third eye. "Now that would serve no

125

purpose," she said. "The forty percent is what you owe her for sleepin' with Ethan."

"But—"

"You aren't just givin' it to that man, are you? You can't be that love struck." Her eyes narrowed as she studied Michael more closely. "Where'd you work before you answered Dee's advertisement?"

Michael's mind went blank. There were probably a thousand dancehalls, brothels, and bars in New York City and she couldn't think of the name of one. She thought her hesitation would be her undoing, instead Kitty put another explanation to it.

"My God, you're new to this, aren't you? You just answered that ad to get out here. I'll wager you don't have no more sense than a gaggle of geese headin' for the choppin' block about what's in store for you."

"That's a good assessment of the situation."

"Hell, you don't even talk normal." Kitty shook her head as if she could barely take in this turn of events. "You better stay close to me else you're in for a passel of trouble. What Dee didn't know won't hurt her much. You *can* dance, can't you? You weren't so foolish to answer her ad without at least knowin' that."

"I can dance."

"Kick?"

How hard could kicking be? "I can kick."

"Line dancing?"

"I know the Virginia Reel," she said, thinking of the two lines that were formed for that dance.

Kitty rolled her eyes, threw up her hands, and sank into the wing chair. Her curly flaxen hair bobbed with the force of her drop. "Lord, this is going to be harder than I thought. I wish I hadn't taken a likin' to you. Don't even know why I should when you lassoed the man I've had my eye on for five months now."

"You and Ethan . . . you never . . . that is, you haven't . . ."

"Never. I think he feels a little funny about it since I'm Obie's kid sister. Doesn't seem to bother anyone else around here. Thought I might have a chance with him when he got back from huntin' down Happy, but no, I just ended up with Happy."

Michael tried to imagine Kitty, fresh of face, full of hope and spunk, agreeing to lie with cynical, mean-spirited Happy McAllister. It was a troubling vision. Kitty seemed to read her mind.

"Happy's not so bad. There's three or four others I could name that treat me worse. Not that I've ever complained to Obie. He'd call them out in the street and then where would I be? He'd get himself killed or Houston would have to put him in jail for a few weeks." She shrugged. "Enough about me. When you've been here a while you'll get used to the way things are. And one of the things you'll have to get used to asking Ethan for money. It's all fine of him to pay for your clothes and the like, but you can't give forty percent of a hat to Detra. She'll want cash. Have you thought about what you want to charge?"

Michael blanched. Before her life had been turned upside down she had been a respected reporter for a reputable paper. Now Kitty was telling her that in Kelly's Saloon she was no more than a prostitute who could serve drinks and dance. And she had yet to prove she could do any of those things.

"No, I can see that you haven't," Kitty said, watching Michael's face closely. "Most of the girls ask for five or ten dollars a poke. I like to get at least twelve—this is a mining town, after all—but I'll settle for eight if they're down on their luck. Eight's my final offer. I take a man to my room if I want to, not because I'm forced. This is a saloon, not a bordello. Dee wants her share if she knows her girls are making money on the side, but she doesn't push the trade. Seein' that Ethan's already got an arrangement with you, she'll want her cut. You can't get by just dancin' and peddlin' drinks to the customers, 'specially when they're goin' to be all over you like bees on honey."

Michael determined she was going to have a very frank discussion with Ethan Stone. "I'll speak to Ethan," she said.

"Don't look so worried, honey," Kitty said consolingly. "He'll pay. At least until he tires of you. And the way he had you screamin' last night, it don't seem like an arrangement either one of you is goin' to quit soon."

Michael was beginning to believe her scream the night before wasn't quite the rebel yell that Ethan had described it.

"Just listenin' to you got Happy all hot again. I made a tidy fortune last night." She giggled. "He couldn't get enough of me."

Michael was also revising her opinion about Kitty Long being only a slightly soiled dove. "Perhaps I should ask Ethan for ten," she said.

Kitty shook her head. "No. Ask for twelve, just like I do, but be prepared to take a little less. Say nine or ten. That way he'll feel he's won more than just you for the night. And don't give anything away free and don't run a tab like you was servin' drinks. If word got around that you were treatin' Ethan then others are like to expect the same. It wouldn't be good for you after Ethan's gone. You have to consider your future prospects. That's only good business sense."

It was an interesting slant, Michael thought. Kitty Long: the prostitute with the heart of a cash register. It made for better copy than those penny pulp stories where a dance hall demirep was likely to be confused with a long suffering charity worker. Fiction. Bah! Life was so much more interesting . . . and infinitely more strange. "I'll accept ten," she said.

"Good for you," Kitty said.

Michael got out of bed and slipped into the robe. The sleeves were too long and she had to roll up material at the waist and tie the belt tightly to keep from tripping over the hem. It wasn't Dee's robe. She didn't ask who donated it because she didn't want to know the answer. "Where did Ethan go?"

"He does some handy work for a widowed woman just outside of town in the mornin' and usually by the afternoon they've got some work for him at the mines, blastin' out a tunnel. That's what he is, a blaster. You probably knew that, though."

"I knew that," she lied. He probably blew up safes. That's what he did. Taking people's winnings, their wages, their pensions, and their rainy day money. Ethan Stone was a son of a bitch. "Breakfast?" she asked, putting her hand to her stomach as it growled loudly. She was ravenous.

"Downstairs in the back. There's a kitchen. You've got a few minutes yet."

Michael pointed to the tub. "What should I do with that?"

"Use the bucket to throw some of the water out the window. When the tub's light enough to move you can drag it down the hall to the storage closet so the next person who needs it can find it."

"I can't empty it here. Ethan told me the window's

129

stuck."

"Since when?"

Kitty walked over to the window, tapped it along the frame and pushed. It lifted easily. Cold air swept through the room and she slammed it shut quickly. "Just goes to prove how far you can trust *any* man." She went to the door and opened it. "I'll expect you in the kitchen in a few minutes and afterwards we've got a routine to learn. We do our show at eight and again at ten thirty. In between you'll have to mingle with the customers and push drinks. Don't worry. Pushin' drinks ain't hard and the minglin' comes easy after you've had a few yourself."

"I don't drink."

"You will," Kitty said. She wasn't smiling. "You may even learn to like it."

Michael stared at the door for a full minute after Kitty closed it. Ethan Stone blew open mine tunnels and train safes. Detra Kelly was a madam who preferred to be called a proprietress. Kitty Long was a shrewd young businesswoman whose stock had gone public. Nathaniel Houston led a gang of murderers and still found time to run for sheriff . . . and win.

What in God's name had she gotten herself into? How soon could she get herself out?

The kitchen was noisy and crowded. Only one woman beside Michael and Kitty was dressed in something other than a flimsy chemise, drawers, tights, and a corset. The robes they wore were tied loosely at the waist and sheer to the point of being inconsequential. They appeared to be eminently comfortable as they sat around the large knotty pine table trading casual remarks about the night that had passed and their plans for the day.

130

"This is Michael . . ." Kitty turned to Michael. "I'm sorry. I don't think I know your last name."

She couldn't say Dennehy. Houston may have been familiar with her byline on the *Chronicle*. She couldn't say Stone. Kitty and the others weren't supposed to believe she was married to Ethan. She said the first name that came to her mind. "Worth." Michael had never wanted to depend on her father for anything. It struck her as ironic that in a moment of great fear she had grasped for his name as she would a life line.

"Michael Worth," Kitty repeated. "You might have seen her last night. She's the one Ethan carried in here over his shoulder."

There were several nods, a few smiles, and general laughter.

Kitty grinned. "Don't mind them. They're jealous." She pointed to each of the women. "That's Carmen at the head of the table." Carmen raised her sloe eyes to Michael and gave Michael a sly whisper of a smile in greeting. Michael had no difficulty divining the look as a challenge. She had been intimate with Ethan and she wanted to be again. Looking on Carmen as a savior rather than a competitor, Michael smiled brilliantly and openly. "Josie's on her right," Kitty went on. Josie had a round, expressive face that telegraphed her thoughts before she opened her mouth. She was studying Michael as though she might a particularly vulgar looking insect. When she concluded there was nothing to be alarmed about she grinned and pushed a cup of hot chocolate in Michael's direction. "That's Lottie at the sink," Kitty said, pointing to the fair-skinned young woman up to her elbows in dishwater. "And Susan Adams." Susan was closest to Michael. She reached forward with plump, bejeweled fingers, clasped Michael's

131

hand, and pumped it hard. Michael tried not to grimace. Susan's grip squeezed her fingers.

"That's enough, Susan," Kitty said, easing Michael away. "She's not looking for a fight." Kitty encouraged Michael to have a seat and help herself to the spread on the table. There were scrambled eggs, fresh bread, several kinds of jam, bacon, sausage links, and fried potatoes. Michael put a little of everything on her plate.

"Where's Miss Kelly?" she asked when Kitty had finished serving herself. The question effectively silenced the entire table. Even Lottie stopped scrubbing.

"Actually it's Mrs. Kelly," Kitty said.

"And no one calls her that," Josie said. "She prefers not to be too closely associated with the late Mr. Kelly."

"I'm sorry. I didn't know about her husband."

Carmen cinched her robe more tightly around her waist. "Don't know why you should be sorry. You didn't know him."

"I just meant—"

"You wouldn't have wanted to know him," said Lottie. "I never heard anything about him that was good. The only piece of luck he ever ran into was winning this saloon in a card game. It would have gone under if it hadn't been for Dee."

"I thought Mr. Houston owned the saloon," Michael said, smearing a thick slice of bread with grape jam.

"Mr. Kelly later lost it to Houston," Susan said.

"Oh. That must have been . . ." She searched for the appropriate word. ". . . unsettling for Dee."

Laughter jolted the table. When it died down Carmen leaned forward in her chair and tapped her tapered nails on the surface of the table. She looked long and hard at Michael. "Unsettled doesn't begin to describe Detra's feelings about that bastard she married."

Josie giggled. "Murderous does."

There was more laughter and when Michael looked to Kitty for an answer she responded, "They're just warnin' you, Michael. Give Detra plenty of elbow room and if you cross her, run like hell. She killed Harry Kelly."

Chapter Five

The saloon's stage was nothing more than a platform raised two feet above the main floor. The proscenium was bounded by six sheltered tin boxes which held candles and served as footlights. There was no curtain. The canvas backdrop was a painted scene of a mountain lake and the words Kelly's Saloon were written in large script letters just above the distant peaks. There was a small area on either side of the stage where the performers could stand without being seen by the audience. Michael heard the areas being referred to as the wings, but like everything else about the stage, the name was a little too grand for the reality.

In the left wing, just at eye level for most of the performers, there was a small hole which allowed the dancers to peek at their audience. Michael found the hole almost immediately and pressed her eye to it. The saloon wasn't open yet and, except for Detra who was taking inventory behind the bar and Lottie who was sitting at the piano off stage, the place was empty.

Kitty tugged on Michael's sleeve. "Stop staring at Detra. And for God's sake, don't let her see you smoking. She thinks it's vulgar."

Michael stepped away from the peep hole reluctantly. "I wasn't staring at her," she lied, embarrassed to have been caught doing just that. She inhaled deeply on her cigarette and wished she had asked Josie to roll a second one for her. Wetting her thumb and forefinger, Michael snuffed the end. It sizzled. When she was certain it was out she slipped it in a crevice in the wall where she could find it later. She just couldn't bring herself to throw it away. Who knew when she would get another?

Watching Michael's antics with the cigarette, Kitty could only shake her head. "Of course you were staring at her," she said. "Every girl does once they've heard about the murder. Only it makes Dee angry and that's exactly what you don't want to do." She paused then pointed to the secreted cigarette. "Are you really going to smoke that later?"

"Of course I am."

"Aren't you a strange one," Kitty said softly.

Michael waved aside Kitty's observation. "I'm not sure I even believe that story about Dee. You probably made it up."

Kitty shrugged. "Ask Ethan. See what he says."

"I'll do that." She took a quick peek through the hole again and saw Dee carefully adding a measured glass of water to a bottle of whiskey. It suddenly became easier to imagine Dee taking the same care with arsenic and her late husband's coffee. Michael turned away from the hole. "If she really did poison Mr. Kelly, and everyone knows it, then why didn't she go to jail?"

"Because no one cared," Kitty said matter of factly. "You'd appreciate that if you'd known Mr. Kelly."

"But—"

"Enough. I wouldn't have told you if I knew you were goin' to ask so many questions. And don't let it get back to Dee that I told you. I don't want her mad at me."

"She wouldn't poison you."

Kitty looked at Michael as if she had grown another head. "Of course she wouldn't poison me. You take the

135

oddest notions to heart. Dee might send me packin' and that would be worse. Everyone 'round here knows this is the best place to work. Someday I might go to Denver and run a place of my own, but until then this is just where I want to be." Kitty began unfastening her gown. "C'mon. You've got to take that dress off. You can't dance in it."

It was Michael's turn to look appalled. "I've been dancing in gowns all my life."

"Not like this you haven't." She stepped out of her dress, leaving her in a chemise, drawers, calf-length petticoat, and corset. Kitty tapped her foot impatiently. "Do you want me to teach you or not? The other girls will be coming soon and you should know a little of the routine before they get here. They're not very patient."

"Oh, very well," Michael said, exasperated. There was only Lottie and Dee in the saloon. When she thought about it rationally her undergarments were less revealing than the gown Kitty had given her to wear for the actual performance. She hung her dress on the hook beside Kitty's and fought the urge to fold her arms protectively across her chest. "Let's get this over."

Kitty's head tilted to one side as she considered Michael thoughtfully. "What possessed you to answer Dee's advertisement in the first place?"

"Desperation." Michael was relieved to see that Kitty seemed to understand that answer. "I *want* to do this, Kitty," she said. "I'm just nervous." I *don't* want to do it, she thought, and I'm scared to death.

"All right. Let's go." Kitty's plump fingers clamped around Michael's wrist as she led her onto the middle of the stage. "Lottie, just give us the chorus to *When the Sun Shines*. I'll teach that part to Michael first."

Lottie nodded, turned on her stool, and began playing. A light, festive tune filled the saloon. Kitty

136

dropped Michael's wrist and took her through the steps slowly, showing her the saucy sashay around the borders of the stage while pretending to twirl her parasol. Kitty's expression was at once demur and sly, shyness used as an open invitation.

The steps were not difficult for Michael to follow. The routine consisted primarily of several turns about the stage with the parasol in different positions, a few waltz-like twirls with the parasol as a partner, and some toe-heel steps that made a pleasant clicking sound on the floor while the parasol was used as a cane.

"She's got the steps nicely," Lottie said, watching Michael while she played. "But her smile's just awful."

"Don't I know it," Kitty said, glancing sideways at Michael as they went through the shuffle steps. "Two-and-three-and-four-and . . . quickly, Michael. And-light-on-your-feet-and-smile-like-you-mean-it."

Michael laughed.

"That's better," Kitty said encouragingly as Michael's smile grew more fulsome. "Much better. Just forget there'll be fifty miners, give or take a half dozen, in here tonight, and that most of them will be watchin' you 'cause you're the new girl."

Michael's feet tangled almost immediately. Her smiled was forced down by rising panic. "Oh, Lord," she said softly looking out at the sea of empty tables and chairs. Tonight it would be swimming with men looking to her for entertainment. Handsome faces, plain faces, leering, respectful, or hopeful, every aspect of expression would be there in their eyes. "I don't think I can do this, Kitty."

"Sure you can," Kitty said, aware that Dee had stopped polishing the bar counter and was watching them. "Dee's looking this way," she said under her breath. "Remember 'desperation.' It'll help."

It did. Michael thought of all the things she was des-

137

perate to do: escape Ethan, escape the saloon, escape the mountain town. She had a story to write, testimony to give, and friends' deaths to revenge. Surely she could stand humiliating herself in order to achieve those ends. How was she to accomplish any of it without first gaining the trust of people like Kitty and Lottie, who didn't understand her circumstances, or like Houston and Happy who thought they did, or finally, of Ethan, who knew more about her than she would have wished?

Michael managed a small smile as Lottie started up the chorus again and demonstrated the routine to Kitty without faltering. She felt Dee's watchful eyes on her, felt the other woman's animosity though her expression remained unchanged. Even when Dee's concentration returned to polishing the long mahogany bar, Michael sensed her activity was merely a pretense and that her interest was still on the stage.

After nearly an hour of rehearsal they were joined by the other dancers. Practice continued for another hour while they taught Michael the main body of the routine, including the line kicks that Michael realized would expose a considerable length of her legs when done in the short gown and thigh-high tights. Joined arm in arm, the dancers raised their knees high and kicked out and up, alternating legs as they gradually made their line form a small circle, going round and round, faster and faster, until one of them lost balance and the group seemed to implode, falling in a heap of arms and elbows and a flurry of petticoats and ruffled drawers.

Laughing as they untangled themselves, they didn't hear the light, appreciative applause that was offered in their direction. When they saw Houston standing at the end of the bar nearest the stage they laughed all the harder. Everyone except Michael. Feeling her face flame under the steady regard of Houston's black eyes,

Michael disengaged herself quickly from the others and practically dove into the wings to retrieve her gown.

"She's still a trifle modest," Kitty said to no one in particular. Laughter rolled through the group again. Houston merely smiled.

"It's rather refreshing," he said.

Carmen got to her feet and dusted off her behind, turning and twisting, making a display of it for Houston's benefit. "Too obvious?" she asked, tossing him a sassy smile over her shoulder.

"Much too obvious," he said. "But very nice."

"Thank you."

Detra came out from her office in time to hear the last exchange. "Let's go, girls. There's plenty of work for you to do. Carmen, you can start with the floor in here. Kitty, the spittoons. The brass rail needs polishing and the mirror needs wiping." She held up one hand when they started to protest that they needed more rehearsal time. "You've been doing those songs for two weeks now. You know them as well as you need to."

"But Michael needs—" Josie's objection was met with one of Dee's most frosty stares. "Well, I hope she doesn't embarrass the rest of us," she mumbled, getting to her feet.

"I don't see how she could," Houston said as Michael returned to the stage. "She wasn't the one who caused that fall. It seemed to me that Susan couldn't keep the pace."

Susan huffed a little while Dee glared at Houston. After a moment Detra turned on her heel and marched into her office.

Houston grinned, completely unrepentant. He took off his hat, dropped it on the counter, and ran his fingers through his light hair. "Go on, girls. You heard, Dee. She has work for you to do."

139

Michael spied the broom leaning against the upright piano. "I'll sweep," she said. She gave Carmen a wary glance. "Unless you want to."

"Be my guest. I want to talk to Houston anyway."

Houston pushed away from the bar and shook his head. "No, Michael. I want to talk to you. Carmen can sweep." His brows came up as the door to Dee's office was slammed. He looked once in that direction but his thoughts were masked. When he returned his attention to the stage Carmen was already getting the broom and Michael was alone. "Down here, Michael. We can sit at one of the tables."

Michael ignored the hand he offered to help her down from the stage and took the short ramp instead. It was more difficult to pretend she hadn't seen that Houston was amused by her gesture. To spare herself more of his smug ridicule, Michael accepted the chair he pulled out for her.

"Do you want a drink?" he asked.

"No, thank you. I don't drink."

"I was thinking of coffee. Lottie will bring it from the kitchen."

"No, nothing," she said hurriedly. The last thing she wanted was one of the girls waiting on her. She needed to join them, not be set apart. "If you want something, I'll get it."

Houston placed a hand over Michael's forearm, stopping her from rising. He sat down and removed his hand only when he was certain she wasn't going to bolt. "That's better. I don't want anything either."

Michael's eyes strayed to the star on Houston's shirt. She tried not to show her disdain. "Is this official business, Sheriff?"

He chuckled. "There's not much in the way of official business in this town. Nothing ever happens here." He stared at her hard for a moment. "At least not officially."

"I'm beginning to realize that."

"Good."

"Then what is it you want?"

Houston shrugged. "Just some conversation."

"You didn't have to single me out for that."

"Yes, I did."

She heard sincerity in his tone and saw something earnest and warm in his coal black eyes. He had strong, even bold features. His dark eyes and brows were a startling, even arresting contrast to the light, pale ash color of his hair. He was not nearly as handsome as he was compelling, and Nathaniel Houston, Michael admitted reluctantly, was very, very handsome.

And like everyone who worked for him, he was also a murderer.

Michael had the oddest sensation that he knew precisely what she was thinking. She recalled Ethan's warning to stay away from Houston and Detra's animosity. She met Houston's direct gaze and saw the warmth had been replaced by a cold, fathomless, and implacable stare that communicated both a warning and a threat. Here, then, was the killer. Here was the man she meant to see hang.

"Ethan's not in favor of you dancing," he said.

"That's not what Kitty told me this morning."

Houston thought that over. "You're still Ethan's wife."

"That was a long time ago."

"Meaning?"

"Meaning it was a long time ago. Nothing more, nothing less." She lowered her voice so none of the girls engaged in tasks around them would hear. "I think for myself, Mr. Houston."

"Houston. Just Houston. Or Nate. I don't fancy being a mister anybody." He leaned forward in his chair and placed his forearms on the tabletop. "Tell me

141

something, when Ethan walked out on you, were you in love with him?"

Michael's eyes dropped away. She stared at her hands for a moment trying to formulate the best answer. "That's very personal," she said.

"Were you?"

"Yes." She hoped she sounded as if she had given the answer reluctantly.

"Are you still?"

It came quite naturally to look at Houston as if he were mad.

He laughed at her. "Guess not. You forgiven him yet?"

"For walking out on me? I forgave him for that years ago. For bringing me to this forsaken place? Never."

"But you intend to stay with him."

"Do I have any choice?"

Houston didn't say anything for a moment. His look was considering as his eyes drifted over Michael's face. He made a slight nod of approval as he saw her flush under his thoughtful scrutiny. "You may have another choice," he said, pushing away from the table and standing up. "I *do* find your modesty refreshing." And more than a little intriguing, he thought. "If you'll excuse me, I have to see Dee."

Michael watched his retreating back, frowning. Had he meant she may have a choice to leave or a choice to change partners? The former was appealing and unlikely. The latter was something she didn't want to think about.

She came out of her reverie as she was tapped on the shoulder. Carmen thrust a broom in her hands. "As long as you're done jawin'," Carmen said, "there's your share of the work to be done. Customers start driftin' in just before noon."

Michael was glad to take the broom, relieved for something to do. It gave her the opportunity to become familiar with the saloon and later, when she swept the dust onto the wooden sidewalk and then onto the street, it gave her her first breath of real freedom.

She counted sixteen tables in the saloon, each with three, four, or five chairs. The mahogany bar with its brass footrail and cuspidors went nearly the length of the room. A large mirror had been mounted on the wall behind it and there were shelves of liquor on either side. Glasses, towels, and aprons were kept below the bar. A roulette wheel took up one corner of the saloon and a pool table took up another. The cues were hanging in a rack beside the largest elk's head Michael had ever seen. The wallpaper was a sumptuous red and gold in a richly detailed print. Milk-white glass globes hid the burning gaslights and the clock above the entrance to the dining room ticked off the minutes quietly.

Sweeping off the sidewalk, Michael observed the location of the livery and the mercantile. Horses and guns. Knowing where to find each was absolutely essential.

"What do you think you're doing?" Dee asked from the doorway to the saloon. Houston was directly behind her.

"Sweeping." Michael knew a moment's triumph when she glimpsed the last vestige of panic in their faces.

"Get inside," Dee snapped. "And don't leave the saloon again for any reason." She pushed Houston out of the way and went back to her office.

"Don't give me any reason to think you've left again," Houston said. His voice was as hard as his eyes. "Detra will be the least of your worries."

Michael's sense of triumph disappeared. Even though they had found her easily and she had given no indication she was doing anything but her chore, she realized her action had made them more wary, not more trusting. Discouraged, she followed Houston back into the saloon.

She wasn't able to see her entire reflection in the mirror above the bureau. In a way it was a relief. What she could see made her want to scream in frustration. Kitty had come to her room after dinner to assist her with rouge and powder and hairpins. Michael didn't recognize herself when Kitty was finished. Her lips were painted bright red, her cheeks rouged just a shade less so. Kitty arranged her hair more loosely than was Michael's preference, letting the curls spill freely where they would. Michael was successful in convincing Kitty the pink taffeta bow was too much, but as a victory it was hardly satisfying. Not when Michael still had to contend with the gown.

It was every bit as tight as she thought it would be and the stiff whalebone corset constricted her breathing. Putting her hands on her waist, Michael decided it was too small to contain the organs inside it. Which led her to the conclusion that it was indeed her heart that was in her mouth. Against her better judgment Michael pulled a chair over to the chest of drawers and stood on it. The view of what she would be presenting below stairs did not give her any confidence.

Her breasts were too exposed by the low curved neckline, her arms and shoulders too bare without benefit of gloves or a shawl. The hem of the skirt fell just below her knees and the white stockings and high-heeled boots, from what she could see, made her legs seem impossibly long.

Michael jumped down from the chair and pushed it back against the wall. "I can't do this," she said to the empty room. "I can't go downstairs like this. I can't dance in these shoes. I can't kick in this dress. My God, they'll see *everything*." Michael had brought her partially smoked cigarette from the morning to her room and squirreled it away. She got it out now and went to the window and opened it wide. Sitting on the sill, she lit it and drew the smoke in deeply. She simply didn't care who observed her from below. Exhaling slowly, Michael stared down at the street without really seeing any of the activity. She imagined herself on stage. "Those miners are going to see everything even if I don't kick."

She wished Dee had allowed her to serve drinks in the afternoon with all the other girls. After Houston left Detra decided it would be better if Michael spent the afternoon and early evening in her room, just as much to get her out of the way as to offer her up as a surprise for the miners later. Michael had been happy to retreat earlier. Now she wished she hadn't. She could have gotten used to the stares gradually, used to the pinching and poking. Now she would have to face it all at once, along with the whistling and hooting and namecalling, and she would have to be pleasant, even pretend to enjoy some of it.

"Another minute," she told herself, waving smoke outside so it wouldn't cling to her dress or the room, "and I'll probably just wake up and laugh about this nightmare." She waited. A minute passed and she had to admit there would be no waking up because there was no dream.

Kitty poked her head in the door. "You look grand!" She saw the cigarette. "Get rid of that! Dee will have a fit! C'mon, we'll take the backstairs so no one sees you before time. What a sight you are! They're about goin' to pop themselves when they see what Dee's ordered up for them from the East. Listen." She cocked her head to one side. "You can hear 'em downstairs askin' for us to get started. Kind of warms you, don't it? And won't Ethan like how you cleaned up so well!"

Michael's head snapped up. "Ethan's back? He's here?"

145

Kitty nodded. "Hmm-mm. Downstairs sittin' at a table with Houston. Just came in a few minutes ago from the mines. Are you comin' or not?"

Putting out her cigarette, Michael came to her feet slowly. "I'm coming."

Ethan's eyes wandered around the saloon as he nursed his beer. He was dog tired and had little patience for the rowdy crowd that filled Kelly's. He glanced at Houston. "You here as the owner this evening or as the sheriff?"

"Both. In either capacity I figure Jake and I will throw out half a dozen men tonight." Houston reached in his shirt pocket and pulled out a leather notepad and two pencils. He laid them on the table and pushed them toward Ethan. "You know anything about this? Lottie found them when she was washing Michael's things."

Masking his concern with indifference, Ethan picked up the notepad and began leafing through it. Though he examined the book casually he was looking for any reference to the *Chronicle,* Michael's position there, or her real name. He saw nothing that could serve to endanger her. "It's a diary of her trip," he said. "Michael's always kept a diary."

Houston nodded. "See that she doesn't keep a diary of this little side excursion. I don't want her writing down anything that could cause us trouble later."

Ethan offered up the notepad. "Do you want to keep it?"

"No. But I want to look at it from time to time. Michael doesn't have to know. I find her observations interesting." He leaned forward, turning his shot glass slowly between his thumb and forefinger. "I'm going to give you a chance, Ethan, that I don't usually give other men when I see something I want. I'm going to tell you about it before I have it safely in hand."

Ethan finished the last of his beer and set down his glass. "I appreciate the gesture, but you're not going to tell me anything I don't already know. Your interest in Michael is pretty evident. Detra sees it, too."

"I'm not concerned with Dee. I'm wondering about you. Do you really still think of Michael as your wife? Even after four years?"

"Would it stop you if I did?"

"I don't know."

"And I don't know either," Ethan said. "But, you see, it doesn't matter, because she *is* my wife."

"She was going to marry that reporter."

"She thought I was dead."

"You still could be."

Ethan considered Houston's threat a moment. He had come to know his man well in the last five months and he believed Houston was bluffing. "Where would be the challenge for you then? You want her, but so do I. I'm not going to warn you off her, Houston. You've seen enough of Michael to know she makes up her own mind." He raised his glass for a refill, closing the subject. When no one came to take his order he realized all the girls were getting ready for the entertainment. "As long as I can't get another quick beer," he said, "I'm going up. Michael must be half out of her mind from being trapped in the room all day."

"She wasn't in there all day."

Ethan had started to rise but Houston's words brought him back to the table. "What do you mean?" He put Michael's notepad and pencils in his coat pocket. "I told Dee that I wanted Michael locked in. I even gave her the key."

"You settle it with Dee, but I was still here this morning when Dee sent Kitty up to Michael with clothes and instructions to come down for breakfast and rehearsal."

147

"That bitch," he swore softly. "She knows I didn't want Michael dancing."

"Dee can defend herself, but she had a point about getting Michael involved. Michael's supposed to work for her."

"She can serve drinks. I told Dee that. Just not yet."

"You don't trust Michael, do you?"

"I'd be a fool to."

Houston nodded. "She swept her way right out of here after rehearsal this morning."

"She was outside? Without Dee?" Ethan looked down at his empty beer glass and wished there were another swallow in it. He lowered his voice so that Houston had to pull in closer to hear him. "She only needs a few minutes head start to leave Madison. Less than that to tell someone a story about No. 349. No one might believe her at first but she'd plant a seed in their mind. Sooner or later they'd realize the truth."

Houston's reply was cut off by the piano. Lottie was banging out the introduction to *When the Sun Shines*. The crowd hushed almost immediately in anticipation.

"I'm going to strangle her," Ethan said softly.

"Who? Detra?"

"Her first, then Michael."

Houston brushed aside his concern. "Let the men enjoy looking at her. You can afford to be generous. After all, you get to bed down with her."

Ethan didn't comment. His blue-gray eyes were fixed on the raised platform where the dancers would appear in another moment. There was a roar from the crowd as Susan shuffled on stage, twirling her parasol and blowing kisses to the miners. She was followed by Carmen and Josie and Kitty and finally by Michael. The steady roar erupted into wild applause as the men became aware of the new face and figure on the stage.

"Oh God," Ethan sighed, shaking his head. "Would you look at her?"

"I am." Houston glanced at the other tables. "So is everyone else. Quite a change from the priggish schoolmarm I first laid eyes on."

Ethan's thoughts were along the same lines but he kept them to himself. Even at the distance he was from the stage, Michael looked as if she had applied her face paints with a heavy hand. He had never thought the other women looked garish with their bright lips and rosy cheeks, but seeing the same effect on Michael made him revise his opinion.

His eyes strayed from her face to her gown. She was showing more leg than any of the other dancers and no less of her breasts. He winced as she linked arms with Josie and Kitty and raised her legs in a high stepping kick. Her petticoats flew up and seemed to stay there a moment after her legs came down. It was a movement repeated over and over again as Lottie pounded out the ditty on the piano. He tried to single out her voice among the dancers and couldn't, then the miners joined in as the chorus was repeated and the task became impossible. It occurred to him that she was probably simply mouthing the words, though why she thought she had to was beyond him. Above the caterwauling of the miners, the sour notes that Lottie hit from time to time, and the shrill pitch of the dancers, it didn't matter if Michael was tone deaf.

The dance seemed to last longer than he remembered, but then Ethan had always been able to enjoy it before. Watching Michael, knowing she was burning with embarrassment and rage, made it torture for him as well. Her smile was fixed, her eyes vacant, and as near as he could tell from the enthusiasm of the crowd, he was the only one who realized it. He amended his thinking a moment later. Houston seemed to realize it as well. Ethan saw he was no longer smiling as Lottie played the final chorus and the saloon fairly vibrated with sustained applause and whistling.

149

"Where are you going?" Houston asked as Ethan got to his feet.

"To get her off that stage."

Houston laid his hand over Ethan's forearm and shook his head. "Let her be. The worst's over. You said she could serve drinks." He released Ethan's arm and pointed to his empty glass. "You look like you could use another beer."

Ethan hesitated. Michael was already leaving the stage, following the other girls down the ramp and being swallowed up by the miners eager to get a few words with her. He saw she was managing to make her way to the bar. Raising his glass, he caught her eye. She ignored him.

Houston had seen the exchange. When Ethan sat down again he said, "Looks like there'll be hell to pay."

Ethan's small grunt was all the acknowledgment he offered. "You heard anything official about the other night?" he asked, referring to the robbery.

"News was telegraphed here this morning. Rich Hardy reported it to me right away. I suspect everyone in Madison knows about the robbery by now. Seems it was one of the biggest train heists to date."

"That a fact?" He grinned because it was expected.

"That's what they're saying over the wire."

They continued to talk about the robbery as if they had not been part of it, as if they knew no more about it than what the telegrapher had reported to the sheriff. But between the lines there was another communication, one of success, of congratulation. Ethan participated because he had to, not because he wanted to. It was something of a relief to be troubled by the conversation. It meant he still knew which side he was on.

Detra joined them at the table. She kissed Houston on the cheek but her dark blue eyes were more interested in Ethan Stone. There was too much cunning in

her smile for it to be a sincere greeting. "You men enjoy the show as much as my other customers?" she
asked.

"You deliberately ignored my orders," Ethan said,
making no effort to hide his anger from Dee or any of
the customers who might look in their direction.

"You don't have the right to order me," Detra said.
The look she gave Houston was equally significant.
"No man does. I manage this place and I'll manage it
as I see fit."

"And I own it," Houston said. "Don't push too hard,
Dee. I can push back. You should have honored
Ethan's wishes. He had his reasons for not wanting
Michael down here, not the least of which is that one
word from her can ruin everything."

"You should have thought of that before you
brought her here." Detra fiddled with a black curl at
her temple, twirling it around her finger before tucking it neatly behind her ear. "Instead of risking everything—"

"Lower your voice," Houston snapped. "Or it won't
be Michael that sees us ruined." He took Dee's wrist in
a firm grip and stood up, taking her with him. "I think
you need a little more attention." He pulled her hard
against him and lowered his mouth. One of the miners
started pounding on his table and the drumbeat was
soon picked up by others. It lasted until Houston
scooped Dee up in his arms and carried her through
the crowd back to her office.

Ethan decided Houston had probably saved Dee's
life by getting her away from the table. Ethan had
come as close to hurting Detra, *really* hurting her, as he
ever had anyone. If the woman questioned again why
they hadn't killed Michael at the robbery, he wasn't going to hold himself back. It didn't occur to him to
question his anger at Dee and what it said about his
feelings toward Michael. Ethan had gotten used to not

examining some things too closely, or feeling things too deeply.

"Refill?" Michael asked, lifting a pitcher of beer above Ethan's glass.

He nodded. "Join me?"

"I can't. Dee will—"

"Dee's busy," he said, pointing the office. "Houston's seeing to her." Ethan thought it would have been impossible to see Michael blush beneath her painted face. It wasn't. "Sit down." He took the pitcher from her and poured his own drink while Michael sat. His eyes glanced briefly in her direction and took in the neckline of her gown and everything that was rising above it. "Not what you're used to wearing."

"No, it's not."

"Pink's not your color. Not with your hair."

Her hands rose self-consciously to her hair. She felt a few loose pins and attempted to stick them back in place. She stopped because Ethan was shaking his head as he watched her.

"The problem's not your hair," he said. Her hair was so fine it made the rest of her look tawdry. He took a long swallow of beer. "Let's go upstairs. You don't belong down here."

"I'm not sure—"

Ethan was about to ignore her objection when they were interrupted. Ralph Hooper was standing next to Michael's chair, shuffling his weight nervously from one foot to the other. "Like to know if I could get a dance with you, ma'am, that is if Ethan here don't take no offense. She's been tellin' everyone she's spoken for and I saw you carry her in here yesterday, so I know the truth of it, but I was just wonderin' about a dance."

Though Michael hardly understood it herself, she looked to Ethan for permission. The action so appalled her that without waiting for any indication from him, she stood up and offered her hand to the ruddy, broad-shouldered miner. "I'd be pleased to." And when his wide, open face split with a happy grin she suddenly realized she meant it. She turned to Ethan. "I won't be long."

Watching her go, Ethan raised his glass and took another long swallow. He had time, he thought, and she had left the pitcher behind. He might as well work on it. There was little chance she'd return to the table any time soon. One dance would lead to another . . . and another. The glass was pressed to Ethan's lips so it was difficult to see that he was smiling. Damn. Didn't she just look like she was enjoying herself.

Ralph Hooper eventually had to let her go and another miner took his place. Lottie continued accompanying on the piano, playing the tunes that were called out. There were rousing jigs, country dances, polkas, and lilting waltzes. Men claimed the other girls and the partners moved from the main floor of the saloon where they had to negotiate the maze of tables and chairs, to the stage where they had the freedom to rollick in any direction.

Ethan saw that she was graceful. Even during the lively jigs and highstepping country flings, Michael's movements were lithe and light. She swayed and turned and jumped as if buoyed by the air rather than being restrained by it. Her partners were not nearly as adept as they were enthusiastic, but when she waltzed with them her command of the dance made their form look almost elegant. The laughter and clapping and spirited singing all but drowned out the music. It didn't seem to matter to Michael. She never once lost the rhythm of the dance, never once faltered on her feet.

Never once . . . until Ethan became her partner.

His hand on her waist tightened, supporting her. He turned her lightly in the three-quarter time of the waltz. "Don't stop smiling now," he said. "The others

153

will think you don't want to dance with me."

"I don't."

"Pretend," he ordered succinctly. "Because when this dance is over, you're finished down here. I'm taking you to our room and let everyone here think what they like."

"You mean think what you want them to think."

"Look around you, Michael. Either they think you're my personal property or you'll be doing a far more intimate dance with most of them before the night's out. Is that what you want?"

She smiled sweetly and replied through her teeth. "You know I don't."

His hand slid a little further up her back. "Then stop suffering this. I'm not the worst partner you've had tonight."

It wasn't his dancing she found fault with. It was the way his long fingers seemed to burn the skin at her back and the way his other hand engulfed hers. He seemed closer to her than any of the other men yet he held her at a respectful distance. He seemed to be aware of every part of her although his eyes never left her face.

The tempo of the dance changed as Lottie played a few connecting bars from waltz to something more lively. "This is it," Ethan said, placing both hands on her waist. With virtually no effort he lifted her over his shoulder. The immediate reaction of the miners was loud and prolonged booing. When they saw Ethan wasn't swayed by their objections and they remembered he had blasted open two new tunnels for them only that day, when they saw he hadn't checked his gun at the door, and when they recalled Nathaniel Houston was Ethan's friend, they let him pass.

Outside the door to his room Ethan set Michael down. She was furious. "Did you have to do that? I can walk, you know. I'm not one of your damn saddlebags."

His eyes dropped to her mouth as she swore. He opened the door and gestured with his hand, ushering her in. "Go on," he said. "Inside. Before they change their minds downstairs and decide to come after you. You keep swearing at me and I might just let them."

"Oh, go to hell," she said. But she hurried inside nonetheless.

"Wash off that war paint."

"It's your fault that I have it on in the first place."

"It's not," he said, closing the door. He noticed the latch had been fixed and hooked it. "But it doesn't matter. Wash it off anyway."

Reaching the washstand, Michael turned on him. "I let you order me around downstairs because it was for my protection. I'll be damned if I'm going to let you—" She stopped as he approached her, flinty purpose in his eyes. She pressed herself against the washstand and felt the pitcher and basin behind her wobble. "What are you . . . what do you wa—" He reached around her— to steady the washstand, she thought—but when he pulled away he was holding a slim bar of soap. Somehow he made the gesture appear threatening and Michael felt some of her bravado fade.

She tried to snatch the soap from his hand but he held it up and out of her reach. "I can wash my own face," she said impatiently.

"It's not your face I'm thinking about."

She saw his eyes drop pointedly to her mouth. "You wouldn't."

"Is that a challenge or are you asking for clarification? Either way, know this: one more cuss word and you'll be tasting soap for a week." Michael didn't say a word in reply. One corner of Ethan's mouth lifted in a sardonic smile. "I'm of a mind to wash your mouth out for the words you're *thinking*."

She glared harder and gave him a push with the flat of her hands. He dropped the soap and Michael managed to get it first. Hoping he choked on his laughter, she turned back to the washstand and poured water in the basin. She scrubbed her face hard, first with just the soap, then with a lathered cloth.

"Here," Ethan said, tapping her shoulder. He slipped a towel into her hands and took the wet cloth. "Before you sand away your skin."

Michael patted her face dry. "There's no satisfying you." She realized too late the meaning he could give her words. He was already looking at her oddly, his eyes moving from feature to feature, studying her face as if he didn't quite know what to make of it. "I didn't mean . . . that is, I didn't—"

"I know what you meant." He turned away, taking off his gun belt and hanging it up. "More's the pity," he said softly.

Michael was quite sure she hadn't heard him correctly. More to the point, if he had said it, she didn't want to hear him correctly. Ethan Stone frightened her and not entirely in the way he meant to. He threatened her life, he threatened to wash her mouth out, he threatened her with other men, yet what filled her with dread was her reaction to him when he wasn't threatening at all.

Taking Ethan's nightshirt out of the bureau, Michael slipped it over her head and over her clothes. Once she was covered she began removing her gown, petticoats, and tights. Ethan, she noticed was sitting in the wing chair, his legs stretched out, his eyes closed, not paying her the least attention.

Ethan thought if she didn't finish soon he would strip the clothes off her back himself. She didn't mean to be provocative. That's what bothered him: she hardly seemed to be aware of the way he was fighting her attraction now. "I'm going to get the tub," he said gruffly. "I'll be back in a few minutes."

Michael shrugged indifferently. When he was gone

156

she permitted herself a small smile. He had left his gunbelt behind. She wondered if he was trusting her not to use his Colt on him or if he simply believed she didn't know how. Michael didn't dwell on Ethan's reasoning. Instead she used the time he was gone to wash herself at the basin and set the fire in the stove. By the time he returned with the tub and buckets she was getting comfortable in bed.

Ethan paid her little attention while he was filling the tub. He warned her when he was going to undress and grinned as she dove under the covers. He was still grinning when she began to emerge cautiously at the sound of his splashing. "Thanks for stoking the fire," he said. "I appreciate it."

"I did it for me."

"I still appreciate it." He raised a leg, propping his heel on the edge of the tub and began scrubbing.

Michael watched him because there was nothing else to do with her eyes. She had nothing to read, no picture that might entertain her interest, and she was too wary to sleep.

"I've been wondering about that Drew fellow," Ethan said without looking at her. "Was he really your fiancé?"

In spite of the fact there was no one else in the room, it took Michael a moment to realize he was talking to her. "No," she said. "I wasn't engaged to him or anyone else from the paper."

"But you were traveling with all those men."

"Do you have a point, Mr. Stone?"

"Are you pregnant?"

Michael blinked widely at the question, not quite believing she'd heard him correctly.

Ethan spared her a small glance. "Do you have an answer, Miss Dennehy?" he asked sarcastically.

Michael sat up. "I am *not* pregnant."

"Why are you so offended? It seems a fair enough

question. You lived in close quarters with the other reporters. Did you share a bed?"

"You *would* think that."

"Let me ask it another way, Michael. *Could* you be pregnant?"

Michael's knuckles were white where she clutched the comforter. She spoke after she had reined in the first rush of anger and even then it was in carefully measured tones. "It's none of your damn business, you simple jackass."

Ethan paused in his scrubbing and looked thoughtfully at the soap in his open palm. He also gave Michael the first steady look since he'd begun bathing. The threat was clear. "I'm not interrupting my bath to clean out your mouth. Neither am I going to forget."

"Oh, go to hell," she said tiredly, lying down again. "I don't care what you do."

Ethan surprised himself by laughing at her last pathetic show of defiance. He certainly couldn't interpret it as a challenge. "I'll take this all to mean that you couldn't be pregnant," he said.

"Suit yourself."

"I always do." He began scrubbing his chest and took pleasure in the passing of several silent minutes. "Lottie found your notebook and pencils when she washed your clothes," he said casually.

It was difficult for Michael to temper her excitement or her interest. "She did?" she asked with more eagerness than was her desire.

"I'm not sure why, but she gave the book to Houston. He asked me about it." He ran the bar of soap up and down the length of his right arm then took his time rinsing it.

"Well?" she demanded impatiently.

"Oh," he said as if he'd forgotten they were discussing anything. "I told him that you've always kept a diary."

"Did he believe you?"

"You're still alive, aren't you? I hate to say it, Michael, but that's the only measure we have of what Houston believes." He saw her face pale. She turned on her side, drawing her knees protectively toward her chest. Her eyes were accusing.

"You enjoy frightening me. You never miss an opportunity."

"You're wrong. I just figure fear will make you a little more cautious. Your book's in the pocket of my coat. It's yours if you want it back."

"The pencils?"

"I'll return them only if I get to read everything you write. No surprises, Michael. In the unlikely event you leave Madison, you're not going to write something you can use against any of us. Houston's also going to be interested in what's in that book of yours."

What choice did she have? "All right," she said reluctantly.

"The pencils are with the book. Lower left hand pocket. Your spectacles are in the upper right." Ethan had a glimpse of long legs and fair skin as she threw back the covers. The nightshirt fell quickly as she stood.

Michael sat cross-legged on top of the covers as she skimmed the contents of her notebook. Her spectacles rested near the tip of her nose and there was a faint line between her brows as she read. Frustrated with her hair which kept falling over her shoulders and getting in her way, she finally pulled it back and held it in place with one hand. Both pencils had been nested neatly behind her right ear.

"Oh, Lord," Ethan said softly when he looked up and saw her. Her mouth had flattened in a way that was becoming familiar to him; the frown was not disapproving, merely thoughtful. He had a sudden urge to do something about that serious mouth

159

of hers. Like kiss it.

The notion was enough to make Ethan attend to his back.

Michael glanced up when she heard Ethan wince. "What's wrong?"

He dropped the washcloth as his hand went to his shoulder. His fingers searched gently around a tender spot on his back. "It's just a bruise," he said, trying to tilt his head at an impossible angle to see it.

Michael closed her book and placed it on the bedside table. She scooted off the bed and padded softly over to the tub. "Let me see."

"It's nothing."

"Be quiet, and move your hand." Michael knelt behind him. There was a bruise the size of her fist near his shoulder blade. There were also inflamed abrasions and scratches. "Hand me the cloth," she said in no nonsense tones. "This needs to be thoroughly cleaned. The soap, too. Do you have any alcohol in here? A touch of that wouldn't hurt."

"For you or for me?"

"I'm not that squeamish, Mr. Stone."

"Ethan," he said. "I'm naked. I'm in a tub. You're wearing my nightshirt. You've already slept in my bed. I think you should call me Ethan."

"Where's the alcohol, Ethan?"

"Bottom of the wardrobe."

"Thank you." She found it quickly and returned to his side.

Michael washed the cuts carefully, gauging the pressure of her fingers by the sudden tensing of muscles in Ethan's back. She gave him the bottle of whiskey.

He took a long swallow. "God, what are you doing back there?"

"You have bits of thread from your shirt in the cuts. I have to get them out if you don't want an infection." She waited until he finished taking another drink.

160

"Save some of that for these cuts. I plan to wash them out with it."

"You're enjoying this."

Michael stopped working and rocked back on her heels. "Do you want me to send for a doctor?"

"No," he said after a moment. "You go on with what you're doing."

She leaned forward again and ran the damp soap cloth over his back. "How did this happen?"

"I was blasting out a tunnel this afternoon. I guess I set the fuse too short."

"I guess you did," she said softly.

"I dove for cover when the rocks started flying. I don't remember anything falling on me. It must have happened when I hit the ground."

"Give me the bottle back."

He handed it to her, clenching his teeth for what he knew was coming. His fingers curled around the edge of the tub.

She was mercifully quick about it.

"You can let your breath out," she said, moving around to the side of the tub. She gave him the bottle again. "Here, have another drink. I'm all done. You're going to live."

"I knew I was going to survive the injury," he said lowly. His eyes held hers. "I didn't know if I was going to survive your attentions."

Michael stared at him over the top of her spectacles. One of his hands reached for her, slipping beneath her hair at the nape. He held her gently, just steadying her, feeling the panicked heartbeat in the pulse of her neck. He didn't pull her toward him. Instead, Ethan was the one to lean forward.

Chapter Six

His lips tasted faintly of whiskey. They moved over Michael's slowly, sipping, learning the texture, the shape. The hand at her nape exerted no pressure. The choice was hers and she remained where she was. Her eyes closed. His mouth was firm and the kiss was warm. He searched without hunger, without demand. His touch was persuading.

Michael's lips parted under his. She felt the damp roughness of his tongue as he traced the soft inside of her upper lip. She tasted him again as he ran his tongue against the ridge of her teeth. Her mouth opened a fraction more. Water from his arm dampened the front of her nightshirt. A rivulet curved past her throat and between her breasts. It was as if he had touched her there too.

Her lips were more than pliant beneath his touch. Her mouth was yielding. She thought nothing. She felt everything.

Neither of them heard the door open. Detra stood just inside the room watching them a moment before declaring her presence by clearing her throat. "I knocked," she said as Michael pushed back from the tub. Ethan's arm fell away from her neck.

"What do you want, Dee?" he growled. He cursed himself for not securing the door when he came back

162

with the tub. Out of the corner of his eye he could see Michael was forcing a composure she didn't feel. Her spectacles had been pushed up the bridge of her nose and her shoulders were set straight and stiff.

"Customers are asking for you downstairs," she said to Michael.

"She's not going down again," Ethan said. "She's here for the night. And while we're at it, Dee, tell Michael whose idea it was that she should start dancing tonight."

Dee fingered a curl at her ear. "I don't see what harm it's done. She was a success. They like her."

"Too much. She's not going down again tonight."

Dee's dark blue eyes made a leisurely, insulting inspection of Michael. "I think my customers thought you'd be through with her by now." She saw Michael suck in her breath and smiled. "Appears you're only starting to thaw this block of ice."

"Don't let us keep you, Dee," Ethan said, his eyes flinty.

With a cheeky smile, Detra pivoted on her heel and made her exit without bothering to shut the door.

"Get the door, Michael," Ethan ordered. When she simply sat there he barked at her again. "The *door*, Michael."

Michael scrambled to her feet. She latched the door quickly and hurried to the bed, turning away as Ethan reached for a towel and started to rise from the water.

"Don't let Dee bother you," he said. "She's just trying to gauge the threat you are to her. The more possessive I am, the happier she is. She's counting on me to keep you away from Houston."

She nodded slowly, not quite meeting his eyes. "Then, thank you. I wouldn't have wanted to go back down there tonight. Do those men really think . . . what Dee said?"

"Probably. We've told them you're my mistress, remember, not my wife. I suppose they think I should be a little more accommodating. Share you more."

"You mean they think *I* should be more accommodating."

"Something like that." He fastened his drawers and rubbed his hair briskly with the towel. "The other girls do more . . . entertaining. It's natural for them to expect the same from you."

"What about Detra?"

He shook his head. "She's Houston's woman."

"Perhaps if I was Houston's woman . . ." She let the sentence trail away.

"You wouldn't have to worry about the men. I told you before: Detra would kill you."

"Is it true she poisoned her husband?"

"So you heard the story. That didn't take long." He checked the fire in the stove. "I can't say if it's true one way or the other. It supposedly happened long before I got here. I don't have any reason *not* to believe it though. And if you think I'm saying that to frighten you, you're right." Ethan got the blankets from the wardrobe and snapped them out beside the bed. He took one of the pillows from the bed and tossed it on the floor, then blew out one of the lamps, leaving the one on the bedside table for Michael. He stretched out on the floor. "Houston was asking me questions tonight. About you. About me. About you *and* me. He let me know he wants you."

Michael moved to the edge of the bed and peered down at Ethan. She considered telling him Houston had had a similar conversation with her earlier in the day. She decided against it.

"But he thinks I'm your wife."

"It doesn't weigh that heavily on his mind, Michael. He thinks he's done his part just by telling me his intentions. I can't say that I'm all that eager to fight him over you."

Michael hoped they killed each other. She took off her spectacles, folded the stems carefully, and laid them aside. Patting down her hair, she found the pencils and put them aside also, then she turned back the lamp. Michael lay on her side, one arm curved under her head, the other hugging the pillow. "I don't want you to kiss me anymore."

"Tell me that when I'm kissing you and I'll stop."

"Do you think I can't?"

"I don't know. Shall we find out now?"

"No!"

Ethan chuckled. "Don't worry, Michael. The moment's past. I'm miserably tired, my shoulder aches, and I have to do some more blasting in the mines tomorrow. Go to sleep."

She bristled at his directions. "I'm tired of your orders." She was physically exhausted but mentally alert. Sleep seemed impossible.

"Fine. Don't go to sleep."

Twenty minutes later he heard her breath catch in a soft snore. Ethan removed the bullets from his gun, put them in the drawer, and returned to his bed on the floor.

She was the most irritating woman he'd ever known. Most of his dreams that night were about kissing her.

Ethan was gone again when Michael awoke. It became a familiar pattern over the next two weeks. Ethan's bed on the floor was always removed, his shaving instruments put away, and his clothes from the day before were stuffed in a laundry bag just inside the door. He always left Michael fresh water in the pitcher and sometimes a note on the table telling her if he planned to be back early or late from the mines.

Michael realized that over time she had become, if not precisely comfortable in Ethan's presence, then accustomed to it. There were times that she forgot she was not free to come and go as she pleased, times when she was almost content to be in Ethan's company. When she realized she was feeling that way she fought against it . . . and Ethan. The evenings that started out the best ended in the worst arguments.

Rehearsal for the evening's routines was just after breakfast. Michael took part because she always danced in the first show, if not the second. After the first night it seemed useless to pretend she had never taken part in the evening's entertainment. When rehearsal was over Michael did her share of the chores, whether it was polishing brass or watering down the liquor. Detra was never far away while Michael was working on the main floor. It was Detra's continual presence that reminded Michael she was a prisoner in the saloon.

The other girls warmed to Michael's presence in varying degrees. Kitty was invariably kind, Josie just a little less so. Lottie and Susan were the most helpful during rehearsals but didn't talk much to her outside of them. Carmen made no secret about wanting Ethan in her bed again. Her jealousy could have taken a venomous turn except, unlike Detra, Carmen tempered her feelings when Ethan wasn't around.

No one in Madison was enterprising enough to start a town paper so most of the news that reached the community came from the telegrapher's office and was passed by word of mouth. It was inevitable that someone always got the story wrong and just as inevitable that no one really seemed to care. Occasionally papers were brought in from Stillwater. The most reliable news came from Denver's *Rocky Mountain News*.

There were several accounts over a period of time about the robbery of No. 349. It was a chilling experience for Michael to read about her own death along with that of her colleagues. She was never identified by name, only as a passenger from the East, with no mention of her work for the *Chronicle*. She supposed she should have been thankful for the anonymity which protected her, yet mostly she was just angry that the reporter hadn't gotten the story right.

There was something else about the accounts that bothered her, but the only conclusion she could draw from it was so fantastic, and so at odds with what she had witnessed with her own eyes, that it couldn't have been true. Yet as time passed, the more credible the incredible seemed.

"You're frowning."

Michael didn't raise her head, only her eyes. She looked at Houston over the rims of her spectacles. His face was cast in shadow as he blocked sunlight from the window behind him. "Was I?" she asked. "I hadn't realized." She glanced around the saloon. Dee wasn't at the bar but Kitty was sweeping off the stage and Lottie was practicing a new piece at the piano.

Without waiting for an invitation, knowing better than to expect one, Houston pulled out a chair and seated himself next to Michael. He nudged one of the papers Michael had in front of her and skimmed it briefly. "Where did you get these?" he asked.

"Ethan gave them to me. He said there was nothing in them I couldn't read. Is there some problem with that?"

"No, no problem. I can't see why you'd want to though. Reporters never get their stories right. Worse, what they don't know they make up."

There was a shade of bitterness in his tone that Michael had never heard before. "Is that why you wanted all those reporters killed? Did you hate them personally or was it principle in general? The only good newspaperman is a dead one?"

Houston drew back slightly, surprised by her effrontery. His cold black eyes narrowed as the line between his brows deepened. "You don't know a thing about it," he said finally.

Michael had half suspected he would hit her. He looked as if he wanted to. "Tell me," she said quietly.

He considered it for a long moment. "Some other time."

"All right." She saw that she had surprised him again by not pressing the issue. She also had no doubt he would eventually tell her. Michael knew she might have to advance her questions and then retreat a half dozen more times between now and then, but in the end she would know something important about Nathaniel Houston. "Would you like some coffee?" she asked. "There's some fresh back in the kitchen. It's no trouble to get it."

"Let's both go back."

Michael hesitated. She looked around the saloon again wondering who might be in the kitchen. "I'm not sure . . ."

Houston leaned back in his chair. "You don't like being alone with me, do you?"

"I . . . I'm not . . . no, I don't like being alone with you."

"At least you're honest." He placed his large hand over her wrist, stood up, and pulled Michael to her feet. "C'mon. I can smell that coffee. Besides that, I have something for you."

Michael frowned, wondering what he meant. She began gathering up the papers.

Houston held her fast. "Leave them. They'll be safe right where they are."

Michael obeyed reluctantly.

In the kitchen she poured coffee for Houston and herself. "Have you had lunch?" she asked. "There's some cold chicken here somewhere."

"Sit down. You don't have to wait on me like I'm one of the customers."

"No, you're the owner."

"Which means I can get whatever I want when I want it." He pushed out a chair that was at a right angle to his.

Michael ignored it and chose one that was directly across from him. "You said you have something for me."

He smiled, reaching across the table to flick back a curl that had fallen against Michael's cheek. Even before he touched her he realized she was steeling herself not to flinch. He hoped that what he had for her would soften her view of him. "You're as greedy as Dee," he said.

The criticism stung. "I didn't mean —"

"I know." He withdrew his hand and flipped it over, palm up, showing her it was no longer empty. "I have this for you."

Michael stared at an ivory cameo framed in gold filigree, not quite believing what she was seeing. Slightly dazed, she lifted one hand to her ear as if something else might appear. Her hand dropped away slowly. "It's my brooch," she said. "The one you took on the train."

Houston nodded. He reached for her hand and dropped it in her palm, then folded her fingers around it. "I meant to have it as a memento of a rather remarkable encounter. It seems unnecessary with you here."

Tears pricked her eyes. Michael told herself that she shouldn't be grateful for receiving something that was hers in the first place. She told herself that she should give him the sharp edge of her tongue. "Thank you," she said quietly. She bent her head, blinking rapidly as she fiddled with the pin. She felt Houston's forefinger under her chin, forcing her to look up.

"Here," he said, taking the brooch from her shaking fingers. "Let me." He came around the table and fastened it to the center of her high collar. "This is what you were wearing on the train."

"Yes."

His dark eyes slid over her briefly. "It suits you."

Michael was very much afraid he meant to kiss her. She ducked her head quickly. He stood there a moment longer, looking down on her bent head while her heart beat madly with fear and uncertainty, then rounded the table and returned to his seat. Michael grasped for any conversational gambit. "I've been asking Ethan if I could venture out in the afternoons," she said, the words fairly rushing out. "Has he asked you about it?"

"He's mentioned it. Ethan's busy in the afternoon. Who would you go with?"

"Dee?"

"I don't think so. Not often anyway. She's tired of playing nursemaid to you."

"You could always let me go alone."

Half of Houston's mouth lifted in amusement. "I don't think so."

"Then one of the other girls?"

"They don't understand the importance of keeping you close and I'm not taking them into my confidence."

Michael's shoulders slumped a little. "Then there's no one."

"No one besides me, you mean." He folded his hands around his coffee cup, warming them.

"I wouldn't want to bother you."

"It's no bother. I make rounds every afternoon. Talk to the folks, make sure they know I'm around if they need me. I'm not a bad sheriff, Michael."

He really believed it, she realized. As if taking care of Madison somehow compensated for the fact that he robbed trains and murdered innocent people. It was such an appalling concept that Michael was struck dumb.

"This afternoon, for instance, I'm free to escort you."

"It's my turn to work the bar."

"I'll talk to Dee."

"I don't think—"

"Talk to Dee about what?" Detra asked. She was standing on the threshold of the kitchen, two ledgers in the crook of her arm.

"I'm taking Michael out for the afternoon. She's been cooped up in here too long."

"You're a fool, Houston. She means to go the first chance she has and you're playing into her hands." Dee put her ledgers on the table and poured herself a cup of coffee. "What's Ethan say about you sniffing after his wife's skirts?"

Michael set down her cup. It clattered in the saucer, nearly covering the small choked sound that came to her lips. "I'll be at the bar."

"Get your coat," Houston ordered. "We're leaving now. I'll wait for you at the bottom of the stairs."

Michael fled the room. When she was gone Houston turned to Dee. "Your jealousy isn't flattering any longer, Dee. It's boring. I suggest you do something about it." He left the kitchen.

Detra stared after her lover. "I intend to," she said softly. "I fully intend to."

Ethan was lying on his back on the floor, his head cradled in the palm of his hands. Except for the dim light from the stove and the lamp on the bedside table, the room was dark. Michael was sitting up in bed, recording the day's events in her diary. Ethan read it regularly, usually when she wasn't around, and thus far had found nothing objectionable in it.

"Are you almost done scribbling up there?" he asked. "I'd like to go to sleep."

"So?" Michael leaned over the edge of the bed. Her spectacles slipped down her nose. "Go to sleep."

"Can you write in the dark?"

"Of course not."

"Well, I can't sleep with the lamp burning."

"I'll hurry."

"Please." He listened to her scribbling a little while longer. He was getting used to the sound, he realized. It was part of their nighttime ritual, just like taking turns with the bath, making up his bed on the floor while she brushed out her hair, or keeping the fire in the stove from going out. "Are you writing about your outing with Houston?" he asked.

"I suppose Dee told you about that?"

"No, Houston did. He must have been feeling generous today. Taking you out *and* giving you that brooch."

"Did he tell you about the brooch?"

"No, he didn't have to. I saw it lying on the bureau and I remembered that Houston had kept that part of the bounty for himself."

"It was mine in the first place. He took it from me."

171

"And he gave it back?" Ethan made a soft whistling sound. "He really *does* want you." He heard Michael's pencil scratching stop momentarily as she felt the impact of his words. Inside, Ethan's stomach was roiling. Houston was stepping up his pursuit. Putting up a credible front of indifference, Ethan asked, "Where'd you go on your walk?"

"Just up one side of the street and down the other," she said, her words clipped.

"What did you talk about?"

Michael waved her notepad over the side of the bed so he could see it. "Would you like to read it now instead of waiting for morning when you think I'm sleeping?"

"Know about that, do you?"

"You're not so very clever."

He wondered if she knew that he emptied his gun every evening. He didn't ask. "I don't want to read it now." He had come to enjoy reading her observations over a cup of coffee in the morning. She was witty and astute and gave a good account of the things she saw. She was also a fine writer. "Tell me about it."

Michael laid the pad and pencil aside and felt herself relax just thinking about the afternoon. "We were only gone for an hour, perhaps not even that long. Oh, Ethan, you can't imagine . . . just breathing the air . . . It was . . . *liberating*. I would have gone mad being trapped here another day. Houston was charming, of course. He put on his best face. You know, the gentle, solicitous one where he appears genuinely interested in what a person has to say. He introduced me to some of the respectable women in town. They were courteous, more so because of Houston, I think. Once they realized I was one of Dee's girls they removed themselves rather quickly from the conversation."

"What did Houston do about that?"

"The same thing I did. Pretended not to notice." Michael rolled over and turned back the lamp. "It's been an odd experience here in Madison," she said. "I've been treated respectfully most of my life. Unless someone knows my family very well, my own morals are never questioned. Yet here, because so many people think you'll eventually tire of me, I'm touched without my permission and propositioned several times a day. I'm sought by married men and snubbed by married women. Houston wants me and Detra wants to kill me." She sighed. "It's not an arrangement I would have asked for myself."

Ethan stared at the ceiling. "Don't you think I know that?" he asked, more to himself than to Michael.

Michael scooted closer to the edge of the bed. "Houston took away the Denver papers you gave me," she said. "He was careful not to let me think he'd done it, but he got me out of the saloon and into the kitchen and when I returned to the table they were gone."

"One of the girls probably threw them away."

"I'm sure that's what happened. I'm just as sure Houston engineered it."

"Does it matter? You've read the accounts before."

"Why did you give me the papers, Ethan?"

His tone became impatient. "I thought you'd be interested, that's all."

Hardly all, Michael thought, if her suspicion was true. "It was kind of you." She heard him grunt softly, either in negation or acknowledgement, then he turned on his side away from her, signaling the end of the discussion. "Good night, Ethan."

"Night."

Ethan watched Michael slip out the door before he sat up and jerked on his trousers and boots. He didn't bother with a shirt and shrugged into his coat instead, taking just another few seconds to check his bureau drawer for the bullets. They were still there. Michael had left with his empty revolver.

He wasn't completely surprised by her action, only by the speed with which she was able to accomplish it. Her clothes had been hanging on the inside of the wardrobe and she dressed in the dark without bumping into anything. Ethan still didn't know what had woken him, but was thankful nonetheless. At best, Michael only had an inkling of the dangers she faced, or how quickly she would face them.

He supposed it was something she had seen earlier during her walk with Houston that led her to believe she could make an escape now. Although Ethan hurried he was only at the foot of the staircase when he heard the commotion on the sidewalk outside the saloon.

"You can put her down, Happy." Ethan said as he stepped outside. He raked his hair back from his forehead with his fingers, a sure sign he was out of patience.

Happy had hoisted Michael on his shoulder much the way Ethan had had occasion to do in the past. Michael, however, was fighting Happy for all she was worth, kicking and flailing and cursing. "She'll run!"

"She won't. Will you, Michael?"

"You bastard! I swear I'm going to—"

"You swear too much," Ethan said. "But we'll discuss that privately. Go on, Happy, put her down. She's not running away from Madison. She's only running out on me."

Happy hesitated. The punch Michael landed on the small of his back decided him. Grunting with pain and anger, he pushed her off. He grinned when she landed hard on her behind. The heel of his boot came down on her hand when she started to get up. "Stay put," he said roughly. He didn't press hard, but the weight on the back of her hand increased just enough to let Michael know he could seriously injure her. He spit once and addressed Ethan. "What do you mean she was runnin' out on you? Looks to me like she was hell bent on reachin' the livery over yonder. Leastways that's the direction she was headin' when I scooped her up in the street."

"I doubt she knew where she was heading, Happy. We had a fight."

"She was flashin' your gun at me."

Ethan was glad for the cover of night because he felt himself pale at Happy's revelation. "What stopped you from shooting her?"

"I remembered what you said once about takin' out the bullets."

"You took a chance."

"Damn right I did."

Ethan reached in the pocket of his coat and held up one of the bullets for Happy's inspection. "I've got them right here. The gun wasn't loaded." He jumped out of the way as Michael kicked at him and swore. "Where's the gun?" he asked Happy.

Happy jerked his head in the direction of the street. "She dropped it out there. Go on, I'll hold her here. You find it."

It took Ethan a few minutes to locate his Colt. All the while he could hear Michael muttering curses under her breath. Except for the soft sound of her angry voice the main street of Madison was quiet.

"Now, tell me why you're so sure she was just leavin' you," Happy said when Ethan returned.

"Because she caught Carmen flirting with me earlier this evening." That was true, but Michael hadn't said a word or acknowledged in any way that she was bothered by it.

"Carmen always flirts with you," Happy said.

"I was returning her regard."

Happy nudged Michael with the toe of his boot. "That right, Miz Stone? You jealous of your man?"

"Green with it," she said between clenched teeth. She knew Ethan's quick thinking was saving her life. She wasn't ready to thank him for it.

"C'mon, Happy, let her up. There's nothing I can't straighten out with her in private."

"Mebbe you need to put your gun in her holster a tad more often." His coarse eyebrows rose and fell suggestively. "If you take my meanin'."

175

Ethan jerked Michael to her feet, cutting off the epithets she was hurling at Happy. "Upstairs, Michael. I'm right behind you." He turned to Happy. "There's probably no need for you to stay here the rest of the night. She's not going to run out again."

"Better safe than sorry. I don't mind keepin' watch. Ben's turn tomorrow night."

"Suit yourself." He followed Michael into the saloon.

"You are a complete bastard," she whispered harshly. "Don't you put your hands on me. You knew—"

"Upstairs, Michael. Now. We'll discuss this in our room."

Michael pulled her elbow away from his hand and marched up the stairs, her spine stiff with the strength of her anger. As soon as they were in the room she rounded on him. The fact that he was not only latching the door but locking it with the key as well, served to further infuriate her. "You knew Houston had someone posted at the front of the saloon all these nights and you never told me! You showed me those papers from Denver, let me think I could trust you, and you betrayed me! You son of a bitch! I hope you see me in the front row of the crowd when you hang, Ethan Stone, because I'll be there and I'll be cheering!"

Ethan was peripherally aware of the brightness of her green eyes and the high natural color of her face as she vented her outrage at him. He was also vaguely aware that though she would never be beautiful when she was angry he had never wanted to kiss her more. He understood little of what she was saying, even less of what she wanted, but he knew he was tired of hearing her swear.

Taking Michael by the wrist, Ethan dragged her to the washstand. She was too blindly furious with him to understand his intention until the soap was hovering above her mouth.

She tried to twist away from him. "Let me go, you—"

Ethan wasn't certain what name she intended to call him, but he doubted it would be a kind one. He gently

176

stuffed one corner of the bar of soap between her lips. Michael's head reared back. Ethan kept applying pressure and the soap followed her motion. She tried to dislodge it by pushing at it with her tongue but that only made her get a better taste of the vile stuff.

"Had enough?" he asked politely. When she merely glared at him, refusing to answer, Ethan pushed the soap in a little more deeply. Michael's surrender came quickly then, muffled around the rounded edges of the cake of soap, but understandable in spite of that. Although Ethan withdrew the soap immediately, he still kept hold of it. When she tried to get away from him, he held her fast.

"Just a moment," he told her. "I want to be certain you're quite finished. Is there anything else you want to call me? Bring my heritage into question again?" It was difficult to be serious when Michael's face was contorting into a series of grimaces as she tried to get the taste of the soap out of her mouth. "No? Very well. You may rinse out your mouth." He let her go but kept her trapped between himself and the washstand. He poured her a small glass of water. "Here you go. Make certain you spit in the basin and not at me."

That he could read her thoughts so clearly was unnerving. Michael swished the water from side to side in her mouth, glaring at him all the while.

"You look like a squirrel when your cheeks puff out that way," he said.

Michael choked and nearly swallowed the rinse water. She managed to turn and spit in the basin just in time. Ethan's hand came down solidly on her back between her shoulder blades, then patted her heartily as she coughed and sputtered. "Do you mind?" she asked with some asperity. He wasn't hurting her exactly, but the thumping was rattling her heart and lungs.

Ethan stopped. "Sorry."

His apology surprised her. She turned to face him again, uncomfortably aware that he had given her no quarter, that he was still standing as close as he had a moment before. Perhaps he would apologize for something else. "You wouldn't have used that soap on me if you had ever had the misfortune to taste it yourself," she said.

Ethan raised the cake of soap and examined it. He even brought it close to his mouth as if he were seriously considering tasting it. "No," he said finally, setting it down behind Michael. "There's another way." He bent his head and his mouth settled over Michael's. He sipped her lips, sucking gently on the lower one, drawing it out with tender, insistent pressure. She took a step toward him, her hands at her sides, and their bodies remained separated by a small space of air. Her mouth moved under his. His tongue traced her lips, her teeth, and as she opened for him, he tasted her sweetness. Not for anything would he admit he couldn't taste the soap. He drew back slowly, watching her. She seemed to lean toward him, in reluctant pursuit of the kiss, then catch herself and hold her ground. Her darkening green eyes searched his face.

"Well?" she asked shakily.

Ethan shrugged. "I can see why you wouldn't like it," he said. "The soap, I mean."

Her nod was vague, her thoughts far away. "Of course, the soap."

Ethan took a step back and turned away. "I could use a drink. How about you?"

Michael sat down at the foot of the bed. She was going to repeat her standard, 'I-don't-drink,' and thought better of it. "Yes," she said. "I'd like one."

Ethan retrieved the bottle from the base of the wardrobe, grinning to himself. She sounded as if she'd like to fight him for the bottle. He poured a little whiskey into the water glass and handed it to her. Taking a shot glass and the bottle to the wing chair, Ethan sat down. He shrugged out of his coat and tossed it on the footstool.

"You're not wearing a shirt," Michael said. She

178

frowned, taking a large swallow of her drink. She was embarrassed that she had spoken her thoughts aloud and mortified that she sounded so hopelessly idiotic.

"I suppose it's your job as a reporter that's made you so observant."

And trust him not to let the comment pass. Michael finished off her drink and actually enjoyed the rush of fire from her throat to the pit of her stomach. Without waiting for him to offer another, she got up, poured a generous two fingers in her glass, and went back to the bed.

"I was in a hurry to chase you down," he said. "Before you got into more trouble than you could handle. I almost didn't bother with jeans." He saw her take another quick sip. "You can take off your coat, you know. Unless you mean to sleep in it tonight. Or go out again."

Michael put down her glass long enough to get rid of the coat. "I'm not going anywhere."

"Very wise." He knocked back a shot of whiskey. "It was a pretty stupid thing to do, even for you."

She didn't say anything.

"Stop doing that," he said.

"What?"

"Looking at me like that."

Michael still had enough inhibition left to blush, but not enough to keep quiet. "I'm sorry," she said, looking down at the glass she was rolling between her palms. "It's just that I was remembering something Kitty said . . . about you being a beautiful man." She glanced up in time to see a ruddy hue touch his lean cheeks. Her grin was a trifle lopsided and not at all repentant. "Oh dear, I've embarrassed you."

"You've flattered me," he said, "and embarrassed yourself. Little wonder you don't drink much. You trip over your own tongue with just a whiff of the stuff." He got up and took the half-emptied glass from her. "You've had enough. Why don't you get ready for bed?" Ethan threw her the nightshirt she had worn earlier. "Go on. I'll turn my back."

"Oh, very well," she sighed. Michael didn't move to obey right away. Instead she found herself staring at Ethan's naked back, at the angle of his shoulder blades, at the tautness of his skin. She wanted to run a finger down the length of his spine. She wanted to trace it with her tongue.

When Ethan didn't hear her moving he glanced over his shoulder. He was in time to catch her staring at him. He said her name sharply and watched her jerk to attention. "You're playing hell with my patience. Now get ready for bed."

"Yes, sir," she said meekly.

Her display of humility was so out of character for her that Ethan found himself grinning again. What was he supposed to do with her? he wondered. For the past two weeks he could only think about getting his hands around her neck, either to choke her or hold her steady while he kissed her senseless. He'd held himself back from doing either. Until tonight, when he had been desperate enough to do both. "Are you almost finished?" he asked roughly.

She nodded.

"If you're shaking your head, I can't hear you," he told her.

Michael giggled. "That shoots down your theory, doesn't it?"

"What theory?" he asked impatiently.

"The one that says I have rocks in my head. You'd hear them rattle, wouldn't you?"

Ethan turned around then. Michael was just pulling the nightshirt modestly over her knees. She almost looked prim. Almost. But there was her hair which had been loosed from every confining pin and lay across her shoulders and back in all its magnificent splendor. There was the delicate hollow of her throat which was laid bare by the open collar of his nightshirt. Then there was the way her lips came together as she swallowed her

180

smile. His blue-gray eyes slid over her hair, her throat, and came to rest on her mouth.

"I'm about tired of sleeping on the floor," he said in a low voice. Then he came toward her.

Michael was drawn to her feet though Ethan never touched her. She raised her face. Her eyes held his.

"This is when you should tell me to stop." Ethan saw that she never moved. She stood there still as stone, yet he felt her tremble. "Can you?"

Michael blinked once. Her mouth parted slightly. No sound came.

"Can you?" he asked again, his voice just above a whisper.

"No."

She had never thought when she conceived her scheme for escape that it would bring her to this pass, yet against all reason she couldn't conceive of any other place she wanted to be. She understood now that she had been wrong about the articles in the Denver paper, not wrong about their content, but wrong about the significance she had attached to them. Ethan had given them to her for a reason, whether he realized it or not. She had misinterpreted the gesture. She thought he'd meant for her to trust him enough to make her escape. She knew now he'd meant for her to trust him enough to make her stay.

Ethan's hands slid under Michael's hair and rested lightly against the skin of her neck. Beneath the callused pads of his fingers she was incredibly soft. He stroked her from the back of her ear to the curve of her shoulder. His thumbs caressed the soft underside of her jaw. Her hair was a whisper against the back of his hands, silk against his knuckles.

"Touch me," he said. When he saw her hesitate his hands circled her wrists and lifted her fingers to his chest. "Here. Anywhere. If you don't touch me I'll come out of my skin." His eyes had gone from flint to smoke. "It will probably happen anyway."

181

Her fingers explored. Lightly at first, hesitantly, but not reluctantly. She wanted to touch him. When she was being honest with herself she could admit to wanting to touch him for a long time. Her palms curved over his chest, ran softly along his rib cage, and learned about the heat and tension of his flesh. She felt him suck in his breath as her fingers made a light pass across his abdomen. His skin retracted in anticipation of her touch.

"Yes," he said. "Just that way."

Her fingers slid along the edge of his jeans. Her hands disappeared behind his back and moved slowly over his skin. She felt the taut smoothness of him, the warmth and strength of him. Her stroking brought her flush against him and Michael knew the shape of Ethan by the planes and curves of her own body. And yet she had never been so aware of herself as when she was touching Ethan.

Her breasts were fuller, slightly swollen and tender, aching with the need to be caressed by his hands. Her belly felt flat and hard, full of tension. And her hips, where they were pocketed by his thighs, had an emptiness in their middle she only partially understood.

Ethan's hands drifted over the neckline of the nightshirt, his fingers sliding just beneath the material to whisper across her skin. She held her breath as he undid the first button. It made him smile.

He set her back slightly so that he could see what he was doing, enjoy what he was uncovering. He began to widen the gap in the neckline.

Michael's fingers curled around his wrists, gripping him tightly. Her dark green eyes were anxious, imploring. "Please," she said, a catch in the single word. "The lamp. Couldn't we . . ."

"Turn it back?" he asked.

She nodded.

"No." He didn't move and she didn't release her grip. "I want to see you," he said. "All this time . . . I've only imagined." He waited. Warm color tinged her skin. The fingers around his wrists eased slightly.

"All right."

He saw that she seemed surprised by her answer, as if she hadn't known she would say it until it was said, as if her response were against her will. He waited again, giving her a chance to change her mind. She didn't. In the end her hands slipped away from his. "It will be all right," he said softly, brushing her eyelids with his mouth. "I won't hurt you."

A small shudder swept through her. Her eyes fluttered open. "I know."

He nodded. "Then watch me," he told her. "Watch my hands on your skin."

Her eyes dropped from his face to his hands. His knuckles brushed the curve of her breasts as his fingers dropped to the next button. He undid it. His hands slipped inside the nightshirt and lifted slowly, caressing the smooth skin of her stomach then cupping the underside of her breasts. The nightshirt slid off one shoulder. Ethan bent, his mouth took in the tip of her breast and sucked.

Michael's hands came to rest on Ethan's shoulders, not to push him away, but to clutch him. His mouth was hot and wet on her nipple, his tongue sweetly rough. The ache she felt in her breast was deeper now but somehow more deeply pleasurable. The nightshirt slid from her other shoulder as Ethan's mouth moved into the hollow between her breasts. Her fingers lifted and caught the ends of his hair. There was a little tug as she threaded between the strands, stroked, and learned the texture of it. She caressed the nape of his neck. She thought she heard him groan. She didn't trust what she heard anymore, only what she felt. And she knew she felt the hard press of his mouth to her skin in that moment.

The nightshirt fell to the floor. Ethan's arms curved around her back and below her hips. He lifted her easily and set her down on the bed, following her with his body. Pushing her back, he stretched out beside her.

183

One hand rested against her waist. His thumb made a slow arc across her skin.

"So soft," he said. "You can't even know . . ." He bent his head and touched his mouth to her collarbone. His tongue made a small damp spot on her skin. Brushing aside her hair, he nuzzled her neck. His lips teased her skin, drawing it into his mouth, sucking gently. She stirred restlessly beside him. He moved one leg to trap her and his hand slid from her waist to her hip. His fingers curved around her buttock and pressed against her flesh.

Ethan continued to tease her with his mouth. He traced the line of her throat, her jaw, tickled her ear with his tongue. He held her head immobile while he kissed her feathered brows, her eyelids, the arch of her cheeks. When he finally settled his mouth over hers she was hungry for the taste and feel of him.

The kiss she returned was hard. No longer just sweetly eager, Michael was fully responsive, opening her mouth under his to return the fullness of his kiss measure for measure. It was she who pressed for a deeper kiss, sweeping her tongue along the line of his teeth and into his mouth. When she moved this time it was not to get away but to get closer. Michael arched against Ethan's chest, slipping her arms around his shoulders, keeping her fingers threaded in his hair. The pressure of his body was an exquisite sensation everywhere he touched her. She rubbed against him.

"Whoa," he chided softly, raising his head. The centers of her eyes were black as polished ebony and so large there was only a sliver of emerald surrounding them. Her mouth was damp and beautifully swollen. He kissed her lightly. Then again. "God, you're sweet. I don't think — " He didn't finish as he started to sit up.

"Ethan?"

He bent again and kissed her swiftly. "I have to get these boots off. The jeans, too. And if I don't slow us down I won't be able — " He cursed softly as the left boot proved to be a tougher customer than the right one.

Michael was unhappily aware of her naked body stretched out on top of the bed. When Ethan had been covering her it didn't seem so brazen somehow. With his back turned as he worked on the boots, Michael slipped between the sheets. They were cool to her flushed skin. "Won't be able to what?"

"Won't be able to last more than three seconds inside you," he said bluntly.

"Is that so bad?"

He looked over his shoulder while he worked off his jeans. One of his dark brows was arched skeptically. "It is if you want any pleasure." He saw her frown. Her well-kissed mouth flattened just a little. Ethan managed to kick off his jeans. They cartwheeled in the air and landed on the wing chair. Turning back the lamp, Ethan slipped under the sheet and comforter and warmed Michael's feet with his. "Is that it, Michael?" he asked, searching her out with his hands. His thumb brushed one nipple. The sound she made in the back of her throat was still audible. "Is that why you explode in my arms? No man's ever pleasured you?"

"No man," she whispered. She felt the heat of his mouth. She closed her eyes and knew that in another moment he would touch her with his lips. His tongue would be sweet and insistent and curious. She would give him whatever he wanted. "I *do* explode in your arms." She wasn't sure she liked the idea.

"You don't sound happy about it." That, at least, he understood. She thought he was a robber and a murderer. She was denying every value she held dear so she didn't have to deny him. He didn't want to think about it. He didn't want her to think about it. That's why he kissed her hard and long and sweet and deep.

Ethan's knee insinuated itself between Michael's legs. His hand trailed lightly from her breast to her thighs. He cupped her mound with his hand and pressed when she jerked against him reflexively. "It's all right," he whis-

185

pered, taking her mouth again. His fingers sought her out, searching, stroking, pleasuring. She was moist and warm. He wanted to use his mouth but he held back and was satisfied for now with the urgent sounds she could not contain.

He moved so she could feel how hard he was against her belly. He wanted to be inside her desperately. Instead he used one finger. She gasped. Her fingers dug into his upper arms but her body accommodated his seeking. Her movements became less restless and more purposeful.

"That's it," he encouraged as she moved her hips against him. "Will you take me now?"

"Yes." The sound was a little eager, a little panicked. Ethan's mouth was on her breast then, soothing the panic, playing to the eagerness. He laved her nipple with his tongue, worried the bud between his lips and tugged. Tension radiated just under the surface of her skin. She felt it in the tips of her fingers, in the length of her legs, and most especially between her thighs where his hand continued its intimate caress.

Ethan moved over her, covering her with his body just for a moment. The sheet slipped down his back as he positioned himself between her thighs. He helped her raise her hips and before he realized she was clutching the sheet in a white-knuckled grip, he was inside her.

She was so tight. Too tight. And he knew he was hurting her when it was the very thing he promised not to do. He held himself very still, denial making his features hard and angry, and his eyes, even in the dim light, burn with a blue-white intensity.

"Why?" he asked roughly as her body tried to accommodate him. "Damn you! Why?"

Michael couldn't pretend she didn't know what he was asking. Her fears of being too clumsy to pass as experienced were borne home. If he didn't know for certain, he at least suspected that until a moment ago she'd been a virgin. "I didn't know it would bother you," she said. She squirmed slightly under him.

He practically growled. "For God's sake, don't move."

"You said yourself no man had ever pleasured me."

"I didn't mean that no man had ever had the opportunity."

It didn't seem prudent to tell him to be more clear in the future.

Chapter Seven

"Ethan?" She said his name hesitantly. Her hands came up to touch his face. She felt the tension in his features beneath her fingertips. "Don't you want me now?"

He shut his eyes and tried not to think of how good it felt to be inside her with her hands on his face and her legs curved against his thighs. Even as he started to withdraw he felt the hot, moist center of her tighten around him. "What I didn't want was everything complicated by a virgin." He swore as her body, probably without her even being aware of it, tightened around him again. He couldn't contain the thrust that followed. He was aware that Michael moved with him. "Damn you," he said. "Tell me to stop."

"I told you I wouldn't," she said. More softly she added, "And I'm not a virgin anymore."

Her husky voice did what her hands and legs couldn't do: pushed Ethan over the edge. "It's that sweet mouth of yours," he said, slanting his mouth across hers. "It's always getting you in trouble."

His thrust was hard and sure. He wanted to take his time, to draw out the pleasure. It was much too late for that. He needed to take her swiftly, needed to feel, not think. His hips quickened as a force outside himself seemed to take over. The pleasure was there because Michael met him thrust for thrust, hungry and as needy as he. That loving could be so mutually greedy and satisfying was a new experience for Ethan. Her hands clutched and caressed him, her mouth tasted and teased, and when she reached the point of pleasure's end her mouth opened under his and he felt the rush of tension pass from her into him. His name was on her lips. He swore he could taste her wonderment. The shudder that shook her became his a few moments later. She stroked his hair as he spilled his seed.

Neither of them moved for several minutes. Finally Ethan raised himself away from her. The bed creaked. He wondered if it had creaked the entire time they were making love. Probably. He hadn't noticed.

He kicked a boot out of the way as he headed for the washstand. He thought about lighting a lamp but decided Michael wasn't quite ready for that. When he was finished cleaning himself he carried fresh water and cloth to Michael's side. "There might be blood," he said. "You may want to wash."

When he sat on the edge of the bed he was close enough to feel her stiffen. "Mortified or scared of me?" he asked frankly.

"Mortified."

"Do you want me to wash you?"

"God, no!" She sat up, thankful there was only a little light in the room from the stove. "Turn your back. And stop grinning. I know you're grinning. And looking smug. Unbearably smug. Is your back really turned?"

"Absolutely."

She breathed a little easier. "I don't think I'm bleeding, but there's something that's—"

"That's me."

Her head jerked up. "What?"

"That's me. My seed. What you took from me and into you. Hasn't anyone explained these things?"

189

"Of course they've been explained," she snapped, tossing the cloth back in the basin. Droplets of water splashed Ethan's back. He reached for the basin and carried it back to the washstand. Her softly stunned voice followed him. "It's just that the reality is so much more . . . *real.*"

He tamped down a smile. "It is that." He pulled on a pair of drawers and passed Michael her nightshirt. "Put that back on. You may just get some sleep that way."

She cocked her head to one side, not certain she understood. "You mean . . . again . . . this very night?"

Ethan shrugged. "As you so poignantly pointed out earlier: you're not a virgin any longer. Move over. No matter what does or doesn't happen between us, I'm not sleeping on the floor anymore." He stoked the fire while Michael put on the nightshirt. When he returned to the bed there was a space for him. "You don't have to sleep way over there."

Her move toward him was a trifle cautious. "I'm new at this."

"You don't have to remind me. The question is why?" He was turned on his side, his head propped on one elbow. His hand seemed to gravitate of its own accord toward Michael's hair. He sifted the wild curls with his fingers.

"Why what?" she asked.

"Why there's never been anyone before me."

"You'd have been more comfortable with that, wouldn't you?"

"Hell, yes."

"Are you afraid I'll want marriage?"

He shook his head. "If you recall, I offered that your first night here. You turned me down flat. I don't fancy things have changed that much." He found another curl and twisted it around his finger. "What about those fellas you traveled with on the train?"

190

"I worked too hard to make them accept me as one of the boys to allow them to see me as a woman. I wanted to just be a *person*. But it isn't possible sometimes. It's newspaper*men*. The good ol' *boys*. Even on the poker table kings are high. I graduated from a college for women but most of the professors were men. I was at the top of my class and I had to start at a position below men who weren't nearly as good as I was. I didn't mind starting at the bottom, only I thought they should have been there too. I've scrambled and scratched and made them notice me at the *Chronicle* for what I could *do*. Not for what I am."

"But you *are* a woman."

"You don't understand," she said with husky urgency, trying to make her point. "It's not that I don't want to be a woman. I just want the same opportunities as a man. I want to walk the streets alone without being considered a streetwalker. I want to work in a newsroom without my presence being newsworthy. I want my name to mean something aside from my husband's. I want to vote for the next mayor of Tammany Hall. And even if she's a complete idiot, at least I'll know I had some choice in the matter of putting her there."

Ethan thought about that. "And what about the other things men have to do?"

"I suppose you're speaking of wars," she said, sighing that she was not eloquent enough to make him understand. "It seems that invariably the argument turns to war. Have I given you any reason to think that I wouldn't fight for something I believed in?"

Ethan's fingers paused in their sifting of her hair. "No," he said. After a moment he added, "Quite the opposite, in fact."

His admission stunned her and quite helpless to call them back, tears stung her eyes. She brushed them away impatiently. Tears always seemed to lend their

191

weight on the side of a woman's frailty.

Ethan saw the sparkle of tears, felt the hurried swipe of her hand across her face. He leaned over and touched his mouth to her closed eyes. He tasted the sweet and salty wetness. He found her mouth and kissed her watery smile. "Still," he said, "why me?" Why would you allow me to be the first man in your bed?"

"You're not going to let this rest, are you?"

"No."

She sighed. "Very well. There are a lot of reasons, I suppose. For you I wanted to be seen as a woman. I thought it might be to my advantage. I've seen how the women here manipulate the customers, teasing and flirting and eventually getting what they want. It doesn't always have to end up in the bedroom. The men are often satisfied with a smile or a companion who simply listens to them. But sometimes it needs to go beyond sharing a drink and some companionship and I thought that would be true in your case."

"Wait a minute," he said. "You're telling me you deliberately set out to manipulate me."

"More or less."

Ethan just shook his head, bewildered by her confession. "You have a lot to learn about feminine wiles. You can't be so honest about your motives and still expect to be manipulative."

"Exactly," she said triumphantly.

"Exactly?"

"Hmm-mmm. I abandoned the entire idea. Don't you see? Feminine wiles, as you call them, simply didn't suit me. Oh, I can be wily, I think, but I had so much trouble with the feminine part. The one time I really wanted to be noticed as a woman, and I couldn't make it happen."

Ethan's dark brows nearly rose to his hairline. "Not be noticed as a woman? What in the world are you talking about? Houston's been dogging your steps since he got his first good look at you. Detra sees you as a rival. The miners take a dance with you every chance they get. When you kick up your legs on stage no one with eyes in their head thinks of you as anything but a woman."

"But none of those people will help me. I needed *you* to notice me. I thought you were the most likely one to help me get away."

"So you thought a virgin sacrifice was in order?"

Michael didn't know whether to slap his face or laugh. She did neither, counting to ten instead. "I told you I abandoned the idea. Not only couldn't I get you to notice me, I wasn't certain I wanted you to."

"I seem to recall a few kisses."

"I haven't forgotten them either, but I didn't know what I wanted then. The thought of you in my bed then was abhorrent. By the time I realized there might be some advantage in it, you didn't seem to be interested."

Ethan couldn't remember ever *not* being interested. Apparently he'd been more successful in hiding his thoughts than he'd suspected. "So you gave up trying to seduce me because you thought you couldn't do it, you weren't certain you wanted to, and you didn't have any real assurance that I'd help you escape."

"I never said the last thing you mentioned."

"No, I did. Because it's true. I won't help you get away from here." It was too dangerous. She couldn't do it on her own and he wasn't ready to go with her. He couldn't tell her those things.

"I realize that now." The feel of his fingers in her hair, against her scalp, was so gentle, so soothing. She felt as if she could give herself up to him. Then he reminded her that he wasn't so different from the men he rode with. He seemed bent on making her understand he wasn't her hero. "I suppose I didn't take the right meaning from those articles you gave me."

"The articles? You mean the ones about the robbery? From the Denver paper?"

She nodded. The movement brought his thumb in contact with her lower lip. He ran it along its length. Her tongue touched the very tip. She heard his breath catch.

"Michael?"

"Yes?"

"If you're wanting me to notice you as a woman right now, you're doing a helluva job."

"I am?"

In answer he found her hand and brought it to his groin. She could feel the heat and hardness of him through his drawers.

"Oh, my," she said softly. "Does it hurt?"

Her question elicited something between laughter and a groan. Ethan leaned over and pressed his mouth and body against her. His hands pushed up her nightshirt. Her hands were tugging at his drawers. "You're sure?" he asked. His hungry mouth was against her ear.

"Please . . . yes . . . I want you."

There were no preliminaries this time. She was ready for him and Ethan drove into her hard. Her heels pressed into the bedding as she lifted for his thrusts. The pads of her fingers pressed whitely into his arms. Her mouth sought his. Their tongues matched the energy and motion of their bodies. His hands stroked her. He couldn't touch her in enough places. Her hair. Her breasts. Her mouth. The sensitive inside of her elbow. Her skin was fragrant, musky. It was his own scent he smelled, the scent of him on her while he was in her deeply, filling her, touching her so intimately that he was part of her. And she held him, rocked with him, and accepted from him what she had never accepted from any man. She clung to him and there were soft keening cries at the back of her throat, urgent little murmurs that spoke of her pleasure, her passion. She felt the sleekness of his muscled back, the tension that rippled through him as her hands caressed. There was the wetness of her mouth on his shoulder and at his throat, her fingers in his ebony hair, her calves stretched out beside the length of his. She twisted beneath him, rising, falling, arching in her need. His long beautiful fingers were in the thickness of her hair. He whispered her name and his breath was hot on her face. She tasted her name on his lips. His whiskey soft voice held secrets and pleasure.

Michael shuddered. The long line of her neck was exposed as she arched with the force of her release. Her body strained with the fullness of her pleasure. She felt the cadence of Ethan's rhythm change, the stroking became more shallow and furious and then the final thrust and the tension in every part of his body as he spilled himself into her.

Their breathing was harsh, their bodies damp. Ethan turned so that Michael could lie comfortably on her side and rest against him. His hand slipped beneath the neckline of the nightshirt and felt the steady strength of her heart. He brought her hand to his. The beats were in unison.

"Are you all right?" he asked after awhile. "I didn't hurt you, did I?"

"No. No hurt."

"I was rough."

"I didn't mind." She touched his shoulder, exploring with her fingers. "I think I was rough back." She found a small indentation on his flesh. "Did I *bite* you?"

"Old wound," he said, raising her fingers to his mouth. He kissed the tip of each one in turn. "But you did bite me." He didn't need light to know that she was embarrassed by the revelation. He could feel the heat in her cheek against his chest. "I didn't mind. I've never been with a woman who enjoys loving the way you do." And he hadn't, he thought. Michael was the most completely sensual woman he had ever known, in or out of bed. She liked to touch things. He'd seen her hands smooth over the folds of a dress she was putting away. She ran her fingers around the corners of her notepad whenever she closed it for the night. He thought she was familiar with the texture of most everything she saw because it was part of her nature to touch. She liked the cold, the heat. She'd sit at the window watching snow fall for hours if he didn't make her turn in. He'd seen her working in the kitchen taking hot pies from the oven, holding them just below her face so she could inhale the steam and the fragrance. She'd sat at the table one Sunday morning with a mug of hot chocolate in her hands. Between sipping it so delicately, enjoying the sweet aroma, and warming her hands, she'd let it grow mostly cold. He'd thought then that no one had ever enjoyed simple pleasures the way Michael did.

"Is that a bad thing," she asked, "to enjoy it so much? My mother says it's not."

"Your mother's a wise woman then."

"I wonder," Michael said lowly, more to herself than to Ethan. "Some people think my mother's a whore."

Ethan wondered what he was supposed to say to that. "I've mostly been with whores," he said finally. "If they happened to enjoy it, they still enjoyed my money more."

"It was never about money to my mother. It was always about love. Love made her stupid." Bitterness tinged her voice. "It won't happen to me. I won't let it."

It occurred to Ethan that she was trying to convince herself. That meant in some corner of her mind she was afraid it *could* happen. Mary Michael Dennehy

196

feared taking the same path as her mother. Ethan stroked her hair. When he spoke his breath ruffled strands of it. "You won't let it," he repeated softly.

"I love my mother."

"Hmm-mm."

"But I don't respect what she became for him."

"Him?"

"My father."

Ethan said nothing. His hand slipped to her shoulder. He caressed her lightly, soothingly, without sexual intent. In a few minutes she was asleep. A little while after that so was he.

When they woke it was just dawn. Light spotted the room through the checked curtains. The stove was cold. They were making love.

Michael blinked widely. "How did —"

"I don't —"

"It feels —"

"Good. Do you —"

"Want it?"

"Yes."

"Yes," she said.

His groan was captured by her mouth. His hips ground against hers. They spoke all the while, in half-sentences, finishing uncompleted thoughts for each other, never erring in the interpretation. He seemed to know precisely where to touch her to get the response he wanted. She seemed to know just how to caress him to make him want her more.

She couldn't be this soft, he thought. He couldn't be this hard, she thought. She was eager and filled with wanting. He was hungry and filled her with him. They rolled across the top of the bed, tangling in the sheets. Neither of them noticed when the comforter fell over the side of the bed and onto the floor. They were still warm in the cold room. They were laughing.

His fingers tickled her then his mouth made her burn. She batted at him playfully then her hands clutched him fiercely. She drove her body up against him as he drove into her. He spent first, then held her, stroking, until she shivered with pleasure in his arms.

They slept again.

The sun was only a little higher in the sky when they woke the second time. Without a word of his intentions, Ethan bounded out of bed, slipped on a pair of jeans, and left the room. The banging of the tub as he dragged it down the hall announced his return. Someone from another room yelled for a little quiet. Michael grinned as Ethan came into view.

She held a finger to her lips, slightly swollen with his kisses. "Sunday morning," she said.

Ethan merely grunted. He went after buckets of water and a kettle for heating it.

While he was gone Michael wrapped herself in the comforter and sat in a chair near the window. She pulled back the curtains. There were frost flowers on the panes. She blew on them softly, melting them with her warm breath. Clearing one pane, she wiped away the condensation with the back of her hand and looked out. The sun was shining brightly now but there had been another snowfall during the night. The hitching posts wore thick white caps of snow. It lay still and unmarked on the tops of porches and eaves. It filled the rutted street making it seem smooth as cotton bunting. Icicles just above her window dripped rainbows of color on the sill.

"Your bath awaits," Ethan said. When she didn't move Ethan went to the window. Her head was resting at an angle against the frame. She'd fallen asleep again just sitting there in the chair. "Michael," he said softly. "Sleepyhead."

"Mmmm?"

He kissed her on the mouth, a light and nibbling kiss that engaged her almost instantly. When he straightened he was smiling. "Your bath," he said again. "Or should I use the water first?" He laughed as she jumped to her feet, nearly tripping over herself to lay claim to the fresh hot water. "I guess not." He plopped himself down on the bed while Michael slipped into the tub. "Too hot?"

"No. It's wonderful."

"Too much water."

"No."

Half his mouth lifted in a lopsided grin. "No, I mean there's too much water for me. You're all covered up."

She flicked water at him. It splattered harmlessly on the floor.

"While I'm taking my bath," he said, "you can do something about breakfast."

"Eat it, you mean."

"Bring it here, I mean. Eggs. Two of them over easy. Flapjacks if Lottie's making them. Forget them if they're Kitty's. I wouldn't mind some of that pastry you were baking yesterday. A pot of hot coffee. Bacon would be nice."

"I doubt I can carry all of that."

"You'll have to think of a better excuse. I've seen you manage three pitchers of beer and a tray of glasses."

Michael sighed dramatically. "All right," she said with feigned reluctance. "But only because you let me use the bathwater first."

"I'll keep that in mind."

"That's very wise of you," she said sweetly.

Ethan punched two pillows, making them fuller so he could stuff them behind the small of his back. He leaned against the headboard. "You know you've never told me why," he said with casual interest. "You said you abandoned the idea of trying to manipulate me, but you've never really said what led up to last night."

"Didn't I?" She frowned, trying to remember what she'd told him. She soaped her arm absently. "I thought I mentioned the Denver papers."

"You did. But it doesn't mean anything to me."

"But you're the one who gave them to me to read."

"So? I read them too. There's nothing in them that you didn't already know."

She tilted her head in his direction, her look questioning. "Yes, there was."

"I sure as hell don't understand what you're talking about."

"I admit I was confused at first." Her voice was low so there was no chance she could be overheard beyond their room. "I thought you meant it as a message to me that I could leave."

"You said that last night. You said I betrayed you."

"For stopping me. I did feel betrayed. I thought you were giving me a clear signal to go when I was ready. Instead I discover Happy's outside the saloon just waiting for the opportunity to catch me. You knew he was there. Of course I felt betrayed."

Ethan still didn't understand. He pinched the bridge of nose with his thumb and forefinger and rubbed gently, thinking.

"Then I realized that you didn't mean for me to go, that your message was a little different than that. You simply wanted me to trust you. And I did. *Do*. Last night was proof of that. I would have never let you touch me like that if you hadn't shown me the Denver papers."

"The papers again," he sighed. "What did you read that I don't know about?"

A faint frown line appeared between Michael's

200

brows. Her wide mouth turned serious. "Nothing," she said. "Just the articles about the robbery."

"And?" he prompted. "There must be something else."

"And I know you didn't kill Drew Beaumont."

"What?" Belatedly he realized he had shouted the word. Michael had sunk lower in the tub. Her head jerked back and her eyes widened in surprise. "What?" he repeated more softly. "What makes you say that? You saw it with your own eyes."

"I know what I saw," she said. "But it doesn't make sense because I also know what I read."

"None of those articles mentioned anything about Drew except as a victim."

"Knowing Drew he probably took some perverse pleasure in that."

"What are you saying?"

"Drew wrote the articles."

Ethan shook his head in denial of something he didn't want to think about. "No, he didn't. I killed him. I shot him in the chest and I kicked him over the side of the mountain."

"Just like you and Obie pretended to kill me."

"Yes . . . no! Not like that at all. There was no pretending about Drew. What ever you think you know, Michael, you don't know at all. Drew's dead."

"It's all right," she said. "I won't tell anyone differently. I've seen that some of the others don't completely trust you. My presence has only made things worse for you. But I don't think you have the stomach for murder that they have. That's why you didn't kill me and that's why you didn't kill Drew."

"You're wrong."

"I'm not."

"What makes you so damn sure?" He had to discover if he was vulnerable to the others or only to her. "And don't say the articles. I read them, remember."

In spite of the warm water a chill swept through Michael. He hadn't known. Not at all. He'd given her the papers to read and meant nothing by it. He wasn't asking for her trust, he wasn't asking for her help, he wasn't offering anything. She grabbed a towel and started to rise, wrapping it quickly around her. There was an unfamiliar ache between her thighs as she stood, not unpleasant, just unwelcome now that she understood what she hadn't before.

Ethan watched coldness seep into her, witnessed her withdrawal with his own eyes. She was as defensive as a soldier raising battlements. She slipped into the blood red robe that was Houston's contribution to her clothing. She reached beneath it, pulled off the towel, and began rubbing her hair dry.

"Michael," Ethan said. "Answer me. What did you read?"

Her head snapped up and the towel fell around her shoulders. "Every writer has a style unique to him," she said emotionlessly. "You've read my work in my diary. I'd be surprised if you couldn't recognize my writing at some later time, even if you didn't know I was the author of the piece, or even if I used another name. Writing is that individual. Like a signature. I worked with Drew for two years. I've read hundreds of articles that he's written. I know his style almost as well as I know my own. Drew Beaumont wrote those pieces for the *Chronicle* and they were picked up by the Denver paper, probably by a hundred other papers. Drew finally got his national story because you let him live."

"You must be wrong."

She shook her head. "You can deny it all you like, but it doesn't change what I know. It occurred to me that you only *thought* you might have killed him, that he survived in spite of some wound. But if that were true he would have used his name. This is a story that

202

deserves a byline and Drew would have made certain he got it. When I came upon you your kerchief was around your neck. Drew saw your face yet there's no description of you beyond what is similar to Houston and the others. Drew was close enough to you to have an artist sketch your face later. But there's nothing like that and I asked myself why. There's only one reason that makes sense and that's that he knows I'm with you and he's protecting me by protecting you."

"You've given the matter a great deal of thought, I see." He swung his legs over the side of the bed and started to undress. He noticed Michael gave immediate attention to her hair again, letting it hang down either side of her face while she buried her head in the towel. "And you keep coming to the wrong conclusions."

"I know." Her voice was muffled.

"What?"

Her head sprung up. Her eyes flashed. He was standing beside the tub, naked and unselfconscious about it. That he appeared to have no shame made her even angrier. She threw the towel at him. "I said I know," she snapped.

Ethan caught the towel, knew what he was supposed to do with it, and deliberately pitched it to the floor. He watched her push herself out of the chair and turn her back on him. He slipped into the tub in his own sweet time. "If you know your conclusions are wrong then why do you keep insisting Drew's alive?"

Michael began making up the bed. She saw the stained sheets and angrily tore them off. She went to the wardrobe for fresh linens. "My wrong conclusions aren't the same as yours. Drew *is* alive. I was wrong about other things."

"Such as?"

Michael snapped open a sheet and laid it smoothly across the mattress. With swift, economic motions she made triangular creases at all four corners and tucked it under. "I believed you knew it was Drew's writings in those articles. An unfortunate assumption on my part. From there I concluded it was safe for me to leave. We both know that was incorrect. I believed then that you were asking me to trust you, telling me in the only way you could that I could at least rely on you. Do you think I would have gone to bed with you if I hadn't believed you didn't kill Drew?"

"Lower your voice!"

"Don't shout at me!"

Ethan forced himself to take a calming breath. "Get another bar of soap for me, please." He held up the sliver she had been using. "This is useless."

Michael found one and threw it at him. It slipped through his fingers and knocked him hard in the chest. She winced, knowing it must have hurt, and waited to see what he would do. She half expected him to come out of the tub and force her to eat the thing. She hated the fact that he could still frighten her.

Ethan watched her face, saw her fear, and held his temper. Things could be, if not precisely simple for him, then at least more pleasurable, if he would tell her the truth. He could, he reasoned, but then he'd live each day wondering if she'd do something to give him away. He wanted to trust her. It said more about him than it did about Michael that he couldn't. He hadn't the least desire to take inventory of his failings now. It was enough that he knew they were considerable.

"Stop trying to make me into something I'm not," he told her. "There's only one reason you leaped to all those fantastic conclusions and that's because last night you were right where you wanted to be: in my bed and not alone. You were sick and tired of your virginity, curious to know a man, and you thought, 'why not?'" Why not give it to the only man who's not

204

pinching your behind when he has the chance? Lady, that doesn't make me a gentleman, only particular. The same goes for spending night after night on the floor beside your bed. I'm a robber, not a rapist. I'm not a kind man, merely a patient one. I could have waited a lot longer for you."

"You arrogant bastard."

He ignored her. "Or satisfied myself with one of the other women if you'd never come around at all. You're the one that made all the excuses. You had to have me, but you had to have me fit your idea of what's right and proper. You're attracted to me therefore I can't be a killer. You want me in bed therefore I can't be ruthless."

Ethan gave her a hard, flinty look, his eyes narrowing on her pale face. "I'm both those things. You'd do well to remember that."

Michael's knuckles were nearly as white as the sheet she was holding. "I won't forget," she said dully. Inside her there was an emptiness so deep and abiding that she ached with it.

"I'm also more honest than you, Michael," he said, his voice a whiskey whisper now. "I've thought about what you would be like in bed since the first time I laid eyes on you. I wanted what happened last night. And I don't regret it this morning. If you were braver, you wouldn't regret it either. You'd come to me again in spite of what I've told you is the truth."

"I'll sleep on the floor first."

Ethan didn't say anything immediately. After a moment he shrugged. "You'll have to. I'm not giving up my bed."

Ten minutes later, after Michael finished making the bed and dressing, she left the room carrying the stained sheets from their night of lovemaking. Ethan watched her go. He leaned back in the tub and rested his head against the high back. Somehow he didn't think she was going to bring him breakfast.

"You're looking very bright-eyed this morning."

Michael rounded on Houston. "What do you mean by that?" she snapped.

He laughed, holding up his hands in a gesture of innocence and surrender. "It's just an observation, not an accusation. You were attacking those plates so energetically. Calm down. Don't throw one of them at my head."

Michael realized she was indeed treating his comment as if it were an indictment. He didn't know how she had passed the night and wee morning hours with Ethan. She forced a smile and hoped it appeared genuine. "I'm sorry. Have you had breakfast?"

"About an hour ago. I've been up since just before dawn. The Grant brothers were coming off a two day drunk and decided to shoot up the south end of town. Didn't you hear it?"

She shook her head and started in on the dishes again. "Was anyone hurt?"

"Jack took a bullet in the foot from his own gun. The Grant boys would be less dangerous if they *could* shoot straight. Trouble is, no one knows what they're aiming at or if they'll hit it. Seems like I'm called down that way at least once a month to put things right."

"What did you do with them?"

"Charged them with disturbing the peace for the umpteenth time and took them to jail. Relieved them of their guns. They'll sober up by afternoon but I'll make them stay at least until Tuesday. They go back to the mines then. They'll be fine until they get a few days off together."

Michael glanced at Houston, a question in her eyes. "You could be such a good sheriff."

"I *am* a good sheriff."

206

"No, I mean—"

"I know what you mean. But one doesn't have much to do with the other."

"How can you say that?"

"Is this what you and Ethan argue about?" he asked, changing the subject.

"One of the things." Michael added hot water from the stove into the sink.

Houston pushed out a chair from the table and straddled it, resting his arms across the top rail. "What about last night?"

"So you heard about that," she said with a casualness she didn't feel. She kept her hands busy so he wouldn't see them trembling.

"Happy told me right away. He said he thought you were making for the livery."

"I might have been going in that direction, but I wasn't going *there*. I don't know if I really thought of going anywhere in particular except away from Ethan."

"You had his gun."

She nodded. "But he had the bullets. Necessary self-protection on his part. I was mad enough to shoot him last night."

"You were lucky Happy didn't shoot you. Those were his orders."

"Your orders you mean."

Houston shrugged. "I won't let you compromise us."

"So I'm to be a prisoner here in Madison for the rest of my life?"

Houston wouldn't commit himself. "We'll see."

Michael really did have an urge to throw a plate at his head. She scrubbed harder.

"I see you're wearing the brooch," he said, pointing to where it fastened the collar of her shirt.

"I suspect you'll see me wear it often. I told you it meant a great deal to me."

207

"I notice you don't wear any other jewelry though. No earbobs. No rings."

"If I'd had anything like that on the night of the robbery you'd have taken it, too."

"And you'd probably have it back by now. So where is your wedding ring?"

"I took that off years ago, Houston. When my marriage was over." Michael decided this experience was making her an adept liar. She had never thought of herself as particularly quick when it came to deception. Now she was not only passing quick, but rather smooth as well. She bent her head a little more to hide her smile.

"What about your engagement ring?"

"Drew and I hadn't announced our engagement officially. We decided against a ring until we did."

"But you were traveling with him."

"I didn't need a ring to do that."

Houston ran his fingers through his light hair. "You're a puzzle, Michael." He watched her for several more minutes, saying nothing. When she was finished with most of the work he stood up, pushed the chair aside, and cupped her elbow. "Let me take you for a walk."

Michael hesitated. She wanted to go outside desperately but she doubted Ethan would let her. "I don't think so, Houston. Ethan wouldn't . . ."

"Forget about Ethan. He doesn't even have to know." He drew her away from the sink. His smile was light and boyish. "I'll get you one of Dee's coats and you won't have to go to your room for yours."

His mood was infectious. Sometimes it was difficult to remember the danger. "All right. I'd love to go out."

"Good."

Once they were on the sidewalk Houston slipped his arm through Michael's. "There are icy patches," he said when she looked at him oddly. "I don't want you to fall."

She didn't know how to protest without making a scene, so she said nothing. She didn't know that from Ethan's vantage point at the window above he could see them arm in arm as they walked away.

"New snow's beautiful, don't you think?" she said. "Everything's clean and quiet. You can look behind you and see where you've been, but when you look in front of you and there are no tracks, it's like being an explorer. Every which way is filled with possibilities. On a day like this when there's sun *and* snow, well, I think it's just about the most perfect thing."

They were crossing the street as she spoke. Houston stopped in his tracks and pulled her up with him. He stared at her upturned face, the dark green eyes, the rare wide smile dimpling at the corners, the skin as smooth as milk. "How the hell did he ever walk away from you?" Then Houston kissed her. In the middle of the broad, deserted street, blanketed with snow and silence, he kissed her with something akin to reverence.

Michael's hand went to her mouth. She touched her lips gently while staring at him widely. "You shouldn't have . . . I don't . . ." Belatedly she realized her hand was shaking and not from the cold. She turned quickly and began retracing her path to the saloon.

Houston caught her elbow. "No, wait. It won't happen again. Not here at least. Please, don't go back. We'll walk. That's all. You wanted to get out, didn't you?"

"That's all I wanted."

"Just a walk," he said. "I promise."

She hesitated again and thought she should be guided by that hesitation and return to the saloon. Instead she permitted him to take her arm again and lead her away.

Their walk took them along same routes they had

209

taken before. None of the shops were open. The few people they saw were on their way to church. Michael would have liked to join them but she didn't ask and Houston didn't offer. His questions were always casual, as if he didn't really care if she answered, but Michael sensed the opposite was true. In spite of the kiss, in spite of his gentleness, his boyish eagerness, he was determined as the grand inquisitor to trip her up in some manner. He might want her, but he didn't trust her. In that, at least, he was not so different from Ethan.

Michael was marginally successful in turning the tables. She had no idea if he answered any of her questions truthfully, but he didn't bother avoiding them. In part he seemed to be flattered by her interest. Vanity was something Michael could, and did, exploit.

She learned that he was originally from Virginia and that he still had distant relatives there. He was an only child. Neither of his parents were alive. Although he evaded directly talking about their deaths Michael gathered they had been stricken suddenly. His father had owned a large bank in Richmond, his mother gathered the most important people for her parties. They were well-respected and they were proud.

"You see," he said, opening the door to the saloon for her. "We have more things in common than not."

Michael gave her skirts a little rustle to dislodge the dusting of snow that clung to the hem. "It doesn't surprise me. I tend to think I'm a lot more like other people than I am different. We simply don't travel the same roads is all."

"Sometimes our paths cross." He brushed a bit of snow from her shoulder.

"Yes, sometimes our paths cross." Michael waited for him to remove his hand then she excused herself. "I've got to return this coat to Dee and see about starting work."

Houston let her go. He watched her disappear into Dee's office, then he slipped out the front entrance.

Detra Kelly was sitting at her large mahogany desk when Michael walked in. She looked up from her ledgers at Michael, then went back to the books. "I'm surprised you had the nerve to return my coat yourself. I'd have thought you'd wheedle Houston to do it for you."

Michael thought it best to ignore Detra's digs. She was spoiling for a fight. An hour earlier Michael would have been more than happy to give her what she wanted. She slipped out of the coat and folded it over her arm. "Where would you like me to put it?"

"On the hook behind you. Be careful. It's already dripping on my carpet. You could have treated it as if it were your own."

"There are six inches of new snow outside. It was impossible to keep it dry."

"You should have thought of that before you had Houston commandeer it."

It was going to be very difficult to avoid that fight, Michael thought. She hung up the coat and spread out a newspaper on the floor to catch the water. "That should suffice," she said. "I'll see to cleaning out front now."

"Not so fast." Dee leaned back in her chair. She laid down her pen and pointed to the cabriolet chair in front of the desk. "Sit down. I want to talk to you. The saloon can wait. It's Sunday morning. Even the miners around here wait 'til afternoon before they come sauntering back in after a Saturday night." She pointed to the chair again. "Sit."

Michael sat. Without realizing it, she fingered the brooch at her neck. It had a calming effect. It also drew Detra's attention and her anger.

"What did you promise Houston to get that

211

brooch?" she asked.

"Nothing. It was mine. He merely returned it."

"Houston doesn't *merely* do anything."

"I don't pretend to understand his mind. More to the point, I don't wish to. He returned the brooch and I accepted it. There was no more to it."

"He's made little effort to hide the fact that you interest him. Everyone's seen it." Dee rose from behind her desk and disappeared into her adjoining apartments. "Would you like a cup of tea?" she called back.

The offer caught Michael off guard, and she hesitated.

Dee's mouth lifted in a slow, sly smile. "So you've heard the stories about Mr. Kelly. Oh, no, don't bother denying it. All the girls hear the stories sooner or later. With you I suspect it was sooner."

"I'd like some tea, thank you."

Dee's laugh was low and husky. "Of course." She returned within minutes with a tray carrying a pot of tea and two cups. "I wanted you to see me pour. Both cups filled from the same pot, both of us drinking the same brew. You can choose either cup. It makes no difference to me."

"This isn't necessary. I don't believe the stories."

Dee paused and gave Michael a hard look, her deep blue eyes dark and searching. "You don't? That could prove unfortunate. One should always be cautious, don't you think?"

"Cautious, yes. Gullible, no." Michael took one of the cups, added a dollop of milk and a little sugar.

Closing her ledgers, Detra pushed them aside and prepared her own cup. She sat in her chair again, holding herself with the regalness of a queen. "I don't want you alone with Houston anymore."

"I'm hardly ever alone with him."

"You were yesterday afternoon and again this morning. There were probably other times I didn't know

212

about."

"Nothing around here escapes your notice, Dee."

The smile appeared again. It was a cool one. It did not reach Dee's eyes. "I'm not easily taken in by flattery." She sipped her tea. "Don't underestimate me, Michael. I may not have your education or your prim and proper manners, but what I want, I get, and what I get, I keep. If I were you I'd concentrate on holding onto Ethan instead of setting your cap for Houston. If you're not careful Carmen will have Ethan and you won't have anyone. Happy doesn't think much of you. Your life won't be worth a tinker's damn if Ethan leaves you again."

"I managed when he walked out the first time," Michael said, matching Dee's frosty tones. "I'll manage again. I'm not so convinced as you, Dee, that I need a man. Perhaps that's what Houston finds interesting."

"Challenging," she corrected.

Michael shrugged. "It doesn't matter. The truth is, I'm not chasing Houston. I'm not interested in him. I don't want anything from him. You can—"

"Even your freedom?"

"What?"

"Houston can give you your freedom. Doesn't that interest you?"

Michael sensed a trap. She refused to step in it. "I don't want anything from Houston," she repeated.

"That isn't what it looked like to me," Dee said. "Just above an hour ago you were kissing him in the middle of the street." She waited. Michael said nothing. "Do you deny it?"

"What would be the point? It happened. But he was kissing me. If you have a problem with that take it up with Houston." Michael took a drink of her tea then set the cup and saucer down. "If there's nothing else, Dee . . ."

"But there is. I want your promise that you'll stay

away from Houston."

"As much as it's possible, you have it."

"You *make* it happen."

Michael stood up. "I'll be in the saloon if you need me," she said. She forced herself to exit slowly. Dee would be so satisfied to see her trembling.

Michael saw little of Ethan throughout the day. He didn't have to go to the mine but he did work for several hours at the widow's ranch. He was still gone at supper and his absence did not go unremarked by the others. It seemed everyone knew about the fight she and Ethan had had the evening before. Happy had been busy spreading the tale of her thwarted attempt to take Ethan's life, or at least his manhood. The story became more convoluted and more divorced from the truth each time it was repeated. Michael let everyone think what they would, neither denying nor confirming. Between performances that evening she sat at one of the tables with Ralph Hooper, Billy Saunders, and three more of their friends and tried to drink herself into a stupor.

Chapter Eight

"Don't you think you'd better go up?" Ethan asked her, taking a seat at the table where Michael was holding court.

"Awww," Billy drawled, "Let 'er stay. Can't you see she's havin' a good time?"

"A good time," Michael repeated. She propped her chin on the back of her hand and smiled.

Ethan felt the full force of that smile. It had already enslaved every man at the table. "She can't even hold her head up."

"Sure I can." The words slid together. Michael giggled. "Sure—I—can," she enunciated clearly. She raised her head, folded her hands neatly in her lap, and straightened her shoulders. "See? I'm quite fine. Would anyone like another beer? I'll get a pitcher." Without waiting for a show of hands, Michael excused herself and wended her way to the bar.

"How long's she been drinking?" Ethan asked the men at large.

Ralph shrugged. "I suppose since the end of the first show. She hasn't had more than three beers."

"It doesn't take more than one for her."

"I saw her take a shot at the bar a while back," Billy said.

Both of Ethan's brows kicked up. "Oh, God," he

groaned, rubbing his chin. "The head she's going to have."

Michael returned with the beer, poured drinks all around, and filled a new glass for Ethan. "Oh, stop looking so critical," she said. "I didn't spill a drop, did I?" She sat down. "It's your fault I'm like this anyway . . . your fault I'm here at all."

Ethan guessed what significance the others would put on her statement. He'd heard the story about their fight that was making the rounds. He also knew perfectly well that she wasn't referring to anything that had happened yesterday. One word about the robbery and he was going to have to do some incredibly fast talking. "Let's go on up, Michael." He reached for her hand.

Michael snatched her arm back. "I have another dance to do."

Ethan was losing patience but he was aware of the harm antagonizing her could do. "You can come back downstairs for it."

Michael was feeling belligerent. She turned to the others at the table to take up her cause. "You don't want me to leave, do ya, fellas? Weren't we just talkin' about our own poker game before Ethan got here?"

Billy looked uneasily at Ralph. Ralph traded looks with Jim and Jim with Calvin and Ben Tyler. "You know, Michael, seems like I'm plumb empty in the pockets," Billy said. "Wouldn't be much of a game with me in it."

"I'm not feelin' very lucky tonight," Jim said.

"Me neither," Ben chimed in.

"I'm tapped out, too," Calvin said.

"Can't have a game with jest the two of us," Ralph told her after everyone had backed down.

Michael fixed them each with an accusing stare. "Cowards," she muttered. "It's all right." To the amazement of everyone at the table she reached inside her

216

bodice and pulled out a deck of cards. She fanned them expertly and began shuffling. "I know lots of ways to play solitaire."

Ethan felt every other man's eyes on him, waiting to see what he would do. Michael's steady defiance was eroding his patience and the respect he was afforded by others. "She has a mind of her own when she's sober, fellas," he said, shrugging off her actions. "When she's drunk she sits on it."

Laughter erupted around the table. Ethan grinned. Michael glared at him. "There's only one ass at this table," she said. "And if I were over there —" she pointed to Ethan's lap, "— *then* I'd be sitting on it."

Silence reigned for several seconds then Ethan began to laugh. "Come here, Michael, I'll see if I can't accommodate you."

"A pompous, braying ass," she told the others, ignoring Ethan's overture.

He jerked her chair close to his and lifted her easily onto his lap. She tried to wiggle off. Her movements merely made him hard. She quieted immediately. "That's better," he whispered against her ear. "Now deal the cards. We'll play one hand, then it's upstairs where you can sleep off that swollen head of yours."

"One han." It was difficult to give the hard consonants sound. "Han-*duh*," she repeated. "An' if I win I stay an' I dance." She tossed him a saucy grin over her shoulder. "I'll dance for you, Ethan. Jus' for you."

Ethan wasn't certain he liked the sound of that. That saucy smile boded no good for anyone, especially not him. His blue-gray eyes took in the others in a single glance. What was the chance of her really winning the hand against all of them together? "All right," he said. "But I'm cutting the cards."

"Of course," she said off handedly. "No matter how dumb the dealer looks . . ."

"*Always* cut the cards." The men finished for her in unison.

Michael bobbed her head twice in agreement. "Oooh," she said softly as the room spun a little. She held herself very still for a moment. Ethan's large hands were braced on her waist. Even through her tight corset she could feel his fingers as if they were on her skin. She began to deal the cards. "Five card stud," she said. "One up, four in the hole. Nothing wild. Highest card starts the bidding."

When the cards were out Ralph had the only face card showing. "It's up to you Ralph," Michael said. "C'mon, gentlemen, you'll have to dig a little in your pockets to stay in the game. I'm curious how empty they really are." Michael peeked at her own cards, making sure to keep them out of Ethan's sight. She had a three of hearts up, another three, a king, and a pair of tens in the hole. Two pair. It wasn't a bad hand. It probably wouldn't win though. Ralph in particular was looking very full of himself. She wished she could see Ethan's face. It probably wouldn't help. He had the sort of face that gave little of what he was thinking or feeling away. "All right, gentlemen, name your pleasure. How many shall it be?"

"Two for me," Ralph said. Three of a kind in his hand, Michael thought.

"Three," said Ben. She thought he probably had a pair.

"Four," said Jim. Nothing in that hand, Michael decided. Yet.

"Two for me," Billy said. He looked as he if were hoping for a straight.

"I'll take one," said Calvin. Michael couldn't make him out. Probably a bluff, she thought.

"Dealer takes one," she said. She laid down the card but didn't look at it. "Ethan? How many?"

218

"Three." She snapped out three cards and prayed he came up short.

Everyone tossed more money into the kitty. "Well, Ralph," Michael said. "Let's see what you have. We've bought the right."

Ralph turned over his cards. "Three pretty ladies. Not as pretty as you."

"What a flatterer you are, Ralph," Michael teased. She felt Ethan's hand tighten on her waist. "Ben, what have you got?"

Ben just pushed his cards toward the middle of the table. "Nothing that beats that."

Jim sighed, tossing in his cards before Michael even asked for them.

Billy showed his pair of sixes.

"What about you Calvin?" asked Michael.

"Two pair."

"Too bad." Michael flipped over her cards and fanned them out. "I drew to a full house. Threes and tens." Behind her she was delighted to hear Ethan's low, disgruntled growl. She reached over her shoulder for his cards. He put them in her hand and she showed them to the others. "It looks as if he was going for a straight. What a pity, Ethan." She slid off his lap, bobbled on her feet a moment, and scooped up the winnings at the table. When she sat down it was on her own chair, not on Ethan's lap. Looking hopefully around the table she asked, "Another game, fellas? No? Oh, well." She shrugged, gathering up the cards. She leaned toward Ethan and put the straightened deck in the breast pocket of his shirt. She patted it lightly. "You keep those safe for me, will you? They're my lucky cards."

"Since when?"

"Since I just won with them." There was a little beer left in the pitcher. As she topped off Ralph's glass she noticed Billy was rolling himself a cigarette. "Could I have that one, Billy?" she asked. "And you roll yourself another?"

Billy started to push it across the table toward her when his wrist was clamped hard by Ethan. He glanced up uneasily at the younger, stronger man.

"She doesn't smoke," Ethan said.

"I most certainly do," Michael said. "Just pass it here, Billy. Ethan won't break your wrist."

Ethan sat back in his chair and glared at Michael. "I just may break your neck."

Billy started to withdraw the cigarette but Michael managed to snatch it from under his fingers. "Does anyone have a light for it?" she asked, holding it out between her index and middle fingers. A shred of tobacco fell out on the table and Michael picked it up and stuffed inside again. "You roll yours a little loose, Billy." She glanced around the table. "Well? How about that match?"

None of the men offered one. Ethan's look assured them they would be sorry if they did.

"You'd think you'd never seen a woman smoke before," Michael said, disgusted with them all. "Worse, you think a woman has no right." She dropped the cigarette down her bodice and wrinkled her nose at Ethan. "I'll simply save it."

"Perhaps you *should* have another drink," Ethan said, pushing his glass of beer at her. "One more might put you under the table."

Michael shook her head, smiling sweetly and insincerely. She felt the room spin again but refused to give in to it. Over the general noise of the saloon she yelled to Lottie who was talking to admirers by the piano. "Play something slow and sweet, Lottie! I'm going to dance for Ethan!" Michael's chair scraped against the floor as she pushed it back and came to her feet. Bracing her arms stiffly on the table a moment for balance, she bid them all good evening. She didn't notice the saloon had become very quiet, nor that focus of every man's eyes was on her. Michael only heard the first strains of the lilting ballad and felt only Ethan's stare.

Swaying to the music, Michael wended her way around the tables to the stage. She pirouetted gracefully as she cleared the footlights, raising her arms above her head and turning slowly, elegantly, her back arched slightly and the line of her throat exposed. She turned once, then again, and again, then she was spinning across the stage, still in time to the music, still with the same beautiful symmetry of motion, but it was different somehow, as if she had given herself up to the music and moved because it compelled her to move.

Her feet seemed to make no sound on the platform as she danced. She had a cat-quickness, a lightness of expression that was all feline grace. Her arms and hands stretched out in a shapely arc, extending the soul of the music to her fingertips.

Ethan had had as much as he could tolerate. He stood up and headed for the staircase, determined to let Michael fend for herself when the music ended. She was so hellbent on proving how independent she was. Let her, he thought. He started to climb.

Michael stumbled briefly on her feet when she saw Ethan start up the stairs. She called to Lottie to change the tempo. Michael took up an imaginary partner and started to waltz, twirling about the stage in large elegant curves. At Michael's signal Lottie played faster and Michael abandoned the waltz and her invisible partner. Her steps became quicker, the sway and arch of her body more exaggerated, the dance more frantic. The dreamy quality of her form and movement was abandoned. Her expressive green eyes were sultry. Her hair whipped across her face as she turned and twisted in a frenzied rhythm.

Ethan was near the top of the stairs now. He didn't

221

want to watch what she was doing on stage but he couldn't help himself. And as he watched he realized he couldn't abandon her to the crowd. It would be a miracle if she wasn't attacked right on the stage. Even as he thought it there was a surge toward the platform as the music ended. Michael made a grand curtsy, then dropped to the floor as if she had collapsed from the frantic energy of her dance.

"Dramatic," Ethan said under his breath. He reached for his gun and held it up over his head, coming down a few steps. "All right, fellas," he called. "She's had her fun. It's over." A few men near the foot of stairs heard him and stopped. Lottie glanced up from the piano and pounded out a few minor chords. Ethan punctuated the dying notes with a single shot from his Colt. There was complete quiet after that. Ethan slipped his gun back in the holster. "Come on, Michael. You can dance your way up here now." There was a low rumble of laughter from the patrons as they started to return to their seats.

Michael raised her head and fixed Ethan with a hard stare. She blinked. He seemed to fade in and out of focus.

"Kitty!" Ethan called. "Josie! See if you can't help her up. I don't think she's going to dance again this evening."

Kitty and Josie leaped quickly to the stage. Lottie started playing again and the other girls began serving drinks. Detra had watched the entire drama from behind the long bar. She cast a sidelong glance at Houston who was leaning against the bar across from her.

"You see what she is?" Dee asked.

Houston pushed away from the bar. "I see what she's becoming," he answered. He went to help Josie and Kitty.

Ethan was setting a fire in the stove when he heard footsteps approaching in the hallway. "Get her over to

222

the bed," he said, shutting the stove's grated door. He stood up and turned. It was Houston who was carrying Michael, not Kitty and Josie. "Oh, it's you."

"It's me."

"Put her on the bed. I'll see to her from here."

Houston's black eyes were cold as they rested long and hard on Ethan. "You haven't seen too well to her since she's been here."

"That's odd coming from you. You made no secret in the beginning that you would have preferred her dead rather than company."

"That's before I knew her." He laid Michael on the bed. The covers had been turned back. He raised the sheet around her shoulders as she turned on her side and curled against one of the pillows. "You should take more care with her, Ethan. She'll be mine in a month."

"I saw you kiss her this morning."

"Then you know she pushed me away." He stepped back from the bed. "But she won't do that always. She doesn't know what to make of me." He smiled slowly. "I think I've intrigued her."

"I'm sure you have."

Houston went to the door. "Are you going to fight for her at all?" he asked.

"It depends."

"On what?"

"On whether she wants me to."

Houston thought about that as he stepped into the hallway and closed the door behind him.

Ethan cast a disgusted look in Michael's direction then latched the door. "Why in God's name didn't you just stay in New York? Why aren't you raising babies instead of raising hell?" He didn't expect a reply and he didn't get one. After removing the bullets from his gun, he hung the belt on the hook by the door and stripped down to his drawers to get ready for bed. He took fresh linens and blankets from the wardrobe, laid them out on the floor as he'd done every night except the last one, and tossed down a pillow from the bed.

That's when he deviated from routine. Sliding one arm beneath Michael's shoulders and the other under her knees, he lifted her off the mattress and eased her onto the floor. She barely stirred in the process. He covered her, tucking the blankets around her curled form. "I told you I wasn't giving up my bed again," he whispered.

Ethan extinguished the lamps and slid between the sheets that Michael had already warmed. The scent of her filled his nostrils. It took a lot longer for him to get to sleep then he had ever anticipated.

Michael knew a moment's disorientation when she awoke. When she realized where she was and who it was sleeping just above her, enjoying the soft comfort of the mattress, she made a quietly derisive sound at the back of her throat. She turned on her side, then on her back, then on her other side. She tried lying on her stomach, her arm under the pillow, then her arms at her side. It didn't matter. Nothing worked. Worse, every time she moved the slightest bit her head thudded abominably. She swore she could feel the blood coursing through her veins and rushing to her head, then rushing back to her leaden feet. She was dizzy and light-headed one moment, steady and immobile with heaviness in the next. Blinking hurt.

It was not as difficult to remember what she had done below stairs as it was painful. The vision of herself, first behaving outrageously at the poker table, then later on stage, dancing with such sensual provocation, caused Michael to grimace with embarrassment. She prayed none of it was true. Her fingers slipped under the bodice of her dress and between her breasts. Her horrible suspicions were confirmed when

4 FREE BOOKS

TO GET YOUR 4 FREE BOOKS WORTH $18.00 — MAIL IN THE FREE BOOK CERTIFICATE T O D A Y

Fill in the Free Book Certificate below, and we'll send your FREE BOOKS to you as soon as we receive it.

If the certificate is missing below, write to: Zebra Home Subscription Service, Inc., P.O. Box 5214, 120 Brighton Road, Clifton, New Jersey 07015-5214.

FREE BOOK CERTIFICATE

4 FREE BOOKS

ZEBRA HOME SUBSCRIPTION SERVICE, INC.

YES! Please start my subscription to Zebra Historical Romances and send me my first 4 books absolutely FREE. I understand that each month I may preview four new Zebra Historical Romances free for 10 days. If I'm not satisfied with them, I may return the four books within 10 days and owe nothing. Otherwise, I will pay the low preferred subscriber's price of just $3.75 each; a total of $15.00, *a savings off the publisher's price of $3.00.* I may return any shipment and I may cancel this subscription at any time. There is no obligation to buy any shipment and there are no shipping, handling or other hidden charges. Regardless of what I decide, the four free books are mine to keep.

NAME _____

ADDRESS _____ APT _____

CITY _____ STATE _____ ZIP _____

TELEPHONE ( ) _____

SIGNATURE _____ (if under 18, parent or guardian must sign)

Terms, offer and prices subject to change without notice. Subscription subject to acceptance by Zebra Books. Zebra Books reserves the right to reject any order or cancel any subscription.

she found the cigarette. "Oh, God," she moaned softly. For all the good it did her head to whisper she may as well have screamed the words. She nudged the cigarette under the bed and out of the way.

Michael sat up gingerly, holding her head in her palms as she did so. She clutched the bedframe, then the footpost, and carefully raised herself up on her knees. When she was steady and could stand the drumroll in her head, she slowly got to her feet. Every movement was accompanied by a soft little grunt or groan.

"You sound like you're dying," Ethan said tiredly. He turned on his side to watch her halting progress to the bureau.

"Trust you to state the obvious," she said lowly. "And, for God's sake, don't yell. That's cruel."

"I'm whispering."

"Then do it softer." She leaned against the chest of drawers and closed her eyes. "I don't drink. I *know* I don't drink. I know I *can't* drink. So why did this happen to me?"

As forlorn as she sounded Ethan wasn't moved to help her. "Because you're a willful, stubborn woman with no more sense than a box of rocks."

"That's one explanation." She placed her forearm across the top of the bureau and buried her face in the crook of her elbow. "Don't rush to my aid. I'm sure I can manage."

Ethan wanted to remain angry with her but he was finding it difficult not to laugh. How she could be so pathetic and still find it in her to admonish him with sarcasm and humor defied explaining.

Michael inched back from the bureau and used touch to search out the second drawer with her fingers.

He heard her fumbling in the dark. "Would you like me to light a lamp?"

In her mind she imagined the torturous brightness of a glaring sun. "Don't you dare."

Ethan rubbed his eyes with his thumb and forefinger, glad she couldn't see that he was smiling. "Did you find the nightshirt?"

She nodded, then moaned. "Yes," she said finally. "I found it." She laid it on top of the bureau. With cautious movements Michael pulled the pink taffeta gown she was wearing over her head. She let it drop on the floor, not caring that she'd have to pick up after herself later. The strings of her corset proved obstinate at first. When she finally loosened them she felt as if she had won a major field campaign. Her petticoats followed the dress. Leaning against the bureau again, she rid herself of her shoes, stockings, and garters. Turning her back to the bed, Michael took off her chemise and short pantelets and put on the nightshirt. When she turned around Ethan was sitting up in bed.

"I need a drink," he muttered. He was rock hard. The light from the coals in the stove, though meager, hadn't prevented him from seeing the curve of her hip or the line of her leg. There were twin dimples at the base of her spine, no less alluring than those on either side of her mouth when she favored him with a smile. He found himself lying there, hoping she would turn just enough to give him a glimpse of her breasts. That's when he sat up and ground the heels of his hands against his eyes until sparks of color appeared. He didn't need her tantalizing him when she was as in control of herself as tumbleweed in a dust storm. Ethan watched her wobble to the washstand, a pale, unsteady wraith in her white nightshirt. Sighing, he got up and searched out the whiskey, uncorked it, and drank a long swallow straight from the bottle. He was putting it away when he noticed Michael had finished washing her face at the basin and was heading for his bed.

226

"Oh, no," he said, catching her by the shoulder as she placed one knee on the mattress. "The floor."

She winced at the pressure of his fingers against her skin. "You're not serious. You'd really make me sleep on the floor for the rest of the night?"

"That or share the bed."

Michael looked longingly at the bed, then at her feet where she was standing on the blankets she would have to wrap around her. "You don't mind sharing?"

"I mind like hell."

"Oh. Then I'll take the floor."

He stopped her again when she began to move away. "But not for the reasons you're probably thinking. Go on, get in. And move all the way over this time. As close to the edge as you can without falling out the other side." And just because he knew he could get away with it this once, he gave her a little pat on the backside as she crawled in.

She twisted her head to glare at him and the effort simply made her collapse.

"Well," he drawled, sliding in after her, "it's not far enough, but I suppose it'll have to do."

Michael gently placed a forearm over her eyes as if she could contain the pressure in her head. "Tell me it will be better in the morning."

He gave her a little push to make room for his legs and brought up the sheet and comforter to cover them. "It will be better in the morning."

"Really?"

His laughter was low and slightly wicked. It was also very near her ear. "No," he said. "It will be worse."

It was every bit as brutal as Ethan had warned her it would be. He found great amusement in the fact.

"Shouldn't you be helping the widow this morning?" she asked as they shared breakfast in the kitchen. Be-

227

cause of the earliness of the hour it was deserted except for them. "Or blowing up something in the mines?"

"Like myself you mean?" He cut her off before she could answer. "Mrs. Johnson doesn't need me for a few days. She's got John Gibbs to help her. And there's nothing more for me to blow up at the mine until they clear the rubble away. So you see, I'm here for the day. And probably again tomorrow."

Michael dunked the tip of her hard crusted bread in her coffee, softening it. Even chewing hurt. She would have liked to have slept longer but when Ethan left the bed she woke and couldn't fall back to sleep. He hadn't said a word about her curled all around him. She couldn't even pretend it had been the other way around. It was her arm he'd had to move and her leg he'd had to untangle before he could slip out of the bed. Michael couldn't even thank him for not mentioning it.

"What exactly do you do there?" she asked. The least she could do was ignore his amusement at her condition and resolve to be polite.

"The silver's in veins that run deep underground. I set the explo—" He stopped because she was shaking her head.

"No, I mean at the widow's. Mrs. Johnson?"

"Emily Johnson," he said, nodding. Ethan cut off a bit of steak and speared some scrambled eggs. "In the beginning there was a lot of work to do on the roof. When she and Georgie bought the place it was pretty run down. They did quite a bit but there wasn't time to get to everything." He stopped for a moment, looked away from Michael, alone with his own thoughts, then began again. "I've been laying a new floor for her in places where the old boards have rotted, clearing some land so she can have a garden in the spring. Mostly it's just this and that kind of work.

I do what I can. Usually a few days a week."

"I'm surprised you do it at all. They must pay you well enough at the mines . . . and then there's your other, more lucrative career."

Ethan paused in buttering a slice of bread. "I don't take any money from Emily. Helping her is the least I can do."

The faint furrow between Michael's brows appeared as she raised a question with her eyes. "The least you can do? I don't think I understand."

He looked at Michael steadily, prepared to measure her response. "I killed her husband."

Michael didn't blink. She lowered her cup and set it firmly in its saucer. She thought she had learned just enough about Ethan to know she couldn't assume anything. He seemed to be waiting for her to do just that. "How did it happen?" she asked instead.

Ethan finished buttering his bread. There was part of him that wanted to tell her a lie, make up some story about gunning down Georgie Johnson on the street. It was precisely the sort of thing he wanted her to believe about him. Then he remembered how she had felt against him, her arms and legs curved around him, cradling him against her breasts. He was too selfish to lie. He wanted her there again. He told her the truth. It was a little less ugly.

"I was setting explosives in the mines. It was just after I came to Madison. I picked Georgie to help me out because he'd had a little experience handling dynamite. We were down pretty deep. There was no light save for what lanterns we carried in ourselves. Georgie and I had finished packing the crevices with the sticks and fixed the blasting caps. I was laying down a powder fuse through the tunnel because we'd run out of cord. Georgie was carrying what we didn't need to safe ground."

Ethan took a drink of his coffee, staring off a point

beyond Michael's shoulder. "I don't know what really happened then, don't know what went through Georgie's mind. I figure he remembered something he left behind in the blast area and went back for it. I'm sure he thought I saw him go back. I didn't though. I swear to God I didn't see him go back."

Michael reached across the table. The very tips of her fingers touched Ethan's wrist. He didn't pull away and she didn't offer anything more intrusive or demanding.

"I set the fuse all the way back to the clear area. Georgie wasn't there. I yelled for him. The tunnels play tricks sometimes with sound. I thought I heard him calling me from another level above me. I thought it was safe. I lit the powder."

"Oh, dear God."

Ethan pushed abruptly away from the table and poured himself another cup of coffee at the stove. "Emily was pregnant at the time it happened. She miscarried."

Michael blanched a little.

"It was ruled an accident. Everyone knew Georgie had no business going back in the blasting area after I started to set the fuse. There were other men around who heard the same trick of sound that I did and thought he was safe."

"It *was* an accident."

Ethan said nothing. He raised the pot of coffee, offering some to Michael. She shook her head. He returned to the table and sat down. "I work alone now."

And take risks, Michael thought, remembering the bruise on his back from setting the fuse too short. "Mrs. Johnson doesn't blame you," she said. When his flint-colored eyes narrowed in question she added, "She couldn't have you around otherwise."

"She says the same thing. She tells me I'm doing unnecessary penance because there's nothing to forgive."

230

"She's right."

Ethan wasn't so certain. "Maybe I'll feel different after she's married again and I'll know she's happy and well cared for, with someone to look out for her."

"All the things a woman could want," she said. She heard her own sarcasm and was immediately sorry. "I apologize. That wasn't meant as a snipe at Emily or at you. I don't know why I said it. I wish her every happiness."

Ethan studied Michael's face, saw that she was earnest. "John Gibbs does too."

"That's the man who's helping her when you're not?"

He nodded. "John's been a good friend to her. He'll be a good husband."

Michael pushed her eggs around on her plate. Outside clouds separated in the sun's path. Light slanted in from the window behind Ethan and laid across the corner of the table. "What about you, Ethan? Do you ever think about not robbing trains and being someone's good husband?"

Glancing toward the doors to make certain they were alone, Ethan said, "One doesn't necessarily preclude the other. All I have to do is find a woman who doesn't particularly care that I like blasting safes more than I like blasting tunnels."

"I see," she said coldly.

He laughed. "Don't worry. I don't think you're that woman."

"You're damned right I'm not."

"But I'll wager you think you can change me." Though she tried to hide it, he saw his remark had struck a chord with her. She was still trying desperately to justify her attraction to him. "You'll realize soon enough that you can't force people to be what you want. I used to think I could stop you from swearing."

231

Before Michael could think of a suitable reply, Ethan was gone from the room.

Houston found Michael in the saloon in the afternoon, picking out a ditty on the piano. There were only seven customers at the bar and few more back in the dining room. Kitty was tending bar and carrying on an animated conversation with her brother and one of his friends.

He leaned against the upright and watched her for a few minutes. "Head still ache?" he asked. "Ethan says it was throbbing this morning."

She glanced up once then continued playing. "It's better." She hit a sour note and winced with exaggerated expressiveness. "Unless I do that."

"Dee might have some powders back in her apartment. Do you want me to get something for you?"

"Powders from Detra's cupboards?" Michael raised one brow skeptically. "No, thank you. I don't think so."

"I take it you've heard about Mr. Kelly."

"I've heard. Is it true?"

Houston shrugged. "Doctor here in town says it was a heart attack. I don't know any different."

"Is there something in particular you want, Houston? Dee's in her office if you're looking for her."

"I wasn't," he said. "I cleared my desk of paperwork, made my rounds, and left the next crisis for my deputy to handle."

"Jake will do fine, I'm sure."

"So I thought you might like to go for a buggy ride with me. I got one at the livery for a few hours. I can take you to the mines, show you where most of the town is when they're not sleeping or in this saloon." He took off his hat, threaded his hair with his fingers, pushing it back at the temples, then replaced the hat. He looked at her expectantly.

"I don't know, Houston. Dee doesn't —"

232

"Let me worry about Dee."

"But Ethan—"

"You said yourself there's no love lost between you and Ethan. Last night proved it as far as I'm concerned. He's being a dog in a manger when it comes to you. He doesn't want you but he doesn't want anyone else to have you either."

"I make my own decisions."

"Prove it. Come with me. You know you want to. The fresh air will do wonders for your head."

Michael wasn't sure about that, but she did want to see the mines. Against her better judgment she continued to be intensely interested in anything connected to Ethan Stone. If Houston could help her, then she would use him. He didn't need to know they were at cross-purposes.

She stood up. "I'll get my coat."

Ethan was in the room, reading in the wing chair, his feet propped on the footstool, when she went in. He marked his place with his finger, closed the book over it, and looked up. "Going someplace?"

"With Houston. For a buggy ride. Are you going to stop me?"

"You really don't understand, do you? The only way to stop you is to stop Houston. I told you early on that I wasn't going to kill a man over you. I should have added: *or get myself killed.* Is he forcing you to go with him?"

"No."

"Then I'm not forcing you *not* to. Mind yourself though. He's after more than just that kiss you shared yesterday."

"You saw that?"

Ethan nodded. His blue-gray eyes studied her carefully, grazing her face, her throat, her breasts, and sliding down the long folds of her hunter green gown as if he could see what lay beneath. "Now that you

233

have a taste for what happens between a man and woman in bed, perhaps you've decided to try some feminine wiles afterall."

"He's a murderer."

"You'll forget that after a while. You did with me."

Michael slammed the door on her way out.

"Ready?" Houston asked as she came quickly down the stairs. "The buggy's outside."

That gave Michael pause. "You were terribly certain of my answer."

"I was merely hopeful."

Out of the corner of her eye Michael caught Kitty's worried expression as they passed the bar. She smiled back with a reassurance she didn't feel.

Houston helped Michael into the buggy and laid a blanket across their laps. "Here, take my gloves," he said. "The sun's deceiving. It's still plenty cold out here and it'll be worse once we start moving. I'll take it slow."

Michael put on the gloves. "What about you?"

"I'll drive with one hand. You keep the other warm." He thrust it toward Michael. "Go on. Take it." He snapped the reins at the same moment she accepted his hand in her gloved ones. He grinned at her sideways. "That's not so bad, is it?"

She held his hand on her lap. The sun's brightness *was* deceiving. The sky was cloudless. The mountain peaks were crisply outlined against a blue background that seemed too uniformly perfect to be quite real. Even when she tried to breathe in sunshine Michael felt nothing but cold air fill her lungs.

Houston pointed out the frozen lake, the fast running streams that rushed over small dams of ice, the empty nests that were wedged in the crooks of spindly barren trees. After a while he slipped his hand out of hers, transferred the reins, and gave her the cold one to warm.

234

Michael turned slightly. Her knees bumped his. "I thought you would be more respectful of my marriage to Ethan."

"I might . . . if you were really married to him."

She felt a rush of panic. Unconsciously she squeezed his hand a little tighter. What did Houston know? Had she said something, done something to give herself away? Had Ethan been merely setting her up and told the truth behind her back? "I don't understand. What do you mean if I were really married to him?"

"Except for the chance meeting on the train, you and Ethan haven't been together as man and wife for four years. My understanding is that your actual marriage only lasted a few months before he left you. There's not a great deal to respect there, wouldn't you say?"

The first rush of panic subsided and Michael began to breath more easily. It was then she was aware of holding Houston's hand too tightly. She eased her grip and rubbed his hand, pretending her intent all along was merely to warm it. "I *am* married to him, though."

Houston was thoughtful. "But you're holding *my* hand. Tell me, what did Ethan say he did for a living when he first met you?"

Michael was thankful for the conversation she and Ethan had had to share information. She remembered precisely what he'd been doing in New York during the spring they supposedly were married. "He worked in a bank."

Grinning, Houston gave her a sideways glance. "I'll wager he did. More than one of them. Though I doubt he was officially employed."

Michael didn't have to pretend to be shocked. She was. She hadn't suspected the information Ethan had given her was only part of the truth. "You're wrong!" she said quickly. "Ethan wasn't robbing banks then."

"He didn't start after he met me. He didn't find us here in Madison. We found *him*. He'd worked on his own in places like St. Louis and Denver."

"Oh, but—"

"You see, there are things you don't know about Ethan. Things you've never known. Makes it kind of difficult to know who to trust, doesn't it?"

"I thought Ethan was your friend."

"I like him well enough, I suppose. I don't know that I trust him." His black eyes left the road again and studied Michael's face briefly. "I don't know that I trust many people at all. It's always been safe not to."

Feeling his interest was somehow cold and detached, Michael barely was able to suppress a shiver. She was grateful for the silence that fell between them.

The silver mines at Madison had more than a dozen different entrances. Some shafts went down hundreds of feet, others only a few score. Inside the mountain a veritable warren of tunnels and passages had been carved out to pursue the path of the precious metal. Ore was taken from the bowels of the mountain by small dumper cars riding on tracks laid through most of the tunnels. After being refined as much as possible locally, it was carried by mule to Stillwater, the nearest community with access to the railroad. It was not the most efficient operation for the town—some thought there should be a rail spur to Madison—but slowing down the process also meant the treasure would be there for years to come.

Houston helped Michael down from the carriage and led her to one of the entrances where there was no activity. "We're only going to go a short way in," he told her. "Without a lantern it's impossible to see. Unless you want to see more? I can get one."

"No. No, that's all right. I don't think I'd like to go in very far." She allowed him to take her elbow and escort her up a small rocky incline until they reached

236

the adit. After walking only five or so yards into the horizontal mine entrance darkness began to close around them.

"You can see there are other tunnels that take different routes up ahead. Generally there are two shifts of miners working each day."

"Is this area tapped out? Is that why no one's working here?"

"I don't know. Could be. I'm not as familiar with the working of the mines as Ethan. You could ask him."

"Perhaps I will." They had stopped walking. Michael realized she was close enough to one of the inner walks that she was able to feel the cool dampness of earth and rock through her clothes. She glanced toward the entrance and was assured by the rectangular patch of sunlight framed by the supporting wooden beams.

"You don't like this place, do you?" Houston asked.

She thought he was going to take a step back and give her room to move toward the adit. Instead he moved closer so that Michael found her back to the tunnel's wall. "No," she said. "I don't like it much." She thought he would move then. He didn't.

"Ethan says you were studying at a university when he met you."

The change of subject startled her. Michael forced herself to meet Houston's eyes directly. "That's right."

"What were you studying?"

"Literature. I was planning to be a writer."

"Poetry?"

She shook her head. "Novels."

"Have you started one?"

"Dozens. But I never finish. I keep a diary." She mentioned the diary because she knew he knew about it. It would add credibility to lies she had to tell.

"Is that why you were going to marry Drew Beaumont? Because he was a writer?"

237

Michael took a tentative step sideways, hoping to inch herself away from the wall. Houston countered by casually bracing his arms on either side of her shoulders. "I was going to marry Drew because I loved him."

"You haven't mourned him. Except for the first few days on the trail I haven't observed you really grieving for him."

"You don't know what's in my heart."

"Don't I?"

Michael broke eye contact then because she couldn't bear looking at him any longer. His stare was so penetrating that she felt violated. "Why are you saying these things to me?"

He didn't answer her directly. "I wonder sometimes just what you would do to secure your escape from Madison."

"Please, I want to go now." Michael crossed her arms in front of her. Even inside Houston's leather gloves her hands were cold.

"It would surprise me if you didn't," he said pleasantly. He looked around, his gaze resting briefly on the lighted entrance, then the dark tunnel branches, and finally on Michael's shadowed features. "This isn't the sort of place where one wants to spend much time. It's possible to get lost in these tunnels and die without ever reaching light again." He paused, watching his words seep in. "There, I've given you something to think about, haven't I?"

Michael remained mute and refused to look at him.

"Now, let's see what you do with it." He cupped her chin and turned her face toward him, then tilted it upward. "Give me your mouth."

Her lips parted on a dry sob. Behind her closed lids, Michael's eyes burned. Her throat ached with suppressed tears. Houston's mouth was firm, his touch probing. She felt his fingers on the fasteners of her

238

coat and then his hands were inside, running down the length of her, cupping her breasts, molding her waist and hips, pressing against her thighs. He forced her back flush with the wall. His mouth slid to the cord of her neck when she turned her head to avoid his kisses.

Houston straightened. "Look at me." His breathing was harsh. "Dammit, look at me."

Michael raised her eyes slowly and let him see the full force of her anger and hatred.

"You won't say anything to Ethan."

It didn't matter if she did, she thought. Ethan warned her he wouldn't kill a man because of her. Houston didn't know that he wouldn't at least try. "I won't say anything."

"Very wise." His mouth lowered over hers again. "I meant it when I said I like Ethan. I wouldn't want to kill a friend over you." He kissed her full on the mouth. Hard. "I suppose I'd have to kill you."

Michael pushed at his chest and ducked under his arms when Houston rocked back on his heels. She made it a few yards toward the light when she was jerked back by a hand on her wrist and drawn up against him. She struggled briefly, realized the futility of it, and chose to save her strength. The ease with which Houston was able to subdue her humiliated Michael.

"That's better," he said softly. "I've never told you why I have no liking for reporters, have I?"

She was very still, listening, watchful. It was difficult to speak. "No, you've never said."

"When I was ten my father killed my mother, then himself. He held the gun but it was a reporter who pulled the trigger."

All the questions that occurred to Michael were left unasked. Houston spun her around and started toward the entrance. A few feet before they reached it

Obie Long appeared. Michael forced herself not to touch her hair or hurriedly button her coat and give Obie cause to think anything had been happening. It was more of an effort not to reveal her relief at his interruption.

"What is it, Obie?" Houston asked pleasantly.

Michael realized Houston had heard Obie's approach before the younger man was visible. The immediate tension she'd felt in him when he had spun her toward the entrance had vanished. He had been preparing himself for another confrontation. Had he thought it could have been Ethan?

"Jake sent me out to get you. There's been a message over the wire for you. Suppose Jake thinks it's important."

Houston nodded. "And it probably is. I was showing Michael here a little bit of the mines. Why don't you finish the tour for me and I'll take your horse back into town?"

"Sure. I don't mind."

"Michael?"

"Umm . . ." She felt Houston's fingers tighten on her elbow. "That's fine. I'd enjoy Obie's company."

"Good," Houston said. "Then it's settled. Don't keep her long, Obie." Houston released Michael's arm and started to go.

"Wait!" Michael called after him. "Your gloves."

"You'll need them on the drive back."

"No. You take them. I insist." She pulled them off and thrust them at his chest, forcing him to catch them or let them drop to the ground.

"Thank you."

Michael watched him go, knowing his parting smile was intended for Obie's benefit, not for hers. She took Obie's arm. "Houston couldn't show me very much," she said. "He forgot to get a lantern. Perhaps we could find one and—"

240

"Sure," Obie interrupted eagerly. "I'll show you where I've been working since you've already seen part of what Ethan's doing."

Obie's tour lasted another hour. If Michael hadn't had to cope with the memory of her encounter with Houston, she would have found Obie's company enjoyable, even entertaining. He was knowledgeable about the mines, understood the equipment that was used to reach the deepest veins. Michael had observed that although he was shy around most of the women in the saloon, in this environment at least he was talkative and open. She wished she dared ask him questions that had nothing to do with the operation of the Madison mines.

She thanked him when they reached the front of the saloon. "No, don't bother seeing me inside. If it will make you feel better, you can just sit here and watch me go in. I know you have to take the buggy back to the livery." Without waiting for a protest or assistance, Michael leapt lightly from the carriage and went directly into the saloon. She spoke to Carmen and Susan in passing, promising them she'd help with the new dance number before dinner was served. She waved at Kitty who was still serving behind the bar and spoke casually to two customers. Passing Dee's office, Michael was careful not to look as if she were avoiding Detra or mounting the stairs too hurriedly.

Michael pushed open the door to her room with more force than she thought. It rebounded off the wall. She closed it more gingerly, aware of Ethan's eyes on her. He was standing at the bureau, the water basin on top of it, mixing up lather in a shaving cup. Naked to the waist, he had a rolled towel around his neck. He wiped a little lather from his fingers on the edge of the towel and watched Michael's movements in the mirror.

She took off her coat and hung it in the wardrobe.

241

Turning, she formed a steeple with her fingers and blew on them gently, warming them. After a moment she crossed the room, got down on her hands and knees and started searching under the bed, making long sweeping motions with her arm.

"Anything in particular you're looking for?" he asked.

She didn't answer. Her fingers came in contact with the cigarette she'd pushed under the bed earlier and grasped it lightly. Rising, she went to the window and shot Ethan a derisive glance as she opened it a crack. "It never was painted shut."

He continued stirring up a lather. "Imagine that."

Reaching under the frame with her fingers, Michael found the matches and striking paper she kept hidden there. She didn't care that Ethan was watching her. Raising defiant eyes to him, Michael put the tip of the cigarette between her lips, struck the match, and lighted it. She inhaled deeply, realizing only when she saw the cigarette flutter at the end of her fingers how much her hand was trembling. She pulled one of the ladderback chairs closer to the window and sat down, blowing the smoke toward the crack.

Ethan began to lather his face and the underside of his jaw. "I'm surprised you know how to sit in that chair like a lady. I half-expected you to straddle it."

She ignored him, turning more toward the window and away from him, and drew deeply again on the cigarette. Tears welled in her eyes. She stared out the window, past the false fronts and sloping roofs across the street, to the jagged mountain crests that lifted the horizon and supported the sky. A tear fell from the center of one eye and slid smoothly down her cheek. She wiped it away impatiently. It was followed immediately by another.

"Are you crying, Michael?" Ethan put down his brush and the shaving mug. He took a step back from

242

the bureau to see her profile better. "Michael? What's wrong?"

The dark green eyes she slowly raised to him were wet with tears. "I just realized how hopeless it is," she said, the slightest quaver in her soft voice. "I'm never going to leave Madison, am I?"

Chapter Nine

Ethan sat down slowly on the edge of the bed. He was frowning. "Did Houston say something to you this afternoon?"

Michael shook her head. "No," she said, glancing out the window again. "Nothing like that."

He let the lie pass, certain that's what it was. "So what did happen?"

She shrugged. "We rode out to the mines. He showed me around until Obie came with a message for him from Jake. Then Houston left and Obie completed the tour."

Ethan was damn well sure Obie wasn't at the root of whatever was troubling Michael. He began wiping lather off his jaw. "Michael, I think it would be best if you would tell—"

Her laughter was a trifle bitter. "Trust you, you mean. But when I tried that before you made sure you set me straight. No, Ethan, I don't think so. I'm not going to tru—" She looked at him then and what she saw made her stop. Ethan had finished wiping lather from his cheeks and along his jaw. His neck was clear. But he'd left a thick mustache of lather above his upper lip. The sense of familiarity that she hadn't experienced in a while returned. She stared at him hard, reaching for the elusive memory and knowing she was closer to grasping it than ever before.

Ethan didn't know what had triggered her attempt at recollection, but knew the precise moment she remembered. Her lips parted a fraction as her jaw went slightly slack. The struggle that had played out in her expressive green eyes came to a halt. It was replaced for a moment by blankness, then denial, then a sudden start, an almost imperceptible widening of her pupils, as complete recognition filled them.

Michael stubbed out what remained of her cigarette and laid it on the sill. She pulled the window shut. "I know you," she said.

Ethan said nothing, waiting. He wiped away the lather mustache, realized then what had helped her remember, and sighed. "I don't think you know me," he said. "You may have seen me before, but you don't know me." He got up and latched the door to make sure there were no interruptions.

"You're wrong. I know you. You're a Marshall."

"Keep your voice down." He stopped at the bureau on his way back to the bed and washed the last vestiges of lather from his face. Hanging onto the ends of the towel around his neck, he sat down and pulled alternately with each hand, trying to massage out the sudden tension. He was about to point out that Houston was a sheriff, so being a marshal didn't necessarily make him honorable, when Michael continued recounting her memory.

"I was trying to get in to see Logan that day," she said slowly, drawing on the past. "God, it must have been six months ago at least. I was still answering letters then, writing occasional columns for the society pages. There was a special assignment I wanted to work on, a murder trial. I'd been giving a lot of thought to an aspect of the story no one else had used. But I needed Logan's permission to proceed with it.

"I'd been screwing up the courage all day to see him. I finally thought I could do it only to discover

245

that he was busy with some people. I caught a glimpse of you just as you walked into his office. I must have made some comment about it to Logan's secretary. That's when he told me you were a Marshall."

Faint color touched her cheeks as she recalled the more embarrassing moments of that afternoon. "I barged in to see him hours later, never suspecting he was still in a meeting. He gave me quite a dressing down then pointed out that he had company." She smiled ruefully. "I would have been happy if the floor had opened up and swallowed me. I remember turning around and seeing there were three men in the room. It's odd what goes through one's mind at times like that. I thought: tall, dark, and handsome." She glanced at Ethan's face and saw the ruddy color appearing just beneath his skin. "Before you flatter yourself too much, you were only the dark one. The older gentleman was tall, the younger one handsome."

Ethan's flinty stare widened slightly. He *had* been flattering himself. "As you say, it's odd what goes through one's mind. I remember thinking the pencils in your hair looked ridiculous."

Without a thought to what she was doing, Michael patted down her hair.

"I've become accustomed to them since then," Ethan said.

Her hands dropped to her lap again. For a moment she couldn't quite meet his eyes. "How are you related to Logan? I know he has a brother Christian, but others in his immediate family are dead. At least that's what I always understood."

Related to Logan? Ethan wondered. What was she talking about? Why would she think he was related to Logan Marshall? It wasn't until he heard himself complete the thought that he understood the problem. Marshall. Marshal. She'd made a natural assumption six months ago when she was told he was a marshal.

246

She had no reason to change it unless he gave her one. Ethan wasn't certain he was going to do that yet. Caution was still his best defense.

"A distant cousin," he said.

Michael nodded. "I thought it might be something like that. You have a little of their look. Black sheep strain, I'll bet."

"Hmmm-mm."

"Is your first name really Ethan?"

"It's Ethan. Ethan Stone. I'm a Marshall on my mother's side."

"Does Logan know what his black sheep cousin does to put money in his pockets?"

Ethan's drawl became more pronounced. "What do you think?"

"I doubt it."

Some day, Ethan thought, Mary Michael Dennehy would not be so easily led into jumping to conclusions. At the moment he was glad it was still possible. He played to her suspicions. "You're right. He doesn't know."

"So what were you doing at his office that day I saw you?"

"Trying to negotiate a business deal."

"Who were those other men?"

"Just some people interested in the same deal."

"You make it sound like a poker game. *Deal* this and *deal* that."

He laughed lowly. "It was rather like a poker game."

"Did you win?"

"I'm still playing out my hand."

There were still tear tracks on Michael's cheeks. She took a cloth from the washstand and bathed her face quickly at the basin. Looking at Ethan over the wet cloth she held up to her cheeks, she asked, "Does that mean what you're doing now has something to do with the meeting that afternoon?"

"That's one way of interpreting it."

Michael wondered how many others there could possibly be. She didn't ask because she knew better than to expect a straight answer from Ethan. "Houston and the others don't know about your connection to the *Chronicle,* do they?"

"It's not much of a connection. I'm the black sheep, remember? As for the meeting, no, they don't know about it or that I was in New York then. But I'd have less problem explaining it than you would. They'd want to know how you came to be in the *Chronicle*'s offices. I don't think you'd care for them to know, would you?"

"I think Houston already suspects."

Ethan slowly pulled the towel from around his neck. His narrowed, hooded eyes followed Michael back to her chair. "He suspects what?" he asked slowly.

"That I'm a reporter, or at least *my* connection to the *Chronicle* is more than simply being Drew Beaumont's traveling companion."

"Traveling companion? You were supposed to be his fiancée."

"Houston asked me about my engagement ring the other day. I had to say something. I told him the engagement wasn't official."

Ethan swore softly. "What exactly did he say to you this afternoon? And don't say it was nothing."

"Just *things,*" she said. At his sharp, angry look Michael recounted Houston's rather one-sided conversation with her. She told Ethan nothing about the physical confrontation that had taken place, only the verbal one. "It was all very veiled," she said. "Threatening without being specific. I don't even know why I'm telling you. You've threatened me with as much yourself. You probably told him what works best with me. I share one terrifying dream with you about falling into blackness and the next thing I know, I'm being threatened with eternity in a mine shaft."

Ethan had forgotten all about the dream until now, but he saw that she hadn't and the threat that Houston used, for all that it had been coincidental, clearly terrified Michael. He got up, opened the first drawer of his bureau and found a handkerchief. He gave it to Michael. "Here, you're crying again."

"Thank you." She hadn't even been aware of it.

He wondered what had happened between last night when Houston berated him for not caring well enough for Michael, and this afternoon, when Houston's own behavior had taken a dramatic turn. Had Houston discovered something, had Dee filled his ears with some lie about Michael, or was it just his manner of keeping her under his thumb?

Standing over her, Ethan placed one hand on the top rail of her chair. The tips of his fingers laid gently against her shoulder. "We've come to a crossroads, you and I, where one of us has to trust the other, even if it's on blind faith. As much as I might like to tell you certain things, I can't. My obligation to protect you conflicts with allowing you to know more. Therefore—"

"Therefore it has to be me who trusts you," she finished for him. "And when I did that you threw it back in my face. When I tried to find something good to believe in, you belittled me as if I were a schoolgirl in the throes of her first infatuation."

It was an apt description. Michael was reaching to him to steady her tilting world. It was natural, perhaps inevitable, that she felt something for him. In other circumstances, he reminded himself, she wouldn't have given him more notice than she'd ever given any man who didn't belong in her world.

"Well, I don't think so." She went on. "I'm not prepared to accept anything you have to say on blind faith. You'll have to give me something more to believe in." She raised her face to him, waiting.

"I didn't kill Drew Beaumont."

Michael sighed and shook her head. "That doesn't serve your case. The time to admit that has already passed." She stood and took a step away, intending to go around him. He blocked her path. "Yes?"

Ethan wanted to tell her. His mouth opened a fraction, the sun lines at the corners of his eyes deepened. There was tension in every line of his body, then it was gone. "No," he said finally, "I can't. I'd be trading your safety for time in your bed. I thought I was that selfish, perhaps I'm not. In any case, you deserve better."

Michael hesitated, moved by the desire that made him want to tell her something and the self-denial that held him back. "If you told me something, anything, to help me trust you, what is it you're afraid I might do?"

"Give the information away by some small misstep. It wouldn't be purposeful. I trust you that much. But it really wouldn't matter about the motive. If it happened you'd be dead."

"Is Nathaniel Houston your friend?" she asked, watching him closely.

Ethan didn't answer immediately. Finally he said, "Houston's using me to get something he wants. I'm using him for the same reason."

"But is he your friend?" She was unaware of the pleading look in her eyes. "Do you like him, admire him?"

"No. None of those things." He paused. "Is that what you needed to hear?"

"It's enough."

"It will have to be. If I respected Houston less, I'd tell you more."

Michael understood. It was the danger Houston represented that Ethan respected, not the man himself. "It's enough," she repeated.

Outside dusk was slipping quietly into Madison, silhouetting the surrounding mountains and bringing up the flames in gaslighted rooms along the main street. Ethan drew the curtain closed. Michael began taking the pins from her hair.

"Let me," he said.

"All right." She dropped her hand to her side and waited, anticipating, her eyes searching his face as he approached. Thick lashes shaded the darkening centers of his eyes. There was an intensity in their cool depths that held her immobile. Inside she trembled.

Ethan stopped just inches from her and raised his hands. His fingers barely touched the downy strands of hair at her nape. He heard her breath catch. "Do I frighten you, Michael?"

"When you look at me that way . . ." She shook her head, unable to finish. Unselfconsciously she tilted her face toward his cupped hand, rubbing her cheek against his palm. ". . . you make me want you."

It was Ethan who felt air swell in his lungs and burn before he could take another breath. His fingers tangled in her hair. He pulled at the pins, unwound the thick coil and combed through it with his fingertips. Silky, curling strands of copper, gold, and red spilled over his hands. He lifted her hair over one shoulder and let it fall and buried his face against her exposed neck. Her skin was as beautifully soft as it looked. He tasted. He sipped. Her arms went around him, holding him, stroking his naked back with the lightest touch of her tapered nails. She traced the length of his spinal cord. Her fingers dipped just below the waist of his jeans and circled around to the front. She fumbled with the button fly.

His mouth was hot on her skin. His tongue damp. Ethan's teeth caught her earlobe and worried it gently. His lips brushed her temple and he felt the faint racing of her pulse. Trailing across her forehead, he touched her feathery brows, her closed lids, the arch of her cheeks. His mouth teased the corner of her lips. Her mouth opened, hungry and demanding. She ground her lips against his mouth, pressing her tongue against his, making no secret of what she wanted.

Ethan was struck by her open and honest passion. There was no one else like her in his experience. Her reserve vanished in the face of her desire. She was without guile, untroubled by the depth of her wanting. Her fingers had managed the buttons on his jeans. She parted the material and pushed at his drawers. He had to capture her wrists as she captured him.

"I'll throw you back on the bed and toss up your skirts if you keep that up."

"I wouldn't mind."

"I would." His voice was husky, whiskey smooth. "I want to look at you."

Her smile was artless, not seductive, her pleasure genuine. She helped him with her buttons as he backed her toward the bed. He pulled the hunter green gown over her shoulders. She wiggled out of it as he tugged at the laces of her corset. She felt the mattress at the back of her thighs and dropped, lying back, supporting herself with her elbows while she raised one leg at a time for Ethan to make short work of her shoes and stockings. Grinning, he tossed them blindly over his shoulder. The shoes thumped, the stockings fluttered.

He was beside her on the bed then, rolling so that they stretched diagonally on the bed. Their mouths touched. Clung.

He pushed at her chemise, baring the smooth skin of her abdomen. She raised her arms over her head so he could pull it off. It went the way of the stockings. His knuckles brushed the tips of her breasts. The pink nipples seemed to darken to rose as they hardened.

Ethan bent his head. His tongue flicked the tip of one nipple. She moved a little impatiently beneath him. He attended the other breast, laving the sweetly tender flesh with the edge of his tongue. She arched. Her fingers curled in his hair, holding him to her. The suck of his mouth radiated fire.

Their legs tangled. The clothing that remained was quickly discarded. When their legs touched again it was flesh against flesh. She reached for him intimately and Ethan watched her hands close around him.

"Take me into you."

She opened her thighs and guided him. Ethan watched her watching them. "You are so beautiful." He was deep inside her. She was tight all around him. Her fingers passed into the taut flesh of his buttocks.

He kissed her. The play of their tongues was a prelude to the play of their bodies. Her mouth slipped from his as she gasped her pleasure. She trailed damp, tasting kisses along his jaw and down his neck. Her hips lifted to his rhythm. She tightened as he withdrew, opened to him as he thrust again.

He spoke her name, whispered it against her skin. Her hair spilled across the comforter. It wound around his fingers. She bit her lip to hold back the sounds of her pleasure. He nudged her mouth open with his, tasted her husky little cries, and let her hear his. Pleasure hummed between them.

Tension tugged at their skin, drawing their bodies taut, making them responsive to the slightest touch. Michael felt as if she was standing on the edge of the very emptiness she feared. It was Ethan who was encouraging her to go further. She listened to him. She leaped.

He didn't desert her. His arms held her, his body cradled her, his voice soothed her. The pleasure was intense. Sharing his was equally satisfying.

After their breathing calmed Ethan started to move away.

"Don't leave me just yet," she said.

His lips brushed the corner of her mouth. "All right. In a little while." He liked the touch of her fingertips sweeping across his back. When he moved later she didn't protest, but rolled with him so that her body curved against his and her head rested in the crook of his shoulder. They managed to get between the sheets with the least amount of fussing.

Michael looked up at him. She absently smoothed back the hair at his temples. "You have some strands of gray here. Did you know that?"

"What I know is that I didn't have so many a few weeks ago."

"Meaning, I suppose, that I'm responsible."

He shrugged. "You decide."

She nudged him lightly in the ribs with her fist. "What's wrong?" she asked when she heard him swear softly. "Did I hurt you?"

Ethan was looking past Michael's shoulder to her breasts. Her skin was faintly reddened there as if she'd been brush burned. "Did I do that?"

Michael looked down at herself, saw the same flush he saw. "It doesn't hurt," she told him. "It's my fault anyway. I interrupted your shaving." He started to sit up to remedy that fact immediately. Michael pushed him back down and trapped his legs beneath one of hers. She snuggled. "That's better. I don't mind the little bit of beard." It had been pleasantly rough against her skin. She stroked the underside of his jaw lightly with her knuckles. "You could grow your mustache again. It doesn't matter if I see you with it now."

"I'll think about it. I've become —" He broke off when there was a knock at the door. "What is it?" he asked impatiently.

It was Carmen's voice that came through the door.

"I'm looking for Michael," she said. "Is she with you?"

Michael started to answer only to have Ethan's hand clamp over her mouth. "She is," he called back. "And she's occupied." At the very moment one of her hands was running across his flat belly.

"Well, let her go, for God's sake. She promised to help with the new dance number."

Ethan tightened his hold on Michael when she began to squirm, trying to get away and answer Carmen herself. "She's not going downstairs at all tonight. She's still recovering from yesterday's bout with the bottle."

"She looked fine to me a while ago."

"Relapse," Ethan said tersely. Beside him Michael was shaking with laughter, at least he hoped it was laughter, not anger.

"Dee won't like it," Carmen called through the door.

"Dee doesn't have to like it." He thought he heard her harrumph her disagreement before she walked away. Ethan waited until he was certain Carmen was down the hall before he slowly lifted his hand from Michael's mouth. She *was* laughing.

"Shhh." He gave her a quick kiss, silencing her. "Someone might hear." He brushed her hair away from her cheek and where it touched her throat. "How *are* you feeling? You had quite a lot to drink yesterday."

The memory, not her head, made her groan. "I'm fine now. Could you doubt it?" She smiled. "But if you really want to protect me, you'll never let me drink like that again."

"I couldn't stop you. In case it hasn't been pointed out to you before, Miss Dennehy, you're a very strong-willed individual."

"My father's influence."

"Oh?" He was curious. He knew only bits and pieces about her family, not much more than the fact that she had one. She had mentioned precious little

255

about her father. "How's that?"

"He doesn't let very much get in his way," she said. "He's been riding roughshod over people most of his life."

"Your mother included?"

She sighed. "Most especially my mother." She glanced up at him. "Don't misunderstand. He loves my mother. Quite desperately, in fact. And, for all his character flaws, she loves him just as desperately. It's the reason she accepts his decisions, no matter how much they pain her or go against what she was raised to believe. She loves him that much."

Ethan recalled something Michael had said to him before. "Why would some people think your mother's a whore?"

"I said that, didn't I?" She paled a little with the memory of her harsh indictment. "I shouldn't have. It doesn't matter what people think. I know the truth."

"And that is?"

"My father's married."

Ethan frowned. "Of course—"

"But not to my mother," she said. "She's been his mistress for twenty-five years, a wife to him in all ways except legally. She's borne him five daughters. She's comforted him, encouraged him, fought with him, and loved him. None of it could change the fact that she knew him first when she was a servant in his home. He was already married. My mother never tried to plead ignorance of that fact. She accepted him for what he was. Not only was he married, he was . . . *is* . . . Presbyterian. He's quite wealthy. She wasn't. His family was here before the revolution. My mother's Irish accent is still very evident. It was an odd pairing from the beginning, I suppose, but somehow it survived."

"You think it shouldn't have?"

"For my mother's sake I'm glad it has. Except for

the place she has in her heart for each of her daughters, he's her entire world. But I resent him sometimes. I resent how he could walk in and out of our lives, how time spent with him, even as a child with my sisters, was always snatched, as if we were keeping him from something more important. I used to think it was his wife that took him away. As I grew older I understood it was just as much his work."

"He paid for your education?"

She nodded. "Mary's too. And Rennie's and Maggie's. Skye will be going soon herself. My father never let us want for anything. There was never a birthday forgotten or a Christmas when he didn't send gifts to our home. We were encouraged to study, to do well in school. Perhaps because he knew the struggles we would face as bastards, even as women."

"Michael . . ." He said her name softly.

"It's all right. I know I should feel blessed by his attention — my sisters don't all share my resentment — but I can't help feeling that he shortchanged all of us."

"And yet you are who you are because of him." Independent. Reserved. Strong-willed. Determined.

Her laughter was dry, humorless. "I know. I set out to avoid my mother's mistakes and somehow became my father. That's something to think about, isn't it?"

Ethan squeezed her lightly. "Hm-mmm."

"Meeting you has been good for me, Ethan."

"Oh?"

"The things I've done with you . . . the feelings . . . it helps me . . ."

"Yes?"

"I understand my mother better. It was so easy to sometimes condemn her in my heart when I never had to make the same choices."

He stroked her shoulder and could not find it in himself to wish he had given her other choices. She did not appear to regret the decisions she'd made.

257

"What's your mother's name? Another Mary?"

She smiled. "No. It's Moira. Her naming us all Mary was her way of trying to atone for her transgressions. She hasn't been inside a church for years, but she's deeply religious. Mary Francis, my oldest sister, completed her vows two years ago and became a nun with Little Sisters of the Poor. That seemed to help Mama. She felt as if she had offered something back to the church."

"Your sister's a sister?"

"Hmm-mm. Oh, I see. It's made you uncomfortable. Jay Mac had the same reaction at first. He's so very protestant and the idea of one of his daughters becoming a nun was a little discomfiting. He never really had any say in the matter though. If you think I'm strong-willed, you should meet Mary Francis. She's every bit as plain a speaker as our father and so calm about it that you don't realize you've been tongue-lashed until you hear yourself apologizing."

Ethan was only listening now with half an ear. Her mention of one single name made it nearly impossible for him to hear anything else. "Jay Mac?" he asked. "Your father's John MacKenzie Worth?"

She sat up, tucking the sheet under her arms and across her breasts as she did so. Michael nodded. "You know Jay Mac?"

Ethan pushed himself up and leaned against the headboard. Know him, he thought, *I'm all but working for him!* He could see himself in Logan Marshall's office again, working out the details of the plan with Marshall, Rivington, and Carl Franklin. Jay Mac hadn't been there, but he was at the heart of the scheme, the majority stockholder in Northeast Rail Lines and the client Franklin represented in the discussion. Had Jay Mac not been called away on some personal matter, he may have well represented himself at the meeting. Ethan could only imagine what would have happened if Michael had burst in on them then.

"I know *of* Jay Mac," he said truthfully. "Naturally I've never met him."

"Never robbed anything of his?" she asked slyly.

His look was stern. "Michael."

"I'm sorry." She leaned forward and kissed him on the mouth. "I just think it would be a wonderful irony if you had. He has banks, you know."

Ethan ignored that. "I thought Jay Mac had a son."

"You're thinking of Elliot. That's Papa's nephew. His brother's son."

"What about Mrs. Worth?"

"Nina? She's not any part of our lives, at least not directly. I find myself feeling sorry for her, then calling myself a traitor for having those feelings. She's childless, fills her days with good works. Jay Mac rarely speaks of her around us; but we always feel the tug of her as he prepares to leave."

"Why didn't you mention who your father was before?"

"I never mentioned who my mother was either. I can't see that it matters at all."

"Jay Mac's capable of turning the country inside out looking for you."

"I did tell you that my family would be trying to find me. You assured me they'd only discover I was dead."

"Jay Mac's not the sort of person who will stop if there isn't a body."

"I see his reputation *is* far reaching."

Ethan wondered how successful Logan Marshall and the others would be at restraining him. Jay Mac Worth's interference now could only make things more difficult for his daughter, not better. "I just wish you had mentioned it before," he said.

"When I didn't trust you? I don't think so. You know what the others would do if they found out Jay

Mac was my father. They'd demand money from him and my body would still never be found."

He reached for her then and held her tightly. The shiver that had begun with her words passed into him. He absorbed it, felt her fear touch his own. John MacKenzie Worth's money, power, and influence couldn't protect her in Madison. Only he could do that.

"I'm not going to let anything happen to you," he said.

"I know. I think I've always known."

"Even when I was threatening you?"

"Well, perhaps not then, at least not consciously. But that sense that I knew you in some way was always there. It probably made me feel safer than I had any right to feel." She kissed his shoulder. Her lips slid along the edge of his collarbone. She kissed his neck, his throat. Her mouth moved lower, down his chest, across his nipples, teasing him with her teeth and tongue the way he had done to her.

He watched her make a path across his belly while her hands dipped beneath the comforter to stroke his thighs. He pushed away from the headboard and lay back. Michael moved with him, sliding down his body to lie on top of him.

"I like this," she whispered against his skin.

"So do I." Her hair was a beautiful cascade of curls framing her face. It brushed his abdomen and then his thighs as she moved still lower. The first tentative, intimate caress of her mouth made him think he would come out of his skin. His fingers tightened in her hair. His words were husky and encouraging. She made him hot and hard and she seemed to know what he wanted, what would give him the most pleasure, without ever asking. No woman had ever done for him what she was doing, leastways without seeing his money first.

"I've got to take you now," he said hungrily, drawing her up, "or I won't . . ."

"It's all right."

"No, it's not. I want to pleasure you." When she started to move to lie beside him, he stopped her, holding her firmly at the hips. "No, not that way. Like this," he said. "I want you like this."

Her emerald eyes darkened as she looked down at his face. She lifted her hips and when she lowered herself down on his belly she was filled with him and he was part of her. He gave himself up to her rhythm and control, finding it the sweetest surrender he'd ever known. His hands caressed her pink-tipped breasts. Her own hands fluttered to his abdomen. His muscles rippled beneath her touch. She rocked faster as her own pleasure began to rise and rode the crest as if it were wild white water. He arched beneath her, driving into her deeply one last time as she collapsed against him. She was laughing unevenly, out of breath with passion and pleasure, and spreading small kisses on his face and neck.

"Oh, Ethan," she sighed. "Should I enjoy this quite so much?"

"Yes," he said. "Always." But always with me, he wanted to say. *Only* with me. He let her slide off him and covered them both with the sheet that got wrapped around his legs. Dusk had deepened outside and darkness was encroaching on the room. Ethan lighted the bedside lamp. His stomach growled.

"I'll get you something to eat," she said, starting to rise.

"Only if you're going to get something for yourself."

Tapping her finger lightly against his lower lip, she flashed him a brilliant smile. "Are you saying you don't need me to wait on you?"

The impact of her smile seemed to drive into his

belly and force air from his lungs. "Are you saying you want to?"

Her smile faded slowly, becoming a shade wistful before it disappeared. "We've both changed a little, haven't we? It's probably good there's no future for us. I might come to like doing for you and stop doing for myself. You'd most likely come to resent it, what with me home all the time with the children, singing and playing the piano, doing needlework and such. You think a little differently now. I suspect all those normal female things would come to grate on your nerves after awhile."

He winced at the memory of asking her if she ever did any normal female things. She was right, they'd both changed a little. "I suspect that's the way it would be," he said after a moment. He held her hand and kissed her fingertip. He thought he would have been relieved to know, all silly reasons aside, that Michael understood they had no future together. He found he was not.

"What would you like from the kitchen?" she asked, sitting up.

Ethan followed suit. "No, I better get it. Once you're downstairs they'll have you out on the floor. I'll have to pull ten fool men away from you, haul you upstairs as a show to the others, and I'll still never have anything for supper. It seems less trouble to get it myself."

"Well, when you put it like—" This time it was Michael who was interrupted by the knocking at the door.

"She's still occupied, Carmen," Ethan called. "Save your knuckles." The chuckle on the other side of the door did not belong to one of Dee's girls.

"It's Obie, not Carmen," he said, leaning against the door. "And I want you, not Michael."

"Damn," Ethan said softly. He slid out of bed and

pulled on his jeans. Behind him Michael dove under the covers. He threw her her robe and made sure she had it on before he unhooked the latch. Obie almost fell in the room when he opened the door.

"You could've warned me," Obie grumbled, straightening his lanky frame and tipping his hat toward Michael on the bed. She smiled wanly, a bit embarrassed by his presence.

"You shouldn't stand around with your ear pressed to other people's business."

Obie hadn't intended to eavesdrop at all. Still, he flushed guiltily. "I wasn't . . . that is, I didn't . . ."

"Get on with it," Ethan said.

Obie looked uneasily at Michael then spoke to Ethan. "Houston says to tell you that there's a . . . a poker game in Dee's apartments this evening. He wants you to be there."

"A poker game?" Ethan realized he was a bit dazed or he would have understood the significant look Obie had given him earlier and was giving to him again. "Oh, a poker game. I understand. I'll be there." He started to shut the door, pushing Obie gently toward the hallway. "What time?"

"Seven-thirty."

Ethan frowned. "It must be close to that now."

Obie nodded. "You have a little less than an hour."

"All right. I'll see you then." He closed the door. "Well, that's that," he said, turning to Michael. We'll both have to go down to the kitchen if we want any supper. There isn't time for me to get it and bring it up here."

"Why do you have to be at Houston's poker game? And why have it in Dee's apartments when you can play just as easily in the saloon?"

"But then we'd have folks wanting to join us, or watch at least. It's a special, private game. No outsiders."

"Oh," she said. "I see." It wasn't about poker at all. It was about robbery. "Then I suppose I can't play."

"Absolutely not." He stooped to pick up their discarded clothes, laying his over his arm and throwing hers at the bed. "Some other time perhaps." He grinned at her. "You're a helluva poker player, aren't you? Who taught you?"

"My father."

He knew it. To be taught poker by John MacKenzie Worth, it boggled the mind. "All your sisters learned?"

Michael's head came through the neckline of her chemise. She straightened the waist. "Of course. We all played together."

"Don't tell me. Mary Francis was the best."

Michael bent her head and concentrated on the laces of her corset.

"Well?" he asked.

"You told me not to tell you," she said with an impish grin. "The truth is that Mary Francis is best at most everything. She's the one who sings like a bird and plays the piano so sweetly it can bring tears to your eyes. She's not pretty, mind you, not Mary Francis. She's beautiful. And kind and smart as a whip."

"Then why . . ." He let his voice trail off and his question go unasked.

Michael finished for him. "Why did she become a nun? Because she *is* the best at everything. God wanted her more. It wasn't a choice. It was a calling." Her smile was gentle as she saw Ethan trying to puzzle it out. "You'd understand if you knew her."

Ethan accepted what Michael said because he knew he'd never meet her sister. He shrugged into a fresh shirt and sat down in the wing chair to put on his sock and boots. "Before I go sit down at the table with Houston, I'd like to hear a more complete version of what happened this afternoon."

Michael paused while smoothing her stockings over

264

her legs. "I told you what I remember he said." She adjusted her garters and pulled down the hem of her dress as she scooted toward the edge of the bed. She ticked off several points of the conversation on her fingers. "He told me that the reason you were in New York during the spring we supposedly met was because you were robbing banks." There was neither denial nor confirmation from Ethan. "He said I would find the mine very unpleasant if I had to spend any length of time there." Except for a slight narrowing of Ethan's eyes, there was no response. "And he said that his father had killed himself and his mother, but that a reporter pulled the trigger. Those are almost his exact words, I think. Do you know what he meant?"

"Houston's father was accused of embezzling from the bank he owned. The case was aired and judged in the papers by a reporter who wasn't connected to all the facts. His apparent source turned out to be the real embezzler. Long before the trial was held though, the Houstons were disgraced publicly. What Houston didn't tell you was that his father shot him, too. He was ten, I think. Took it through the shoulder. He passed out. His father thought he was dead and that's precisely what saved his life. The drama and scandal was played out in the papers as well. It took Houston years to piece together what happened. *That* is why he has no love for the fourth estate."

"He told you all this?"

"Some. Some I found out on my own. I like to know who I'm working for." He stood, tucking his shirt into his pants. "But that isn't what I meant when I asked for a complete account of what happened today. I think Houston did more than threaten you. Now, what happened?"

She went to the bureau and began to coil her hair, pinning it up carefully. "I don't know what you mean."

"Don't dissemble now, Michael. I know . . . wait,

did Houston tell you not to say anything to me?" Her pause gave her away. "I see that he did. Look, you've already told me things he said, why not the things he did?"

"It was nothing."

He came up behind her, put his hands on her shoulders, and caught her eyes in the mirror. "Then why are you shaking?"

She hadn't been aware she was until she looked carefully at her own reflection. She finished pinning her hair and lowered her hands to her sides, leaning back against Ethan. "He was solicitous during the ride," she said in a small emotionless voice. "It wasn't until we got to the mines that he changed. At first it was only his words that were threatening. Then it became his hands."

"He hit you?"

She shook her head. "He put them on me. Touched me. He . . . he kissed me."

"Did you want him to?"

Michael pushed away from him, stung by his question. She escaped to the wing chair and sat down. "How can you say that?"

"It wasn't a statement. It was a question. I had to know, Michael. You left with him of your own accord."

"That doesn't mean I wanted him touching me."

Ethan sat down on the footstool and leaned forward, his forearms on his knees. "What else happened?"

"Nothing. He just kissed me . . . touched me. I don't know if he intended to do more. Obie came with the message."

"Did he frighten you enough to make you stay away from him?"

She nodded.

Ethan was quiet. He knew a rage so intense that it

266

burned him. He swallowed it all because it wasn't for Michael to see.

"What are you going to do?" she asked. His eyes were so cold, she thought. They could burn her with their coldness.

He stood and strapped on his gunbelt. When he heard her soft gasp he realized what decision he appeared to have made. "I always wear this below stairs, Michael. As for Houston, I'm not going to do anything." Yet, he finished in his own mind. "I'm going to play a few hands of poker and drink a few beers. That's all. I'm sorry for what happened to you today at the mines, but I'm not sorry for what it taught you."

Michael said nothing. She stood and preceded him out the door when he opened it for her. They ate in silence in the kitchen, relatively undisturbed by any of the girls who wandered in and out to get something for the customers.

"I may as well help out in the saloon," she said, dropping their dishes in the sink. She pumped some water and let it splash over them. "I don't think I could stand being upstairs tonight by myself. They'll need the help anyway if Dee's going to be with you."

"She will be," he confirmed.

"All right, then. That settles it." She heard Ethan's chair scrape against the floor then felt him just behind her. His hands touched her waist lightly. He leaned forward and placed a kiss on her cheek. It was a gesture she had seen her father do at least a hundred times with her mother. Michael smiled faintly, closing her eyes.

"You'll be fine?" A slight inflection at the end made it a question.

"Yes. You go play poker." She felt his hands drift away slowly, reluctantly. Then he was gone.

Ethan was the last one to enter Detra's private dining room. Everyone else who was expected was already sitting around the large oak table. They all made some acknowledgment of Ethan's presence. He closed the door, sealing off the dining room from the rest of the apartment, and took the empty chair between Jake and Obie. Ben Simpson was absently shuffling a deck of cards with no intent to deal them. Happy had a chew under his lip and a spittoon by his chair. Without ever taking his eyes off his half-brother's hands, he spit and accurately hit the cuspidor. Detra gave him a sour look and muttered something about her carpets. Houston was leaning back in his chair, his legs stretched out beneath the table. His black eyes hadn't left Ethan's face since he'd walked in the room.

"I think we can start," he said. "Ben, deal one hand. Obie said it was a poker game. We may as well make it look like one. Ante up, fellas, and keep a little money in front of you."

Money was tossed in the center of the table as the cards were dealt. A few bills and coins were kept at each man's side, next to the cards that were never picked up.

"Michael's not coming back here," Ethan said. "She's working out front this evening."

"Better safe . . ." Houston didn't bother finishing the homily. "I got a wire today. Coded, of course. We're being asked to take No. 486 on her way to Cheyenne. Cooper'd like it done the week of the 20th. He has business in San Francisco later in the month. He'll be on the train going west then."

Jake whistled softly. "Did I hear right? He wants us to hold up the train he's on?"

Ben shrugged. "Sorta makes sense. Houston promised we could meet him sometime. Ain't no better way than to pluck him clean."

Houston nodded. "And there'll be a shipment of silver from the Salina mines. Not as much as we brought in last time, but enough to make it worth the risk."

"How much you figure?" Happy asked.

"Thirty, forty thousand." There was a general murmur around the table. "Same terms, of course. We split sixty percent between us. Forty percent goes back to him."

Obie's fingers stopped drumming against the table top. He frowned slightly.

"Something wrong, Obie?" Houston asked. "You have some objection?"

He thought about it a while before he spoke. "Well," he drawled, "it don't seem right somehow. The risk is always ours. Seems like forty percent is a lot to give back for information when we could pick the trains ourselves."

It wasn't Houston who answered, but Ethan. "We wouldn't be nearly as successful and the risk would be much greater. Because of Cooper we generally know how much is going to be on the train, how many men are guarding it, who we might expect to encounter. Pretty difficult for us to find that sort of thing out without raising suspicion. My life's worth my share of that forty percent."

Ben nodded. "It's true what you say, but he mucked things up last time out. We shoulda been warned about the cars from the *Chronicle*."

"Which is why we'll meet with him this time," Houston said. "Happy, you tell him what happened with the *Chronicle*. Coop only knows what he's read in the papers. Obie, you tell him what you think about his forty percent. Maybe we can renegotiate something more favorable."

Obie looked uncertain at first, glancing around the table to see if he could count on support. He finally nodded. "I'll do it."

Houston smiled. "Good."

"The 20th's only ten days from now," Happy said. "Not much time to plan. We took No. 349 when we thought the time was right. Coop didn't dictate then."

"I think this is different," Ethan said. "I know I've only been with you since you decided you wanted 349. You brought me on board because of the safe. But there were . . . how many? . . . five, six trains you stopped before I joined you?"

"Six," Happy said. "Unless you don't count Seneca Valley. Obie don't like to. That's where he shot hisself in the foot."

Ethan waited for the laughter to die down. "What I'm getting at is Coop's provided you with quite a bit of information. Depending on who he is, what his job might be, he could be coming under suspicion. If that's the case, I'd do the same thing in his place: invite you all to rob me."

"The same thing's occurred to me," Houston said approvingly. "It makes sense. If we mean to go on as we have been then this robbery is critical. We have to do it to take suspicion away from the source of our information."

Ben picked up the deck of undealt cards and flicked through them with his thumb. "Sounds all right by me."

Happy spit. "By me, too. Any one got any ideas? Detra? You're usually good for one or two."

Detra stopped twirling a strand of her hair as all eyes went to her. "I haven't had much more time than you to think about it. I don't see how we can use the same ruse as last time to get all of you out of town together."

"We can't," Houston said, putting a period to any more thinking along that line.

"You could all leave separately, though," she said. "Different times, different reasons. Perhaps within a few days of one another. You have a schedule

270

for the train, don't you, Houston?"

"Jake got the latest one this afternoon, right after he got the wire."

"We still have to pick a place to take the train. That will decide the time. We'll need confirmation from Cooper that he's actually going to be on it."

Houston shook his head. "I can't reach him, you know that."

Ethan rubbed the back of his neck. "He said the 486. We'll have to hope he's got it right and they don't change schedules on him." Cooper's identity had frustrated Ethan from the beginning. He was the reason it was impossible to quit after the robbery of No. 349, the reason it wasn't good enough to simply have Houston and the others dead to rights. He needed the man who gave them their information, the man who made it possible for them to take the trains in the first place. Ethan's private money was on Cooper being a dispatcher or someone from the Wells Fargo office who knew about gold, silver, and payroll shipments. So far nothing had turned up a Cooper working in either place. Ethan hadn't really expected it to. Cooper was undoubtedly not his real name.

"What's your idea, Dee, about us leaving at different times?"

"I haven't thought it through, you understand," she said, "but it makes sense that Ben and Happy should go out prospecting together. Happy's always talking about finding placer gold again. After his last 'incident' of getting lost, he'll take Ben along for safety. That will take care of the mules and supplies you'll need. Obie can go to Stillwater for me. I'm expecting some things I ordered from Chicago."

"What about me?" Jake asked.

"If a wire came in for the sheriff's office to look into some leads on the 349 robbery, you and Houston could leave for a few days." Dee's dark blue eyes rested

271

on Ethan. "I'm not certain what to do about you."

"And I'm not certain what to do with Michael," he said.

Houston leaned forward in his chair and folded his arms on the table. "I am. She stays holed up here. I don't trust your wife to be any part of this."

Happy got up, stretched. "Sounds like we got some discussin' to do about that little lady. Hold your fire till I get back from the privy." He opened the door to leave the dining room.

Michael stumbled into the room carrying a tray of glasses in one hand and a pitcher of beer in the other. She steadied herself and looked up, feeling the eyes of everyone in the room boring into her. Her smile faltered. "Kitty just tapped a keg. Drinks around?"

Her hopeful question was met with stony silence.

Chapter Ten

"Shut the door, Happy," Houston said calmly. "And take a seat. Your trip will have to wait."

Happy accepted Houston's dictate. He took the tray from Michael and put it on the table. "You'd better have a seat yourself," he told her.

There was only one unoccupied chair in the room. Happy took it from against the wall and set it squarely next to Houston. Michael stared at the pitcher in her hand and wondered at the steadiness of it. She felt as if she were shaking with ague. She sat slowly in the chair Happy held out to her and set the pitcher down.

"I don't think I understand," she said. "I was only bringing the beer. Kitty asked me to."

"Then why was your ear pressed to the door?" Ben asked.

Michael faced her accuser directly. "I'd like to see you open that door with a tray of glasses and a pitcher. I was trying to turn the knob with my elbow."

"You might have knocked," Jake said.

"With what? My head?" She glanced around the table. No one was amused. "I did tap at the door, this one and the outer one, with my foot. No one answered either time."

"No one heard anything," Ethan said.

"That doesn't mean I didn't do it." They'd had an argument like this before, she recalled, only now the

273

tables were turned. "Obie, are you going to sit there and pretend nothing of the sort's ever happened to you? Just this evening you almost fell on your face when Ethan opened the door. Were you listening then? That seems to be what I'm accused of."

"No, ma'am. I wasn't."

"And I can tell you that what was going on inside that room was a lot more interesting than a poker game."

Ethan tamped down his smile as Obie's ears pinkened. He saw Ben and Jake were grinning. Happy cast him a sly glance. Trust Michael to charge ahead rather than retreat. It was exactly the right strategy to use. Only Houston and Dee remained unconvinced by her explanation.

Houston touched Dee's arm. "Go out and ask Kitty how long it's been since she sent Michael here with the drinks." Dee excused herself. "I'll take that beer now," Houston told Michael.

She gave no indication of wanting to pour it over his head. She served up glasses to everyone while waiting for Dee's return.

"Kitty can't be sure," Dee said, taking her seat again. "She'd only say that it wasn't long. They're busy out front. Michael should be going back. They need her."

Michael picked up the empty pitcher and tray and stood, considering herself dismissed. Houston put a hand on her forearm. Her skin crawled.

"The next time tell Kitty to bring refreshment herself," he said. "You stay out front. We'll be checking from time to time." He let her go. Michael put the tray under her arm and fled the room. Houston looked directly at Ethan. "She stays here," he repeated. "I don't trust her."

"But we'll be gone a few days. How will you keep her quiet?"

"Dee will think of something."

Dee nodded.

Ethan saw there was nothing more to say. It had all been decided before he got to the table. He was quiet for most of the meeting, contributing only when they looked to him for answers about the safe, explosives, or blowing the track. It was agreed that he would make the trip to Stillwater with Obie on the pretense of getting supplies for the mine. Since he did the requisitioning and was in charge of all the explosives, no one would question it.

They looked over the schedule and detailed maps of the territory. Happy's knowledge of the mountains was critical, giving them escape routes that would take them away from the rail lines where it would be difficult to follow. The full moon would be a problem, the weather would always be uncertain. It was fairly certain to be cold; they hoped for cloud cover. There was a trestle the train would cross on the night they wanted to stop her. They elected to take the train just before the trestle, then send it on, cutting off any possibility of a reverse chase by destroying the side span. Ethan would set the explosives the day before. Obie would cut telegraph wires as 486 came down the side of the mountain. A bonfire would alert the train to trouble. The boarding procedure would be similar to the last robbery but this time Ben and Ethan wouldn't be passengers. They'd make their assault on the mail car after the train had stopped. There would be only one guard posted in the mail car. Someone had apparently thought less guards would not bring undue attention to the shipment. It may have worked if not for Cooper.

The meeting ended shortly after two. Ethan took his money from where it lay untouched in the center of the table. He stuffed it in his pocket and followed Obie and Ben out.

Michael was sleeping when he returned to their room. She stirred when he slipped into bed beside her.

He turned on his side and fitted himself against her. One of his arms slid under her pillow. Her hair was slightly damp from an earlier bath. He breathed deeply of its fragrance.

"You're back," she said softly.

"Hmmm." He kissed her gently on the back of her neck. His arm came around her shoulder. She took his hand in hers, their fingers intertwined. "I thought you were sleeping."

"I was. Did you just come in?"

"A few minutes ago. It's after two."

"Did you win much?"

"Broke even."

"That's too bad."

"How long were you listening at the door, Michael?" The question had caught her off guard as he'd known it would. He felt her stiffen and struck again before she had time to think. "There was never any tap. I know I would have heard it. How long were you there?"

"Not long. I swear it."

"You're fortunate Kitty covered for you."

"What she said was the truth."

"What did you hear?"

"Only voices. I couldn't even make out who was talking most of the time. I wasn't *trying* to anyway."

He felt her agitation as she tried to defend herself again. He squeezed her fingers. "All right," he said softly. "All right. We won't talk about it any more."

It wasn't precisely what Michael wanted. She waited, eyes open, staring into the darkness, hoping he would tell her what her fate was to be. When Houston said Dee would think of something, what did he mean? She fell asleep wondering.

A week later she learned that whatever was going to happen would happen soon. Their lovemaking that morning was strained, some part of Ethan's desperation was in the way he touched her, held her, kissed her. She felt it all, not understanding until he left their bed and began to dress. It was then that he told her.

"I'm leaving this afternoon," he said, watching her reflection in the mirror as he shaved. Her skin was damp, the hollow of her throat invited another kiss. Kisses. "I don't want to leave you, but there's really no choice."

"This is about your meeting last week, isn't it?" She was kneeling in the middle of the bed, the sheet wrapped around her. "You're going to do whatever you planned that night."

Ethan felt her accusing words like needles at his back. He put down his straight razor and put on a shirt. "I played poker that night, remember? My trip's to Stillwater. I have to pick up an order of supplies for the mine. It will take a few days."

"Happy and Ben have been gone since Monday," she said. "Jake and Houston took some men out on a posse two days ago. Most everyone's returned but Jake and Houston."

"You heard what the others said. They split up to search the canyons. They'll be along directly."

"About the same time you and Ben and Happy all return? What about Obie? Or is he staying here to watch over me?"

"Dee will do that. Obie's got a trip to Stillwater too. No sense in us traveling alone."

He *was* leaving her with Dee. She had almost convinced herself she hadn't heard them correctly at the door that night. "I'm supposed to work here?" she asked, incredulous. "Without your protection? What do you imagine is going to happen while you're gone? Do you think Dee will lift a finger to see that I'm left unmolested?"

Ethan turned around and wiped the last bit of lather from his face. "Don't even think it. Dee won't let anything like that happen to you. She'd have to answer to me *and* Houston. He might not trust you, but he still wants you. You're a puzzle to him and the fact that you've managed to avoid being alone with him since the afternoon at the mines, has mostly served to whet his appetite."

"If it didn't escape your notice I'm certain it didn't escape Dee's."

"I've spoken to Kitty. She'll help you."

"So it *did* occur to you. And you're still going to leave me?"

"Keep your voice down. This is not a discussion you want overheard."

"I don't care," she said, her voice rising. She tossed her hair over her shoulder with an impatient gesture. "It's not right! What about the protection you promised me? What about that? What good is your word, Ethan? While you're out rob—" The rest of her sentence was muffled by Ethan's hand clamped firmly across her mouth.

"Stop it right now," he whispered harshly. "Nothing terrible is going to happen to you." He eased the pressure of his hand.

"I won't be here when you get back," she said rashly. "I'm leaving!"

Ethan put his hands firmly on Michael's shoulders and pushed her back on the bed. He leaned over her. "That's the worst thing you could do. Take that thought right out of your head. You'd be doing what they expect. Listen to me, Michael. There won't be anyone outside this saloon to stop you. You'll even be able to get out of Madison. But not far. You don't know the first thing about these mountains. You don't ride well, a buggy won't go far on these roads before it breaks an axle, and if you don't fall and snap your neck on some narrow trail, the cold will get you and then the wild animals."

The picture he painted for her made her pale and fear made her reckless. "Then I'll tell someone what's going on. I *will*, Ethan."

"Tell them what? That I'm going to Stillwater with Obie?"

Michael looked away. "Let me up, Ethan," she said tiredly. "You know it was just an empty threat. I don't want to see you dead."

"Really? There was a time you wanted to see me hanged. You even promised to be there cheering."

"That's because you stopped me from leaving. And I know you didn't kill Drew. You'll just spend time in prison for everything else you've done."

"We'll see." He bent to kiss her mouth. She turned her head at the last moment and gave him her cheek. Ethan rose slowly, watching her. "I have to go to the mines this morning, but I'll be back before I leave for Stillwater to say goodbye."

"Don't trouble yourself on my account."

He shrugged and started to leave. When he got to the door she called to him.

"Ethan? I'm sorry. I want you to come back to say goodbye."

He paused, his hand on the knob, and looked at her for a long moment, his eyes searching, memorizing. Then he left without a word.

Michael wondered throughout the morning and into the early afternoon whether Ethan would keep his promise. She had difficulty concentrating on the dances they practiced or doing her chores. Lottie kept her busy in the kitchen until she burned a pie. She wandered aimlessly, first picking out tunes on the piano, then doing inventory at the bar. Hidden in the wings on stage, she smoked cigarettes until Dee caught her and raised a ruckus about her disappearing *and* smoking.

Michael finally ended up in her own room. That's where Ethan found her. She was sitting cross-legged on the bed, her notepad opened on her lap. She had one pencil in her hair and was chewing on the tip of the other. Her spectacles were at the tip of her nose. The expression in her eyes was distant, the set of her features thoughtful.

Ethan knew then that leaving her was going to be the hardest thing he'd ever done. Drugging her, the second hardest.

He kicked the door shut with the heel of his boot and set down the tray he was carrying. "Carmen was making hot chocolate when I came in. I thought you might like some."

Michael closed her pad and put it aside, smiling widely. "Peace offering?" He nodded. "You didn't have to," she said. "I'm sorry about this morning." Dropping her pencil, she scooted off the bed and went to the table where he was standing. She put her arms around his waist and hugged him, pressing her cheek to his chest. "I don't want you to go. I'll never change my mind about that. But I want you to come back safely."

He rubbed her back. "It's only for a few days and only to Stillwater."

His insistence on the pretense and what it said about trusting her, bothered Michael. She took a small step backward and looked up at him. There would be no changing his mind. It was there in the flinty, implacable eyes. "Let's have our chocolate," she said, "before it gets cold."

Ethan took off his coat and hat and hung them where he usually put his gunbelt. He sat in the wing chair while Michael nudged the footstool closer to the chair and sat there. She already had a cup in her hand. "No," he said, "that one's mine. This is yours. It's sweeter, the way you like it."

She traded cups. "Thank you." She blew on her cocoa lightly, watching the liquid ripple, then sipped it cautiously. "It's good. And hot."

"What I said this morning, Michael, about nothing terrible happening to you while I'm away, I meant it."

280

"I know you mean it. I don't understand how you can enforce it."

Ethan didn't answer. Instead he encouraged her to drink her chocolate.

Michael found his insistence amusing. "Cocoa kisses," she said. "That's what you want."

He leaned forward and removed her spectacles then the pencil from her hair. Her cheeks reddened when she saw the pencil. "I don't want to stab myself in the eye," he said, dropping it on the table.

Michael raised her face. His kiss was sweet. When he drew back she said, "Is Obie waiting for you?"

"We have time."

Her eyes darkened. "Good." She finished most of her drink and set it down. She moved from the stool to his lap, took his cup, and put it aside also. "Kissing you is one of my very favorite things," she said.

"I'm flattered."

Smiling, she nuzzled his neck. His arms went around her. His chin brushed her temple. Her mouth found his. They kissed slowly, sipping, tasting. They kissed for a long time, unhurriedly because passion was not at the center of their desire. Closeness was.

He held her, stroking her shoulder and her back, learning the curve of her body with his palms. He heard her sigh. Kissing her closed eyes, Ethan helped her to her feet, came to his own, lifted her, and carried her to the bed. She protested that she could walk. Ethan ignored her. He wasn't so certain. The drops Dee had put in her cocoa were working more quickly than he expected. He needed to stay with her until she fell asleep, assure himself that she would be all right. Then he could leave, he thought. It would tear at his insides, but he could do it.

"I thought you liked kissing me," he whispered, lying down beside her.

"Mmmm." She moved sleepily, sinuously against him. "I do. I like it very much."

His fingers played in her hair, pulling out the pins and fanning it out across the pillow. "That a fact?"

She murmured something again, seeking his mouth. He obliged her with a long, leisurely kiss.

The last thought Michael had before she lost consciousness was that Ethan had never promised nothing would happen her, only that it would be nothing terrible.

Ethan laid the back of his hand across her forehead and then her cheek. Her skin was slightly warm, a little flushed. Exactly what Dee had told him to expect. Her breathing was strong and even and her pulse was good. Detra had done only as she said she would. "I'm taking you away from here when I get back," he whispered. "I'll have done everything I set out to do."

And some things besides, he thought to himself. Falling in love had never been part of his plans.

He got his coat and hat and left the room, locking it behind him. Downstairs, in Dee's office, he handed over the key. "It worked like you said it would. A little faster than I thought."

Detra pocketed the key. "She's probably a bit more susceptible than other people. I'll reduce the dose."

"You're sure this won't harm her?"

"You've asked that a hundred times already and the answer's the same. It's perfectly safe. I've used the drops myself when I have trouble sleeping. She'll feel tired and groggy with repeated use. She'll think she's sick, that's all, and that's the way I'll explain it to everyone else. She won't be out of her room while you're gone. That's safest for everybody."

Ethan tugged his hat lower over his forehead. It shaded the hard look of his eyes. "Listen to me, Dee. I want to be sure you understand that it's not Michael's fault that Houston's still interested in her. She's gone out of her way to avoid him. You must have seen that for yourself."

"So?"

"So I want you to guarantee Michael's safety while I'm gone. If anything . . . *anything* . . . happens to her you'll answer to me." And I'll make you wish I'd killed you quickly. He didn't have to say it. Dee's faltering step backward told she'd read what was in his mind.

"Unless she rolls out of bed, nothing's going to happen to her."

"You better make sure even that doesn't happen."

Dee skirted her desk, putting some distance between Ethan and her. "You really are a fool for her, aren't you?"

"Could be, Detra," he said, walking away. "Could be."

When Michael awoke her mouth was dry and her temples throbbed. Her head felt so heavy she could barely lift it. She turned on her side and opened her eyes slowly. Kitty was sitting in the wing chair with an embroidery hoop in her lap. She looked up when she heard Michael stirring.

"Aaah, you're awake. When you didn't come down for dinner Dee sent me up to check on you. We were worried. You have a little fever." Kitty went to the bed and sat down on the edge. She touched Michael's cheek. Her fingers were very cool against Michael's skin. "What hurts?"

"Nothing," Michael said, her voice just a thread of sound. "Everything." She had a terrible taste in her mouth, slightly bitter. The chocolate gone sour, she thought. "Could I have a glass of water?"

"I have tea right here," Kitty said, jumping up to get it. "Is that all right?"

"Anything." Michael touched her throat. It seemed swollen at the curve of her jaw and neck. She tried to push herself upright. Kitty had to help her, plumping the pillows so Michael could rest against the headboard.

"That better?" She handed Michael the tea. "There's a little lemon drop in it. That's always good for a sore throat."

"How did you know I had a sore throat?"

"Your voice is just a croak. Oh, you mean how did I know to have the lemon drops on hand? Dee mentioned you might be a bit off in the throat. She was here just after Ethan left, I think."

Michael sipped the tea. It *was* soothing. "What time is it?"

"After six."

"Six! But that means I've—"

"Hush. You're getting yourself excited over nothin'. They're managin' just fine downstairs without either one of us. Dee's helpin' out more than usual and that's not killin' her." She grinned. "Ralph Hooper's been askin' for you. I think he's kinda sweet on you."

"Ralph's nice, but you're the one he likes."

Kitty blushed. "Go on. He never comes to my room."

"But does he go to anyone else's?" She drank some more tea to cut the rawness in her throat. "You know he doesn't."

"Sssh. Don't talk so much. Ralph's always askin' to dance with you."

"Because I'm taken," she whispered huskily. She set the cup down on her lap and let Kitty take it away before it spilled.

"You want more? I can get you something else."

"No . . . nothing. I feel so weak." Her eyes closed. She wanted to touch her throat again but her arms were like leaden weights. "He's shy."

"What?"

"Ralph. He's shy."

"Oh, we're back to that, are we? C'mon. Lie down again. You're as weak as the runt of the litter."

Michael smiled weakly as Kitty fussed over her.

"Would you like another lemon drop? Dee swears by

them." Kitty didn't bother to interpret Michael's murmur as acceptance or protest. She pushed the extra lemon drop Dee had given her into Michael's mouth. "Here. Suck on this. It'll help."

Twelve hours after leaving Stillwater, Ethan was setting explosives on the sidespan of the South Platte trestle. Two trains would cross the span before the one they wanted to stop. It would be just after midnight when No. 486 engineer would signal her approach. It was still light enough for Ethan to see what he was doing without a lantern. He had plenty of time to do thorough job.

Obie helped him, hunkered down on the abutment, passing the dynamite that Ethan had bundled earlier. Ethan knew the stress points, the wooden ties that held the most weight. A quick examination of the trestle showed him it had been built hastily, without much regard for good engineering. It supported the trains, but the weight was not distributed as evenly as it should have been. Ethan guessed that when the trains came rolling on, the entire structure vibrated like a plucked banjo string. He was doing everyone a favor blowing it up. They'd be forced to rebuild. Perhaps they'd do a better job of it this time.

He set five separate fuses using miner's safety cord. It burned evenly, even when slightly damp, so that Ethan would know how much time he had between lighting the fuse and detonation. After the robbery he wanted to give No. 486 enough time to cross the trestle before he blew the sidespan. He wanted himself and others to be clear of the blast as well.

Ethan climbed from the sidespan, moving with the agility and grace of a spider, and onto the abutment. "That should do it," he told Obie. "Everything else ready?"

"You had the hard part. Nothin' much for the rest

of us to do but wait. Happy's got a little encampment set up over the ridge there. Ben says there's fresh hot coffee."

"We may as well go then."

Their waiting horses managed the rocky incline with the sure-footedness of mountain goats. It only took them minutes to reach the others. Happy had chosen to make camp in a flat lay of land sheltered by pines and a ridge of rock. The men were sitting around the small fire. Bacon sizzled and spit in an iron skillet. The aroma filled the crisp evening air. Ethan and Obie joined them.

Houston handed Ethan a cup of coffee. "I figure when the train stops because of the bonfire, you and Ben can come down on the roof of the mail car from the ridge. Pitch a stick of dynamite in the overhead vent. That'll either flush out the guard or kill him. Either way, you're in."

"Ben agree to that?" Ethan asked.

"I got no problem with it."

Houston raised the collar of his coat against the wind. "Is there a problem on your side, Stone?"

"No problem."

"Good."

Later, when they had finished eating dinner, Ethan excused himself from the card game to get the explosives he would need.

Engine No. 486 was only ten minutes off her posted schedule. She was running early. Caleb French was in the cab, pounding his engine as was his nature, keeping his fireman busy swinging a shovel from the coal tender to the furnace. When he saw the bonfire that was built across the tracks he regretted the speed he'd forced from his powerful engine. He had no real faith that he could stop her in time.

The wheels of the train flattened against the metal

rails as French threw the reverse lever. In the cars behind him he knew passengers were being thrown from
their seats. Baggage was being pitched to the floor.
Without looking out the window of his cab he knew
that the whine and squeal of metal against metal was
showering the gravel bed and ballast with blue and
white sparks. His fireman had found a handle to
clutch and was holding on with bloodless fists. He
imagined his conductors were flat on their faces by
now and his brakemen near powerless to help him.

Caleb French was only sure of one thing: he and his
fireman weren't going to jump. He was staying with
his engine.

Watching the approach of No. 486, Ethan began to
wonder if all their planning would be for nothing. "If
that train doesn't slow soon," he said to Ben, "we've got
to clear the tracks as best we can."

"You're crazy!"

"Maybe, but we came to do a robbery, not mass
murder. They'll jump the track and take the mountain
if we don't. You forget who's on that train? Cooper
will be dead, too."

"Aww, hell," Ben muttered. He watched the speed-
ing approach of No. 486 with heightened interest.

Caleb French thought he'd been part of a miracle
when he finally brought 486 to a halt only thirty yards
in front of the fire. Then Jake Harrity entered the cab
with his raised gun and French knew he was about to
pay for the lives he'd saved.

On the roof of the mail car, Ethan and Ben moved
with cat-like quickness. Ben jerked open the roof vent
while Ethan lighted the fuse on the stick of dynamite.
They yelled a warning, took cover on the roof of the
adjoining car and waited. The side door of the mail
car opened almost immediately and they saw the
guard jump out. Ethan slid down the side ladder and
leaped off the sill slip, tackling the guard before he
could orient himself. He cuffed him solidly on the jaw

and let him thud to the ground. He disarmed him, pitching the carbine well out of reach, then he climbed into the mail car.

Ben joined him a moment later. "What the hell happened to the explosion? I thought for sure—"

Ethan held up the stick and pretended to examine it. "Look, the paraffin wrapping's cracked. The explosive must be damp." He tossed it at Ben who jumped out of the way. Ethan chuckled. "Easy, Ben. It can't hurt you like that."

Ben snorted and grumbled his displeasure. "Hope you checked the stuff on the trestle better than you did that one. We're lucky the guard scared at the sight of the stuff."

Turning away to check the safe, Ethan knew he'd been lucky. He had counted on the guard being frightened enough of the lighted stick to make the jump. Ethan had cracked the paraffin seal and wet the explosive mix of nitroglycerine and guncotton himself. Ethan knelt in front of the safe and began taking cartridges from his coatpockets. "You know, Ben, if it gets much colder, that trestle's not going to blow."

"What the hell you talkin' about?"

"Dynamite freezes at 40°. It feels colder than that now."

"Fine time to be tellin' me. Does Houston know?"

"I thought he did. We discussed the problems with the weather, remember?"

"Just hurry it up."

"Oh, these sticks are all right. Don't worry about the safe."

Ben shifted his weight from one foot to the other, as if the impatient movement could hurry Ethan along. As with most everything, Ethan would not be hurried.

He had pried away the safe's dial with a small iron crowbar, leaving a spindle hole opening. Cracking open a stick of dynamite, Ethan packed the hole with the charge, a mixture of nitroglycerine and other fillers like gun cotton, wood pulp, and sodium nitrate. He searched his pocket for the sliver of soap he'd brought along. Spitting on it, he gummed it up enough to serve as an adhesive so that he could affix the detonator. After placing the tiny blasting cap in the soap and sticking it against the powder charge, Ethan ran the safety fuse a few feet away from the iron door. "Better go get the mules, Ben," he said calmly. He lit a match using the lantern the guard had left, cupped it to steady the flame, and blew out the lantern. "This won't take long."

Swearing, Ben jumped from the mail car. Ethan started the fuse and followed a few seconds later. He left the car's side door open a few inches and ticked off the seconds in his mind. When the explosion came only Ben jumped.

Grinning, Ethan opened the door, hoisted himself inside, and examined the safe. He'd been very fortunate to set a well-balanced charge. The locking bolts were pulled back and the door had flown open. There was no need to set multiple charges. The only damage he was able to detect in the safe was a small bulge in the front plate where he had packed the charge. "I'll be damned," he said. "Would you look at this."

Ben lighted the lantern. He didn't spare a glance for Ethan's handiwork, his eyes were filled with the sight of the bullion and payroll sacks. Jake had a similar reaction when he joined them. Working like a fire brigade they emptied the safe with efficient ease.

Jake readjusted the kerchief around his face. "Let's go see this Cooper fella and then get the hell out of here."

They walked along the outside of the train to reach the car where Houston told them to meet. Keeping with the theory that an engine pulling a few number of cars would attract less notice, No. 486 had only three passenger cars. The one preceding the caboose was a private car. Ethan, Ben, and Jake passed below the windows of dozens of subdued and resigned, if not frightened, passengers. They entered the private car.

"These are the others?" Cooper asked Houston. He was sitting in a large red leather chair. Brass tacks followed the curve of the wide arms. The tips of Cooper's nails tapped lightly against tacks, making a tiny clicking sound in the otherwise silent car.

He was a large man, not tall, but solidly built. There was evidence of a slight paunch where his silver-threaded vest was pulled taut across his belly. His neck and jowls, which may have given a better indication of his age and health, were covered by thick side whiskers and a full beard. His hair line was receding on either side of his center part. The curling ends of his handlebar mustache were stiffly waxed.

Ethan's glance assessed Cooper's expensively tailored clothes, the gold watch chain that hung in a swag from his vest pocket, the polished shoes, and manicured nails. No dispatcher here, he thought. No menial clerk for Wells Fargo. Hell, the man looked like he could own Wells Fargo. Ethan felt his stare being returned. He looked up into a pair of eyes so pale they were nearly colorless. He knew he would never forget those eyes.

"These are the others," Houston said. "Obie and Happy have already said their piece to Cooper. They're finishing with the passengers. He's not interested in less than forty percent."

Ben looked around the plushly appointed car and said what was on his mind. "It don't seem to me that a little less than forty would set you back none."

"On the contrary," Cooper said in a rich, deep baritone, "I have so much more to lose." The sweet of his mustache rose a little as he smiled. "I think you wanted proof from Houston that I exist. You can see that I do. You can be certain of my continued help as long as you are equal to the task. I have large plans for my share of the money, gentlemen." There was an ivory knobbed ebony cane resting against the arm of his chair. He picked it up and laid it across his lap, stroking the smooth wood absently. He turned to Houston. "You'll deliver my money in the same manner as always?"

Houston nodded. "I wish you could take it now. It would save me a trip to Denver."

It was the first Ethan had ever been able to learn how Cooper recovered his share. There was probably a transfer through a bank in Denver and the actual account wouldn't prove too difficult to find.

"Far from giving me the money, you're going to have to take something from me." He handed over his gold watch and chain without another thought and slipped the emerald ring from his pinkie. "Take these. I'm sure a few of the other passengers remember seeing them. Feel free to overturn some things in here. It will be more impressive." His pale glance encompassed all of them. "Oh, and I suppose it should look as if I've struggled. No one hearing this won't believe I didn't put up a fight."

"You sure?" Houston asked.

"I'm sure." He stood, leaning lightly on the cane, making it clear it wasn't necessary, but simply an affectation.

Houston stepped forward but Ethan got there first. "Let me," he said. Before Cooper could blink a protest, Ethan hammered him in the jaw. He dropped like a stone in the blood red chair.

"I think you broke it," Jake said.

Ethan shook out his fingers. "Glass jaw."

Houston was laughing. "I bet nobody's ever done that to him. C'mon. We've got a train to get moving. Jake, get Obie and Happy. Let's go."

It was then that the first shots were fired.

Jake jumped out of the private car and crouched down, using the horses and mules for cover. Ethan and Houston followed suit. Ben stayed behind long enough to overturn a few pieces of furniture and blow out the lamps.

"What the hell's going on?" he whispered, joining the others. "Where'd those shots come from?" Even as he spoke a bullet whined above his head. He ducked a little lower.

"That answer your question?" Jake asked. "Those rocks over there. Just about the same place we were camped."

Houston nudged Ben. "Ben, you and Jake find a route around, see how many there are and try to cut them off. If we can scare them out of here, fine. If not, kill them. Ethan and I will get the others."

Ethan followed Houston between the cars to the protected side of the train. Running quickly forward they encountered Happy using the train wheels for cover.

"What happened?" Houston demanded.

Happy shrugged. "Hell if I know. I was standin' at this end of the car. I could see Obie standin' in the other. Too much damn light in the cars, that's what it is. There was a shot, glass broke, and Obie went down. I think one of the conductors got his gun. I jumped. We gotta get outta here."

"All right. Happy, stay with the mules. I'm going up to the cab and see about firing up the engine. Jake better have cleared the track. Ethan, what explosives do you have left?"

"A few sticks, some black powder."

"Put it to good use then. See if you can't help Ben and Jake flush them down here to the train."

Ethan understood immediately. "The train goes over the trestle and we blow the trestle."

The trio split. Ethan circled round the caboose and took the general route that Jake and Ben had taken. In the dark he was in as much danger from a shot by Jake or Ben as he was from whoever else was firing on the train. It was probably a safe assumption that the

292

shots were from a posse. How the law had chanced upon the robbery was more difficult to figure out. Even if Michael hadn't been depending on Ethan's help in Madison, Ethan doubted he would have risked surrendering. He was unlikely to convince anyone that he was a federal marshal and the trees in the area looked plenty high enough to accommodate a lynching.

His best, in truth his only, alternative was to follow Houston's plan and hope to God that it worked.

"You're damn lucky I didn't shoot you," Ben said as Ethan came up on him.

"Don't I know it," Ethan whispered, settling down against the rocks. Ben and Jake had found a good protected location on higher ground. "How many are there?"

"Five that we know of," Jake said. "Pretty damn hard to see them. 'Course they're havin' the same problem with us."

"One of them's a sharp shooter," Ethan said. "Happy says Obie went down." Oil lamps inside the cars made the movements of the passengers visible. A few paced restlessly in the aisles. Most sat in the seats, their faces pressed against the window as they peered out, searching for some sign of their rescuers or a gun battle. "Houston's firing up the engine. We've got to move them to the train."

"Any ideas?" Ben asked.

Ethan reached in his pocket and pulled out a cartridge. "Several of them," he said.

"Oh, hell," Ben groaned. "Be careful with that, will ya?"

Setting a blasting cap and a short fuse, Ethan struck a match to it and pitched it over the rocky incline. He realized one of the men below saw the streak of light and recognized it for what it was. There was a shout and then a lot of scrambling for cover as the dynamite exploded. There was more noise than damage but

Ethan was the only one who really understood that.

Thinking the entire gang of robbers behind them, the posse moved quickly in the direction of the train. Ben and Jake fired a few shots to encourage them. Their fire was returned but it was random and without focus. The posse clearly didn't know where their quarry was located.

Ethan set another stick of explosive and sent it sailing over the ridge. The posse split and ran again. The lights from the cars illuminated their path as they got closer to the train.

"Right where we want them," Ethan said calmly. He took his last cartridge out of his pocket, set the fuse, and waited.

"Damn, look at that," Ben said, pointing to the engine. "Houston's got it goin'!"

No. 486 rolled forward slowly, in fits and starts, straining against the track that had already damaged her wheels. As she began picking up speed Ethan threw his last stick. The fuse was so short it exploded in midair. They could see four men take refuge on the train. A fifth joined them a few seconds later.

Ethan scrambled down the rocks, half running, half sliding. The train was pulling away. He ran behind it, leaped, and caught a ride on the back of the caboose for a few hundred yards. Then he jumped. He hoped Houston had already done the same. It was too late now. The train was crossing the trestle and it was vibrating as fiercely as Ethan suspected it would.

He found the fuse cords quickly, marked by the stone mound he had made earlier, and struck a match. They caught immediately, burning at an even rate toward the packs of dynamite nested in the trestle beams. He watched the progress of the train, a bulky shadow a shade darker than the surrounding night. The rattling of the cars, the steady churning of the engine, receded as distance yawned between Ethan and the train.

From behind him, down the tracks, Ethan heard Houston shout for him. "In a minute," he called. "I want to be certain this—"

The explosions, almost simultaneous, cut off Ethan's sentence.

"Blows," he finished when the dust and timber settled. No. 486 was safely on the other side but there would be no coming back. Standing on the edge of the abutment, he shook his head as he examined the damage he had wrought. "I guess it wasn't too cold."

Houston called him again. Ethan turned. "I'm coming."

They found Obie lying on the canyon side of the track where the passengers had pushed him after he'd been shot. He was unconscious, not dead. Ethan and Houston supported Obie between them and headed for where their horses were hidden. Ben was waiting there with the mules. He helped them strap Obie into his saddle then mounted himself. Jake and Happy joined them a few minutes later.

They were somber as they rode. There was no sense of victory in eluding the posse, only a question of how the law had come to be there in the first place.

Happy said what the others, except Ethan, were thinking. "Your wife's behind this, Ethan. She's the reason Obie took a bullet, hell, the reason we *all* almost took one."

"You're crazy, Happy. Michael didn't do this."

"You're the one who's not thinking straight," Ben said, taking up his brother's argument. "We caught her listenin' at the door the night we were makin' our plans. I never did believe she didn't hear nothin'. Tonight's bad business is proof I was right."

"Michael couldn't have done it," Ethan said. "She's been drugged the whole time we've been gone. I gave her the first dose myself so she'd be easy for Dee to handle. She'll still be drugged when we get back. There's no way possible she could have told anyone, even if she knew anything. Which she didn't."

Houston slowed his horse and let Ethan come up beside him. "So what do you think happened?"

"The possibility that makes the most sense to me is Cooper set us up."

"Cooper?" It was clear by his tone that Houston hadn't considered that. "Why?"

"I don't know why. Perhaps he's not as happy with the arrangement he has with us as he appears. Or perhaps he simply wanted to remove any suspicion from himself by making certain we were killed during this robbery."

Houston was silent for a long time. The others were also considering the possibility of betrayal at Cooper's hands. "It's worth looking at a little more closely," Houston said.

Obie died on the trail. They buried him near a stretch of limber pines and covered the grave with needles. They agreed that Kitty could have Obie's share from the robbery. There had to be a story to cover for his disappearance and Kitty would have to support it. The money they would offer her was meant less to compensate for the loss of her brother than it was a bribe for her cooperation. No one anticipated there would be trouble from Kitty. She was a realist.

They returned to town separately. Jake and Houston went to the jail first, tending to the business of the town before they tended to their own. Ben and Happy took the mules and money and headed for their cabin. It was left for Ethan to go to the saloon. It was left to him to tell Kitty.

She seemed to know. When he walked into the saloon alone and sought her out even before asking about Michael, Kitty knew what Ethan was going to tell her. She took the arm he offered and allowed him to lead her into Dee's office. Kitty sagged weakly against the door as Ethan closed it behind them.

Detra stepped into the office from her apartments. "What's happened?" she demanded, her eyes darting between Ethan and Kitty. "Is it Houston?"

Ethan gave Dee a quelling glance. His expression softened when he faced Kitty again. "I'm sorry, Kitty," he said. He helped her away from the door and into a chair. She leaned against him heavily, barely able to support herself.

"How?" she asked weakly.

"It was an ambush." He heard Dee suck in her breath but paid her no attention. He hunkered down beside Kitty's chair and took her hand, squeezing it gently. "Obie was on the train when it happened and none of us could get to him. The passengers pushed him off. We found him, bandaged the wound, and carried him back. He'd lost too much blood, Kitty. He couldn't make it all the way back to Madison."

Numbness stole all expression from Kitty's face. She stared blankly at her hand in Ethan's as if there were no connection between herself and the story he told.

"We buried him on the way back," said Ethan. "I can take you there some time if you'd like." He paused. "No one in Madison can know how it really happened, Kitty. You understand, don't you? We have to tell people that Obie—"

Dee interrupted. "Damn it, Ethan. This isn't the time to work out a story between you. Can't you see she's in shock?" Her skirts rustled as she rounded her desk and came to stand just behind Kitty. She placed a hand on Kitty's shoulder. "Come with me, Kitty. You can lie down in my bedroom. You don't have to talk to anyone about this right now." Kitty allowed herself to be nudged out of the chair. Dee's dark blue eyes locked angrily on Ethan's. "I'll be back as soon as Kitty's settled. Don't go anywhere. I want to talk to you." When she saw his brows rise slightly at her tone Dee offered the information that would assure his compliance. "It's about Michael."

Ethan was sitting on the edge of Dee's desk when she returned, negligently turning the pages of her open ledger. The first thing she did was close the book over his hand.

"Nothing in there is your affair," she said.

"I was just passing time, Dee."

She put the bookkeeping ledger in the middle desk drawer and locked it. "I knew this would happen," she said, lowering her voice to prevent Kitty from hearing. "If there was an ambush, that bitch wife of yours is to blame."

Ethan stood. "What are you saying? Michael's here, isn't she?"

"She's here now, but she caused us some trouble a few days ago."

"It was your responsibility to see that wasn't possible. What kind of trouble could Michael cause when she was drugged?"

"She disappeared for a few hours. We couldn't find her. Don't look at me that way, Ethan. It happens sometimes. The powders I gave her don't always have the same effect on people. Remember how quickly she slept the first time? I told you I would reduce the dose and I did. Too much, it seems. It took time to find the proper blend." Detra paced the length of the room as she talked. "It's not my fault that any of this happened. I told you from the beginning that you shouldn't have brought her here. She's not one of us, Ethan, and she never will be. I know she talked to someone while she was gone."

"How do you know, Dee? Did you see her?"

"No, I didn't, but—"

"Did someone say something to you?"

"No, but—"

"Where was she while she was gone?"

"I don't know, but—"

"I don't want to hear anymore about it," Ethan said. "Michael *didn't* betray us."

Dee started to say something, felt Ethan's hard stare on her, and thought better of it. Her mouth snapped shut.

"I'm going to see Michael myself. You better have taken good care of her, Dee." He held out his hand for the key to his room.

Dee gave it to him. She watched him leave. "This isn't the end of it," she said softly as the door closed behind him. "Not the end at all."

The saloon was quiet with only a dozen customers there at midday. Someone called to Ethan as he mounted the stairs. Ethan pretended he didn't hear. He had no desire to engage in any conversation about Obie or Kitty or his trip to Stillwater. The key grated loudly in the silent hallway. Ethan pushed open the door.

Michael was lying in the middle of the bed on her back. Her face was pale, her eyes closed. Bluish color tinged her lips. The skin on the back of her hands seemed remarkably white, almost translucent. Her breathing was shallow, quiet.

Ethan tossed his hat on the wing chair as he approached the bed. He shrugged out of his coat and threw it aside also. "Michael?" Sitting on the edge of the bed, Ethan reached for one of her hands and took it in his. Her skin was cool. "Michael? It's Ethan. I'm back." He watched her head turn slowly toward him. There was a faint smile and her lids fluttered open. Her eyes were unfocused.

"Ethan," she said softly. She felt him move, leaning closer to hear what she said. "I'm glad. No more drugs."

"No," he said. "No more drugs." He slipped an arm under her shoulders and helped her sit up. She leaned heavily against him. "We have to leave here tonight, Michael. It's time."

"Time," she repeated sleepily.

"Michael. Do you understand what I'm saying?"

How much had Dee given her? Ethan wondered. Surely there'd been no need for Michael to be all but oblivious to her surroundings. "Michael, Dee says that you went somewhere while I was gone. Did you talk to anyone? See anyone?" He watched her struggle to make sense of his questions. Could he trust her answer? "Nevermind. It doesn't matter. We're leaving together."

The door to the room banged open. Houston and Jake stood on the threshold, Dee just behind them. The men looked grim. Detra's smile was complacent.

"We need to talk about her," Houston said, jerking his chin toward Michael. "Dee says she's the reason Obie's dead."

Chapter Eleven

They sat around Dee's dining room table. By some unspoken agreement they took the same chairs they had while planning the robbery. Obie's chair was left in the circle, unoccupied by anyone. It served as a reminder of betrayal and as focus for their anger.

Michael was forced to sit beside Houston and across the table from Ethan.

"This is ridiculous," Ethan said. "Look at her. She can barely sit up. You can't expect that she'll be able to defend herself."

Happy stared out the window at the darkening sky. A storm was moving in. A few inches of snow would cover their tracks. He wondered if it mattered. Had Michael done more than warn someone about the robbery? Had she identified them to the law? "I don't think it matters much if she can defend herself," he said. He glanced at the cuspidor beside his chair and spit. "She got you to speak for her, don't she?"

"I wasn't here," Ethan said. "Neither were you. It seems to me we have Dee's word and nothing else."

"My word should be good enough," Dee said sharply, glancing around the table. "I tell you she was missing for a few hours. I know I locked her in at night but somehow she got out. It was three in the morning when I went to check on her and found her gone. It was nearly six when I caught her sneaking in the back door."

Michael pulled the shawl she was wearing more closely about her shoulders. She stared at her lap, shaking her head slowly. "It's not true," she said quietly. "Not true. I never—"

"Oh, for God's sake," Dee said, throwing up her hands. "How can you deny what—"

Ethan slammed the flat of his hand on the table. Dee's chin came up defiantly but she stopped talking. "Let Michael at least finish," Ethan said. "Let's hear what she has to say."

Michael raised her eyes. She looked at Houston, not Ethan. It was an effort to speak. "Detra's lying. I never left my room. I couldn't. I was too sick. I barely remember anything since—"

"There!" Detra said triumphantly. "You see. She says herself that she barely remembers. Well, I tell you she was gone. I don't know who she spoke to on her little trek from the saloon but you can be certain she spoke to someone. You wouldn't have had a posse meet that train otherwise."

Ethan pushed back his chair. "This is ridiculous. You assured us that your damn powders would keep her bedridden for the length of our trip. Now you're saying that it didn't happen that way."

"It was a problem with the amount," Dee said. "When she came back I increased the dose. It was only this morning, when I anticipated your return, that I could reduce it again. You can see for yourself that she's shaking off the effects. In a few hours it will be as if she'd never taken anything at all."

Ethan found that difficult to believe. Michael's speech was slurred, the cadence uneven. He had forced her to drink three cups of coffee while they waited for Happy and Ben to join them and she still had little command of her posture. Though she denied Dee's accusation, she seemed to not understand the

302

gravity of her position. It worked in Dee's favor. "Michael says it didn't happen," Ethan said.

"Are you sayin' Dee's a liar?" asked Ben.

"I'm saying that something's not right here. Even if Michael was gone for a few hours in the middle of the night, where would she go? What would she say?"

Houston held up his hand, stopping Ethan. "You know damn well she knows too much. She heard our conversation the night we were planning. She had plenty to tell someone."

"Who?" Ethan asked. "Who the hell would listen to her?"

"Ralph Hooper," Dee said. "Why not? He's one of her favorites. Or Billy Saunders. Someone not only listened to her, someone believed her. Can't you see the evidence that's in front of your face, Ethan?"

"There *is* no evidence," Ethan said.

"I heard plenty," Happy said. "It ain't safe to have her around. I said so from the beginnin', didn't I?"

Michael tried to get up. Houston pulled her back and kept his hand on her forearm. "I didn't leave," she said again. "Never left at all."

Silence greeted her words.

Ethan stood and went to the window. He faced the others and pressed his back against the cool panes of glass. His arms were folded in front of him. "I still say there's no evidence," he said finally. "We can't ask Billy or Ralph or anyone else for that matter without giving ourselves away. I think it was Cooper himself who betrayed us, not my wife."

Houston and Dee exchanged glances. There was a slight nod from Houston and Dee rose, left the room, and returned less than a minute later with a half a dozen newspapers under her arm. She gave one to Ethan and dropped the rest on the table.

"Perhaps these back issues of the *Chronicle* will convince you, Ethan," Houston said. "Dee did a little investigating on her own and received these a while ago.

I wasn't sure then. I was still willing to give Michael the benefit of the doubt. I can't ignore this."

Ethan unfolded the paper. "What am I supposed to look for?" he asked, knowing the answer. "This issue's dated more than two weeks before the 349 robbery."

"That's right," Houston said. "And I think there's a story in the bottom right corner that's particularly interesting."

Ethan bluffed with impatience. "Just tell me what the hell it's about. I don't want to hear about your mysteries now."

Houston passed out other issues to Ben and Happy and Jake. He pushed one in front of Michael. "Look at the reporter's name, Ethan," he said. "Every issue I have has at least one story by her, one story that she reported from the touring *Chronicle* car."

Jake found one in his copy. "The Plains' Truth by Mary M. Dennehy," he read with some difficulty. "Is that what you meant, Houston?"

"Precisely what I meant." Houston looked at Michael. "That's your work, isn't it?"

Michael stared at the article he pointed to in her paper. She wondered what she was supposed to say. "Yes," she said finally. "I wrote that." She retained the presence of mind to look sorrowfully in Ethan's direction. "I'm sorry, Ethan. I couldn't tell you. I wanted to . . . I was afraid."

Ethan could hardly believe she was trying to save him. His startled expression was real enough. "Michael, I don't think this is—"

She rested her head in her hands. The pain in her eyes was genuine, but it was physical, not emotional. "I should have said something . . . let you know why I was with the *Chronicle* . . . I couldn't . . . I just couldn't. Not after what you did to Drew."

"He wasn't your fiancé," Houston said. It was not a question. He was satisfied that he already knew the truth.

Michael shook her head. "He was a friend. A colleague. Please, I need to lie down. I don't feel well. I think I'm going to be sick." A small choking sound convinced everyone. Dee rushed her out of the dining room and into the apartment's tiny kitchen.

"Well?" Houston asked, leaning back in his chair. "What's to be done?"

"Jesus," Ben said. "A reporter. She's a goddamn reporter."

Happy tossed his paper toward the center of the table, disgusted by the revelation. "How the hell did you figure this out, Houston?"

Ethan wanted to know the same thing. He skimmed the article quickly and discovered the answer. It was the journal that Michael kept that had betrayed her. He remembered what she had said about writing being as individual as a signature. This was her work. Houston had read the notes she kept and recognized it as well. He only listened with half an ear to what Houston was telling the others.

"Dee's really the one you have to thank," Houston said, finishing his explanation. "She ordered the papers from New York. Woman's intuition, I suppose."

A woman scorned, Ethan thought. That's what had prompted Dee's search for information about Michael. Now he was faced with the problem of what to do about it.

Dee returned to the dining room. "She's resting at the kitchen table."

"Jake, keep an eye on her," Houston ordered. Jake left the table and stood guard in the doorway between the two rooms.

"Is that really necessary?" Ethan asked. "She's not going anywhere in her condition."

"That's what we thought before," Happy muttered. "It don't seem like you know your wife very well."

"She lied to me the same as she did all of you," Ethan said.

305

"Did she?" Houston asked. "I've been wondering about that."

"What the hell's that supposed to mean?"

"Just that I've been wondering." Houston refused to say anything more. He looked at Happy. "What do you want to do about her?"

Happy spit. "Only one thing we can do," he said. "Question is when and how."

"It'll be dark soon enough," Ben said to his brother. "And the mines don't tell no tales."

"You're not serious," Ethan said. "You've proven nothing except that she's written a few stories for the *Chronicle*. That doesn't have anything to do with us. There's still only Dee's word that Michael left here at all. No one knows if she talked to anyone. I'm telling you, it's probably Cooper. We're fools if we trust him again. Let me talk to Michael when she's not drugged. I think there's more to this than we know."

"Sounds to me like you're sweet on her," Happy said. "And thinkin' with what's between your legs instead of what's between your ears."

"He's more than sweet on her," Dee said, sitting down on Houston's lap. She looped one arm around his shoulders. "I think Ethan's in love with her. Isn't that right, Ethan? Fallen in love with your wife all over again?"

"Shut up, Dee," Houston said. "Well, Ethan, do you have a problem with what Happy has planned for Michael?"

"It doesn't matter if I do," Ethan said. "When I signed on I agreed to majority rule. It appears I'm out voted." And out numbered, he thought.

"Then you won't mind helping Happy," said Houston. "It would go a long way to show that you're still one of us."

Ethan hesitated, knowing he could not appear eager after stating his opposition to the plan. He pushed away from the window. "I'll help," he said finally. "If that's what it takes, I'll help."

It was better to have no questions than to think of a plan to answer them. To that end Michael's belongings were packed and removed from the saloon when there was no one to witness it. Detra used more sleeping powders to make Michael, if not entirely compliant, then at least less resistant. She knew that all around her plans were being made and carried out and she was powerless to stop any of it.

The saloon was quiet, the street dark, when Ethan carried Michael out. He placed her in the back of the buckboard wagon that Happy brought around. She shared the space with a trunk of her clothes, her journal, pencils, and spectacles. There was no one up in the middle of the night to monitor their progress through town or bear testimony to the fact that Michael was not leaving of her own accord. Some miners might wonder at her leaving without a word to them, but no one would suspect it was anything but her own decision to do so.

Happy brought the wagon to a halt just outside the adit of the same mine Michael had visited with Houston. "You take her on in," he said. "I'll bring the trunk."

Ethan had to wait at the entrance for Happy to bring a lantern then he followed the older man inside. Happy led him to where the tunnel branched in different directions. Ethan set Michael on her feet and let her lean heavily against him. She was shivering but Ethan suspected it was more in response to the cold than from any awareness of danger. Her eyes were dark and unfocused, her limbs weak.

Happy raised the lantern to look at the three tunnels available to him. "Which one leads to the deepest shaft?" he asked, poking his head inside the entrance to the first tunnel.

"You're looking at it." Ethan's hand dropped casually to his gun. "Be careful, Happy. A dozen or so steps in that direction and you'll be falling down it." With Happy's attention occupied, Ethan took his gun from the holster and held it by the barrel. "You satisfied that no one's going to find her body accidentally?" Ethan inched forward, pulling Michael with him. He raised the butt of his Colt.

"Can't see how they could," Happy said. He lowered the lantern and began to turn toward Ethan in the same motion. The butt of Ethan's gun caught him at the base of his skull and he dropped to his knees instantly. The lantern fell out of Happy's hand as he lost consciousness. The light flickered and went out.

Ethan placed his Colt back into the holster and swung Michael in his arms. She whimpered like a small, wounded animal. "It'll be all right," he said against her ear. "I'll make this all right." He turned toward the entrance. The tunnel was relentlessly dark, so much so that beyond the entrance the night sky seemed more blue than black. Even without the lantern Ethan was able to make his way unerringly toward the outside.

He was standing on the threshold when they appeared. Ben, Jake, and Houston were waiting for him. They blocked his escape. With Michael in his arms it was impossible to go for his gun.

"I lose," Houston said calmly as Ben struck a match. The flame briefly illuminated his features. The harsh light softened when Ben put the match to the lantern he carried. "I told the others you wouldn't chose her over us. Seems I was wrong. You cost me quite a bit. Suppose I won't get any part of your take from the last robbery."

"I guess that means I don't get my cut," Ethan said.

Houston grinned at Ethan's unruffled tones. "Never doubted that you were a bright one. Best blaster we've ever had." He saw Ethan was having difficulty holding

308

Michael. "Jake, get his gun." When that was done he indicated that Ethan could lower Michael. Houston drew his .45 and leveled the barrel at Ethan's chest. "You'll have to go back the way you came. Take Michael with you. Ben, you can go on ahead a little with the lantern and see to your brother. Jake, start setting the charges."

Ethan wrapped his arm around Michael's waist and supported with his hip. Her head lolled against his shoulder. "Happy's going to have a headache," he said. "Nothing else. I didn't kill him."

"Didn't think you would. That's why Happy was willing to risk it. Except for that incident with that Drew fella, Happy said you were pretty reluctant to kill. Went out of your way, he said, to avoid it. You know Happy. He gets an idea and then he's hell bent on proving it."

"You were all certain I'd do this," said Ethan.

"I wasn't," said Houston. "Like I said, I believed in you. Damn shame. I hate to be wrong. But I've been that twice. About you. About her. I liked Michael. You know I did. I wasn't even willing to believe Dee when she said there was something not quite right. In the end I couldn't ignore the evidence of my own eyes. Michael's a reporter. She would have turned us all in sooner or later. The problems we had at the last robbery prove she was prepared to do it sooner."

"That wasn't Michael," Ethan said. "Look at her, Houston. She can barely stand. This is how Dee kept her the entire time we were gone. Michael was no more able to talk to anyone than a baby. I'm telling you, it was Cooper who set us up. If I didn't believe that I wouldn't have tried to help Michael get away. Do you really think I'd let her write anything about us?"

Houston kept urging Ethan and Michael deeper into the mine with little prompting motions of his gun. "It doesn't matter what I think anymore," he said.

"I'm letting the others make the decisions where you're concerned. Majority rule, remember? They don't trust you. I don't see how I can." His black eyes darted to Ben. "How's Happy? Do you need help?"

"He'll be all right," Ben said. "Like Ethan said. I can get him out myself." He set the lantern firmly on the ground and with some effort managed to lift his brother over his shoulder. "I'll be back to get the lantern as soon as I put Happy in the wagon."

Houston nodded. "See how Jake's coming with the explosives." He gave his full attention back to Ethan. "I suppose it's too much to expect you to set the charges."

"If it's your plan to bury us in here, then it's too much to expect."

"Too bad. You're the expert at this sort of thing. Jake's liable to blow off his fingers."

"That *would* be a shame," Ethan said coolly.

Houston found himself smiling. "I'm going to miss you, Ethan."

Ethan shrugged. He lowered Michael to the ground and let her lean back against one of the supporting wooden beams. She was still shivering. After a questioning look at Houston for approval, Ethan took off his coat and tucked it around her shoulders.

"Almost finished," Jake called from the entrance.

The shout distracted Houston momentarily. Ethan took the only opportunity he had. He leaped.

They were evenly matched in size and strength. The gun was Houston's edge until Ethan managed to deliver a blow to Houston's wrist and dislodge his grip on the weapon. It fell to the ground and was kicked out of the way as they fought. Ethan scrambled for it once, throwing his body at the Colt, knowing he had no chance without it. Houston hauled him back, catching him in the midsection with a powerful punch. Stumbling backward, Ethan pulled Houston with him. They toppled together, rolling across the cold,

310

hard ground. Their hats were pushed away. Ethan's fingers tangled in Houston's hair. He was able to hold Houston's head steady long enough to deliver a bone jarring blow to his chin. Stunned, Houston's grip relaxed and Ethan went for the gun again. There was a shout behind him. He recognized the voice as Jake's but he had to ignore it. The gun was everything.

His fingers were within inches of closing around the maple butt when he was struck from behind. Starbursts of pure white light flickered in front of his eyes and he thought he heard himself groan. Then he saw nothing, heard nothing. It was over. He had lost.

Ethan tasted dust in his mouth, grit on the inner side of his lips. He breathed it in, choked. He coughed weakly. The pressure inside his head was intense. Pain was not isolated in any particular place. He felt it everywhere, most sharply at the crown of his head.

He opened his eyes. He couldn't see anything. At first he thought he was blind. Then he remembered the mine, the fight, Houston's plan to bury him alive. He wished he were already dead. It would have been less painful. He slept.

It was the insistent whisper touch across his cheek that woke him. He thought it was a spider and tried to brush it away. It returned. He ducked his head, trying to avoid it. The movement sent a rush of pain to his head. There was a ringing in his ears. He groaned.

"Ethan?" Michael said. "Ethan? Are you awake?"

Everything was black when he opened his eyes. This time he did not think he was blind. He knew that his eyes would never adjust to the sort of relentless darkness he was experiencing now. Light was required for vision and there was not even a sliver of it in the mine. The blackness was total.

The gentle sweep of fingers across his cheek stopped. He heard his name again. By slow degrees he became aware of other things. He was lying on his side, his head cushioned against the softness of Michael's lap. One of his hands rested on her knee, the other was tucked awkwardly under him. His left shoulder was numb. The coat that he had given to Michael earlier was wrapped around him now. If she was cold he couldn't tell. He was the one shaking.

"Michael?" he said softly. He heard her sob once at the sound of her name, then she was leaning forward and her mouth found his forehead, his temple. She kissed his hair. He felt her tears on his skin. "It's all right, Michael. God knows why I'm alive, but I am."

Michael sucked back her sobs and swiped at her eyes with the back of her hand. "Don't you die on me, Ethan. I'd never forgive you for that. I'll harangue you in eternity. Follow you to hell if I have to."

He searched out her hand, found it, and squeezed. "That's all the reason I need to stay alive." He sensed, rather than saw, her watery smile. "How long have we been here?"

"I don't know. Several hours I think. It's impossible to judge time."

"What happened after Jake knocked me out?"

"Oh, you remember that. I didn't know if you would."

"It's hard not to. I've got a lump the size of Pike's Peak on the back of my head." He brought her hand up to feel it. "Careful."

Her fingers explored gently. "Jake didn't hold back. So much of what I remember is fuzzy, but that was quite clear to me. I tried to reach you but it was useless. I had a sense of what was happening and no ability to stop it. I could barely move my arms and legs then. Houston got to his feet, brushed himself off, and thanked Jake for his help."

"Did he pick up his gun?" Ethan thought there

might be some use for it, even if they could do nothing but fire off a few rounds to alert someone to their existence.

She nodded, realized he couldn't see that sort of reply, and answered. "Yes. Houston got his gun. I thought they might kill us then but they ignored both of us. I didn't understand their intentions."

Ethan checked his disappointment about the gun to protect Michael from the hopelessness he felt. "You didn't realize Jake was planting explosives?"

"I heard them talking about it but I couldn't make sense of what they were doing. There was no warning. It just happened. I didn't really see anything. The ground rocked and the support beams in here shuddered. Some of them collapsed. The roar was deafening and the smoke and dust was thick enough to taste. For a moment I couldn't breathe. It was as if all the air had been sucked out with the force of the explosion."

"You probably didn't imagine that. It could have happened for an instant."

"I was unconscious for a while. I know that." She hesitated. "Are we going to suffocate in here?"

"No. There's plenty of air." For now, he added silently.

"What are we going to do, Ethan?"

"I don't know." He struggled to a sitting position. "I must have wrenched my shoulder fighting with Houston."

"You might have," she said. "But I don't think so. You were half-buried by debris during the explosion. I had to move a beam off your shoulder."

"How the hell did you do that?"

"I'm not sure. It took me time to find you in the dark. I was on my hands and knees sweeping the ground, looking for you. Your legs weren't covered. I found them first and I was able to get rid of the rocks fairly easily. Then I came across the beam. I couldn't move it. I sat there, feeling sorry for myself and you. I worked myself up into a fine state of anger, I can tell you. Oh, Ethan, what you could have done with a cake of soap." She smiled when she heard his low chuckle. "I don't know what came over me then. I attacked that beam and it came away with all the difficulty of a toothpick. I was so surprised I almost dropped it."

Ethan winced as he imagined the pain and damage that would have caused him. "Thank God you didn't. I think my shoulder's dislocated. Can you help me?"

"What do you want me to do?"

"Take my arm." It took them a moment to find each other. "Use both your hands, Michael. That's it. Firm around my wrist. Don't let go until I tell you. Better yet, don't let go until my shoulder's back in place."

"How will I know?"

"You'll hear it."

"Oh, God." She released his wrist immediately. "I don't think I can —"

"Don't you dare quit on me now." He felt her fingers close around his wrist again. "Good. Now hang on." Ethan used his free hand to direct the movement of his shoulder and arm bone. He yanked hard, glad Michael couldn't see his painful grimace, and pushed the ball joint into his shoulder socket.

Michael heard the sound and let go. "Ethan? Are you all right?"

He grunted softly. "Give me a minute." He imagined the corners of his mouth were taut and white with strain. Gradually the radiating pain disappeared and left only a mild throbbing. "I'm fine." He leaned against her and rested his head on the rock behind them, catching his breath from the sudden exertion. "We need to take stock of our situation, Michael. I'd like to believe it's only been a few hours since Houston and the others buried us in here, but I have a feeling it's been a lot longer."

"How can you know?"

"You. The drugs Dee gave you have finally worn off. That couldn't have happened quickly. You said yourself you were unconscious after the explosion. You have no way of knowing how long that was. It could be daylight outside now."

"Is that important?"

"It is if we're going to get out of here and away."

"Won't there be anyone looking for us? Some digging from the other side?"

"You know Houston's put together some story to explain our disappearance. Everything of yours was already taken out of the room we shared. There's a trunk in here somewhere that belongs to you. I wouldn't be surprised if they packed up my things as well. It will look as if we left Madison together."

"What about the collapse of this mine entrance? That will draw some attention, won't it?"

"Perhaps. It's doubtful anyone will examine it long, especially when they haven't got a reason. We've been expecting this adit to collapse for weeks now. That's one of the reasons I stopped working in here. I needed the entrance shored and there wasn't any hurry to do it."

"Then we're not going to be rescued."

"No, we're not." He found her hand. "Do you have any idea how far back we are from the entrance?"

"None. I stopped investigating when I found you. Do you think we can dig our way out?"

"I don't know. It depends how much damage was done and how many feet of rock lies between us and the opening." He started to get to his feet but Michael held him back.

"No, don't leave me. I can't stand this darkness. I'm afraid, Ethan."

He hunkered down beside her as she came to her knees. His arms went around her shoulders and she pressed her face against his chest. His fingers touched her hair. It was matted and gritty with the same powder and dust that covered them elsewhere. "I'm not going to leave you, Michael. There's nowhere for me to go even if I wanted to. It's all right to be afraid. I'd be worried if you weren't."

She raised her head slightly. "I'm sorry I'm being so . . . so . . ."

"Female?"

Michael swallowed her sob. "You'll be sorry you said that. When we're out of here I'll remember that you said that and I'll make you sorry for it."

He loved her perfect indignation. Ethan kissed the crown of her head and hugged her more tightly. "That's something to look forward to. Now help me find the proper direction of the entrance. We'll talk to each other all the while so you won't feel as if I'm deserting you." He released her slowly. "Can you do that?"

"I can do whatever you want," she said quietly.

"And *I'll* remember that." Ethan helped her to her feet. "Are you oriented at all? Do you know the approximate direction of the entrance?"

Michael's eyes darted around. It was the same no matter where she looked. Blackness seemed to penetrate her very soul. She found Ethan's hand and cautiously led him a few feet to her left. "I think this is where you were lying." She searched with her foot. "Yes, here's the beam I moved. When Jake hit you your head was toward the entrance. This should be about right. I suppose you were at least ten feet back from it then."

"Stay here," Ethan said. "Facing just the way you are now. I'm going to climb over the rocks and see if I can't reach the entrance."

She was reluctant to give up his hand. "Don't forget to talk."

"I won't." Ethan waited for her fingers to drift away from his. He began to examine the face of the obstruction, feeling for the smaller rocks and pushing them out of his way. "I can talk about most anything," he said. "What do you want to hear?"

"Tell me about growing up. Where you lived, what you did. You've never told me more than a few sketchy details."

"That's because I knew you'd never be asked. People aren't generally as curious as you."

"It's not a bad thing for a reporter to be."

Ethan wrestled with another beam, pushing it out of his way. Rocks slid. The debris shifted and Ethan heard the groaning of some of the support timber. He stopped, listened.

"You're not saying anything, Ethan."

"Oh." There were no more sounds that would predict another collapse. He proceeded carefully. "I told you my parents died of typhus when I was ten. I'd always lived in Nevada until then. My father had followed the rush for gold to California then the silver strike to Nevada. Friends of my parents wrote to my father's brother in Texas. He lived in a hide-hut encampment in the northern panhandle and he took me in. He didn't feel any particular responsibility to me. I didn't eat much and I could shoot straight. Mostly I skinned buffalo for five years. Are you certain you want to hear this?"

"I'm certain. Not about the skinning. I don't think I'd like to know about that. What did you do at the end of five years?"

"I answered an advertisement I saw in Amarillo. Someone was looking for brave young men." His laugh was self-mocking. "I fancied I was one back then. There was a preference for orphans. I knew I was qualified on that count. I could ride and shoot and didn't mind hard work or long hours in the saddle. At fifteen the adventure seemed everything I could want."

"I don't think I understand what the job was."

Ethan was crawling along the top of the debris. There was very little room between him and the roof

317

of the mine. He was only able to go a few feet before he realized his way was blocked again. There was no chance they could dig through all the rubble to reach the entrance. The support timbers groaned again. It was too easy for Ethan to imagine the structure collapsing on him and burying him under hundreds of feet of mountain this time. He began to push himself out again. "Mail carrier," he told her. "Nothing special. I just carried the mail."

"Just carried the mail," she said softly to herself. Some quick calculations gave her the answer she needed. "You were fifteen, you say?"

"Hmm-mm."

"That would have been 1860."

"That's right."

"Carried the mail," she said again, shaking her head at his modest description of his job. "You were a Pony Express rider."

Ethan slipped on some rocks. The smaller ones scattered and rolled. The clatter seemed like a series of cannon shots in the absolute darkness and the danger was magnified in his own mind and Michael's. He paused, waiting for everything to be quiet again. "Yes," he said evenly. "I rode for the Express."

Michael's fingers curled and uncurled in the folds of her gown. It would have been easy, even comforting, to give into hysteria. Instead, she forced herself to match Ethan's calm. "It must have been terribly exciting."

"It was damn hard work," he muttered. Then he remembered what it had been like at fifteen. "But you're right, it was exciting too. Every young man then wanted to ride. I was lucky."

"Where was your run?"

"In the Sierra Nevadas, through Carson Pass to Sacramento. That was the last leg. I handed over the letters to a steamship captain and they were taken to San Francisco by water. The 85 miles through the mountains was the hardest part of the journey. I've heard other riders say it was the worst stretch on the entire route. I don't know about that. At least I wasn't chased by the Paiutes across Utah and Nevada." Ethan reached solid ground again and waved an outstretched arm in front of him to find Michael. He took her hand. "We may as well sit down," he said. "It's no good trying to get out that way. I need to think."

Michael let him guide her to a natural seat in the fallen rock. She sat beside him, not giving up her grip on his hand even when his fingers loosened around hers. "What made Carson Pass so difficult?" she asked, needing the reassurance of his voice.

Ethan leaned carefully against the rocks behind him. He put an arm around Michael's shoulders and let her shift closer to him. "Winter," he said. "Drifts could reach twenty feet. The winds lashed at you like a water soaked whip. The cold was numbing. To body *and* mind. Thank God my mustang generally had more sense than I did. Somehow I always got through with my *mochila*."

"*Mochila?*"

"Spanish for knapsack. It was a leather rectangle with four *cantinas* — pouches — for holding the mail. The *mochila* slipped over the special lightweight saddle we used and could be changed quickly when we traded mounts. We were only allowed two minutes for the exchange. Usually it didn't take that long."

Michael knew that slim wire cables stretching from pole to pole across the country were able to accomplish what harsh weather and Indian raids could not: the end of the Pony Express. But for a year and a half the service and its riders had captured the fancy of America, and Ethan Stone had been one of them. "You would have been just a little over sixteen when the service ended," she said. "What did you do then?"

"I had saved most of my money — fifty dollars a month was good pay — and I headed east. I had some notion about going to school. Ended up in the war instead."

"But you were just a child!"

Her protest, as if she could protect him from what he had already experienced, touched him. "I was closer to seventeen by then," he reminded her gently. "And there were men younger than me who served in the unit."

"You should have gone to school."

"You weren't there to boss me around."

Michael turned her cheek against Ethan's shoulder. Her fingers threaded in his. She wished she could see if he was smiling. "I was only ten. You wouldn't have paid me any attention."

Ethan wondered how true that was. Her methods of persuasion probably differed in those days. She wouldn't have harangued him with her logic back then. She would have kicked him in the shin. He imagined she had been making people pay attention to her all of her life.

"What did you do in the army?" she asked.

"Is it so important that you know everything about my life?" He meant the question as a tease and he asked it with laughter in his voice.

Michael felt tears prick her eyes. It was a moment before she could answer. "Yes," she whispered gravely. "I want to know everything. I don't want us to be strangers when we . . . when we . . ." She tried to move away so he wouldn't feel the shudder of her repressed sob.

He held her close instead. "All right," he said. His mouth was against her hair. He kissed the crown of her head. "What do you want to know?"

"What you did," she repeated. "Were you a cook or a scout or a soldier on the front line?"

"None of those things, though I suppose scout comes closest to describing what I did. Mostly, I just blew things up." He knew he had startled her. "Now, why does that surprise you? You must have wondered where I learned to use explosives. Actually, back then we didn't have dynamite. We used pure nitroglycerine when we needed to get rid of a bridge or stop a train. Very unstable, highly explosive. That's when I learned to cultivate patience and a steady hand. None of the men I worked with were ever killed or maimed by enemy fire. They blew themselves up."

"That's horrible."

"That's war."

Michael absorbed the truth of his statement in silence. She imagined the dangers he had faced, the meager rations and living conditions, the constant threat of death with the slightest misstep. Minutes passed before she asked, "Were you blue or gray?"

"Blue. Not from any particular guiding principle though. It was more a matter of geography. I was in Philadelphia when I enlisted. If I had wanted to attend William and Mary instead of the University of Pennsylvania I probably would have been a reb."

"What stopped you from going to the university?"

"I said I had saved *some* money. Not nearly enough as it turned out. And then there was the problem of my own schooling. Up until then what I knew was what I'd been taught by my mother. It was her dream that I should go to an eastern school someday. I suppose I was just trying to please her. I found out I wasn't rich enough or smart enough. Seemed like riding and fighting was what I knew best. The war was another opportunity to prove it."

"But eventually you were able to go to school," she said.

"How do you know that? I never said—"

"Ethan, I've known all along you were educated. At least more educated than you pretended to be around the others back at the saloon. It's in your speech, in your manner. I know you said that you were self-taught after the eighth grade, and I accepted it because it was clear you wanted me to, but it never fit with the things I saw with my own eyes and heard with my own ears. So where *did* you go to school?"

He hesitated. The truth—all of it—couldn't hurt now. At the very least he owed her the truth. "The University of Pennsylvania finally accepted me. I had to get a whole lot smarter and richer first, and I had to survive four years of fighting, but somehow I managed all of it."

"How?"

"One of the men I worked with, a Cornishman by birth and a miner by trade, was an expert with explosives. Connell Penwyn was his name. I was his apprentice throughout the war and that's what kept me alive. He was a careful, thoughtful man. He had come to this country with the hope of making a rich strike out west. He said he never found his golden vein and when war came he went east to fight, earn his fare back to Wales, and planned to live out his life on the other side of the Atlantic.

"That's what he told me, anyway. I never had any reason to doubt him. He was my mentor of sorts, not educated himself, but wise in his own way. Connell encouraged me to read more and since I didn't have anyone to write, and no one wrote me, he thought I should keep a journal. It was rather crude, nothing like your writing, but it forced me to practice skills that had been rotting since my mother died. Connell bought me books to read with his pay and in return I read aloud. He thought it was a fair exchange. I thought he was a trifle touched to be spending his passage money on me, but I was too selfish to protest. Some of the things I read were law books. Connell had great respect for justice. Just laws had leveled kings, he told me, and raised the common man. Laws also had to be enforced, he said, by fair and decent men. I think in his own mind he saw himself as

Diogenes in the New World, searching for an honest man."

"Were you one in those days?"

"Connell thought so. It helped that he thought I saved his life."

"Did you?"

Ethan shrugged. "I killed the rebel sniper that was aiming for Connell's jar of nitro. It was my life, too. Connell never cared about that and he never forgot." Ethan's fingers absently stroked Michael's hair. "When the war was over he told me he wanted to pay for my schooling. It seems Connell had his own ideas about the truth. He hadn't found a gold vein, but a silver one. He'd never told another soul about it because he'd known there'd be another rush west for riches if he did. He figured his claim was perfectly safe as long as he kept his secret. Only another determined Cornishman would have been able to track the black-coated silver ore, or even know what it was. I stayed in the east after the war and Connell went back to the Rockies. Six months, almost to the day he left, I received the first of many money drafts in my name. The amount stunned me. I could have attended the university twenty times over with the money he gave me and kept on giving me."

"You never thought about taking the money and doing something else with it?"

"No. I wanted to go to school. Law school. I thought that would please Connell." Ethan chuckled. "I aspired to the bench naturally. I imagined that Connell would like the idea of having a judge in his pocket."

Michael straightened and pulled away from Ethan. She peered at him in the darkness, frustrated that she couldn't see his face or that he couldn't see hers. Her voice was sharp. "Are you telling me that you have a law degree?" she demanded.

"Well, yes," he said. "I went to school. I graduated.

Four and one half years ago as a matter of fact. 1871. I went to New York afterwards. I thought about setting up a practice there."

"That's the time you told the others we were supposed to have met."

"Yes. I told you I was in New York then."

"You told me you were working in a bank. Houston told me you were robbing them. Who in the *hell* are you, Ethan Stone?"

He sighed. "You would have liked this better if we had remained strangers. You're glaring at me, aren't you?"

She smiled sweetly, gritting her teeth. "You know me so well."

Ethan found her hand again, thankful that she let him take it. "I *was* a lawyer. I still am, though I don't practice."

"That's understandable given the company you keep."

He ignored her comment. "I was only in New York a few months when I received word that Connell had died. Murdered, actually. Killed because of dispute over his claim. And I decided then that I didn't want to be a lawyer or a judge. I wanted to be the man who made the difference at the lowest rung on the ladder. I went west again and got myself elected sheriff in the mining town where Connell lived. I made it my first order of business to find his killer. As it turned out, there were two, and finding them was the easy part. Gathering enough evidence to bring them in took another year. During that time they were stripping the claim as quickly as they could, thinking I would never be able to do anything about it. They never knew there was any connection between Connell Penwyn and me."

Ethan's voice was distant, thoughtful. "The day they were sentenced to hang they still thought it was about the money."

324

"I don't understand."

"Connell left the Silver Slipper Mine to me. It was in his will and my connection to him all came out at the trial. There was a bias on my part that their lawyers naturally tried to exploit. They contended I'd manufactured the evidence to end the dispute and take back the claim. It was never about that, not for a moment, and luckily the jury believed me. I would have happily given up the Silver Slipper to have Connell back."

"You vindicated Connell's belief in justice."

"Perhaps."

"Then why," she began imploringly, "why did you throw in with Houston and the others?"

"It's not what you think, Michael. I know how it's looked to you, how I *wanted* it to look, but I've never really been one of them. There's been a number of times that I've wondered if I'd gone too far, helped them too much, but it seemed there were no other choices." He could almost feel her confusion and even without being able to see her he knew her head was tilted to one side, her brows drawn together, and her serious, questioning expression had flattened the beautiful shape of her mouth.

"You made a natural mistake," he said, "on the occasion of our first meeting."

"On the train?"

"No, at the *Chronicle*, when your publisher's secretary told you I was a marshal."

Michael tried to think what error she could have made. "I don't think —"

"You assumed I was a relative of Logan's. A very natural assumption if you didn't know my job, and you didn't. Michael, I've been a U.S. Marshal since right after the Silver Slipper affair was settled. I threw in with Houston, as you called it, because in order to beat him I had to join him."

"Marshall," she said softly. *"Marshal."*

Ethan had no idea how she managed it in the complete blackness of their surroundings, but the flat of her free hand found his cheek with the accuracy of an eagle swooping down on its prey. She tore the hand he had claimed away and stood. When her voice came to him it was from several feet away.

"How could you?" she demanded, her voice and body shaking with rage. "How could you let me think, no, how could you *want* me to think every horrible thing about you?"

"I admitted I didn't kill Drew." He rubbed the side of his face. It was no lady-like slap she had delivered, but a real blow. His cheek tingled as blood rushed to the area and suffused it with heat and color.

"You admitted it *after* I confronted you. Long after. And you went out of your way to make certain I thought the worst of you! You abducted me! You took me away from that train when—"

Ethan stood himself now. "When Obie would have killed you!" he thundered. "Have you forgotten what you were about to blurt out? Do you think I wanted you tagging along, getting in my way, giving me something else to worry about? Do you think I'd be trapped in this goddamn mine right now if it weren't for you?"

The words spilled out and he was helpless to call them back. In their wake the silence was as absolute as the darkness surrounding them.

Ethan took a step toward where he thought she might be. Stones scraped beneath his boot. "I didn't mean—"

"Shut up," she said quietly. "And don't come near me." If it had been daylight Michael's tears would have blinded her. Now they had no effect. She stumbled, groping her way in the dark to put more distance between her and Ethan. Disoriented quickly, she simply dropped to her knees and wrapped her arms around her, rocking slightly, comforting herself as if she were mother to her own child.

Her crying was painful to hear, wild and wounded, and the more she tried to hold it back the more it made Ethan ache. In the end it didn't matter that she didn't want him near her, there wasn't anybody else. Her sobs guided him toward her and covered the sound of his approach. He knelt beside her and when she fought him he just held on more tightly, gentling her with his voice and his hands, and letting her feel his strength as something solid but not overpowering.

"Michael." He said her name softly, over and over, a litany of penance to ease his soul. "I didn't mean it. Do you hear me, Michael? It's not your fault. None of it. Not what happened the night of the robbery, not that we're here now. It's mine. I should have thought of something besides taking you away from the train. I should have figured out a way to get you out of Madison. But I didn't want to quit without finding out who was helping Houston with the robberies. I let that rule my common sense and jeopardize your safety." His voice was husky beside her ear and though she was stiff and unyielding in his arms, she was quiet. "And I didn't really want to let you go . . . I love you, Mary Michael."

Michael slumped against him. His hold relaxed when he knew she wasn't going to fight him any longer. How could she? she thought. She loved him.

Ethan accepted the words she said, not really believing them. It was the danger, he thought, the threat of death, the need to give all that had come before and all that still awaited them some sense of rightness. She believed that she loved him and it was enough for Ethan. It was more than he thought he had any right to expect.

"I love you," he said again. She couldn't have been any closer to his heart in that moment if she had crawled under his skin.

Chapter Twelve

It was a mutual decision, made without a word passing between them. Darkness cloaked them. They were insensible to the color that touched their features. They felt the heat. He couldn't see her parting lips but he heard her sigh. She was blind to the mouth that hovered over hers. She tasted it instead.

It was frantic, reckless lovemaking, desperate and urgent. She fumbled with the buttons on his fly, he raised the skirt of her gown and pulled at her drawers. The press of his mouth was insistent. Her lips ground against his, eager and wanting.

She said, "Come into me."

"Take me," he said.

She did, straddling him as he lay back. A single thrust joined them. Michael's hands slid under his shirt and stroked his warm skin. He pulled at the neckline of her gown, rending it. Neither of them cared. He bared her breasts, cupped them, caressed. She leaned forward. His mouth was hot and damp on her skin and the suck of it tugged at the very center of her womb.

His fingers pressed into her buttocks, guiding her, encouraging her movements, forcing her pleasure. She shimmered with her release, crying out his name. The tension that was in every line of his body, in the hard thrusts that filled her, exploded. He held her tightly, kissed her harder, felt the sense of urgency fade, and still could not let go of her or stop wanting to love her.

She eased herself down beside him, sensing that he needed to know her strength now. Her fingers flitted across his cheek, his forehead. She brushed aside the strands that laid across his brow. "I'm not so afraid now," she said. "Really, I'm not. There are thousands of places I'd rather be but not without you. I mean that, Ethan."

And she would die meaning it, Ethan thought, if he didn't get her out of the mine. But once she was out, once she had time to think about it, she would realize it was as she had said once before. They really had no future together. It didn't matter if he was a thief or a marshal. She was Jay Mac's daughter. When she saw things more clearly she wouldn't have him as a gift, or be allowed to.

"I never said anything to anyone about the robbery," she said. "I wanted you to know that."

"I know it. You heard more at the door than you admitted though."

"That's true. But it wasn't planned. I caught a few words and then I couldn't help myself. I really never learned enough to tell anyone, and whatever Dee gave left me without any strength. I could hardly lift my head for four days."

"I wish we hadn't had to do that. My purpose was to protect you while I was gone. I knew you wouldn't be able to get away. It's too bad Dee didn't have the dosage right at the outset. You wouldn't have wandered off and she couldn't have accused you of turning us in. No one would listen when I tried to tell them it was Cooper all along."

"You're not listening to me," Michael said. "I could hardly lift my head. I *never* wandered anywhere. Dee's lying about that."

329

"To what purpose?"

"To exactly this purpose. She got rid of me. It was her aim all along."

Ethan thought about that. It had been Detra who sent to New York for the back issues of the *Chronicle*. Dee, who had suggested the sleeping powders as a way to keep Michael compliant and silent during the robbery. Dee, who had been jealous of Houston's interest in Michael from the very beginning. "Houston could have been killed," he said. "Obie was."

"I think she was willing to take that risk."

"Why didn't you say anything when Houston confronted you?"

"I tried to defend myself," she reminded him. "Even to my own ears I sounded pathetic. Who would have believed me anyway? You're not certain yourself." The flat of Michael's hand stroked Ethan's side. "It's not important now. It will never be important unless we find a way out of here. What can be done, Ethan? Is it so very hopeless?"

It was. But he could not tell her so bluntly. Perhaps if he explained their situation aloud he would think of something, if not, then she would know the worst as well as he. "This adit branches into three very different routes."

"I remember. This is where Houston brought me."

Ethan sat up, helping Michael up in the same motion. He cradled her between his legs, her back against his chest, her body circled by his arms. "If you're facing them, the one on the left descends by a shaft some two hundred feet. The tunnel goes less than twenty yards. Hard rock walls, all of it. The vein just petered out. It was there and then it wasn't. I'm not certain the hoistway even works any more; it's been a long time since anyone's been down there.

"The middle tunnel has a shaft that's about a quarter as deep. The miners came across some water and decided it wasn't worth pumping out to get at a less than a promising vein. When other parts of the mountain are tapped out, they'll come back and decide to get rid of the water."

Michael shivered. That's when they'll find us, she thought, our skeletons bound to each other in just this pose. She said, "It's good to know we'll have something to drink." But her voice trembled and her attempt at humor was too forced to be funny.

His chin moved slowly back and forth in her hair and against her scalp. "The last opening doesn't go down at all. I was following a vein that started to take a turn upward. It took me a while to realize that I was coming close to the surface again. I stopped blasting, afraid I might force a collapse. We needed to get more support timber in here. That's what I would have done this week if Cooper hadn't directed Houston to take the train."

"How close to the surface?" asked Michael. "Close enough to dig?"

"No. It's not like that. I'd have to blast first. Get through some more hard rock."

"Oh."

"I must have half a dozen crates of giant powder back in that tunnel. It was a good storage place. Blasting caps in a separate box. A spool of Bickford safety fuse. Everything." He laughed humorlessly. "Everything but a match. I know enough about blasting to keep the matches well out of the way of the explosives. I wish now I—"

"I have a match."

"—had thought a little less—"

"Several of them."

"—about safety." He paused, certain he hadn't heard correctly. "What did you say, Michael?"

"You said there was a trunk of my belongings in here," she said.

"Yes."

"Then I have some matches."

He was stunned into silence.

"I didn't know we had anything to light," she said simply. "A single match wouldn't have been very useful."

Still not believing what he was hearing, Ethan slowly shook his head. "No, it wouldn't have."

"It's because of my cigarettes," she said. "I've wanted one so badly, but then I made this bargain with God. I know it's horrible but I couldn't help myself."

"What sort of bargain?"

"That if He got us out of here alive then I'd never smoke again. I thought I should show a good faith effort by not lighting one now."

Ethan hugged her tightly, laughing, kissing the back of her head, her neck. "Oh, sweet Michael!" It was wonderfully just, he thought, how her bargain saved the matches and how the matches would save them. He might have been willing to bargain with the devil himself to bring about their escape. Michael was much wiser than he.

"You're not angry?" she asked.

"Angry? Because you have matches?"

"Because I didn't tell you about them."

"You didn't know." He placed his hands lightly on her shoulders. "All right. First we have to find the trunk. It would be better if we searched systematically—on our hands and knees. We can use a grid pattern, sweeping out with our hands. There's no need to hurry and no danger of taking a tumble down one of the shafts if we're careful. Can you do that?"

She hated the thought of being separated from him again in the dark. For one moment she actually regretted telling him about the matches in her trunk. "I'll help." Her voice was small.

He knew how frightened she was. "You don't have

to help me," he said.

"No. It will go faster if we both search."

"We also have to figure out what we're going to light with the match. I can't set explosives in the dark and I can't work by a lighted stick of dynamite." He thought a moment. "Happy carried a lantern in here. When I knocked him out I remember it fell and went out."

"That's right, but it's no good, Ethan. I kicked it when I was scrambling to find you. I know it lost most of it's oil. I smelled it."

"Take off your petticoat, Michael."

"Ethan!"

"Take it off," he repeated. "And tear it in strips. I'll find a piece of timber we can use and we'll make a torch. If we're lucky we'll come across the spilled oil and lantern in our search for the trunk. We can soak the strips in the oil." He could sense her skepticism. "It will work, Michael. I *know* it will."

And when he said it like that, she believed him. Absolutely.

Michael peeled off her petticoat and tore it into strips. The activity kept her busy so that she did not dwell on the fact that Ethan had moved away in his search for a piece of suitable timber. She hummed softly while she worked so that he could find her with relative ease when he had finished his task. The song was *While the Sun Shines.*

"Are you going to miss the stage?" he asked.

"Never." She smiled then because he laughed. Michael went back to humming.

It took Ethan several minutes to find something they could use. Taking the cotton strips from Michael, he fashioned a torch, then they parted again to begin their individual search for the oil and the trunk. It was harrowing work, even though they moved slowly and cautiously. There was always the sense that the next movement they made would send them into one of the

333

shafts. Their search was methodical: Ethan took the north-south route; Michael the east-west. The totality of the surrounding darkness made it difficult for them to manage a straight line as they crawled along the mine floor. The tendency for each of them was to move in a circle.

Michael found the broken glass from the lantern first, then she found the oil. Ethan joined her and they found the trunk together. Opening the lid, Michael searched through her belongings carefully, feeling the fabric of each garment until she came across the skirt she had been wearing on the train. Squirreled away in the hem she located four matches and two flattened cigarettes. Sighing, she left the cigarettes where they were and retrieved the matches.

"There are four," she said. "Do you have the torch ready?"

"It's ready. Just give me one. I'll have to find a good dry rock to strike it on." Their hands touched in the dark, held briefly, then Ethan accepted one of the matches. He moved away.

Michael wasn't aware she was holding her breath. She heard the matchhead scratch against rock then saw, actually *saw*, the spark. She had not realized a tiny fragile flame could burn with such intensity. It hurt her eyes to look at it and yet she was unable to look away.

Ethan held the flame to the oil soaked cotton. The flame ate away at the matchstick, burning his finger-tips. In spite of the instinct to toss the match, he held on. The frayed edges of the cotton strips caught the flame first. They fizzled and crackled and shriveled in red hot threads of fire. Ethan dropped the match in the same instant the torch took up the heat and light.

Though neither of them wanted to, they both had to look away from the light. Their eyes adjusted slowly, painfully, and when they stared at each other they both were squinting. It wasn't important. Neither was the fact they were nearly black with dust and grime. What captured their attention was the set of their happy, stupid grins. Ethan held the torch away from them as Michael launched herself into his arms, laughing and hugging and kissing his blackened face.

"This won't burn forever," he reminded her gently. "We have work to do."

She nodded, drawing away reluctantly. "What do you want me to do?"

Ethan got to his feet and held out a hand for Michael, pulling her up. He knew she didn't need the help. It was simply an excuse to touch her again. He didn't let go of her hand, brushing his thumb across her knuckles. "I want you to follow me into the tunnel. I need to set the explosives. You'll have to hold the torch while I work."

"You'd have a more difficult time getting me *not* to follow you," she said.

He smiled. "I thought so."

The tunnel was wide enough for three men to walk abreast. Michael didn't venture far from Ethan's side as she watched their shadows flicker on the hard rock walls. Ten yards before the tunnel's abrupt end, Ethan stopped her and passed the torch.

"Stay here. There's enough light for me to work if you don't move off." He placed his hands on her shoulders and kissed her cheek. "You understand not to come any closer."

Looking past Ethan's shoulder, Michael saw the box of blasting caps, the spool of safety fuse, and the crates of dynamite. She nodded. "I'm fine just where I am."

"Then we're both fine." An unexpected spark was the last thing he needed. The danger was not so great as Michael thought but setting her fears aside could make her less cautious. Ethan wanted to err on the side of safety.

His work was both patient and methodical. He examined the rock walls carefully first, determining where to lay the first charge. He wasn't certain he could break through to the outside with a single blast and several blasts carried the danger of a massive rockslide that not only could block their exit, but alert any nearby miners. A rescue would be very short-lived if Houston heard about it. Ethan knew his orientation to time was completely gone. He could only hope that when they found a way out it was the night sky that greeted them.

Ethan's tools were limited. He had only left a crowbar and hammer behind with the crates. Now he wished he'd left at least a knife. Using the crowbar, he cleared packed dirt from the crevices around the rock. Without a drill, or even a pick, he couldn't create holes within the rock for placing the dynamite sticks. Explosives set like that would have shattered the rock. What he had to do could shatter the tunnel.

Carefully considering the number of sticks he needed for some sort of impact, Ethan set the fuses and inserted blasting caps into the side of each stick. He examined the fuses again, knowing if he had timed them to go off properly it would help create a cavity of loose rock he could blow out into the tunnel. They might have to clear some debris away before he could set the next charges, but it wouldn't be an impossible task, not like what blocked the main entrance.

"We have to clear these supplies out of here," he told her. "It will take several trips. If you can roll the spool down the tunnel I'll take the blasting caps."

She looked at the large spool she was expected to move while carrying the torch and then at the small box that he picked up.

Ethan intercepted her questioning glance. "These little copper tubes contain fulminate of mercury. It's the jolt from one of them that sets off the dynamite.

Handled carelessly they can blow off a finger, a hand, and a box of them mismanaged will blow us both to kingdom come." He pointed to the spool of safety fuse. "That, on the other hand, is not going to hurt you unless you trip over it."

"I think I'll just take care of this spool," she said as if it had been her idea all along.

"Good for you."

On the second, third, and fourth trips, Michael only had to carry the torch and the tools. Ethan hauled the crates of dynamite. They put the explosives and equipment in the antechamber for safety then Ethan went back to light the fuses, taking the torch with him.

Michael sat on her trunk in the dark, ticking off the seconds he was gone on her fingers. She counted thirty before she heard him yell 'fire in the hole' and another ten before he joined her again. They dropped behind the trunk for the minimum protection it offered and waited.

And waited.

"How much longer?" Michael asked, every line of her body tense with anticipation.

"It should have gone off by—" The first explosion shook the ground beneath them. "Now." Dust billowed out of the tunnel and the flame of their torch flickered madly. Ethan shielded it with his body.

"Is that all?" she asked. It hadn't been very loud, more of a thud and rumble, like distant thunder.

Before Ethan answered there were two subsequent explosions. The ground seemed to roll under them again. When everything was still and silent Ethan stood. "That's all," he said, brushing himself off. It was a gesture of habit and made no impact on the layers of dust covering him. He smiled ruefully when he realized what he was doing. "Let's have a look at the damage."

As they neared the end of the tunnel they had to pick their way over the muck from the explosion. Ethan raised the torch and examined his work. "It didn't have much impact," he announced after a moment. In spite of the fact that he had expected it, disappointment was clear in his voice. "We'll have to try again." He glanced at the torch, wondering how much longer they could expect it to burn. "How many matches did you say you had?"

"Three now."

Ethan hoped he wouldn't need even one of them. They worked quickly, carrying back the supplies. Ethan set new charges, peeling back the paraffin wrapping on the dynamite and molding the malleable sticks into shapes he needed. Carving out new crevices with the crowbar and hammer, Ethan tamped the explosives into place. He set more charges, knowing it might be his last chance to work with light.

They protected themselves as before. This time when the dust cloud rolled through the tunnel their torch was extinguished.

Coughing, her eyes watering, Michael searched the trunk for another garment. She found her shirt-waist blouse and tore it as she had the petticoat. Wrapping it around the burned out torch, Michael rolled it in what was left of the oil and gave it back to Ethan with a match to light.

They were halfway to the site of the explosion when the torch failed them again. Ethan found Michael's hand. "It will be all right," he said.

"It will," she said softly.

He squeezed her hand. "I meant to reassure you, but thank you." He led her slowly and carefully deeper into the tunnel, using the wall as a guide.

"I could light a match," she said.

"No. It would be a waste. I might need it to set off another charge. We could still need both of them."

338

They groped their way over the debris, stumbling a little, and knew they had reached the end of the tunnel. Ethan let go of Michael's hand and began to examine the rock face with his palms, searching for structural damage that could lead them to the outside.

Michael stood very still, peering hard in Ethan's direction, trying to imagine what he was doing. His hands slid over the rock; his finger dug into new crevices. He pulled away loose stone, flinging it behind him so carelessly once that Michael had to dodge the rock.

It took her several seconds to realize what she had done and what it meant. "Ethan!"

He paused in his task. "Did I hurt you?"

"No! I jumped out of the way, Ethan. I saw the stone!"

Ethan spun around. He stared at her, stared at her hard, and slowly the shadow of her form began to take shape.

It was not light, not in the sense that it was bright and white or concentrated in a beam. It was light only in the sense it was less dark. "Where's the light coming from?"

Michael raised her head and looked around, searching out the source. Suddenly her eyes caught a vein of dark blue, just a sliver of something that was different than what surrounded it. She squinted, trying to make it out, and swayed slightly on her feet. That's when she saw the pinprick of light, the beacon that was beyond her reach.

"It's a star," she said softly, awed by her discovery. Tears blurred her vision. "Ethan. I can see a star."

He came to stand directly behind her. Mimicking the angle of her head, Ethan raised his eyes. Never again would he think of the night sky as black, he thought. It was filled with light, beautiful blue-white light, glistening, pulsing, points of light. "That's our way out," he said quietly, solemnly. There were tears in his eyes as well.

He set her away and reached in his pockets for the sticks of dynamite he brought with him. He let Michael peel back the waterproof wrapping while he cut off the proper lengths of fuse with his teeth. He plugged the vein of light with dynamite, plunging them into darkness again. Working by touch alone, Ethan inserted the blasting caps and set the fuses. The cords were longer this time to give Ethan and Michael ample chance to get far away from the center of the explosion.

Ethan made Michael start down the tunnel before he lighted the fuses. He caught up to her and half-carried, half-dragged her toward the adit. They tripped over the trunk in their rush for safety. That and the explosion sent them both sprawling.

"Are you all right?" he asked.

"Winded." She sat up, wrestling impatiently with her gown as it tangled beneath her. "You?"

"I'm fine." He stood. "Michael? Where are you? Let's see if we've done enough damage this time."

Michael was kneeling over the trunk, rummaging through it. She found her journal and her brooch. "I'm ready."

Ethan had been listening to her movements. "You're not getting a cigarette, are you?"

She laughed. "No. A promise is a promise."

At the end of the tunnel the blue velvet night sky opened to them. Giddy with the enormity of what they had accomplished, they hastily constructed a small mountain of stones out of the muck to raise them nearer the opening. Ethan lifted Michael and pushed her through. He followed a moment later.

They didn't do anything but breathe the fresh, cold night air and stare at the heavens.

"You're shivering," he said.

"I don't care." She hugged the notepad to her breast. Her teeth chattered. "I d-don't care," she said happily.

Ethan stripped off his coat and gave it to her. He held her close, pressing a smile against her hair. "We can't stay here. I can't imagine we have more than two hours left before dawn. The miners next shift will be starting soon."

She nodded. "Where are we going? The livery?"

"No, not to town. We'll go to Emily's. She'll give us horses and supplies. We need to get to Stillwater, Michael. You understand that, don't you? There's really no help for us here in Madison. Houston's well liked. I'd be dead before I could prove the case against him and the others."

"I understand." She put her hand in his and let him lead the way.

Stillwater was a mining town, bigger and rougher than Madison, with twice the population and less than half the laws. Even so, an hour and a half since dawn's first light, when Ethan and Michael rode down the frozen mud track that was the main thoroughfare, the town was relatively quiet, the street almost deserted of traffic.

Ethan secured both horses to the rail in front of Walter's Boarding House. He helped Michael dismount and escorted her inside. Mrs. Walter, going through the motions of registering them like a sleepwalker, set out their keys and waved them on up to the separate rooms Ethan had requested. They were only marginally more clean than they had been since leaving the mine, thanks to Emily John's hospitality, but Mrs. Walker asked no questions about their sorry appearance. Her lack of concern made Michael wonder about the condition of the rooms.

Ethan carried the satchel of fresh clothing that Emily had given them and mounted the stairs behind Michael. Outside the door to her room he passed it to her. "You take this," he said. "I have to find the sheriff and the telegrapher."

"Ethan. You should get some rest."

He shook his head. "You'll have to sleep enough for both of us." He kissed her forehead.

Michael wouldn't let him go so easily. She raised herself up and kissed him full on the mouth. "Separate rooms?" she asked.

Ethan straightened. His blue-gray eyes searched her face, saw the uncertainty she tried to mask in the lightly asked question. "We're not in Madison any longer," he told her gently. "This isn't Kelly's Saloon and you aren't really my wife."

She was unaware that she was looking at him hopefully, she only felt it in her heart. He would say it now, she thought, he would make his proposal. But he said nothing and the moment passed. Her eyes dropped away and the chill that clutched her heart took possession of her entire body. She fumbled with the key to her room, her hand shaking as she applied it to the lock. Ethan's hand closed around hers and guided it. The door opened.

"Thank you," she said, not looking at him. Her voice was small, only seconds away from breaking.

Ethan stepped back as the door closed behind her. He stared at it, wondering if he should go to her. He had seen the look in her beautiful green eyes, known what she was thinking as if she had said it aloud. Ethan turned, jamming his hands in his pockets, and started down the stairs. There wasn't time and it wasn't the time.

Ethan found the sheriff sleeping off a two day drunk in one of his own cells. It took a pot of hot coffee and bucket of ice water to bring the man around. Sheriff Rivers offered no apology for his condition but was philosophically good-humored about the cure.

Ethan introduced himself but once Rivers was sober the man required proof. They went to the telegrapher's office and kept the clerk busy for more than an hour with a steady stream of dots and dashes between Stillwater and Denver and eventually New York and Washington. Satisfied eventually that Ethan Stone was precisely who he said he was, and very much in authority as a federal marshal, Sheriff Rivers was moved to offer his reluctant cooperation and participation in gathering the posse.

Ethan doubted he could have counted on Rivers's help if the crime against Houston hadn't been theft of the payrolls and bullion from mining camps. Rivers, an ex-miner himself, still had respect for the old laws of the mining camps that meted out justice quickly and firmly, although not always so wisely. Most offenses wouldn't have bothered him overmuch. The theft of the miner's payroll and bullion, some of it from Stillwater itself, was a heinous crime to his way of thinking. The attempted murder of Ethan and Michael, the murders of the *Chronicle* staffers, didn't bother him quite as much. He hadn't known any of them. He *understood* gold and silver and the sanctity of a man's livelihood if not his life.

The posse Ethan commanded counted forty men in its ranks. They were all formally deputized and cautioned to bring in Houston and the others alive. Ethan wanted his case against Cooper, the man who made the raids so easy for Houston, to be backed by Houston's own testimony.

The arrests were surprisingly easy, even a little anticlimatic to the men who rode with Ethan and expected a shoot out. Happy and Ben were caught cleaning fish in their cabin outside of Madison at dusk. Jake was alone in the sheriff's office. Detra was serving drinks behind the bar, answering the questions her customers put forth about Michael and Ethan's elopement with complete aplomb, each well-rehearsed lie coming smoothly to her lips. She didn't falter until she actually saw Ethan standing at the end of the mahogany bar with his gun drawn. She was caught between two deputies before she could manage to call a warning to Houston. He stepped into the saloon from the office when the place fell silent.

Ethan and a dozen deputies were waiting for him.

"I asked for his star, then his gun," Ethan told Michael.

"You never said it in quite those words before. Is that what you're going to tell the jury?" she asked. They were sitting in the dining room of Mason's Hotel in Denver, sharing dinner while Ethan reviewed some of the testimony he was likely to give in the morning.

Fourteen days had passed since Houston's arrest, eleven since the prisoners had been moved to Denver for trial. The men were housed in the local jail; Detra was quartered in Peak's Hotel with a guard at the door day and night. Ethan had insisted upon a change of venue. Lynching was almost a certainty if the prisoners remained in Stillwater and a fair trial in Madison was out of the question. There was also the matter of getting as circuit judge to hear the cases in a timely manner. A fair and swift trial could only take place in Denver and the city was happy to entertain the notorious.

The *Rocky Mountain News* ran daily stories about the gang, uncovering the past of all its members. The results were a mixed bag of accuracy, tall tales, and supposition. All of it read as fact.

There was little danger of Houston and the others becoming folk heros, not when they had stolen from the miners themselves. The paper made a point of reminding Denver citizens about the murder of the *Chronicle* reporters and called for hanging all gang members with the exception of Detra Kelly. In Dee's case they came across the rumor of Mr. Kelly's untimely death and demanded a full investigation.

Drew Beaumont had returned west to cover the story for the *Chronicle*. As a witness in the trial, Michael could not in good conscious put her name to a single story about the gang. Worse, in her estimation, was that she had become part of the story, a source of information rather than a reporter of it. She was heartily sick of the questioning, not only from reporters, but from the prosecuting attorneys as they challenged her testimony in preparation of their case.

Tonight, when Ethan had proposed they have dinner together in the hotel, Michael accepted because she wanted to pretend there was nothing momentous happening on the morrow. On the eve of the trial it was an impossible pretense to maintain.

"I asked for his star, then his gun?" Ethan repeated, questioning her this time. "Why should I say it that way?"

Michael cut a bit of her rainbow trout and lifted it to her mouth. "It emphasizes Houston's betrayal," she said. She tasted the trout. It was light and flaky, quite delicious. She only wished she could enjoy it more. "He violated a trust to the people of Madison. By asking for his star first you made him answer for his abuse of authority. I think that's how the jury will hear it. It's something they'll remember when they're deciding Houston's fate."

"I hope so." Ethan searched Michael's face. Her complexion was pale and there were faint shadows beneath her eyes. Her skin looked drawn and tight, her eyes were remarkable only for their lack of expression. He didn't know if she was sad or hurt or angry or anxious. She only seemed weary. "Have you heard from your family today?"

She shook her head. "There was a telegram from Mama and my sisters yesterday. They're anxious for me to come home. They've read everything Drew's written but it isn't enough for them. They need to see me to know that I'm really safe."

"In their place I'd want the same thing." Yesterday, he thought, his eyes clouding. Yesterday she had received a telegram and he hadn't known about it. They were only two weeks out of the mine, two weeks distant from a time they shared everything, and she was talking to him in the polite tones of a casual acquaintance. "And Jay Mac?" he asked. "What have you heard from him?"

"Another threatening telegram ordering me home." She smiled faintly. "Papa doesn't think I should have to testify. I can imagine he's furious that he can't influence the prosecutors to see things his way." Her smile faded. She pushed food around her plate for a moment, then set down her fork and gave up the pretense of eating. "You should have told me about your connection to my father," she said, raising her eyes to his. Her green eyes held no accusation, only a certain sadness. She fingered the brooch she had saved from the mine. "Why didn't you?"

"There never seemed a good time."

"When we were trapped in the mine you told me you were a marshal. Why not the rest?"

"It wasn't important."

But it was, Michael thought, and she had had to learn it from Ethan while he was explaining it to the state's attorneys. The nature of his business in Logan Marshall's office all those months ago had finally become clear. The only deal he had offered anyone that day was his promise to end the series of train robberies that were plaguing the Union Pacific in Colorado, Nebraska and Wyoming, and make it possible for inves-

346

tors to see profits in expanding the routes. "You were essentially working for my father," she said. "I'd say that was important."

"You're father didn't hire me, Michael. Neither did Logan Marshall. I'm employed by the federal government. The idea for becoming part of the gang was actually Joe Rivington's, the Secretary of the Interior's man. Marshall supplied the contacts we needed to create some stories about bank robberies in Missouri and Colorado, all of which described a clever safe blaster. Houston found me as a result of those stories. Carl Franklin, representing your father and Northeast Rail Lines, offered contacts with all the lines as the search continued to identify and locate the man who was supplying information to the robbers. Long before we knew the identities of anyone involved in the robberies, we understood their approach to the crimes. When I failed early on to learn about Cooper I had to become more a part of Houston's gang than I, or anyone else, had ever intended.

"Cooper eluded us because we were looking for a small cog in the machinery. No one expected him to be a respected vice-president and major stockholder with the Union Pacific. It was your father who recognized the description I telegraphed to his office. Those pale eyes were as unforgettable as I thought they might be."

Michael nodded. "Peter Monroe and my father attended Harvard together. I imagine they've had a number of business dealings over the years. I understand why Mr. Monroe wouldn't have used his own name with Houston, but why Cooper?"

"Apparently Monroe's grandfather repaired barrels and casks for a living. Monroe thought he was being common and coy by using the name."

"And his motive for engineering the robberies?"

"The simplest one: greed. He had ideas of ex-

347

panding into his own rail line."

"He's been arrested?"

"Four days ago in the San Francisco offices."

Michael picked up her tea cup. It was cool to the touch but she sipped it anyway. "I wish you had told me," she said after a moment.

"About Monroe's arrest?"

She shook her head. "About Jay Mac. About his involvement in your scheme."

"It wasn't a scheme. It was a plan. And I told you, I didn't really work for Jay Mac Worth."

"Of course you did. You risked your life to make my father richer. He'll put his money down in Colorado rails and reap the profits now that you've helped clear another obstacle."

"A lot of people will benefit."

She snorted delicately and her tones were icy when she spoke. "Now you sound like my sister Rennie. She knows all about profits and losses and how many people will benefit. Jay Mac will be at the top of the heap, I can tell you that."

A muscle ticked along Ethan's jaw. "I want to know what's wrong with you," he said. "Why you're being so damnably provoking."

"Keep your voice down," she said quickly, glancing around at the other diners. The privacy of their corner table was not assured by the potted palms and hothouse flowers that surrounded them. She put her cup down and her hands drifted to her lap. Beneath the table she nervously pleated the linen napkin. "I wasn't aware I was being provoking at all."

But she knew it was a lie. She wanted to make him feel something, some regret for not being completely honest with her when he had had the chance. This wasn't about Jay Mac. He was merely an excuse, the thing she could talk about when what she really wanted to say was 'why weren't you honest

348

about loving me?'

"Are you nervous about the trial?" he asked.

The trial. She wanted to scream, rail at him. She didn't care about the trial. No, that wasn't true either. She did care, only not as much as she cared about him never touching her any more, never kissing her, never acknowledging by so much as a gesture that they had once been lovers, or that he had ever said he loved her. She remembered his words when she asked about the separate rooms in Stillwater. "This isn't Kelly's Saloon and you aren't really my wife." It seemed there was no place for them anywhere outside of Kelly's Saloon. Not Stillwater. Not Denver. Certainly not New York.

"I suppose I'm nervous," she said. "A little."

"The courtroom will be full."

She shrugged. "The trial has national interest."

"Have you thought of how you're going to respond to questions about us?"

Her beautifully feathered eyebrows rose a fraction. "What about us?" she said coolly. Hidden from his view were her fingers frantically pleating the napkin, knuckles nearly as white as the linen. "There's nothing to tell. Nothing happened."

It was what he expected to hear at the trial, but not now, not in the relative privacy of the dining room, when they were alone for one of the few times since the arrests. Ethan felt as if he'd been kicked. "I see," he said. His eyes searched hers, caught her glance and held it. He could not tell what she was thinking, the emerald eyes were more blank than guarded, more resigned than challenging. "That's the way you remember it?" he asked.

"Don't you?" She waited. Tell me now, she wanted to say. Tell me that you love me. Make me believe it wasn't about offering comfort when you thought we would die.

He remembered that she had said she loved him.

He had tried to caution himself then that she was merely throwing him a bone, that she had said it as a means of salving her own conscience. But he hadn't wanted to believe that, not really. His fingers raked his dark hair. A heavy ache settled in his chest. "The same," he said quietly, looking away from her.

"Then there's no reason for either one of us to be nervous, is there? We've only to speak the truth."

"There's bound to be speculation," he said.

"There always is," she said with credible indifference. When he didn't say anything silence settled uncomfortably between them. The remainder of her meal grew cold. Ethan ate very little of what was left of his. The waitress came and cleared the table. They accepted her offer of coffee and pie because they were reluctant to leave and didn't know how to go on.

"When do you think I'll be able to go home?" she asked. "That was the gist of Mama's telegram yesterday."

Apple pie tasted like ash in his mouth. "A few weeks. I suspect Houston's trial will take the longest. Dee's may be a close second. The cases against Happy, Ben, and Jake will be quick. They may even be tried together."

"Peter Monroe's?"

"Cooper has to be extradited here first. That could take a while. It shouldn't matter to you. You don't have to give any testimony in that case. I'm the witness who can identify him."

"Then you won't be going to New York any time soon." Was that she, Michael wondered, who sounded so calm? How could her heart, beating wildly, not lend its vibration to her voice?

"No," he said. The coffee was too hot for his mouth. He didn't care. "Not any time soon. I don't have any business there."

"I thought . . ." She faltered and started again,

more briskly this time. "I thought you might have some dealings with Joe Rivington."

"If I do, it will take me to Washington, not New York."

"Of course . . . I didn't think of that."

"This is where I'll be settling, Michael. Colorado will be my home."

"Denver?"

"Most likely. It's at the center of my jurisdiction."

She nodded. He would hate New York if he had to stay there any length of time. It was probably just as well that there was no discussion of marriage. She was east and he was west. It had been so easy to forget in Kelly's Saloon. She had just been his then. Her smile was wistful. And he had been hers.

"Something amusing?" he asked softly.

"No," she said. "Just a wayward thought."

Ethan knew all about those. He wanted to touch her hair. Gaslight softened the burnished frame of it around her face. He imagined his fingertips trace the arch of her cheekbones, sliding along the line of her jaw. His thumb would pass over her lower lip, caress the pout. The tip of her tongue would touch him. Her eyes would darken. He would . . . Ethan stopped. Michael's eyes were regarding him steadily, as if she could read his thoughts. He reined them in. She didn't want any part of him now. She'd made that clear by going out of her way to avoid him and spending most of her time with Drew Beaumont as soon as he got to Denver.

He pointed to the pie she had barely touched. "Are you finished?"

She flushed self-consciously. "I'm not very hungry." She almost asked if he wanted it then saw he hadn't finished his own. Michael placed her napkin beside her plate. "I should be returning to my room. I have a story to finish for the paper."

351

"I didn't realize you were writing about the trial for the *Chronicle*."

"It's not about the trial. It's about dance halls in mining towns. Something with which I'm well acquainted. I have enough material in my journal for ten or so different articles. Mr. Marshall's going to run them as a serial in the Sunday edition."

She'd never be satisfied with the *Rocky Mountain News,* he thought. "I'll escort you to your room," he said, starting to rise.

Michael let Ethan pull out her chair. She stood. "That won't be necessary." Over his shoulder she caught sight of Drew standing in the hotel lobby. "I see Drew. He'll walk with me. Our rooms are on the same floor and I need to talk to him about something anyway."

Ethan couldn't find any good reason to object. Drew had seen them and was already approaching. Ethan didn't want to be thanked one more time for saving Drew's life. He bid a curt good evening to Michael, took his hat, and brushed past Drew without a word.

"What's the matter with the marshal?" Drew asked, taking Michael's arm.

She stared after Ethan a moment longer. "Just the trial," she said finally. "He's anxious for the trial to begin."

For fifteen days Denver hung on every word of the trials. Denver was not alone. People all over the country were interested in the story of a sheriff and a deputy who robbed trains, the woman who was his mistress and who may or may not have murdered her husband, the half-brothers who prospected for years in the Rockies with nothing to show for it except what they stole, and everyone's connection to the vice-president of Union Pacific who had hit upon the plan to add to his personal fortune.

The courtroom was filled to capacity every morning, with people waiting in the hallways in the vain hope that someone would excuse themself from the proceedings and the vacancy might be taken. Judge Clark Tucker presided over the madness that ensued, raising his gavel in a threatening manner at the unruly crowd rather than banging it. The *Rocky Mountain News* reported Tucker wore a gun beneath his robes but no one would confirm it, least of all the distinguished judge himself.

True to Ethan's predictions, Houston's trial lasted the longest. It was there that the story of Michael's abduction unraveled and was bared for public scrutiny. Houston's lawyer contended the fault lay with Ethan Stone, not with Nathaniel Houston. He argued eloquently that the man who had placed her in danger was the one who had taken her from the train, not the one who allegedly led the robbery. It was also the defense's contention that the incident at the mines was an accident, the result of a landslide and not attempted murder. He proved that Houston had not ordered the deaths of the *Chronicle* reporters by bringing witnesses from the robbery who could testify to Houston's whereabouts on the train when the cars had been uncoupled.

The courtroom was quiet while Ethan testified but it was nothing to the silence that held the gallery still when Michael took the stand. Under oath she recounted the story of the robbery of No. 349 and her abduction, the way in which Marshal Stone had been careful to maintain his cover for the others but reveal himself to her. Many of the things she was asked to relate by the defense were more damaging to Ethan's reputation than to Houston. It was not Houston who made her work in the saloon or kept her locked in her room. It was not Houston who stopped her escape. She told of being drugged, though she could not say with certainty that Houston had ordered it. The prosecution gave her time to explain that what Ethan had done had been done to protect her; Houston's attorney did everything in his power to make the jury forget that. Her state of mind at the time of the mine incident was called to question again and again and the defense beat her down until she admitted she was not certain of the early events of that night. When she left the stand she was pale and her hands trembled. Drew escorted her out of the courtroom. Ethan did not look up at her as she passed.

After four days of testimony and two days of deliberation the verdict was returned. Houston was found guilty on all counts of robbery. He was cleared on the murder charges of the *Chronicle* employees and the attempted murder of Ethan and Michael. Sentencing for the robberies alone would see him in prison for forty years, but the prosecution had been seeking the death penalty.

When the verdict was read Houston reacted as if he had won, as indeed Ethan felt that he had. On his way out of the courtroom, surrounded by guards, Houston swiveled his head in Ethan's direction and smiled. It was full of promise, full of threat. Ethan bore it without blinking. He didn't react at all until he saw Houston seek out Michael. It was the expression in Houston's obsidian eyes that made Ethan's blood run cold, but it was his wink that nearly raised Ethan out of his seat. He looked back three rows at Michael. Her head was bent. He couldn't tell if she had seen Houston's suggestive leer or not. It was certain that Drew had. The reporter was staring after Houston while his hand flew across his notepad.

The circumstances of the death of Mr. Kelly were never introduced at Detra's trial. If the jury had read any of the accounts in the newspaper, or if they knew her father had been a druggist, they gave no indication of it. In Judge Tucker's courtroom she was strictly on trial for her part in planning the robberies. Ethan provided the main testimony against her. Michael's story came strictly from what she had heard at the door as the robbery for No. 486 was being planned. Detra's attorney provided plenty of people, including Kitty Long, who supported her business-like acumen in running the saloon and her fairness in dealing with employees. Miners from Madison bore witness to the fact that she was well thought of in the mining town and honest with the games she ran in the saloon. The twelve man jury liked her as well and they were not convinced she was as critical to the planning as Ethan would have had them believe. She was, after all, only a woman. They found her guilty but the honorable Judge Tucker only gave her two years.

Ben, Happy, and Jake were tried together. Ben and Jake received the same sentence as Houston. Happy, on the strength of Michael's testimony that he had admitted his guilt in the deaths of the *Chronicle* staffers, was sentenced to hang.

Michael did not attend the public hanging three days later. When they cut Happy McAllister down, Michael was somewhere between St. Louis and Pittsburgh, headed home.

Chapter Thirteen

John MacKenzie Worth swiveled in his large leather armchair as the door to his office opened. The deep burgundy leather held the aroma of cigar smoke. It was the way he liked it, even before he'd given them up seven months earlier. He'd bargained with God for the safe return of his daughter. His wife thought he'd finally given them up for her. In deference to years of Nina's nagging, he let her believe it. Now Nina was encouraging him to get rid of the chair. He was holding firm there.

Jay Mac's secretary entered the office filled with self-importance, his demeanor as stiff as his blackened mustache. "Your two o'clock appointment is here," he said. "He's brought someone with him."

"Show them in, Wilson." He looked beyond the secretary's shoulder and saw two men approaching the office's threshold. "Nevermind. They've found their own way." He stood up, came around his desk, and dismissed Wilson while holding out a hand to his visitors.

They both looked bone weary, stiff from days and nights of train travel to which neither was accustomed. They did not have the appearance of men who tolerated confinement, much less enjoyed it.

Ethan Stone found his hand taken firmly in Jay Mac's. The older man looked him squarely in the eye and studied him long and hard. Jay Mac's face remained impassive. Here was the man, Ethan thought, who taught Michael how to play poker. Ethan relished the idea of sitting across a table from Jay Mac some day himself, just to see who bluffed better and who folded first.

On this occasion Ethan gave the round to Jay Mac. It was impossible not to look into the face of Michael's father and not see Michael. Ethan knew for a moment he had actually flinched from the directness of Jay Mac's implacable green eyes.

John MacKenzie Worth was several inches shorter than Ethan but it was something Ethan noticed only as Jay Mac was turning away. Michael's father was slender and there was an aura of authority and power that lent him a stature that didn't physically exist. He had a head of thick dark blonde hair, turning to ash at the temples. Threads of the same lighter color sprinkled his side whiskers and mustache. His face was a trifle broader than Michael's but they shared the same seriously set mouth. Unlike his daughter, Jay Mac's spectacles were kept in the breast pocket of his jacket when he wasn't wearing them.

"This is Jarret Sullivan," Ethan said when Jay Mac greeted the man who had accompanied him. "I've asked him to help. We go back a few years together, since the Express days."

Jarret shook Jay Mac's hand. He was as tall as Ethan, slightly broader in the shoulders, but leaner overall. Long-limbed, he held himself loosely, so that he appeared lithe rather than powerful. There was a sense of calm surrounding him, a lazy watchfulness that made him seem more relaxed than he actually was. A faint lift of one corner of his mouth signaled Jarret's sometimes cynical, sometimes genuine, amusement of what went on around him. He was

357

never as removed from events as his remote, dark blue eyes seemed to indicate.

The deep sapphire eyes were a startling feature in a face that was tanned and weathered by the sun. The sharply cut jaw and patrician nose gave him the arrogant air of a blue-blood. The beard stubble on his chin and jaw made him look dangerous. His hair was dark blond, too long at the nape for New York fashion, but somehow suited to him.

"Sullivan?" asked Jay Mac, finishing his assessment. "That's an Irish name, isn't it?"

Jarret had little patience for Jay Mac sizing him up, but in deference to Ethan he made an attempt to answer politely, in a credible Irish brogue, keeping his disdain in check. "County Wexford on ma da's side."

Jay Mac chuckled, removing his hand. He indicated the chairs in front of his desk and asked Ethan and Jarret to be seated. He stood, leaning back on the edge of his desk, and lifted the black lacquered box of cigars beside him. Raising the lid, he offered them to his guests. "I gave them up myself," he said. "But I wouldn't mind smelling one burning. I don't think that would be going back on my promise."

Ethan passed but Jarret took one. "Promise?" Ethan asked.

Jay Mac closed the lid, clipped and lit Jarret's cigar. "I made a bargain to stop smoking if God returned my daughter safely." He missed Ethan's start of surprise as he vicariously enjoyed Jarret's second hand smoke. After a moment he straightened, sighed, and went around the desk to his chair. He sat down and gave Ethan his full attention. "I got your telegram five days ago," he said. "It seemed to me God was going back on His word. I never said as much to Moira or Mary Francis. They'd be sorely disappointed to hear me talk that way, but it's what I've been thinking. Tell me, Mr.

Stone, how much danger is my daughter really in?"

Ethan glanced at Jarret who was stretched out comfortably in his chair, his long legs crossed at the ankles, giving every evidence that he was enjoying his cigar. Ethan couldn't affect such calm. There was tension in every line of his body. It was an effort to remain seated when what he wanted to do was pace the floor. His only concession to the agitation was to lean forward in his chair. "If I didn't believe that Houston and Detra would come looking for her, I wouldn't have wired you or come here myself," he said. He hadn't heard from Michael since she left Denver. There had been no letters or telegrams, nothing to indicate that she ever wanted to see him again. "Michael will need protection. I don't believe for a minute that Houston and Dee will slip away quietly and live the rest of their lives in anonymity. If you'd seen the look Houston gave Michael as he was being led away after sentencing, you wouldn't believe it either."

Jay Mac picked up the letter opener on his desk and tapped the flat of it lightly against his palm. Those who knew him well would have recognized the agitation and anger in the gesture. "I didn't want her testifying at their trials," he said with an edge of sharpness in his tone. "That should have been your job alone."

"She would have been subpoenaed," Ethan told him. "She was a witness to almost everything."

"I have you to thank for that, don't I?" He slapped the letter opener a little harder against his skin. "And if you don't think I could have kept her from testifying, you're seriously underestimating my influence."

"You couldn't have bought me, Mr. Worth." Ethan's blue-gray eyes did not waver from the railroad tycoon's. John MacKenzie Worth was one of the hundred most powerful men in the country and at this moment it mattered nothing at all to Ethan. "I don't want your money."

This time it was Jay Mac who looked away. He tossed the letter opener on the desk. It skittered across the surface and spun like a compass needle before it fell still. "I was just blowing off steam."

The admission was nearly an apology. Either seemed surprising coming from Jay Mac Worth. Ethan nodded once, accepting it. "You never tried any bribery at all, did you?"

"My daughter knows me too well. She warned me not to do it. Warned me, not asked me. Michael would cut off her right hand before she *asked* me to do anything for her. She insisted on testifying; said it was her privilege and her right. Stopping her would have meant losing her, Mr. Stone, and that's the one thing I won't have. Michael and I don't always see things the same, but God knows, I love her."

Ethan didn't doubt that. Very briefly there had been the sheen of tears in Jay Mac's eyes as he spoke. It would have been clear to the meanest intelligence that Jay Mac loved his daughter. "I've come to make certain she stays safe, Mr. Worth. You and I are not at cross purposes here."

Jay Mac relaxed slightly. He leaned back in his chair, breathed the pungent aroma of Jarret's cigar smoke drifting in his direction, and met Ethan's direct gaze again. "Your telegram was short on details. There's been nothing in the local papers about the escape. Even the *Chronicle* didn't pick up the story."

"I asked Logan Marshall not to run it," Ethan said. "I thought it would be too alarming for Michael to learn about it that way. It was better that she hear it from you. You've told her, haven't you?"

Jay Mac nodded. "Her and her sisters and her

360

mother. They all had a right to know. And they all had questions I couldn't answer."

Jarret picked up an ashtray and knocked a little ash off the glowing tip of his cigar. "Detra Kelly had the help of a guard at the woman's prison. Apparently she seduced him." Jarret's lazy grin deepened. "Dee's a good looker but I don't think it hurt that she promised a sizable share of the robbery money that's never been recovered."

"I didn't even hear about her escape until she aided Houston in his," Ethan said. "That was ten days ago. I wired a message to you as soon as I learned of it. Ben was injured in the escape attempt. He took a nasty fall in the quarry where they were digging. Jake was killed. One report says that Houston took a bullet in his leg, but it apparently didn't slow him much. Dee managed to get him away. They've eluded every search party sent after them."

"Ethan and I split from the main posse and tracked them as far as St. Louis," Jarret said. "I lost them then. The trail went cold."

"New names?" Jay Mac asked. "Disguises?"

"That's a pretty safe bet," Ethan said. "We wouldn't waste time trying to follow them at that point. We needed to get ahead of them."

"Do you think you have?"

"I don't know. Houston and Dee could already be in New York and I doubt we'll find them first. Have you acted on my suggestions in the telegram?"

"Moved my family out, you mean?" Jay Mac asked. Incredulity was clear in the expression. "Mr. Stone, I couldn't have moved Moira and my daughters out of the city this week with anything less than the 7th cavalry. And they're not stationed where I can get them." He put on his spectacles, took his watch out of his pocket and glanced at the time. "Ninety minutes from

361

now my daughter is getting married. They've been planning and carrying on for months now. The news of Nate Houston's escape made them pause for all of a second. They went right back to choosing flowers for the church and arguing about the menu for the reception. Took their cue from Michael, they did, and when she wasn't concerned, they weren't concerned. Or at least pretended not to be."

Ethan wondered if he was as pale as he felt. At the mention of the wedding it seemed that the blood drained from his face and settled in his stomach. For a moment he couldn't breathe or swallow. When Jay Mac offered him a drink he accepted, then knocked it back as if it were water. It burned all the way down and did nothing to clear his head.

Jarret sipped his own drink, watching Ethan out of the corner of his eye. His old friend had it bad, he thought. His deep amusement was partly rooted in the fact he considered himself immune to what was so obviously ailing Ethan. "Ethan told me you have five daughters," he said. "Now which one would it be that's tying the knot?"

Jay Mac's level gaze slipped away from Ethan and fell innocently on Jarret. "Didn't I say? I thought I mentioned it was Mary Renee."

"Rennie," Ethan said softly. His immediate relief was quickly overshadowed by anger at being manipulated. The old codger, he thought. "You wanted me to think it was Michael."

Jay Mac shrugged, putting away the liquor. He carried his own glass back to his desk and sat on the edge. "I needed to know what you felt for my daughter," he said without apology. He glanced at Jarret. "I think he loves her. What do you think?"

"The very same, sir."

Ethan glared at his friend, then at Jay Mac. He ignored the subject of his feelings altogether. "Does Michael know I planned to come here?"

"I didn't tell her," Jay Mac said. "Quite frankly, I was afraid the news would send her packing. That would have been fine, except that she would have been running from the wrong person. There was every chance that Houston and this Dee woman would have found her before you did. I didn't want that to happen."

It wasn't comforting to know that Michael would have gone out of her way to avoid him, yet had no sensible fear of Houston or Detra. He rolled his shot glass between his palms. "Jarret and I discussed a plan on the way here. We think that Michael should go on with her routine, apparently just as she has. That will draw out Houston and Dee. In deference to the rest of your family's safety, however, I think they should leave the city for a while."

Jay Mac was silent. He took another sip of his drink. "I can't say that I like the idea of Michael being used as felon bait and that's exactly what you're proposing. On the other hand, I don't have any hope of convincing her to leave her job at the *Chronicle* for even a day, let alone the weeks or months that it might take for you to flush out Houston. Mary Francis will be quite safe at the convent. Maggie and Skye and their mother will go to my summer home in the Hudson Valley."

"And Rennie will be honeymooning with her new husband," Ethan said.

Jay Mac hesitated. "Well, actually, Rennie poses something of a problem. I'm not so sure she'll agree to leave the city once she finds out you're here."

Jarret dismissed the notion. A wreathe of blue-gray smoke hovered in the air in front of him. He exhaled, blowing it away. "Surely her husband will have some say in that."

"Hollis Banks?" His snort was clearly derisive. "He wouldn't have the nerve to gainsay Rennie. He'll do what she says."

Ethan sunk back in his chair. The double shot of whiskey on an empty stomach loosened his tongue. His tone was faintly accusing. "Don't you have any daughters who do what they're told?"

"Not a one." Although he threw up his hands he didn't sound especially disappointed. "Moira's raised them with a mind of their own, I'm afraid."

Somehow Ethan doubted that was entirely truthful. There was a great deal about Michael that spoke to Jay Mac's influence. He sighed heavily, shaking his head.

Jay Mac finished his drink. "I was rather hoping this business with Houston would have a silver lining."

"How's that?" Ethan asked.

"I thought it might put Rennie's wedding on hold." He pushed his spectacles up the bridge of his nose and looked at his watch again. "Just a little over an hour now. I wish to God she weren't marrying that milksop."

Jarret grinned, making an obvious show of enjoying his cigar. "I take it you'd strike a bargain with God if you had another vice to give up."

Jay Mac blinked at the younger man's impudence. Then he gave a short bark of laughter. "You're exactly right, Mr. Sullivan, exactly right."

Ethan stood. Rennie's wedding wasn't his problem. "Jarret will stay with Michael's mother and sisters in the valley. If you're quite certain that Mary Francis will be safe there's no need for additional protection there. If you don't trust Rennie's future husband to do right by her, then I suggest you hire someone. I'll be

364

with Michael." The manner in which he said the last was almost a challenge to Jay Mac.

Michael's father merely returned Ethan's steady regard.

Jarret put his shot glass on the edge of the desk and followed Ethan's lead. "I suppose we'll meet them all at the wedding then. We're not really dressed for it though." Neither was Jay Mac, he realized. "Should we follow you there?"

Dead silence followed Jarret's question. Ethan knew the reason; Jarret only understood he had inadvertently broached a subject that was meant to be avoided.

Jay Mac went around his desk, drew out a paper and pen from the middle drawer and quickly wrote out directions. The rapid movement of his hand across the page made the slight trembling of his fingers almost invisible. When he spoke his voice was carefully modulated. Only the dark green eyes hinted at the intensity of his pain. "I won't be attending the wedding," he said. "Or giving Rennie away. One of the prices a father pays for siring bastard daughters, I'm afraid." His smile was filled with self-mockery. "Perhaps that's the silver lining. I don't have to see her make the worst mistake of her life."

He blew on the paper, drying the ink, folded it into quarters, and passed it across the desk to Ethan. "The wedding's at St. Gregory's Chapel here in Manhattan. There are also directions to Michael's hotel. She's been boarding at the St. Mark since she returned from Denver. I'm leaving with Moira and the girls in the morning for the summer house. I've hired protection of my own. We won't be needing Mr. Sullivan."

Jarret nodded. "Then I'll stay close to you, Ethan."

Jay Mac shook his head. "I'd feel a lot better if you stayed close to Rennie."

All vestige of amusement faded from Jarret's face. He crushed his cigar in the ashtray. "On her honeymoon?"

"Since I doubt she'll agree to leave now, she'll need as much protection as Michael."

Jarret and Ethan spoke at the same time. "Why?"

Jay Mac's head tilted to one side and his sandy brows drew together. His forehead was ridged as he looked at Ethan, puzzled. "You really don't know, do you?" he said. "Michael never told you about Rennie."

Ethan shook his head slowly. "I'm not certain what you mean."

This time when Jay Mac Worth threw up his hands he was clearly frustrated. "That's just like her," he said, more to himself than his guests. "And Rennie would have done the same thing. They've been playing these sort of games with people since they were children. One would think that now, at twenty-four, they wouldn't take so much delight in it, but obviously some things never change. God only knows when she would have thought to tell you."

"Tell me what?" Ethan asked, impatient.

"Tell him what?" Jarret asked, intrigued.

"Michael and Rennie . . . they're identical twins."

Ethan's mouth had opened a fraction. Now it snapped shut.

Jarret whistled softly. "Twins. Imagine that." His black brows rose a little as the full implication set in. "Houston and Dee might stumble on the wrong sister."

Jay Mac's gaze shifted from one man to the other. "Precisely. And that fool Hollis Banks can't protect her. I'm not sure anyone can if Rennie decides to draw attention to herself to save Michael. And *that*, gentlemen, is just the sort of maggot Rennie's gotten into her head." He pushed away from his desk and stood. He took off his spectacles, folded them, and put them in his pocket. "I'd be willing to pay ten thousand dollars to stop that wedding."

"I don't want your money, Mr. Worth," Ethan repeated. He held out his hand to Jay Mac, shook it, and turned to go.

Jarret Sullivan followed suit, but on the point of leaving he turned back to Jay Mac. "About that ten thousand dollars," he said. "I could be very interested."

When the door closed behind them John MacKenzie Worth sat in his comfortable leather armchair and reached for a cigar. He inhaled the aroma and even placed it between his lips for a moment. He'd have to find another way to celebrate his good fortune, he thought. Ethan Stone and Mary Michael. The man hadn't traveled a thousand miles just to offer his protection. If Jay Mac was any judge of character, and he thought he was a good one, then Ethan Stone intended to marry his daughter — and about time, too.

That left Rennie. What would Moira think when she found out he'd offered money to stop the wedding? His mustache lifted as he smiled. She'd come around eventually. On most things she usually did. And the family would survive the scandal; somehow they always managed. Moira would be shocked at first but Jarret Sullivan being at least half Irish would go a long way to soothing her fears.

He put away the cigar and closed the black lacquered box. Tomorrow he'd be with Moira in the summer house. The sort of celebration he meant to have began to form in his mind.

"Why did you tell him you wanted the money?" Ethan asked as they stepped out of the Worth Building and onto Broadway.

"I didn't say I wanted it. Just that I was interested. Aren't you?"

"I don't need it."

Jarret shrugged. "I don't own a silver mine. I can always use ten thousand dollars."

"Then I'll let you be in charge of stopping the wedding. I don't want any part of that. If Rennie's anything like her sister, she won't thank you for it."

"I don't care about her thanks," he said, grinning. "Jay Mac's money will make up for that."

Ethan hailed a hansom and they climbed on. He gave the driver the chapel's address with a curt order to hurry. The May sun was warm but there was a strong wind. Women walked along Broadway holding onto their bonnets with one hand and batting at their skirts with the other. The thoroughfare was crowded with pedestrians, buggies, and wagons. Vendors on the sidewalks hawked vegetables, flowers, and fruit.

They passed Printing House Square on their way to the chapel. Ethan pointed out the *Chronicle's* offices and the white marble French palace that housed the *New York Herald* on the corner of Broadway and Ann. "Supposing you do manage to stop the wedding," he said. "What are you going to do with Rennie?"

"If her mother and sisters are going to be in the valley, there's no reason we can't stay at their home. Don't worry, Ethan. I'll take care of her."

Ethan supposed that if he could trust Jarret with his own life—and he had on several occasions—then he could trust him with Rennie's. "All right."

Jarret glanced over at his friend. He couldn't recall ever seeing Ethan so tense. A jar of nitro would have exploded in his hands. He knew better than to think it had everything to do with Houston and Dee. "What do you think she'll do when she sees you?"

Jamming his hands in his pockets, Ethan leaned back in his seat. "Damned if I know," he said softly.

* * *

Everyone hovered around Rennie in the side chapel. Skye Dennehy was on her knees in front of her sister, making last minute adjustments to the hem of Rennie's gown. Her small oval face was flushed and tendrils of flame-red hair were curling away from the smooth chignon at the back of her head. She mumbled around a mouthful of pins and no one paid her the least attention.

Maggie fiddled with the bouquet, arranging and rearranging the orange blossoms to show them off to their best advantage. Her small, delicate features were taut, her mouth screwed comically to one side as she concentrated on her work.

Mary Francis, her beautiful face framed in the cornet of her habit, fussed with Rennie's hair, tucking hairpins back in place and adjusting the veil. She hummed lightly while she worked, carrying the same tune the organist played in the main chapel, and inadvertently reminding everyone that there wasn't much time left.

The mother of the bride smoothed the satin sleeves of Rennie's gown. Moira's hands shook slightly as she worked, her brow creased with concern. Her dark red hair was covered by a lace scarf. From time to time she glanced worriedly at Rennie.

"A wake is more fun than this," Michael said. She was on her knees beside Skye, threading a needle.

"Michael!" her mother admonished.

"Well, it is," she said, unrepentant. She gave the needle and thread to Skye and carefully plucked the pins from her sister's mouth. "Looking at all of us, one would think the Irish only know how to have fun at funerals. All this last minute fussing because Rennie tripped on the steps and ripped out her hem, soiled her gown, and tossed the bouquet before she was supposed to. If I were a bit more superstitious I'd say this wedding wasn't meant to happen."

Rennie glanced down at her sister, her mouth twisting in disgust. "I'll thank you to keep those kind of thoughts to yourself. I know you mean well, but I've heard all I care to hear from you on the subject of my marriage to Hollis Banks."

Now that Skye's mouth was free of pins she took up Michael's cause. Her young face was earnest. "It's not that we don't like Hollis. Well, it's not that we exactly like him either."

"Schyler!" Moira said, shaking her head in despair. Where had her daughters learned to speak their mind so bluntly? It was Jay Mac's influence, she thought. And he wasn't here to see what he had wrought. "She didn't mean it quite that way, Rennie."

"Yes, I did," said Skye. "Hollis is all right, I suppose, but he's not the sort of man I imagined you'd marry."

Rennie snorted delicately. "I can only guess at what you conjured in that head of yours. Hollis suits me just fine. He's kind and gentle and smart and—"

"He's after your money," Mary Francis said with serene confidence.

Moira gasped at her eldest daughter's pronouncement.

"Actually," Maggie said, shaking the bouquet at Rennie, "he's after Jay Mac's money and thinks you're just the Dennehy who can get it for him."

Moira fanned herself. She wished she were a woman given to fainting spells because she would have liked to have had one right then. As it was her daughters completely ignored her.

"This is a fine time to be telling me," Rennie snapped.

Michael stabbed the collected pins into a pincushion. "We've been telling you all along. You

370

didn't want to hear."

"You should be supporting me now. You should be happy for me, wishing me well." Rennie started to shake everyone off, feeling as if she were being pulled in five different directions. She was only peripherally aware that she had caused them to back away, shamed-faced and sorry for their lack of sensitivity. In spite of the activity all around her, something else had caught Rennie's attention.

Two men stood on the threshold of the side chapel, hat in hand, looking distinctly uncomfortable in their dust-covered and travel-wrinkled clothes. Their gun-belts were jarringly out of place.

Ethan shifted his weight from one foot to the other. Beside him Jarret leaned negligently against the door frame, amused and watchful.

"Is there something we can do for you?" Rennie asked.

It was Michael's voice, Ethan thought, and yet it wasn't Michael. Her face, and yet not hers. If Jay Mac hadn't told him Rennie and Michael were twins, he knew he would have mistaken Rennie for her sister. What differences there were, were so slight as to be virtually nonexistent. Ethan cleared his throat and his eyes wandered past Moira's worried countenance, past Sister Mary's questioning gaze, past Maggie's nervous fingers plucking the bouquet, past young Skye's fiery hair, and finally came to rest on Michael's profile.

"My name's Ethan Stone," he said quietly. "I've come for Michael."

It was not Michael who moved, but Rennie. Gathering the folds of her white satin gown to one side, she squeezed through the circle of her family and approached Ethan, not sparing a glance for the man at his side. She stopped just in front of him and addressed him in a voice that was bitter, cold, and remote. "Marshal Stone?" she asked. "The man who abducted my sister?"

Jarret's eyes were on Rennie. Everyone else was looking at Ethan. "Yes," Ethan said, standing his ground. "The man who abducted your sister."

Rennie's hand swung in a wide arc. A mere inch from Ethan's face the sweep of her arm was halted. Not by Ethan, but by Jarret. He pulled her to one side, twisted her arm behind her back, and yanked her flush against his body. She was stunned into absolute stillness. So was everyone else.

For all of five seconds.

Michael put her hand on Schyler's forearm and raised herself up, turning fully in Ethan's direction. Hands on her hips, the material of her pale blue overblouse was stretched taut across her belly. There was no ignoring the advanced state of her pregnancy. Feeling cornered as Ethan's eyes dropped from her face to her abdomen, she came out fighting, stiffening her shoulders and raising her chin at him. "Tell that man to put my sister down."

Jarret didn't wait for Ethan's directive. Belatedly he realized that he was actually dangling Rennie a few inches off the floor. "Name's Jarret Sullivan, Miss Dennehy," he said politely. He lowered Rennie slowly but didn't let her go. Stepping further into the room, he kicked the door closed behind him. Over the top of Rennie's head his dark blue eyes rested on Michael's abdomen. He glanced at Ethan. His friend had been struck dumb.

Mary Francis found a chair for her mother. Moira looked as if she might faint afterall. Mary slipped the white silk Chinese fan that dangled from her mother's wrist and fanned Moira with it. She watched Ethan consideringly, gauging his reaction to Michael's pregnancy. Mary had wanted Michael to inform Ethan of her condition months ago and Michael had refused. Ethan didn't love her, she had said. Mary thought Michael was wrong then. She *knew* Michael was wrong now.

Maggie's nervous fingers were destroying Rennie's bouquet. Looking down at what she was doing, she sighed, took aim, and pitched the flowers at Ethan. They missed their mark and bounced harmlessly off Jarret's shoulder.

"Maggie!" Rennie wailed, trying to loose herself from Jarret. "Those are my flowers!"

Skye leaped to her feet, picked up the abused bouquet and waved it threateningly at Ethan. "Well, someone needs to do something . . . *say* something." She looked pointedly at Ethan.

Ethan was nearly oblivious to everything going on. He only had eyes for Michael. "Is there somewhere we can talk?" Now he looked around him and added significantly. "Privately?"

"I don't want to talk to you," she said firmly. "Now or later. Private or not. I know why you're here and it has nothing to do with me or my baby. This is about Houston and Dee escaping. Well, you'll just have to find them on your own Marshal Stone, because I'm not interested in helping you!"

"Michael!" Five voices, almost identical in pitch and degrees of horror, chorused her name.

Trust her own family to turn traitor, she thought. "How did you find us?" she demanded.

"I've already talked to your father today."

"And he sent you here?" It was a conspiracy.

"Yes, he sent me, but he didn't tell me what I might expect. He left it to me to find out for myself. How could you, Michael? Why didn't you tell me?"

Her face flushed. "I am not having this conversation in front of my family!"

373

"Then tell me where we can talk alone!"

"I don't want to be alone with you!"

"Then we'll discuss it now!"

"Ethan! We're in the middle of my sister's wedding!"

Schyler's head had been turning back and forth between the combatants. She looked to Ethan now, awaiting his retort, and was disappointed when Jarret answered.

"That reminds me," he said. He let Rennie go, slipped out the door, and closed it without another word.

"Well, I like that," Rennie said sarcastically. She straightened her gown and rearranged her veil. "Who *is* that man?"

"I've never seen him before," Michael said. "But if Ethan claims him as a friend, you'd do well to stay away."

"He's my deputy," Ethan said, ignoring Michael's slur. "And when your mother and sisters go to the valley tomorrow, he'll be staying with you."

Rennie blinked widely. "Staying with me? Not likely. Hollis and I will be staying at his parents' home and your deputy isn't welcome."

Michael looked at her sister, dismayed. "Rennie, what about your honeymoon? You don't mean not to go?"

"Of course I mean not to go," she said firmly. "I'm not leaving you alone here while those criminals are free. I may even be able to help. There's no reason you should put yourself or the baby in danger, not when I can take your place."

"I won't have it." Michael punctuated her statement by stamping her foot. "You're not going to do anything of the sort."

"Oh dear," Moira whispered.

Mary Francis sought the calming influence of her

374

rosary beads.

Maggie and Schyler exchanged knowing glances.

Ethan wished he could pull out his gun, fire off a few rounds, and be done with all the arguing. "You," he said sharply, pointing to Rennie, "not another word. I'm here to take care of your sister and that's what I plan to do. I've discussed it with Jay Mac and it's settled. Jarret will be looking out for you and there will be absolutely *no* heroics on your part."

Michael stared at Ethan, her mouth slightly parted with surprise. "You can't speak to my sister that way," she said.

"It seems he just did," Mary Francis said practically. She stepped away from Moira and turned on Michael. "And he's making some sense. You've not taken anything having to do with those criminals seriously. I, for one, am comforted that Mr. Stone is at least willing to look to your best interests. You've ignored Papa's warning and you've been thinking of no one but yourself since you learned of the escape."

"Mary," Michael said imploringly, "how can you say that? I've been anything but selfish. I've tried not to interfere in Rennie's wedding plans or make any problems any part of your lives."

"That's just it," Mary said. "We're *family* and you're treating us all as if we're strangers. Do you think any of us is really unconcerned simply because you wish it that way? Look at Mama, Michael. Do you think she's not worried about you? And Rennie. Rennie's prepared to take on the world on your behalf. Do you think she's underestimating the danger to you? Skye and Maggie and I have talked. We're all afraid for you, Michael, but you're so intent on going on with *your* life that you've failed to see how it's effecting everyone else."

The room was silent. Michael stared at Mary,

blinking back tears. She looked helplessly at her mother, then at Rennie. Maggie looked away guiltily and Skye plucked at the bouquet. Was it true? she wondered. Had they all been going through the motions of their lives because she didn't want her own disrupted?

"Oh, I'm sorry," she said, tears trickling past the corner of her eyes. She shook her head as if she still could not believe what she had done. "I'm so sorry."

They all started to approach her but it was Ethan who reached for her first. He hesitated, uncertain she would accept him, yet feeling that if he didn't touch her now he would surely die from wanting to. His deep whiskey voice was a mere whisper as he said her name.

Michael turned. Her eyes held his. She had wondered for months what she would do when she saw him again. Never once, not in her day dreams or night dreams, had she willingly stepped into his outstretched arms. She did so now and it was almost as if it were happening to another person.

Ethan's arms folded around her gently, lightly. She didn't reach for him or attempt to hold him. She didn't rest her cheek against his shoulder as she would have done in the past. Neither did she try to push him away.

Skye slipped Ethan a handkerchief. He brushed at Michael's tears and kissed her forehead. Her hard belly pressed against his middle and he felt his child kick. His breath caught and he waited, wanting to feel it again.

Something of what he felt, the enormity of the responsibility, the wonderment of the moment, showed on his face. Moira and Mary nodded approvingly. Schyler grinned. Maggie sighed wistfully. Only Rennie frowned. It was borne home to her that she would never share a moment like that with Hollis Banks. She couldn't imagine Hollis being so deeply or spontaneously touched. Suddenly she ached inside.

"I'd like to take Michael to her home now," Ethan told them. He pressed the handkerchief into her hand. "I can't adequately apologize for what's happened here today . . . or anything that's come before it." He looked at Moira. "I love her. I want you to know that. I'm not going to let anything happen to her or anyone she loves."

Michael felt as if she had been moving through fog and suddenly it was lifted. He spoke so convincingly of love she almost believed him. It was as if they were in the mine again. He'd felt he'd had no choice then but to say he loved her. What choice did he have now? He was facing down her mother and four sisters. He'd probably expressed similar sentiments to Jay Mac and received a pat on the back for it. "I can't leave," she said, stiffening a little. "Rennie's wedding."

Ethan was distinctly uncomfortable. His hands fell away from Michael and the sun lines at the corners of his blue-gray eyes deepened as he winced. "About the wedding," he said slowly, avoiding looking at anyone directly. He'd have rather faced a herd of stampeding buffalo, a blizzard in the Sierras, or Nathanial Houston with his gun drawn, than have to explain what Jarret was most likely doing. "You see, I had a conversation with Jay Mac today," he began again, "and he expressed some doubts about the impending marriage."

"Ethan," Michael said, "what's going on? What have you done?"

"I haven't done anything," he said. "But Jarret, well, I think he's gone off to strike a deal with Hollis Banks. I doubt there's going to be a wedding."

Everyone started talking at once. Loudly.

377

Ethan listened as long as he could stand it then he jammed on his hat, opened the door to the chapel, picked up Michael, and strode out with her in his arms. No one tried to stop him.

"You won my mother over in there," Michael told him. "My sisters are, to varying degrees, appalled by and enamored of your behavior. If Rennie commits murder it will be completely justified and I will hold you responsible."

Ethan grinned. He gave her a little bounce in his arms to distribute her weight better. "You could put your arms around my neck," he told her.

"Hmmpf."

He glanced down at her. She wasn't helping him in the least. Her arms were defiantly folded in front of her and she had that familiar stubborn and mutinous set to her mouth. God, how he wanted to kiss that mouth!

Jogging lightly down the stone steps of the chapel, Ethan caught the hansom driver's attention. The hack jumped down from his perch and opened the door to the cab. The man had a generous smile and it widened fully as he tipped his hat to Ethan. "Seems like I just got you to the church on time." The hack's eyes dropped to Michael's burgeoning belly and his smile faltered. "Then again, maybe not."

A small horrified gasp escaped Michael's lips. She wriggled in Ethan's arms, hoping to get him to set her down. He did, but it was only to get her inside the hansom. She climbed in, spurning his help or that of the driver, and sat in the corner of the closed carriage. She heard Ethan thank the driver for waiting and give him the St. Mark Hotel as their destination. Then he stepped inside. At least he was wise enough to take the leather bench seat opposite her.

A hundred questions occurred to her. She stared out

the window rather than ask even one.

"Your father told me you were living at the St. Mark," he said. "From the way he said it, I gather your living quarters weren't quite so nice in the past. Did Logan Marshall give you a raise when you returned?" His question was met with silence. "I can't imagine Jay Mac would have approved of you living anywhere that wasn't reasonably comfortable. He probably offered to support you in the past." She turned her head long enough to glare at him and then went back to looking out the window. "But you'd never accept anything from your father, would you?"

"You don't know anything about it."

"I think I do," he said quietly. "Jay Mac said you'd cut off your right hand rather than ask him for anything. But I also saw how he likes to wield his influence and control. He offered ten thousand dollars to stop your sister's wedding. I imagine that's the sort of thing your father's been doing for years."

She didn't say anything for a moment, but pressed her forehead to the cool pane of glass. The colorful parade of pedestrians on the boulevard blurred as she blinked back tears. Impatient with herself, she swiped at her eyes. "All my life," she said. She shook her head slowly, sadly. "How could Jay Mac do that to Rennie?"

"He was afraid your sister was making the biggest mistake of her life."

"Other people would have the right to learn from their mistakes," she said bitterly. "Jay Mac's daughters have to fight for the right." Her laughter was short and humorless. "When he found out I wanted to be a reporter he used his influence to get me a position at the *Herald*. I told him I wouldn't work at the *Herald* if they made me city editor. I got the job on the *Chronicle* on my own." She paused, then added quietly. "At least I think I did. When Jay Mac's your father it's

379

difficult to know what you've earned and when the deal's been cut behind your back."

"It's because he loves you."

She nodded. "That's part of it. But he also feels guilty. Five bastard daughters is quite a burden, even for a man of Jay Mac's wealth and influence. It's his conscience he's trying to appease." Michael looked at Ethan now. "Rennie won't thank him for what he's done. It doesn't matter that he was right about her making a mistake. I thought so, too. We all did. But we respected her enough to allow her to go through with it."

"You were trying to talk her out of the marriage when I got there."

"Of course," she said simply. "But it's not that same as offering a . . . a *reward* for stopping it. Only Jay Mac would be that outrageous. Rennie has a mind of her own. She should be allowed to use it."

"Like you."

Michael shrugged and turned away again. "Like me."

"Why did you never tell me Rennie was your twin?"

One of Michael's hands absently stroked her distended belly. "In the beginning . . . I don't know . . . habit perhaps. Rennie and I liked to see people's astonishment when they saw us together for the first time. It was always our natural inclination to avoid telling people about the other one. Later, as I came to know you better, I couldn't tell you."

"Couldn't?"

Her hand stopped moving across her abdomen. "Couldn't," she repeated. "I wanted too badly to be unique in your eyes." The moment the words were out she knew she had said too much. Without sparing Ethan a glance to gauge his reaction, Michael's beautiful mouth flattened and the faint worry line appeared between her brows. The subject was closed as far as she was concerned.

Ethan was not of a similar mind. "There's no one else like you, Michael. There couldn't be. Not even Rennie." He paused and added softly. "Not to me." He watched, waiting for some response, but there was nothing. It wasn't so much that she was ignoring him, but that she was telling him what he had to say was unimportant to her. Sighing, Ethan looked away himself and stared out the window.

The St. Mark Hotel was an impressive white marble residence on Broadway. Although the management was careful to call their clientele guests, never tenants, and treat them accordingly, fully two-thirds of the occupants maintained a permanent address there. It was a prestigious location, known for its gracious living quarters and the family atmosphere. There were reading and dining rooms open to the public but the St. Mark also reserved private areas for guests only.

Ethan didn't need to see his rumpled reflection in the glass entrance to know he was out of place. The furtive glances of the other guests assured him that he was. Crossing the wide lobby with its polished mahogany paneling and crystal chandeliers, Ethan followed Michael to the registry desk. She asked for the key to her room then looked at Ethan expectantly. He didn't understand what it was she wanted him to do.

"You have to register for your room," she said.

He started to tell her he had every intention of staying with her, then thought better of it. It was not the sort of discussion they could have in the lobby of the St. Mark. He signed for his suite, one floor above Michael's, and asked the manager to have his bags brought to the hotel from the train station. He turned to go but Michael didn't follow suit. "What is it now?" he asked impatiently when she continued to stare at him.

"Your gun," she whispered. "You should check it here."

"Like hell."

Michael turned to the harried manager. "It's all right, Mr. Denton. He's a marshal."

"A Marshall?" His nervous smiled eased somewhat. "Oh, well, that's different, I suppose. The St. Mark has a certain affection for the Marshalls since one of them actually designed this hotel. Perhaps we can accommodate . . ." His voice trailed off as Ethan slipped his arm through Michael's and began to lead her toward the staircase.

They climbed the staircase in silence until Michael stopped on the landing of the third floor. "My suite's down this hallway."

"I know. 305. I saw your key."

She hesitated, expecting him to continue up to his floor. He didn't move. "Your suite's one flight up."

He nodded. "That's what it says on the registry."

"Well then?" Michael pointed upward. "What are you waiting for?"

"I'm waiting for you."

"I'm going to my apartment."

"Then I'm going with you."

Michael stood her ground. "Like hell."

Ethan simply took the ground away from her. He scooped her up and carried her down the hallway. He set her down in front of 305 and held out his palm for the key.

"You're not staying with me, Ethan." Ignoring his outstretched hand, she opened the door to the suite herself, stepped inside quickly, turned, and blocked his entrance with her body. Although she was flushed with hot anger, her voice was calm and even. "This isn't Kelly's saloon," she said, "and you aren't my husband."

382

She closed the door in his face.

Numb, as with the immediate aftermath of a punishing blow, Ethan simply stared at the door. He had no idea how long he'd been standing there, a few seconds, or few minutes, when the door opened again. This time Michael pushed a sidechair through the opening.

"If you're going to camp here in the hallway, you may as well have this," she said.

"Michael . . ." Everything else was left unsaid as she shut and bolted the door. Ethan looked down at the chair, grimaced, and kicked the door out of frustration. It held solidly. "Damn her," he said quietly. He set the chair against the wall, sat down, slouched, and stretched out his legs. His arms were folded across his chest and his dusty hat slipped low over his forehead. "Damn me."

Without meaning to he slept off and on. People passing through the hallway woke him up. They looked at him oddly but always without comment. Ethan put his marshal's star on the outside of his coat in the hopes of averting being reported and thus saving himself trouble with the hotel's management. It worked. No one bothered him. He caught sight of his bags being taken to the next floor by one of the hotel porters, but he didn't bother trying to get them. He thought if he could just wait long enough Michael would come around, let him in, and they could talk. He thought he could also get a hot bath, a decent meal, and a bed to sleep in. He wasn't even particular about the order. For a while Ethan considered the merit of picking the lock. He dismissed it when he realized she'd probably find some way to have him arrested. He was no good to her in jail.

On the heels of that thought came another. "I'm not much good to her anywhere," he said, sighing. The pattern of roses on the wallpaper was hypnotic as his eyes traced the swirl of leaves and thorns and dark red petals. Against his will his heavy lashes slowly lowered. He shrugged off the cloak of weariness twice before it covered him completely.

Chapter Fourteen

It was the aroma of baked ham that woke him. His mouth watered. He could taste the texture of the salty meat on the tip of his tongue. The fragrance of hot buttered rolls tempted him. He opened his eyes reluctantly, half afraid he was dreaming, and sought out the source of the delicious odors. At his side on the floor, directly in front of Michael's door, was a tray of covered dishes. Ribbons of steam escaped the silver lids. Ethan breathed deeply and his stomach growled.

He rapped twice on the door. After a moment it opened a crack. "Your dinner's here."

"It's not mine," she told him. "I went to the dining room to eat. I brought that back for you." She started to close the door again but this time Ethan was not being compliant. Michael threw her weight against the door as his intent was clear. She was not quick enough. Ethan pushed from the other side. The tray of food was kicked out of the way, the chair overturned, and Michael did not have to see the cold light in his eyes to know that he was suddenly, blindingly angry. No match for his strength, Michael assessed the situation and calmly stepped to one side. The move was so unexpected that Ethan had to catch the frame to keep from falling into the room.

He glared at her as she serenely walked around him

and picked up the dinner tray. She ducked under his outstretched arm and put the tray on an end table in her sitting room.

"You may eat in here," she said, "but then out you go." She started to walk away only to be brought up short by Ethan's hand on her wrist. His grip was bruising. She turned toward him and raised her face. There was nothing defiant in the gesture, only a certain sadness. "You're hurting me."

Ethan looked down at his hand. His knuckles were bloodless around her forearm. His fingers loosened a fraction and his eyes returned to her face. "I want to hurt you," he said in his deep whiskey-smooth voice. "I want to shake you so badly I'm trembling with it. Why are you acting as if there's no danger? I've never believed you were stupid, Michael. Don't you care what happens to you?"

Michael tried to ease her wrist out of his grip. His fingers hadn't loosened that much. "I don't know what you mean." Ethan didn't so much let go of her as he did throw her away from him. It was as if he couldn't bear to touch her a moment longer. Michael's face paled as she took a step backward and massaged her wrist.

Closing the door behind him, Ethan leaned against it. "I suppose I was giving you the benefit of the doubt," he said. "Thinking you were only *acting* stupid. Do you understand at all the threat that Houston and Detra pose to you? When you let me sleep in that hallway while you blithely went to the dining room, did it even occur to you that perhaps you were putting yourself in danger? Or were you so hellbent on making me seem foolish that risking your life was worth it?"

Frustrated, Ethan raked his hair with his fingers. "What about the baby, Michael? Is it worth risking the baby's life just to put me in my place, just because you hate me so much?"

She gasped a little and her hands went instinctively to her swollen abdomen. She hadn't thought it was possible to hurt anymore than she already did. "How dare you say that to me! You're angry because I *did* slip out right under your nose. It's your pride that's wounded, nothing else. It wasn't a deliberate swipe at you. I was *hungry*. Your incredible nerve to come here this way is not to be believed. You charge back into my life as if you have every right, as if there's not been seven months gone by without so much as a word from you." Her voice rose a fraction and her breathing came faster. Michael's green eyes were luminous with the strength of her own anger. "And to pretend you care so much as *this*—" she snapped her fingers, "—about me in order to capture Houston and Detra is *reprehensible*. Even after all you've done I wouldn't have believed it of you. Until today, that is. Today you proved to me that you are totally without conscience." She pointed to the tray on the table beside her. "Take your dinner and get out now. And get out *all* the way, Ethan. I don't want you lurking in the hallway. If I could blast you out of this hotel I would."

She turned on her heel and headed for the doorway on the left of the sitting room. Without a backward glance, confident that her directions would be followed, she disappeared in her bedroom and shut the door behind her.

Ethan sighed and pushed away from the door. He wondered when she would come out again and discover he had no intention of being ordered around. He sat down on the plump sofa and pulled the tray on his lap, uncovering the dishes and setting the lids on the table. The food was still hot but it had lost much of its appeal. He ate now because he knew he needed to, not because he was particularly hungry. When he was done he set the tray in the hallway and brought in the chair. He bolted the door and turned the key in its

387

lock, then investigated Michael's suite.

The sitting room was decorated primarily in maroon and cream, accented with dark wood and large fringed area rugs. There was a mirror above the mantel that reflected gaslight from the milk-white glass globes on either side. There was a delicate porcelain vase on the mantel filled with fresh pink roses, baby's breath, and greenery.

Ethan took off his hat, tossed it on the sofa, and grimaced as he studied his reflection in the mirror. He could hardly blame the St. Mark's manager for hesitating at the prospect of having him as a guest. He needed a shave and a bath and twelve hours sleep, judging by the shadows beneath his eyes. He swore there were a few more iron gray strands at his temples. Ethan rubbed his chin with the back of his hand and turned away. Shrugging out of his duster, he threw it down beside his hat and unfastened his gun belt. He laid it on the table and continued his exploration.

There was a room opposite Michael's bedroom. She had made it into a study and used it for writing. Books were scattered on top of the desk, stacked on the floor, and lined the window sill. The large overstuffed armchair held more books. The surface of the desk and floor around it were littered with crumbled pieces of paper, the unsatisfactory drafts of her work, he supposed. His hands drifted across the desk, over the papers and books, her spectacles, and finally the pencils. He picked up one, rolled it between his thumb and forefinger thoughtfully. He imagined it tucked in Michael's hair, just behind her ear. The picture in his mind made him smile.

He put the pencil down as his eyes fell on her notepad. The leather binding, slightly worn and beaten was achingly familiar. He picked it up, running his fingers along the spine, hesitating a moment before

388

opening it. He hooked his hip on the edge of the desk and began to read.

Her crisp prose brought it all back to life. He saw Madison so clearly as if he had been standing in front of Kelly's Saloon again, and in some ways, more clearly. Michael made him remember the men behind the hard and ravaged faces she described, the hopefulness in their eyes as they talked of finding the big strike, their pride in the skilled wielding of hammers and drills. She wrote touchingly of Ralph Hooper's shyness as he asked her to dance and frankly of Kitty's philosophical approach to her above-stairs job.

He skimmed the pages, leafing ahead to the point when they arrived in Stillwater. There was no entry about the mine or the arrests. Nothing about the trial or her journey east. Nothing about him. Disappointed, not certain what he had expected to find or how it might have helped him, Ethan started to put the journal aside. His thumbnail slipped along the pages and the journal flipped open to a page where there was a single entry.

He raised the notepad closer and read.

I'm pregnant . . . I'm having a baby . . . I am with child. There's no way to say it, is there, to soften the blow. I can hardly admit it to myself. How will I tell Mama? And Mary Francis? Mama will be so worried for me, Mary Francis so disappointed. Rennie will support me, but she won't understand. Not about this. I don't think I can bear to look at Maggie and Skye, not when I've disgraced my family.

It hurts some, knowing how they'll hurt for me. I think it is probably good to hurt a little now. I haven't felt anything for so long, no pain, no anger, no ache, no fear. The numbness seemed a sweet blessing at first, a way to get through each day pretending confidence and strength, but it is better behind me. I don't think I can heal if I don't care for the wound. No one can help me if I don't acknowledge the wound exists.

It exists.

It sears my heart.

I will have to tell Jay Mac. Tomorrow will be best. No, tonight. I should tell him first so he can be there to support Mama. He will want to find Ethan, of course, and demand that he marry me. I shall have to let him rant and vent his outrage and scheme his schemes and remind him very gently that he's in no position to cast stones. My surname is Dennehy, not Worth. He will be perfectly indignant that I could be so impudent and rightfully so, but it is too late for either of us to change. And neither of us wants to.

Through everything I've never doubted my father's love.

My child will never have the same assurance.

A thin trail of ink followed the final period. There was a smudge where a tear had splashed the page and been hastily wiped away. It wasn't Michael's, but Ethan's. Blinking, sucking in his breath, he closed the journal and set it down. She could have come to him, told him about the baby—not just *the* baby, but *their* baby. He'd always known she hadn't loved him, but that she could have come to feel so little for him that she would keep his child from him left Ethan stunned.

Feeling the numbness she described not as a sweet blessing, but as a curse, Ethan slowly moved away from the desk. He was stepping out of the study when he heard her scream.

For a moment he thought his worst fears had come to pass, but the scream was not about Nathanial Houston or Detra Kelly. The door to Michael's suite was still bolted and locked; his Colt lay undisturbed on the table top. Ethan's heart stopped hammering. It was a different sort of scream, one originating from a vague fear, not a specific one, one he remembered that came to Michael in the middle of the night.

He turned the knob on her bedroom door, and pushed it open.

Ethan stood at the foot of the bed. She was lying across it diagonally on her side. She was still fully dressed, even wearing her shoes. Her gown twisted around her as she moved restlessly. It was clear that Michael had lain down with no intention of falling asleep. The tear stains on her cheek told their own story.

Saying her name brought no waking response. Ethan moved around the bed and sat on the edge. He did not touch or reach for her, but said her name again, this time more firmly than gently. He saw her eyelids flutter, then finally open. For a moment she was frightened of his shadowy figure in the dimly lighted room.

"It's Ethan," he said. He rose from the bed and drew back the curtains at the French doors. Gaslight from the street lamps illuminating Broadway filtered across the small balcony and into the room. He watched the scenes playing out below him, people rushing across the busy thoroughfare, elegant coaches taking their passengers to private clubs, then he turned away from the windows slowly. Michael was sitting up on the bed, taking pins from her hair. Ethan's blue-gray eyes were impassive. "You had a nightmare."

Michael nodded, not looking at him. "I remember."

He watched her comb out her hair with her fingers, an absent, guileless act on her part that sent waves of heat rolling through his middle. "Do you have it often?"

"A few times a week," she said, shrugging. "Since the mine it has more substance." In her dream she had reached out for him and he wasn't there. It was always the same; the emptiness she well and truly feared had come to pass. "The blackness holds more terror." She heard his indrawn breath and paused in combing out her hair and raised her face to him. She was careful to keep her voice calm and even, afraid he would hear the lie and know the depth of her fragile state. "It's all right, Ethan. I've quite accepted it."

391

She put the pins on her bedside table, then got up from the bed and went into the adjoining dressing and bathing room. When she returned a few minutes later all evidence of tears had been washed from her face. She had changed from her gown and was wearing a nightshift and robe. Her feet were bare. "I thought you'd be gone," she said when she saw Ethan still silhouetted at the window.

"Marry me, Michael."

She jerked a little in surprise. Her fingers fumbled with the sash of her robe, tightening it just below her breasts. Her pregnancy became more evident with the gesture. "It's good of you to offer, Ethan," she said without emotion, "but there's no need."

"Perhaps not for you," he said.

For a moment she was hopeful then his eyes wandered to her belly. "I see," she said quietly. "You mean the baby's needs." She walked out of the bedroom. He followed her.

"Why shouldn't my child be assured of her father's love?" he asked from behind her. "The way you were?"

Michael spun on her heel. Except for bright angry color of her emerald eyes her face was pale. She glanced at the open door to her study and then back at Ethan. "You read my journal."

He nodded.

"You had no right!" She hugged herself, the feeling of being violated total. "You had no right," she repeated, more softly this time as accusation was replaced by hurt.

"I know. But I'm not sorry."

At her sides her hands clenched. She wanted to strike him. Instead she struck out. "You complete bastard! You have no decency, no respect. None! I don't need you and my baby certainly doesn't need you!" She looked around her, frantic to put some distance and some barriers between her and Ethan. Her glance fell on his Colt lying on the side table. Before he could divine her intention she had scooped it up and was aiming it at his midsection.

Ethan hadn't moved since her tirade began. He watched her, not the gun. "That's loaded, Michael," he said.

"I hope so." The gun was heavy in her hands. Her outstretched arms were already shaking. "It wouldn't be much of a threat otherwise."

He stood his ground, waiting her out. "Why did you never tell me about our baby?" he asked.

Her brows arched skeptically. How could he not know? "Because you'd offer to marry me, perhaps even force the issue, and I didn't want that."

"I wouldn't force you to marry me. I'd have hoped you'd see the sense of it."

Her laughter held no humor. The gun wobbled in her hands. "Seen the sense of marrying someone because he thinks it's his duty? Well, you've made the offer, Ethan, and I've refused. You're not obligated to do anything else and neither am I."

"Are you going to shoot me, Michael?"

She stared at the Colt for a long moment. Her aching arms were the only connection she had between herself and the gun in her hands. She barely recognized herself and even the part she recognized repelled and appalled her. Michael lowered the gun. "No, I'm not going to shoot you."

Ethan approached her and removed the weapon from her nerveless fingers. He laid it carefully on top of the table then he took Michael's wrists in his hands and held her loosely, drawing her hands to his chest. "Look at me, Michael."

Her eyes came up reluctantly but she could not hold his smoky stare. "I wish you would go," she said wearily. "What do I have to do to make you go?"

"I'm not leaving you until Houston and Dee are

caught and then I'd rather not leave you at all. This isn't all about the baby, Michael, though I'll understand if you don't want to believe me. When I spoke of needs before I wasn't only thinking of our child. I was thinking of me and of what I want. From almost the beginning I've known what you felt for me."

She sucked in her breath a little, and embarrassed, tried to pull away. He wouldn't let her go. "I hadn't realized . . ." she said, her voice trailing off. "I didn't know it was so obvious."

"It's nothing to be ashamed of," he said. "I admit I was flattered. It was difficult to remember that it wasn't real."

Now she pinned him with her eyes, her brows raised in question. "Not real?"

He nodded. "I was your protector — not a good one as things turned out — but there was no one else. It was a natural progression of events that you should imagine yourself in love with me."

"Imagine?"

"Perhaps I should have tried harder to make you see your feelings for what they were, but I liked believing you loved me, and in the mine, when we thought there was no escape for either of us, I needed desperately to believe you loved me that much." He could not understand the growing incredulity he saw in her eyes or the rigid posture in response to his words. "As much as I loved you."

"Loved me? You can say that after the way you've treated me?" Michael tore her wrists away from him now. She stepped out of his reach. "I never *imagined* myself in love with you. I *was* in love with you. If I imagined anything it was that you felt something deep and abiding for me. It didn't take long to have the scales lifted from my eyes. You barely acknowledged me during the weeks of the trial, let alone touched me. I was nothing more to you than a supporting witness, a means to an end."

"That's not true. Yes, I was busy with the trial but I—"

"You were *consumed* by the trial."

"How would you know? You spent all your time with Drew Beaumont!"

"Because you would have none of me!"

"Because I could never have any of you!"

For a while there was only silence. Michael felt the curve of the heavy armchair behind her. She sat down slowly, bewildered. "What do you mean you could never have any of me?" she asked quietly.

Ethan's fingers raked his hair absently and sighed. "You said yourself it was a good thing there was no future for us."

Michael grew very still, remembering her words, despising herself for ever uttering them.

"You're Jay Mac's daughter. Bastard or not, you could marry anyone, someone more like you than different, someone with your fine eastern manners and your love for the city. Your father would want a better arrangement for you than me, and in time, so would you."

"And that's why you never asked me to marry you?"

He nodded shortly.

"But the baby's changed things," she said. "You think I'll have you now where I would have turned you down before."

A muscle worked in his cheek. "I had hoped," he said, his voice strained. "It seems that's not the case."

"Tell me something, Ethan. If Houston and Dee hadn't escaped would you be in New York now?"

Ethan's eyes dropped away briefly, then he looked at her squarely and answered with painful honesty. "No, I wouldn't have come. The hardest thing I've ever had to do was let you leave Denver. That will be nothing compared to leaving you here."

Michael slowly released the breath she'd been holding. "I always thought I'd love a man who didn't make assumptions about my feelings, who didn't make assertions about what I thought. I hoped he'd respect me enough to allow me to make up my own mind and would never hold the circumstances of my birth against me. I may be Jay Mac's daughter, but I'm also Moira Dennehy's. And I'm my own person." She poked herself in the chest with her forefinger as tears gathered in her eyes. "I'm Mary Michael, Ethan. Mary Michael. And I don't want you to leave me behind. I never wanted you to let me go."

The step he took toward her was halting. His hand lifted, almost reaching out to her, then fell back.

Her eyes implored him. "Why won't you believe I love you?"

"Oh God," he said softly. He closed the distance between them, raising his hand to her face. His knuckles brushed her skin in a whisper caress. His eyes darted over her, searching, questioning.

Michael's hand slid over his, holding his fingers against her flushed cheek. "I love you."

She was achingly beautiful to him with her darkening eyes and her tumbled hair. "I never wanted to let you go," he said huskily. "I never *want* to let you go." He bent his head and kissed her softly on the lips.

"Marry me, Michael."

The hint of a rare, wide smile touched her mouth. "Yes."

Houston's restless sleep woke Detra. Tired, she turned on her side and watched him, hoping he would fall into a deep, less painful sleep. The narrow planes of his face were flushed unnaturally; beads of perspiration clung to his forehead and upper lip. Detra touched his brow with the back of her hand. Her eyes darkened worriedly as she felt the unnatural heat of his skin warm her.

Holding up the covers, Dee examined Houston's leg wound. He had insisted she tend to his injury herself rather than seek real medical help. Houston did not want to risk identification at a doctor's hands and the killing which would have inevitably followed. Their trail would have been dirty then, easy to follow, and capture a foregone conclusion. Houston was willing to risk losing his leg rather than losing his life to prison.

Detra scooted out of bed and turned up the flame on the bedside lamp. The small room they had taken in the Bowery was without many amenities, including gas lighting. They had been willing to sacrifice those in return for anonymity in Manhattan's rough and squalid district. The pimps and prostitutes who shared rooms in the sagging clapboard house with them cared nothing about their new neighbors. The portly, ruddy-face landlord cared only about the advance on his week's rent. Detra had been careful not to indicate by either dress or manner that she carried enough money on her to pay the man's rent for years.

Standing at the bedside table, Detra sleepily fumbled with the glass bottles and stoppers that contained Houston's medicine. She used no measure but her eyesight to gauge the amount she poured into the mortar. She ground the grains with a pestle, added water to make a paste, then sat on the edge of the bed again while she cleaned Houston's wound and then swabbed it with the medicine.

His leg jerked once in reaction to her touch and she heard the slight, indrawn whistling sound as he sucked in his breath. He held himself very still for her after that.

"You should have let a doctor take out the bullet," she said. "Not done it yourself. It may come to a doctor anyway, Houston. I'm not certain I can save your leg."

397

"No doctor," he said through clenched teeth. He tried to get a look at the wound on his thigh. Detra was blocking his view as she worked. "Isn't it any better at all?"

"Some, I think. But I don't know if it's going to be enough." She glanced over her shoulder at him. "Lie back down. There's nothing you can do except rest."

"I don't even do that well. I woke you, didn't I?"

She shrugged. "It doesn't matter." When she was finished dressing the wound Detra bathed Houston's face and neck with a cool cloth. "You should sleep again," she said. "I'll sit in the chair so I don't disturb you."

He stilled her hand. His eyes were very dark, hinting at some measure of his pain. "No, I want you here. You won't disturb me."

Perhaps it was gratitude that made him so loving toward her, Dee thought, or perhaps it was the constant, painful reminder of his own mortality. Detra had no desire to examine her good fortune too closely. She rejoiced in the fact that he wanted her at his side. The depth of her own love for this man still stunned her; the thought of living without him nearly paralyzed her with fear.

In her own mind Dee had already proved she was willing to do anything for him. Houston would have agreed. She was responsible for the prison escape, his care, the fact that they made it to New York at all. Dee smiled as she slipped into bed beside him. He barely knew the half of it.

"Have you thought how you'll find her?" he asked, sliding an arm around Dee's waist.

She reached out to turn back the lamp and snuggled gingerly against him, spoon-fashion. "You haven't changed your mind, then?"

"No. Did you think I would?"

"No, not really, I suppose I hoped you would come to your senses on the journey here, but this morning,

398

when we arrived in New York, I knew there was no turning back."

"But you don't agree."

She sighed. "You know I don't. What purpose is served by killing her? We could have been in Canada by now. Or Mexico. I have enough money with us to take a ship to Europe. Killing her is a complication, not a solution."

Houston's hand cupped the underside of Dee's breast. The warm curve of her flesh filled his palm through her thin cotton shift. "Killing her is about a promise I made to myself," he said softly. "It's the only response to betrayal . . . the only proper one."

Dee shivered slightly, but it was not because his thumb was passing across her nipple. It was the chilling calm of his voice that raised her flesh and his talk of betrayal.

"And killing her will make him suffer," he said after a moment.

There was no need to ask whom "him" was. "How can you be so certain? They weren't married, Houston. It was all a lie simply to protect Michael. It wasn't as if he really loved her. You saw them at your trial. Don't you remember what they were like?"

Houston remembered very well but he knew he remembered quite differently than Detra. Ethan and Michael hadn't sat together, hadn't spoken except in passing, but Houston had glimpsed Ethan watching Michael while she testified. The momentary unguarded look on Ethan's face told Houston what he wanted to know. It wasn't so difficult for him to believe. After all, until Detra proved to him that Michael couldn't be trusted, he had been better than halfway to falling in love with her himself. "He'll suffer," Houston told her. "You can trust me, Dee."

She hesitated a mere heartbeat. "Don't I always?"

Moving cautiously, Houston bent his head and

kissed the crown of her black hair. "Now tell me how you plan to find her?"

Dee laid her hand across Houston's. "I'll start with the *Chronicle*. It won't take long after that. Two weeks. A month at the most."

"And no one will know about the poison?"

She laughed softly. "Darling, even you're still not sure about the late Mr. Kelly."

"Well, go on son, this is the time to kiss her."

Ethan grinned. He felt the presence of everyone else in the judge's chambers but he only had eyes for Michael. Bending his head he touched his mouth to hers. Her lips were soft and pliant beneath his, her mouth tasted faintly of peppermint. Her beautiful smile was full of promise when he drew back.

Jay Mac pressed a handkerchief into Moira's hand even as he fought to temper his own emotion. She gave him a sideways look, a watery smile, and squeezed his hand. Mary Francis saw the affectionate exchange between her parents and her own heart swelled with love. No one who saw Jay Mac and Moira together could doubt the depth of the commitment they shared. Mary Francis poked Maggie in the side with her elbow just as Moira leaned into Jay Mac and his hand came around her waist.

Maggie's smile mirrored her sister's as her eyes drifted from the wedded couple to her unwedded parents. She turned to Skye and saw that her younger sister had already observed the same thing. Simultaneously they glanced over their shoulders to look at Rennie. She seemed to have forgotten Jarret Sullivan's hovering presence for the moment because her mouth was curved in a gently wistful smile.

Michael turned away from Ethan and sought out the dear, precious faces of her family. In a moment they were surrounding her, smothering her with hugs and good wishes. Beside her she heard Ethan's low laughter as he was similarly taken into the fold.

"It's the right thing you've done," Moira whispered in Michael's ear. She drew back, took the measure of her daughter's glowing happiness, and nodded. "Sure and you know it, don't you?"

"I know it, Mama." Michael glanced at Ethan. "He's the one."

Mary Francis kissed her sister's cheek. "I suppose he knows you're willful and stubborn and can't possibly honor that vow you made to obey." She looked at Ethan hard, her eyes narrowing momentarily. "You know all of that, don't you?"

"I know it," he said solemnly. "I don't love her in spite of that. I love her because of it."

Mary's features calmed, her beautiful face was serene. She touched the crucifix that rested against her wide, white collar. "Good, because I'll break your kneecaps if you ever hurt my sister again."

"Mary Francis!" Moira admonished, shocked. She cast a significant look at Jay Mac as if to hold him responsible for his daughter's outrageous threat. Jay Mac held up his hands innocently but his eyes were amused.

Rennie drew Michael aside as the rest of the family spoke to Ethan. She searched the face that was so much like her own and found every nuance of expression that made it different. Michael's dark green eyes were radiant, illuminated by some deep happiness within her. There was a becoming blush of color on her cheeks and the normally elusive dimples on either side of her wide mouth were fully evident.

It was Rennie's mouth that had flattened seriously, her eyes that were dark and worried. "Say the word and I'll take your place," she said.

Michael laughed, pretending to misunderstand.

"With Ethan? Really, Rennie, don't you think he'd know?" She looked down at her abdomen then back at her sister. "We're not all so much alike right now."

Rennie took Michael's wrists and gave her a little shake. "Don't you dare make light of me. I'm thinking of you and the baby."

Michael's beatific smile disappeared. "I love you for this, Rennie. There's no one else like you."

"That's quite a compliment coming from my twin."

Michael hugged her sister. "I mean it," she whispered. "There *is* no one else like you. I don't want you to do anything that would place you in danger. I couldn't live with that, Rennie." She stepped back and searched her sister's face. Rennie was making a good show of being calm, but Michael knew better than anyone the strength of the anger that was being suppressed. "I'm sorry about your wedding, Rennie. Not sorry that you're not marrying Hollis, only sorry that it wasn't your decision. You believe that, don't you?"

"You know I do." She jerked her thumb over her shoulder to indicate Jarret Sullivan's shadowy presence by the door. "I wish Mary Francis would threaten his kneecaps."

Michael laughed. "And what about Jay Mac?"

Rennie's emerald eyes shifted from Michael's face to where her father stood in deep conversation with Ethan and Judge Halsey. She shook her head slowly, her expression torn between admiration and anger. "I'm not one to back down from a challenge," she said. "I'll think of some way to outmaneuver him for the trick he's played me."

Michael almost felt sorry for her father. "Good for you, Rennie." She squeezed her sister's hands, offering encouragement. "But don't marry Hollis Banks to spite Papa. You'd only be spiting yourself." Slipping away before Rennie could respond, Michael joined Ethan, the judge, and her father.

After he had drawn her into the circle, Ethan's hands rested lightly at the small of Michael's back. He looked at the grandfather clock standing in one corner of the darkly paneled chambers. It was almost midnight.

Michael intercepted his glance at the clock. "Tired?" she asked, searching his face. The edge of weariness had been taken from his features the moment she agreed to marry him, but it had been impossible to talk him out of waiting. Never had so much been accomplished in so little time. While the hotel sent around bellboys with messages to all the people Michael requested, Ethan soaked in a hot tub and washed away the grit of travel. He shaved as she held up gowns for his opinion. He was partial to the green silk satin with piping along the collar and sleeves the exact shade of her eyes, but she knew she could have worn her dressing gown and he wouldn't have cared. His belongings were brought down from the fourth floor as she shamelessly pressed every employee of the hotel into her service. His clothes were cleaned and pressed and laid out when he was finished in the bathing room. By unspoken mutual agreement, they dressed on opposite sides of the bed, and only came together when he needed help with his cuffs and she with her buttons. Neither of them looked at the bed but they were never more aware of it.

Looking at Ethan now, Michael could see the faint shadow of weariness cross the planes of his face. She wondered if he counted lack of sleep in hours or days. Michael turned to her father. His eyes were warm on hers. She slipped her hand into his.

"It's meant everything to me to be here tonight," he told her.

Michael smiled, shaking her head with bemused affection. "Jay Mac, I'm not at all certain you're not responsible."

403

His thick brows rose slightly. "Responsible for what?"

"For orchestrating Houston and Dee's escape. It set tonight's events in motion."

Jay Mac laughed. "Daughter, you've always credited me with more influence than I have. This is none of my doing."

Michael kissed her father on the cheek. "Twenty-four years ago you chose Judge Halsey as my godfather. I think you had the entire thing planned even then." She hugged the judge, standing on tiptoe to press a kiss to his sharply angled jaw. "Thank you for tonight. It was good of you to do this for us."

The judge sighed and dipped his graying head in Jay Mac's direction. "As you said. The man's had it planned for years. It's hard to stand in his way."

"Don't I know it," she said. Michael fell back into Ethan's loose embrace and she looked at her father. "Rennie's going to challenge you, Papa."

John MacKenzie Worth smiled widely. "Then that's something to look forward to, isn't it?"

Ethan plucked the pins from Michael's hair. His fingers sifted through the tumble of burnished curls before she laid her head against his shoulder. The hansom cab swayed, rocking its occupants gently as it rolled down Broadway to the St. Mark Hotel.

"Jay Mac looked nearly apoplectic when Rennie caught my bouquet," Michael said sleepily. "Did you notice that?"

"I don't think it was the bouquet so much as your sister announcing she had every intention of marrying Hollis Banks come hell or high water."

"Your friend Jarret didn't blink an eye."

"He doesn't."

"He was smiling though."

404

"He does that. Lots of things amuse Jarret."

"Not much amuses Rennie. She's so . . . so *serious.*"

In the darkness of the closed carriage Ethan smiled, pressing a kiss against her fragrant hair. "I didn't know Judge Halsey was your godfather."

"You don't think I could have gotten just anyone to marry us tonight, do you? My father has that kind of influence, I don't."

What Ethan thought was that Jay Mac had done everything in his power to see that his daughters were cared for and well-protected. He couldn't give them influence but he provided connections. "I hope I see to our daughter half as well as Jay Mac saw to you."

"Daughter?" Michael snuggled against him. "Do you really think it will be a girl?"

"I'm counting on it."

"Have I told you I love you?"

"Not since you married me."

"I love you, Ethan."

"That's a damn good thing, Mrs. Stone."

She was shy undressing in front of him. After he unfastened the buttons at her back she started to go to the dressing room. He stopped her, slipping his fingers around her wrist. "Don't you want me to look at you?" he asked.

"I look like an apple on legs."

He bent and kissed her mouth. His lips were warm. "It's all right," he said. "I like apples."

Her eyes were uncertain.

Ethan turned her and gave her a small push toward her dressing room. "Go on. I'll warm the bed for you."

He was as good as his word. The sheets were warm when Michael slipped between them a few minutes later. "Thank you," she said, moving closer, curving her body against his. She drew his arm around her

405

thickened waist and warmed her feet against his calves. He didn't move. "Ethan?"

Michael peered in the darkness, raising her fingers to his face and traced the line of his mouth, his cheek. His lids were closed, his lips slightly parted. His breathing was gentle and even. Her smile was tender as she leaned into him and touched his mouth with hers.

In a few minutes Michael was asleep as well.

His mouth was on her breast. His tongue flicked her nipple and it swelled. Her skin was warm and damp where he touched her, the scent of her flesh musky. The taste of her was sweet.

Ethan's fingers curled around her neck. His thumb dipped in the hollow of her throat. The hair at her nape was downy, as soft as a child's, and his touch there made her whimper at the back of her throat. His mouth moved to her collarbone and placed teasing, tormenting kisses along its length.

Michael liked coming awake to the taste of Ethan against her mouth and the feel of him under her palms. Her movement against him was sleepy and sinuous. Her nightshift had been unbuttoned to her waist. It slipped off her shoulders as Ethan's fingers trailed from her throat to her breasts. Her swollen nipples hardened more. His head moved lower and his teeth caught her flesh, worrying the buds gently.

She sipped the air as a frisson of pleasure tripped down her spine.

"Did I hurt you?" he asked.

His voice was husky and it washed over her with its heat and desire. She shuddered. "No, you didn't hurt me. I want you to touch me." Michael arched toward him, lifting her breasts. The suck of his mouth made her gasp again and this time he knew it was pleasure,

406

not pain, that had pulled the small cry from her.

Ethan's hand caressed the swell of her abdomen. His knuckle grazed her distended navel. The baby kicked and Ethan withdrew his hand as if scalded.

Laughingly, Michael drew back his hand. "Feel? There she is again."

"She wants out."

Michael shook her head. "She's just stretching." Her own arms circled Ethan's neck and she uncurled along his length. "Like her mother."

Ethan's mouth slanted across Michael's. He drew in her lower lip, tracing it with his tongue. She opened her mouth under his, sweeping the ridge of his teeth, sharing the same breath, the same husky and urgent cry.

"I won't hurt the baby, will I?"

Reaching between their bodies, Michael's fingers curled around him and stroked the hard, hot length of him. She giggled softly. "Don't flatter yourself," she said. "The baby will be fine." For her impudence she was kissed breathless.

Ethan's hands slid along the curve of Michael's thigh to her hip. His caress was gently insistent and her legs parted beneath his touch as her mouth parted beneath his. His tongue intruded in the same moment as his fingers.

"We've already waited too long, Ethan," she whispered. "I want you inside me."

"Then take me."

She raised his fingertips to her siren's smile and kissed each in turn. She moved to straddle him. His hands fell to her heavy breasts where her nipples had darkened to dusky rose. She guided herself onto him. The tangle of curls that was her magnificent hair fell forward over her shoulders. She began to move. Blueish-tinged shadows laid lightly across her skin. She moved through them like a sylph, caressing the length

407

of him intimately with her body.

Ethan did not take his eyes from her face until the moment of his coming. His back arched, thrusting into her deeply as his eyes, the same blue-gray shade as the shadows, closed in the taut agony of pleasure.

Michael clung to him as Ethan withdrew and turned her onto her back. His mouth trailed over her flushed skin. His hand slipped between her thighs and his fingers passed in a whisper-stroke across the bud that was all sensation. She twisted in her desiring and when she said his name it was as a plea.

His practiced touch became a shower of pleasure. The heat concentrated at the very center of her burst and became a cascade of sparks skittering along the surface of her skin. Tension dissolved and her fingers unwound in his hair and in the sheet she was clutching.

He watched her, loving her abandonment, her wild pleasure. She was so beautiful to him that he couldn't imagine he had ever thought otherwise. Ethan tugged at her nightshirt, pulling it down as he tucked the sheet around Michael. Her breathing quieted and Ethan listened, stroking her hair, her face. He turned on his side and propped himself on an elbow.

"I should have never let you leave Denver," he said. "I'm going to regret it all my life."

She touched his face, brushed the square angle of his jaw with her forefinger. "There are too many things you should never have done, things that I shouldn't have done. I can't find it in my heart to regret them anymore. You're with me now. It's what I want."

"And you must have whatever you want."

Michael's expressive green eyes were solemn. "Absolutely."

He dropped a kiss on her lips. "I didn't mean to fall asleep before," he said. "It's probably not the wedding night you imagined."

"I've never imagined any wedding night. I never imagined any wedding. I thought you were lost to me, Ethan. It's incredible that I have Houston and Detra Kelly to thank for you being here."

Ethan didn't want to think about that.

"I wished I had been braver," she told him. "I wish I had asked you to marry me back in Stillwater."

Ethan smiled, intrigued by the idea. "Did you think about it?"

She nodded. "But I was afraid it was too forward a gesture—even for me." Michael turned on her side, drawing her legs up as the baby seemed to press into her back. "That's not quite true. I was afraid you'd say no."

"I don't know what I would have said, but I know I loved you then." His fingers threaded in her thick hair. Soft strands curled around his knuckles. "And now . . . I love you now."

An abrupt yawn changed the shape of her beautiful smile.

Ethan chuckled. "Go to sleep, Michael."

Beneath the sheet she searched for his hand, found it, and slipped her fingers between his. She closed her eyes. A moment later, so did he. They fell asleep together.

"I have an address for her," Dee said. She was careful not to jar Houston's leg as she sat on the edge of the bed. She pulled a slip of paper from her reticule and handed it to him. "It wasn't difficult to get at all. I merely told one of the secretaries I had an appointment with her at her home and I'd misplaced the address. It was as simple as that."

"The St. Mark Hotel. 305." Houston folded the slip and returned it to Dee. "She wasn't at the offices?"

"Not today." Her deep blue eyes were almost fever-ishly bright as she tried to relate her news calmly. "Perhaps not tomorrow either. There was quite a buzz at the *Chronicle* this morning. I couldn't help but learn what it was about. Everyone was talking."

Houston's tone was dry. A faint white line of pain tugged at the corners of his mouth. "Well? Can every-one in New York know but me?"

Dee stood, put aside her reticule, and took off her coat. In the cracked mirror above the washbasin she fingered her hair, securing a few wayward strands be-hind her ear. She wanted to relish her secret a mo-ment longer, wanted Houston to feel the frustration of waiting, of being dependent upon her. "It seems Mi-chael Dennehy was married last night."

"Married?"

Dee nodded, shooting Houston a sly, sidelong glance. "To Ethan Stone of all people."

Grimacing, Houston pushed himself upright in bed. Sweat beaded on his upper lip. For a moment he didn't say anything, pushing back the pain. "So he's here, then," he said softly.

"Apparently. The announcement will be in the afternoon paper."

"Has he been here all along or—"

"Just arrived," she said. "I had the distinct impres-sion that the people she works with were surprised. Ethan hadn't been courting her."

"Then he's here because of us."

It was the same conclusion Dee had reached. "It seems likely."

"Do you think they're really married this time?"

"I don't know. It doesn't matter though, does it? You wanted to draw Ethan out, to have him suffer. He'll watch her die."

Houston nodded slowly, his black eyes distant as he stared at the yellowing wall opposite him.

"There's just one other thing, Houston."

He turned.

"It seems the new Mrs. Stone is very pregnant."

Michael and Ethan sat in the second floor family dining room of the St. Mark. They were seated near one of the large arched windows at the rear of the room. They could look down and see the parade of bonnets and derbys as people crossed Broadway or alighted from carriages. Dusk was shading the thoroughfare; crowds gathered in front of the St. Mark preparing to take a meal in the hotel's renowned restaurant. Gas lamps flickered on, brightening the street with warm yellow light.

No one shared their table. Ethan thought they must have looked as if they wanted to be alone. The waiter set their plates on the white linen table cloth and served them. Ethan had roast beef and potatoes and carrots. Michael had chosen the honeyed chicken and a salad. Ethan drank red wine with his meat. Michael sipped from a glass of white.

"Are you feeling all right?" he asked. "You're only fiddling with your food."

Michael pushed her plate away. "I'm really not very hungry." Her fingers curled around the stem of the wine glass but she didn't raise it to her lips.

"Is it the baby?"

"No. Baby's fine." She paused, then plunged in. "Ethan, are you really going to follow me around at the office tomorrow?"

"I don't know about following you around. I certainly hadn't intended to get in your way, but I'll be there. Unless you decide not to go back to the *Chronicle,* there's really no other way."

"I have to go back."

"You don't have to work," he said. "I own a silver

mine."

She laughed. "I didn't marry you for your money."

"Well, I didn't marry you for yours."

"What a relief. I only make forty-five dollars a week."

"That's more than I earn as a federal marshal."

"You don't have to work either," she reminded him gently.

But he did. It was no different for Michael, he realized, only more difficult to accept. "I'm trying," he said.

She reached for his hand. "I know. Someday I'm going to take you to hear Susan B. Anthony and Mrs. Stanton speak on women's rights. The world's changing, Mr. Stone."

His grin was lop-sided, his tone dry. "Next you'll be wanting the vote."

Her steady stare and silence was eloquent.

"Oh, God," he sighed.

Pretending sympathy, Michael patted his hand. "Here," she said, pushing her plate toward him. "Eat up. You're going to need your strength."

Chapter Fifteen

Michael scooted off the bed and padded quietly into the bathing room. One hand supported the small of her back as she poured a glass of water. She didn't drink it herself, but carried it back to the bedroom. Skirting the four-poster, Michael stopped beside the rocker where Ethan was sitting. She handed him the water, which he took without a word, and felt his forehead with the back of her hand.

"You're a little warm," she said, lighting one of the lamps. "How long have you been feeling sick?"

"An hour. Perhaps a little longer." He sipped the water. His stomach roiled and he closed his eyes. "I didn't mean to wake you."

"You could have. 'In sickness and in health.' I made a vow."

The corners of his mouth lifted slightly. "I thought we would be married longer than three days before I challenged the sickness part." He sipped the water again, sloshing it around his mouth before he swallowed. There was a painful contraction as soon as it hit the pit of his stomach.

Michael went to the bathing room and returned with a cool, damp cloth. She wiped his face, then folded it in thirds and placed it across his forehead. "Perhaps I should ask the manager to send for a doctor. I could request Scott Turner. He's already seeing me because of the baby."

He handed her back the glass. "I don't need a doctor. It's nothing more than indigestion. I ate all of my meal and most of yours. And mixing both wines didn't help. I'll be fine in the morn—" His eyes opened wide and his face went from gray to ash. The wet cloth slipped from his forehead as he leaped out of the rocker and ran to the bathing room.

Even through the closed door, Michael could hear the sounds of her husband retching. She patted her belly and spoke to her baby. "And aren't we glad we didn't have the chicken?"

Michael gave Ethan a few more minutes alone before she walked in. He was leaning against the washstand. She handed him a clean nightshirt to replace the damp one he was wearing and bathed his neck, face, and shoulders. "It's probably a touch of food poisoning," she said. "The chicken, most likely."

Ethan nodded, grateful that he hadn't bullied her into eating her dinner and regretting he'd been so hungry. He leaned against her, surprised by his own weakness, and let her lead him back to the bedroom. He started for the rocker but she insisted he lie down.

"If anyone spends the rest of the night in the rocker," she said, "it will be me."

Ethan surprised himself again by not arguing. He crawled under the covers, curled fetally on his side, and let her tuck another blanket around him.

"Perhaps if I order some tea and dry toast?" she suggested. "It always helped me with sickness in the mornings."

"I'm not pregnant."

Michael sat beside him and stroked the hair at his temple. "Are you certain? The world's changing, Mr. Stone."

He closed his eyes. "Very amusing."

414

In the morning Ethan was only marginally better. Michael got ready for work in the dressing room so she wouldn't disturb him. When she came out, wearing a plain gray gown with a white smock, her mother's brooch at the collar, Ethan was pulling on his trousers.

"Oh no," she said. "Back in bed."

"If you're going, then so am I."

"That's ridiculous, Ethan. You don't feel well enough to be going with me to the office."

There was a world of truth in that. "Then stay here and take care of me."

"And you're not that sick." She brushed her hair and arranged it carefully at the back of her head. Her spectacles were lying on top of the vanity. She put them on and regarded him over the wire rims as he struggled with the buttons on his shirt. "Ethan, please go back to bed. I've already arranged with the manager to have someone check on you throughout the day. It's not as if you'll be unattended. There's hot tea and toast waiting for you in the sitting room. Jam if you don't want it dry and orange juice if you're feeling up to it. I'll bring it here if you'll put yourself in bed again."

"I'm not letting you go to the *Chronicle* alone."

"What is it you expect Houston to do? Gun me down in the street? This is New York, Ethan. That kind of thing doesn't happen here."

Ethan sat down. His unsettled, empty stomach growled. His muscles ached in the aftermath of his sudden, acute illness.

"Have you given any thought at all to how long you'll want to be my shadow? A few weeks, a month, six months, a year? If Houston makes no move against me in two years, will that be long enough to convince you he means me no harm? We haven't really talked about this, Ethan, but I envisioned our marriage lasting a lifetime. If you're going to insist living in my pockets, we'll be fortunate to get through the next month."

His head jerked toward her, his eyes narrowed angrily. "And if I don't live in your pockets you may not last a lifetime! What's six months or a year compared to forty or fifty more? I want every one of those years with you, Michael. Don't you dare cheat me!"

Michael was silent. Tears welled in her eyes. She took off her spectacles, rested them on the crown of her head, and swiped at her eyes when she couldn't blink back the tears. "I'm being selfish again, aren't I?" she asked. "Just like Mary Francis said. Oh, Ethan, what if I'm not very good at marriage?"

His smile was weak. He patted the space beside him. When she sat down he put an arm around her shoulders. "You're going to be just fine at marriage."

Michael looked at him skeptically, unconvinced.

"Give me fifty years, Michael, and I'll prove it to you."

The *Chronicle* sent around work for her to do in her suite. It had been months since she had been active as a city reporter anyway. Many of her assignments required research and interviews rather than rushing to the actual scene of a story. She collaborated with some of the site reporters to give background and rich detail to human interest pieces. It was a satisfying compromise to the more demanding role she had once wanted for herself.

Michael leaned back in her chair and massaged her abdomen absently as she considered her last sentence. Her spectacles rested on the tip of her nose and there was a pencil nested in her hair. Her mouth was flat and there was the hint of a furrow between her brows.

416

Ethan leaned against the door jamb watching her. His eyes were hooded, his smile secretive.

Her gaze focused on him suddenly. "Have you been standing there long?"

"Not long. A few minutes."

"Why are you smiling?"

"It's nothing," he said. "I just like to look at you."

Michael felt her cheeks grow warm. To cover her embarrassment, she took off her glasses, folded the fragile stems and set them down on her papers. "You must be feeling better." Her eyes traveled over the lean, narrow-hipped length of him. His posture was casual, his arms folded across his chest, one leg crossed in front of the other at the ankle. His head was tilted to one side consideringly and a lock of his ebony hair had fallen across his forehead. His eyes were more gray than blue, but warm, like sun-baked slate. "You look better."

Ethan rubbed his jaw. "I shaved. Took a bath."

"I thought you were still sleeping. You should have called me."

"Perhaps when I'm not so weak."

She shook her head at his logic. "That's why I should have helped you."

He snorted lightly. Ethan had other ideas of the proper time to share a bath with Michael. "I think I'd like that tea and toast now. Have you had lunch?"

"I keep some fruit here. I had some of that. But I'll sit with you while you eat." She pushed her chair away from the desk. Ethan straightened in the doorway to let her pass. He managed to steal a swift kiss *and* the pencil.

The tea was cold but a little honey made it palatable. The toast was bone dry, nearly tasteless, just the way Ethan insisted he wanted it.

"You know, I could order something else for you," she said, pointing to the deep maroon sash that alerted the hotel management to the needs of its guests. "I spoke to Mr. Covington about the chicken."

"He's the chef?"

"The manager. He says no one else has mentioned being ill."

"You're the one that said it was the chicken. I think it was the roast beef and the chicken and the potatoes and the cherry cheesecake." Just reviewing the list of what he'd eaten made him a bit nauseated. He dipped one corner of toast in his cup of cold tea and ate it. "And the red and white wine." The soggy toast seemed to settle well in his stomach. "I'm going to practice moderation in the future."

Before Michael returned to her study to work she arranged a place for Ethan to sit on the balcony outside the bedroom. It was a clear, cloudless day with a breeze that touched the skin warmly. Ethan sat down on the rocker and took the morning edition of the *Chronicle* when she handed it to him. There was a folded blanket lying over the wrought iron railing for his use if he needed it.

"I feel like an invalid," he grumbled.

"You *are* an invalid." She turned her back on him and just missed being swatted by the newspaper.

He knew she was smiling. Unfolding the paper, Ethan started to read.

Michael was finishing up her day's work a few hours later, straightening a pile of papers and notes for a messenger to take back to the *Chronicle*, when she heard the French doors in the bedroom open and Ethan stumble through the room as if he were drunk. She hurried into the bedroom, following the path of fallen papers into the bathing room. Ethan was on the floor hunched over the wash basin. His pale face was drawn, his flesh taut across his bones. Pain had darkened his eyes.

This time Michael sent for the doctor.

"Is it the influenza?" she asked worriedly, careful to keep her voice low. The door to the bedroom was closed but she didn't trust Ethan not to hear her discussion with Scott Turner.

Dr. Turner's features were carefully schooled, masking some of his uncertainty regarding Ethan's illness. His forehead was touched by the golden fringe of his hair. He pushed it back now and faced Michael with steady blue eyes. "This is the wrong time of year for that," he said. "A few months ago I may have thought that, but now . . ." He shook his head. "His appendix isn't tender but I can't rule out the possibility of surgery at some later time."

"Surgery!"

Scott put a hand on Michael's shoulder. "Nothing's definite. I'll want to see him in a few days and we'll talk more then about what's to be done. First, let's try the medicine I've prescribed. I'll stop by the druggist's and have it delivered here. Make certain he gets it three times a day. It should settle his stomach and help him sleep."

She nodded. "He hates being sick; he hates me seeing him this way."

"I understand completely. Give him a wide berth and don't take to heart too much of what he says while he's like this." Dr. Turner's smile flashed. "That bit of advice is probably worth more than all my other services." His hand dropped away from her shoulder. "How about you? Are you able to take care of him? Perhaps one of your sisters could come by and give some assistance."

"My sisters aren't available right now," she said without going into details. "Neither is Mother."

"Perhaps a nurse then?"

"I can manage, Dr. Turner." She hesitated and her glance was worried. "Unless there's some danger to the baby. Should we be quarantined?"

"I see no reason to panic the entire hotel with quarantine now." He didn't answer her question about her child because he didn't know the answer. "Let's keep his diet light. Beef or chicken broth, tea, that sort of thing. Toast if he wants it. Fruit now and again. If he keeps that down you can add a few more items. You say you told the manager about the chicken the other night and no one else complained?"

"No one. Ethan said he'd just overeaten, but you can see that it's more than that."

"All right, Michael. Don't worry yourself too much over this. It's no help to you or the baby. I'll come around in a few days, before if you need me."

At least he hadn't told her not to worry at all. She opened the door for him. "Thank you, Dr. Turner. I appreciate you coming here. I know the hospital keeps you busy."

Ethan called to her then. Slipping back inside the suite, Michael went to see what her husband needed.

Detra was looking demure. Even so she was aware of the eyes that followed her as she carried a tray from the kitchen through the dining room. Her black hair was pulled back in a smooth chignon. No errant strands curled around her ears or forehead. Her dark blue eyes were not enhanced by any makeup; she wore no rouge and only a light dusting of face powder. Her smile was pleasant, not coy or sly. She wore a simple black gown with a white apron that cinched her tiny waist. The tray she carried looked too heavy for her petite frame yet she balanced it expertly on her fingertips and circled the tables with graceful ease.

At the threshold to the dining room she halted and delivered the tray to the waiting bellboy. He was young, eager to please, and just shy enough to shield his appreciative gaze as Dee approached. He took the tray quickly, happy to assist her. The St. Mark seemed brighter since she was around. She was gay and charming. He'd heard Mr. Covington remark that perhaps Mrs. King was more suited to playing hostess in the dining room than serving in it. It looked as if there was advancement in her future.

"Thank you, Bryan," Dee said. "It was a little heavy." She rearranged some of the items on the tray, distributing the weight more evenly. "There, that's better, isn't it."

Bryan nodded. "Where does this go, Mrs. King?"

"Suite 305. Someone there's not feeling well. The camomile tea is for the sick one." She pointed to the silver pot on Bryan's left. "That's this one. The other's just tea and lemon. You can keep that straight, can't you?"

"Of course."

Dee held her breath when the tray bobbled as Bryan turned sharply on his heel, showing off for her. She envisioned the entire tray of food scattered across the floor. It was not the mess that concerned her, but the difficulty of adding her drugs to another pot of tea. She was constantly being watched, not because she had done anything suspicious, but because everyone in the kitchen liked the look of her. In any other circumstance the attention would have been flattering. Now Dee wished she had a third eye or a wart on her nose. "Easy does it," she said softly. "Careful with it on the stairs. Remember, the camomile is on the left."

Bryan knocked on the door to 305. "Your dinner," he said grandly as the door was opened.

"Just put it on the table," Michael said. "I'll take my husband's food into him myself."

"How's Mr. Stone feeling today?" He set the tray down. "Has the doctor seen him again?"

"He'll be here tomorrow." Michael lifted the lids on the food she had ordered for herself. The fish, parsley

421

potatoes, and buttered medallions of carrots were attractively served, but none of it appealed to her. She wished she'd ordered broth for herself as she had for Ethan. She picked up one of the pots, intending to pour herself some tea.

"Oh, no," Bryan said. "I mean, not if that's for you. Mrs. King was very particular to say that it's the lemon and honey tea for you, and the camomile for the one that's sick. The camomile is what you've got in your hand."

Michael had forgotten she'd ordered both. She shrugged. "It's all right. I like camomile as well." She started to pour, then stopped. "Perhaps I shouldn't. There might not be enough for a second cup for Ethan." Putting the pot back down, Michael poured from the other. "Thank you, Bryan. I'll ring if there's anything else."

When he was gone, Michael carried the tray into the bedroom. Ethan was lying on his side with the blankets pulled close about him. He managed a smile when he saw her. She set the tray down and helped him sit up, punching up the pillows to make them more supportive at his back.

"Beef or chicken?" he asked.

"Beef broth."

Ethan sighed. He was heartily sick of drinking his food but the thought of anything more substantial was just as disagreeable. He watched her tear a few small chunks of bread off a fragrant loaf and drop them into his broth. When they were soaked through she handed him the small bowl and a spoon.

"There's tea for you, too. I ordered camomile. I thought you'd like it for a change. It's supposed to be very soothing."

He made a face. "I hate camomile tea."

"There's tea and lemon."

"Just let me get this broth down first," he said.

Michael sat back in the rocker. She watched him pretend it wasn't difficult to eat, yet she saw him grow tired simply lifting the spoon to his mouth. Whatever the illness, it continued to sap at Ethan's reserve of strength. He was gaunt and pale, bruised beneath his eyes. In the first few days he'd forced himself out of bed, taking what exercise he could. Now he needed her support to move from the bed to the bathing room. "Would you like me to shave you after you eat?" she asked.

"No," he said tersely.

"It might make you feel a little—"

"I don't want a shave. I don't want a paper or a book or clean nightshirt. I don't want you measuring me for my funeral suit. I don't want—" He stopped, seeing Michael's stricken look. "I'm sorry," he said lowly. "I didn't mean . . . I'm sorry."

She didn't say anything.

Ethan put down the broth. "I'll take that camomile tea now," he said in the way of a peace offering.

Michael poured a cup for him, and because she knew now he wouldn't take a second cup, one for herself as well. "Dr. Turner will be here tomorrow," she said, "but he'd come today if I sent for him."

A muscle worked in Ethan's jaw as he suppressed the pain of another contraction. He shifted, trying to hide it from Michael, and changed the subject completely. "Tell me what you did today."

"I worked on a story about Madame Demorest. She has her headquarters near here on Broadway so I had the messenger running back and forth with questions for her."

"She's some forward thinking female I take it."

"Forward thinking," she repeated thoughtfully. "Yes, I'd say that describes her. She heads a business that covers the entire country. Her fashion patterns are sent to dressmakers all over and she publishes *The*

Demorest Monthly Magazine. She's quite outspoken on her views."

"Now there's a surprise. I suppose she supports temperance."

"Adamantly."

Ethan shook his head, raising his teacup in mocking salute. "So do I."

"I think you'll be very interested in what she has to say," Michael said primly. "I'm going to let you read the article before it goes to press."

"I'll commit every word to memory." The tea was as unpleasant as he remembered though he promised himself he would drink it for Michael's sake. She gave every indication of enjoying hers. "I'd like you to get my gun, Michael. I want to show you how to use it."

This change in conversation startled her. "I don't think that's necessary, Ethan."

"Humor me," he said. He could barely hold his cup steady any longer, he knew better than to assume he could still hold a gun. He would have to teach Michael how to protect herself.

When she returned with the gun she laid it gingerly on his lap. "I really don't like guns," she told him.

"I seem to recall you pointing one at me not so long ago."

"Yes, but I hadn't the least idea how to make it work."

"I know. You didn't have the hammer drawn."

"And that's important?"

He emptied the chambers of his Colt and put the cartridges aside. "Very," he said. "Now let me show you what to do."

Houston was able to move about with a cane. His limp was noticeable yet, but not disfiguring. He held up the ebony walking stick and examined the silver

424

knob. He pressed a small catch, a spring was released, and a four inch stiletto appeared at the opposite end. "I like this," he told Dee. "I may carry it even when the need's gone."

"I wish you wouldn't. I didn't know about the blade when it was sold to me. Trust you to find it. Apparently anything can be bought here in the Bowery."

Houston carefully pushed the blade back inside and rested his weight on the cane again. "Let's go for a ride," he suggested. "I'm tired being cooped up here. I want to see something beside these walls."

Dee was not completely taken in by the offer. "I know you, Houston. You want to go to the hotel. I don't think it's such a good idea. There's really nothing to be gained by it, nothing you can do. Michael's been holed up in her suite these past ten days. She hasn't been to work at all. I know a doctor's been up there a few times. I've seen him coming and going myself."

"Ethan?"

"I told you I haven't seen him. That's just as well, don't you think? I'm not trying to get myself caught. As near as I can tell he stays with Michael all the time. The devoted husband, every bit as in love with her as you suspected."

Houston was not entirely relieved by Dee's last bit of information, though he managed to ask with credible calm, "If you never see either one of them, how do you know it's working?"

"Because my drugs always work."

He was thoughtful, giving attention to his vest and the cut of his jacket in the cracked mirror. "Do they?" he asked casually. "There was that problem with Michael before. She somehow managed to betray all of us because your drugs didn't work."

Dee's black brows rose a fraction. She wove a loose strand of hair around her finger, twisting and retwist-

425

ing it. "That was different. It was the matter of the amount. Too much at first, then too little. I told you that."

Houston glanced in her direction. His eyes fell briefly on her absent, nervous gesture. "You did say that, didn't you?"

Her hand fell away from her hair. She got off the bed, smoothing her lavender gown across her midriff and hips. The action dried her damp palms. She went to the rain-spotted window and drew back the curtains. "It's a nice enough day for a ride in Central Park. We can go past the hotel if you wish. Sometimes Ethan and Michael sit on the balcony outside their room. I've seen that much with my own eyes."

"Central Park," he said. "Yes, I'd like seeing that. What about you? Do you have time before you have to go to work?"

"I don't work today." It was the first day she'd had off since being hired at the St. Mark. Missing one day now and again didn't concern her. There might be a slight lessening of the pain, but the poison was well into Michael's system by now. Detra was a little surprised Michael hadn't lost the baby yet. She had expected that to have happened by now. The only explanation she had for it was that Michael, because of Dee's work schedule, was not receiving the poison at each meal. Instead she got it at one, or at the most, two meals every day. It was better that way, Detra supposed. It made it that much harder for the doctor to find any specific cause for the illness.

Detra dropped the curtains and turned away from the narrow clapboarded buildings across the street. "Let's go to the park," she said. "You're right about needing to get out of here. The fresh air will do us both a world of good."

* * *

"I don't understand, Doctor," Michael said. "I thought I was coming down with the same thing as Ethan, but I recovered the following morning. That was four days ago. You saw me then. You know what I was like. But I'm fine now and he's growing weaker all the time."

"Don't talk about me as if I'm not here," Ethan called from the bedroom. "Come in where I don't have to strain to hear you."

Michael sighed, but Scott Turner was impressed by his patient's grit. He followed Michael into the bedroom. "Your wife's telling me that she's recovered from her bout and you're not improving. Is there something you care to add to that?"

With some effort Ethan pushed himself upright. "No," he said sourly. "That's the truth. I wish to God someone would give me a little of it. What the hell's wrong with me?"

"Besides being bad-tempered, you mean," Michael said sweetly. "Please, Dr. Turner, don't take everything he says to heart. I'll wait in the sitting room while you examine him. Call me if you need help."

Scott waited until Michael had closed the door behind her before he sat on the bed. He opened his leather bag, listened to Ethan's heart with his stethoscope, and checked his eyes and general color. "Your wife's full of sass," he said.

"Always."

The doctor grinned. "So's mine." He got up from the bed, drew the tie backs off the curtains at the French doors and let them fall. Shadows fell across the room.

"You don't like the sunshine?" Ethan asked.

"Love it. But I want to see something."

Making the room dark seemed an odd way to go about seeing something, but Ethan kept his comment to himself.

427

Scott leaned against the door, his arms folded across his chest. "I enjoy Michael's work for the *Chronicle*. So does Susan. That's my wife. She was very happy when she learned Logan was hiring a woman for his staff."

"You know Logan Marshall?"

"We're good friends. I've known his brother Christian a lot longer but Logan and I have had our share of adventures together. Susan is close to their wives. In fact, Logan's the reason Michael became my patient. When she suspected she was pregnant she went to him to resign. He wouldn't accept it. Gave her my name instead and told her to stay healthy." Scott pushed away from the doors and sat back on the bed. He told Ethan to look straight ahead while he lifted each lid in turn and examined his eyes closely. When he was done he closed his bag, set it on the floor, and moved to the rocker.

"I like your wife a lot, Mr. Stone, so I don't want you to think badly of me for asking this, but you're my patient and I have to consider every possibility."

Ethan grimaced as a light contraction gripped his middle. He slipped under the covers again, raising his head by doubling the pillow under him. "I can't imagine what you want to know."

Scott took a deep breath and let it out slowly. He rubbed the bottom of his chin with his forefinger, his handsome features set solemnly. "Is there any reason you can think of that Michael might want to poison you?"

"A hundred of them," Ethan drawled, amused for the first time in more than a week. "I abducted her, forced her to work in a saloon, got her drugged, trapped in a mine, dragged her into court, let her leave Denver when she was carrying my child, and completely disrupted her sister's wedding. That's some that come easily to mind. Ask Michael, she'll give you the others."

428

"I know a little of your unusual courtship with Michael. What I didn't read in the papers, Michael's shared with me herself. I can see you're not taking this very seriously."

"You're damn right."

"All right, Mr. Stone," Scott said, "but there's some evidence to suggest that is what's happening to you. Your pupils, for instance, are still constricted, even in this darkened room. Your color is ashen. The painful stomach spasms, your inability to keep down much food, and your accelerated heart rate, could all point toward a particular poison. I wouldn't have thought it at all until Michael had similar symptoms a few days ago. I asked her what she had had to eat or drink. She mentioned you had shared some camomile tea. Then she asked me if I thought smoking would be harmful to the baby. It seems she had a powerful craving for a cigarette."

"Michael gave up smoking months ago. She wouldn't go back on her bargain, not that one."

Scott shrugged. "She was coming awfully close."

Ethan reached for a glass of water on the nightstand and sipped it. It seemed he could never get rid of the slightly bitter, acrid taste in his mouth. "I'm not sure I understand your point. If Michael were poisoning me then why would she drink from the same pot of tea?"

"Nicotine. That's the drug I suspect."

Putting the glass aside, Ethan raised himself on an elbow. He waited for a spasm to pass, his mouth flattening at the corners. Dr. Turner had his full attention now. "Drug? You said poison. You didn't mention drugs."

"Didn't I? I suppose that's because almost anything can meet the definition of a poison. I know of a case where a man died from ingesting thirteen ounces of table salt. So, you see, it's all relative. Vary the amount and the innocuous becomes life-threatening."

Scott hadn't thought what he might expect in the way of a reaction to his information, but he knew he wouldn't have anticipated Ethan's laughter.

Pained with laughter and another spasm, Ethan's call to Michael was weak. She appeared at the door within seconds anyway and when she saw Ethan convulsed on the bed she rushed to his side. "What's wrong with him?" she demanded of Scott. "Isn't there something you can give him?"

Ethan took her hand. "It's all right," he said shakily, letting her see his smile for the first time. "It's just that Dr. Turner thinks you're trying to poison me."

Michael withdrew her hand. "I hardly think that's amusing," she snapped. "That's the sort of thing Dee would try, not me."

"I know," he said, smiling broadly now. "I know. Isn't it wonderful?" His attention shifted to Dr. Turner. "I *am* going to be all right, aren't I, now that you know what it is?"

The doctor nodded, bewildered.

"You see, Michael?" The white line of pain around Ethan's mouth eased slightly. "Detra's found us. It has to be Dee."

Michael sat down slowly, her mouth gaping slightly, struck by the perfect insanity of the idea and the inescapable possibility of it. "My God," she said softly. "But how . . . how could she possibly?"

Scott Turner's glance darted between Michael and Ethan. "Are you both saying it *is* poison? And you know who's doing it?"

Ethan nodded. "Why are you so surprised? You're the one who proposed the idea."

"Yes . . . but I didn't suppose you'd both take it so well."

"Well?" Michael asked, incredulous. "I'm not taking this well at all." Her tapered nails scored her own palms as she clenched her fists. The light in her eyes was feral. "I swear it, Ethan. She's going to pay for do-ing this to you."

He held Michael's hand as she started to rise. "Come. Sit here and think for a moment. The worst thing we could do is let her know we've caught on." He looked at Scott. "We need to know what to do now."

"If we can assure that everything you eat and drink is untainted then it's a safe wager that you'll be much stronger in a week. Don't push yourself, Ethan. What's happened to you is serious. I didn't want to be-lieve Michael was responsible but I hoped she was."

"Dr. Turner!" Michael said, appalled.

"Don't misunderstand, Michael. At least when I thought it might be nicotine poisoning I knew I could save your husband. Otherwise . . ." He let them finish his thought themselves. He saw Michael squeeze her husband's hand. "Very well, this is what we'll do." He leaned forward in the rocker, his forearms resting on his knees, and outlined the plan.

When the doctor was gone Michael joined Ethan in the bedroom. He was struggling into a pair of jeans. He looked as if he had already done battle with a clean shirt and the shirt had gotten the better of him.

She sighed. "Ethan, Dr. Turner just said not to push yourself. What do you think you're doing?"

"I'm dressing myself," he said patiently, paying her no mind. "Then I'm going to go out on the balcony — without help — and I'm going to sit in the sunshine and decide how I'm going to draw Detra Kelly out."

"We," she said, following right behind him, pre-pared to catch him if he stumbled. It didn't occur to her that she couldn't have done it. "How *we* are going to draw Dee out."

Ethan wouldn't let himself be baited. He sat down on one of the straight-backed chairs on the balcony and raised his feet against the railing, pushing back so he tipped the chair on its rear legs. Watching him,

Michael could almost be convinced that he was recovering before her eyes. What he was doing, she knew, was only ignoring the pain in his gut. The bruises beneath his eyes hadn't miraculously disappeared, nor had his drawn face suddenly filled out.

She sat down, her back to the wrought iron railing. "It was good of Dr. Turner to make arrangements for our food and drink. I'm sure his wife will see to everything we need."

"It was good of him," Ethan said, "but it's only one part of the problem. I don't think we can assume that I'm Dee's target."

"What do you mean? You're the one who's been sick."

"But that first night, Michael, I ate most of your meal. I drank your wine. We can't be sure it wasn't your food that was tainted. Dee must be an employee here, it's the only possible way she would have access to our food. After I became sick, and you started ordering the broth and tea for me, it would have been easy for her to know where to put the drug. Sometimes I would became more ill after a meal and sometimes not. That's because she doesn't have any method of poisoning all the meals. She's in and out of here."

Ethan's conclusion made sense to Michael. "I haven't been out since you got sick," she said thoughtfully. "She may well think it's me who's been ill. Do you think Houston's with her?"

"It seems likely, but this is Dee's way of working." He chuckled. "I'm beginning to believe those stories about Mr. Kelly are true."

His black humor made Michael wince. "How do we find her? Should I talk to Mr. Covington?"

"No, he may become suspicious and say something to her. If we tell him too much he'd be well within his rights to fire her. We want to keep her close, Michael, but on our terms."

"So what's the answer?"

"Perhaps Dr. Turner and his wife would like to have dinner at the St. Mark a few evenings this week."

Below them on Broadway an open carriage passed in front of the St. Mark. Neither Ethan nor Michael saw Dee point them out to Houston.

Scott and Susan Turner accepted Ethan's invitation to dine at the St. Mark the following evening. They had no difficulty identifying Dee Kelly from the description Ethan and Michael gave them. Trays of food were delivered to suite 305 as usual, but Michael and Ethan ate and drank only from the selection Susan brought. In twenty-four hours Ethan's contractions had almost stopped completely. He was still weak, though desperate as always not to show it. There were signs of withdrawal as the poison was flushed from his body and his ill-temper tried Michael's patience and his own.

After four days Ethan decided he was well enough to take on Detra Kelly.

Michael stood in the doorway to the bedroom watching Ethan dress, exasperated that he was going against Scott Turner's advice. "I don't see why you can't simply bring her here and ask her what you want to know."

"Because Dee won't tell me anything, or rather what she tells me won't be the truth." He passed Michael as he skirted the bed and dropped a quick kiss on her cheek. Out of the corner of his eye he saw she was not mollified. "The simplest thing is to follow her when she leaves here today. If Houston's staying with her then she'll lead me directly to him."

"The police could do this. You don't have to."

"I wish I could be certain you're right. But there are plenty of places in New York where the police don't go

433

without a partner and where they'd be noticed too quickly to be effective. I don't want to risk losing Houston because he sees them coming. Let me find where Dee's staying first then I'll get Jarret to help me."

Michael's arms crossed in front of her, just below her breasts, making her pregnant state more noticeable. "I don't see why you can't have Jarret follow her now," she muttered under her breath. "I don't see why you have to do it."

Ethan raked his hair, weary of arguing. "Because I *have* to."

It was not what Michael wanted to hear. For a moment she blocked the exit from the bedroom as he attempted to leave. Sighing, she stepped aside. "When can I expect you back?" It was another way of asking when she could stop worrying.

Ethan was already shrugging into his light traveling duster. He stepped away from the mantel and looked at himself in the mirror above it. His gun and gun belt were concealed. He made a swipe along the surface of the mantel, cupped the room key, and dropped it in his pocket. "As near as I can make it Dee will be done working at eight. I'll be in the lobby waiting for her to leave."

"There's an employee's entrance. Dee will go that way."

He shook his head. "Not Dee. You're forgetting how well I know her, Michael. She'll walk out of here as if she owns the place." He went on before Michael could find some other point of contention. "Depending on where she's staying, I should be back here in a few hours."

"Eleven?" she asked.

"Don't try to pin me down, Michael. Something could happen to delay me."

"I know! That's why I'm worried."

He took her by the shoulders, searched her face, willing her to believe him, believe *in* him. "This is my job. This is what I do. There's not going to be a confrontation tonight. I only want to see where she goes."

Michael was stiff in Ethan's arms, unresponsive to the kiss he placed on her mouth. She was angry with him, angry with herself because she couldn't stop him. Then between them, the baby kicked, and she knew he felt it because his kiss softened, became more persuasive, more wanting, and she gave herself up to it because she couldn't bear the thought of him leaving with words between them instead of the baby.

Once he was gone Michael sat on the sofa and stared at the door, prepared to wait.

When she heard the knock some forty minutes later Michael's first thought was that Ethan had forgotten something. She unfolded stiff legs and hobbled to the door. Upon opening it, her second thought was that whatever he'd left behind, it couldn't have been the key. She'd seen him pocket that.

"You!" she said. It seemed to her that she had screamed the word but in truth her voice was a mere whisper. Houston had pushed past her, his gun drawn, before she had a second chance.

Michael backed into the room as Houston closed and bolted the door. Her knees caught the back of the sofa and she dropped abruptly. Instinctively her hands crossed protectively in front of her abdomen.

He hadn't changed at all. There was a slight limp in his step but even with the cane, Houston retained a certain swagger. His weather-worn Stetson had been replaced by a gentleman's derby and his clothes were fitting of New York fashion, but Houston was nothing if not a chameleon, she thought. Without principles or ideals he made himself at home anywhere. He dropped the derby in the chair at his side and replaced his gun, a Smith & Wesson pocket revolver, in the leather holster that fit snugly around his shoulder and under his jacket. Jerking back his head, the fringe of his light hair moved off his forehead. His sharp, handsome features were passive, his black eyes distant, and he leaned on his ebony walking stick as he subjected Michael to several long moments of consideration and scrutiny.

"I admit I was surprised that you came to the door so quickly," he said. "Dee led me to expect you'd be bed-ridden. I thought I'd have to pick the lock."

"Where's Ethan?"

Houston shrugged. "Following Dee I suppose. That's what he planned to do, isn't it? I came around the hotel tonight to walk Dee home. I like to do that sometimes. It gives me the opportunity to see you and Ethan. On a nice evening like this it's quite possible that you'll be out on the balcony." He saw Michael shiver at the notion of being watched by him. It was a cold smile that touched his mouth. "Tonight I was going to surprise Detra. Imagine my surprise when I saw her leave and our friend Marshal Stone following a good twelve paces behind. She hailed a hack and so did he." His head tilted to one side as he studied her. "And here is another surprise. You. Looking quite healthy, and quite pregnant. Dee's drugs seemed to have failed again."

"Again?" Michael asked casually, her fists clenching. She forced herself not to glance at the clock on the mantel to give any indication that she was playing for time. If Ethan took a hack then he wouldn't be gone long at all. "Oh, you mean before, when she kept me confined in Madison while you robbed the train. You've always been wrong about that, Houston, always believed the wrong person. I never left my room during that time. I damn well never left the hotel. The only people I talked to when I was coherent were Kitty and Dee. I can't find it in my heart to believe it was Kitty who betrayed you. You draw your own conclusion."

Houston did not make Michael privy to the conclusion he reached. "How did you discover the drugs Dee's been using now?" he asked.

"What drugs?"

He shook his head. "No, it's too late for prevarication. You showed no confusion when I observed that you weren't bed-ridden. You know what I expected to find."

"No, I'm not certain. Was it Ethan you intended to kill? Or me and my baby?" She stood and went around the sofa to the oval walnut table ladened with food, bottled water, and wine. "Would you care for something to eat? A drink perhaps? I have red and white wine. I think there's a bottle of Scotch here somewhere. No beer, I'm afraid." She smiled coolly. "Oh, but you're hesitating. Really, Houston, there's no need. Everything here is quite safe. I wouldn't try something so devious as poison. I'm much more direct than that. Surely you've noticed."

"I've noticed," he said. "It's one of the things I've admired about you."

Michael's eyes dropped away beneath his steady regard.

"I'll take some of that Scotch," he said.

She found the bottle and poured him the drink, careful to avoid his touch when she handed him the tumbler.

He moved his hat, sat down, and took a swallow of his drink. His cane rested against the arm of the chair. "I'd still like to hear how you avoided the poison. Dee assured me there was a doctor in and out of here."

"There was." Michael poised herself on the broad arm of the sofa, resting her hip against the curve. "But he was here to see Ethan, not me. Another surprise, isn't it? I think Ethan got the first dose of Dee's drugs when he finished my meal one evening. After that it was always Ethan who received the tainted food."

Houston nodded slowly. "I see. Then it seems Dee mistook some things she saw."

"Oh?"

"She said that she'd seen Ethan helping you onto the balcony one afternoon."

"The other way around, I'm afraid. I was helping him."

"He was fortunate to have you care for him."

Michael ignored that. "You still haven't killed anyone, Houston. None of this can be laid clearly at your door. It intrigues me the way you manage to elude responsibility. At most you'll get a few more years as Dee's accomplice."

"You're forgetting the escape. I'll get years for that."

"It's not the same as hanging."

"You've never been to prison or you'd know that hanging's preferable." Michael was not quick enough to hide her shock and Houston saw it. "You hadn't thought of that, had you?"

"Are you going to kill me?"

"I don't know. It was my intention when I came here, but seeing you . . . I don't know." His hands curled around his tumbler. "Did Ethan plan to make an arrest tonight?"

Michael was silent.

"How soon do you think he'll be here?"

She remained quiet.

Houston leaned forward, clutching the tumbler so hard the tips of his fingers were bloodless. "Don't be stupid, Michael."

She was enraged. "I'm not going to help you!"

Her passion made him smile. He relaxed slightly. "I could take you with me. I could overlook the fact that you're a reporter, that you're carrying Ethan's child, even that you despise me. Feelings change, don't they?

438

I think there was a time you felt similarly toward Ethan."

Michael maintained her dignity by maintaining her silence.

"Well, Michael? Would you do that? Would you come away with me? We could go to Canada or even Europe. I have money. It wouldn't be as if you'd want for anything."

"I'm quite certain there are trains to rob in Canada."

Amused by her sarcasm and bravado, Houston laughed. "I can't help but like you. I really didn't want to believe you'd been the one to betray us at the robbery, but the fact that you were a reporter, well, that couldn't be overlooked. It was only a matter of time before you found a way to turn us in."

A faint line creased Michael's brow. "You knew it was Detra, didn't you?" she said.

"Let's say I suspected. But then, I also understood her reasoning. She knew how I felt about you. You were a threat to her, a threat to all of us as it turned out. When she gathered the proof that you worked for the *Chronicle* and I didn't act on it to her satisfaction, she felt she had to take a more direct action."

"But Obie was killed that night. You could have all been killed!"

"I know. And Detra would have eventually paid the price for her betrayal, but it would have been *my* price, not Ethan's, not the court's." Houston knocked back the last of his drink. He rolled the tumbler between his palms. "You'll have to make your decision quickly, Michael. Dee and I weren't staying far from here. Depending on what Ethan intended this evening, he could be back very soon. Your answer will determine whether he finds you dead or finds you at all."

It was the perfect calm with which he spoke that in-

439

censed Michael. That he could talk as if he were giving her a choice when there was none at all, that he could threaten her and, in turn, her child, made her insensible of her own safety. Angered beyond reason she pushed away from the sofa arm and reached for the first thing she could lay her hands on.

It happened to be Houston's ebony walking stick.

She thrust it at him, not connecting, but using as if it were an extension of her pointing finger. "Get out of here, Houston! Get out while you still can. And don't ever threaten me or my baby or my husband again. Do you think I'm flattered by your attention? It makes my skin crawl!"

Michael gripped the silver knob head of the cane more tightly as his complete stillness maddened her further. He seemed to be paying more attention to his walking stick than he was to her. "Get out, Houston!"

He dropped the tumbler and reached for his gun.

That's when Michael emphasized her last order by poking him hard in the chest. She was only aware of the stiletto when she saw the blossom of blood on his chest.

Houston looked down at himself then at Michael. She was stepping back from the chair, the cane trembling in her hands, her features set with shock. Blood was spilling through his fingers and across his white cuffs. His face was ashen, the wound mortal, but there was a shadow of a smile at his mouth. "You always surprise me, Michael," he whispered. "I think you would have been very good for me."

Epilogue

She was the only sort of woman he noticed.

In a room full of women Ethan Stone's shaded glance slipped over the brunettes and the blondes and settled on one head of magnificently burnished mahogany hair. She was sitting on the dais, facing the gathering. Her head was bent over her work as she took notes of the meeting, scribbling as fast as the evening's lecturer spoke on the issue of women's rights in the city, in the marketplace, and at the ballot box. Ethan only listened with half an ear, knowing he would disappoint Michael when she asked him later what he thought, but quite unable to keep his mind on anything but the look of her.

Her mouth was flattened in that serious line he knew so well. There was a small vertical crease between her feathered brows. Her spectacles rested on the tip of her nose and when the nub of her pencil grew too dull for writing more, she unhesitatingly reached in her hair for the one behind her ear. He smiled. There was only one left.

Standing at the rear of the lecture hall, leaning comfortably against the wall beneath a temperance banner, Ethan had to imagine the color of her eyes. It was not difficult. He was holding his daughter in his arms and Madison's eyes were the exact dark emerald of her mother's. He shifted Madison in his arms and looked away from her puckered, rosebud mouth back to the grave, solemn set of Michael's.

She looked up suddenly, as if she could feel his eyes on her, and she smiled then, the brilliant, radiant smile that he could feel squeeze his heart. It knocked a beat out of rhythm. His smoke-colored eyes held hers a moment longer and he could have sworn she flushed. And he had only been *thinking* about what he'd like to do with her starched white blouse and her stiff black skirt.

"She doesn't know the half of it," he whispered to Madison. His deep, whiskey-smooth voice carried to the row of women seated nearest him. Three heads turned simultaneously and shushed him sternly. He started to explain he wasn't referring to Elizabeth Cady Stanton, the lecturer. Several other heads turned. In the end Ethan retreated behind a guilty, apologetic look, and raised Madison in his arms, offering his first born up to the cause. The women were not amused by his mocking sacrifice.

"What was all that fussing around you?" Michael asked on the way back to the St. Mark. She held Madison now and tucked the baby's bonnet more closely around her head. The open carriage created a little stir in the humid air as they rode away from Washington Square. "I didn't know you were going to create a scene."

His look of remorse did not convince Michael any more than it had her suffragette sisters. He sighed, sliding an arm around her. "I don't think I made many friends at your rally tonight." He told her what happened.

"Oh, Ethan," she said, shaking her head. "Did you? Did you really hold her up like that?"

"I didn't know what else to do," he said, a little more seriously than not. "I thought they were going to attack me."

442

Michael burst out laughing. Madison blinked widely at her mother then quieted as Michael snuggled against Ethan. "What did you think of Mrs. Stanton? She's a powerful speaker, isn't she? And the way she talks about a woman's right to challenge men as a *duty*, well, it — "

"It gave me chills," he said.

She heard the double-edge meaning in his tone, just as he intended she should. "Have your fun, Mr. Stone, because I know I'm going to enjoy challenging you."

He grinned and laid his cheek against her hair.

Madison was sleeping soundly by the time they returned to their suite. Michael laid the infant in her crib. The study was still filled with books but in addition to the desk there was a crib and among the crumbled papers and and sheafs of notes and pencils, there were also diapers, tins of cornstarch, and tiny booties and bonnets.

Ethan came up behind Michael and watched Madison over her shoulder. "Do you think she'll sleep through the night?" He helped Michael with her coat and laid it over a chair. "Or don't you dare make a prediction?"

"I don't dare," she said, turning as his arms came around her. "She'll do what she wants. She always does."

For a moment, looking at her, feeling the strength of her spirit in his arms, Ethan found it difficult to swallow. "I wonder where she gets that?" His voice was husky.

Michael raised her face and searched his. "I love you so much."

He simply held her, not taking the miracle of having her for granted.

"Don't blame yourself," she said lowly. Her fingers curled around the lapels of his dark gray jacket. "You did nothing wrong."

He wasn't surprised that she had read his thoughts. "I left you. I could have lost you. I'll never forgive myself for letting you face Houston alone."

"You didn't know. You couldn't have known what would happen."

It didn't make it easier to accept. When he had arrived at the suite Michael had been ten minutes into her first contractions and Houston dead just as long. Ten minutes. He could have been there to stop his wife from killing a man and nearly losing her own life by giving premature birth. He *should* have been there.

The hours waiting in the sitting room while she delivered their daughter in the bedroom had seemed endless. Dr. Turner saw to Michael; Rennie sat with Ethan. Jarret Sullivan saw that Houston's body was removed and made Dee's arrest that same night. The most difficult thing for Ethan to believe was that it happened eight weeks ago. It could have been last night, the feelings were so raw, the fear still so palpable.

Michael's eyes held his. "You keep forgetting that you *did* save my life. And Madison's. Ethan, neither of us would have survived Dee's poisoning attempt. If you hadn't been here, hadn't come for me in the first place, I would have died. Don't dwell on what you could have done, but what you did. I do. It means everything to me."

His look was uncertain, skeptical.

"Give me fifty years, Ethan, and I'll prove it to you."

He laughed then, pulled her close and hugged her. "Tell me what Dr. Turner said today."

"Aaah, you do remember. When you didn't ask me earlier I wondered."

"Remember?" He led her away from the baby's crib, through the sitting room and into the bedroom. "Of course I remembered. It's what got me into trouble

444

with those ladies at the rally. I was thinking about you." His fingers began to undo the buttons on her crisp white blouse. Her skin was warm and pale beneath. The curve of her breasts were higher than the cut of her corset. His fingers stilled. "Scott did say yes, didn't he?"

She was too selfish to tease him by making him wait. She was as eager as he, perhaps more. He'd only asked about her visit to the doctor. She'd known the answer since early afternoon. "Yes," she said. "He told me I'm fine."

He bent his head, rested his forehead against hers. "Then there's only one thing I need to know."

"Hmmm?"

"How do I get you out of this skirt?"

It wasn't all that difficult, but she enjoyed helping him, enjoyed the touch of his hands on her skin. His fingers were gentle on the slope of breasts, at the hollow of her throat, and threaded in her hair. His mouth was tender, reverent, and adoring. His self-denial was maddening. She attacked him, pushing him back on the bed, rolling with him, grappling and laughing, loving the feel of the length of him against her, the contrast of their bodies, the planes and curves, the way they fit, the way they moved together, the way the rhythm of their loving thrummed through their flesh.

She could feel the need in him, the wanting, and it was the same in her. It made her open to him, accept his thrust, accept the heat of him inside and hold him close. She wrapped her legs around his flanks and clutched his hard, broad shoulders. His mouth slid across her face, touching her cheeks, her mouth, her closed eyes. He said her name, called her Michael in that deep, whiskey voice of his, gritty and smooth at the same time, and she knew she was loved.

Michael's head rested in the crook of Ethan's shoul-

445

der. She stroked his flat belly. Their clothes were scattered on the floor, over the rocker and lay at the foot of the bed. "It's nice to be hasty sometimes, isn't it?"

"Sometimes it's the only way to be."

She nodded, pressing her satisfied smile against his skin, then kissed him lightly. "We're so blessed, Ethan."

"I know."

Michael settled against him again, a small frown pulling the corners of her mouth down as she considered her good fortune.

"Second thoughts?" he asked when she was quiet for so long.

"What? Oh, no, I was thinking of Rennie. She'll never know this happiness if she marries Hollis Banks. Do you think Jarret . . . no, that would be absurd."

"Absurd," he said. "Jarret's God knows where by now. He's sure to have collected the bounty on Dee. That means he's free to follow someone else's trail."

"He could have had the bounty on Houston. I didn't want it."

"It was better donated to the suffragettes. Not the cause Jarret would have chosen, perhaps, but he wouldn't have minded."

"Well, he does have ten thousand from Jay Mac for stopping Rennie's wedding."

"Maybe he does," Ethan said enigmatically. Ethan wouldn't have put it past his friend to pay off Hollis Banks with the money from Jay Mac. Jarret's sense of business invariably lost to his sense of the absurd.

Michael was suspicious of his tone. "What do you mean?"

"Nothing."

She pinched him lightly. "You're not telling me something."

He grabbed her hand. "There are lots of things I haven't told you. But then what would we talk about

446

on the train ride back to Denver?"

"Talk?" She slid her body over his, her breasts flush to his chest. Michael kissed him full on the mouth. "I have a better way for us to pass the time."

His laughter was cut short as Michael abandoned herself to the moment.

She was the only woman he could have loved.